HOUSE OF DECEIT

N. E. BUTCHER

Book Cover by Lucy M of Cover Ever After

Developmental Edit by Makenna Albert of On the Same Page Editing

1st Line Edit by Sarah Lamb of Sarah Lamb Writing

2nd Line Edit/Proofreading by Jenny Ayers of Swift Red Line

First Edition: October 2023

Identifiers: ISBN 9798987991619 (paperback) | ISBN 9798987991602 (eBook)

For Sydney.
Without you, I never would have written a single word and
this dream would not have been realized.
I love you to the moon and to Saturn.

Per our agreement so I could use her likeness in this book:
This is dedicated to my bestest best friend in the entire
world, Courtney Parker.
You're more than mildly funny and I love you.

Content Warnings: Language, sexually explicit material, mention of spousal abandonment, physical violence (not between main characters), mention of parental death

BEFORE

CHAPTER ONE

CHARLIE

"Where's my story?" I flip through the newspaper, the paper crinkling as I go through it once more. Slamming my hands on the desk, my coworker turns to look at me over our short divider.

"He didn't include my article," I tell him.

"Again?" he asks, disbelief in his voice.

I spin in my chair and look at Mark in his office. He leans back in his chair, feet propped on the desk, laughing at something the person on the other end of the phone says, unaware that I'm weighing if going to jail would really be that bad. Pushing up from my desk, I yell out across the floor.

"Mark!"

The sounds of the office stop. Ringing phones go unanswered. Fingers stop dancing across keys. I'm making a spectacle, but I don't care. Mark looks at me through the glass. I watch as he tells the person on the phone that he must go while dropping his feet from the desktop. He tries to saunter out of his office, but he looks like a slimy cartoon villain in his ill-fitting, black suit.

"What's the problem, babe?"

I push down my revulsion at the old endearment.

"You didn't print my story. Again," I accuse.

"It wasn't up to snuff. Maybe if you would put some effort into your stories, they would be printed." He crosses his arms over his chest and smirks, expecting me to backdown, but not this time.

"Effort? I spent six weeks researching that story."

He scoffs, smirking. I can feel everyone's eyes on me as the insult bangs around in my head, and I temporarily black out.

"I quit." I pick my trashcan up and dump the contents on the floor. "Fuck this, fuck you, and fuck off. I'm done." With my stomach in my throat, I snatch things off my desk and shove them into my makeshift box. Mark scoffs at me, but I ignore him.

"You can't quit," he huffs.

I pause my packing to glare at him. "I just did, you moron."

"You'll be back, Charlie," he spins around, addressing the room, "They always come back. You won't find a better job in this city."

I put my purse strap over my shoulder, grab the trashcan, and try to rein in the desire to stab him with a letter opener. He steps in front of me as I move out from behind my now empty desk, stalling my grand exit.

Venom pours from my mouth.

"I would sell my plasma before I came back here. Obviously, no one else has ever told you this, so let me do the world a favor. You are a waste of a human being. You're mean, stupid, lazy, and probably the devil incarnate. I hope you choke on your nightly frozen dinner for one and die."

With each sentence I utter, his face turns more and more red. I shove past him and stomp toward the door, keeping my strides in check, so it doesn't seem like I am running away. People avoid eye contact with me as I storm out, but I don't care.

"Oh, yeah?" he calls out, regaining his bravado. "What does it say about you that we dated for three years? I might be the worst, but you were the one who begged me to marry you. You're pathetic, and you'll never find someone that makes you happy!"

I shift the trash can and flip him off over my shoulder without missing a single step. The beautiful spring day greets me as I storm from the building. A sense of relief washes over me. That job has sucked every ounce of life from me. I'm a dried-out fruit pit of a human after five years. Writing is my passion, but over the past year I've realized toiling away at this regional newspaper has taken away my love of words so much so that the novel I've been trying to write has been all but forgotten.

Being an author is a dream that I've had since I was a little girl. I excelled at all of my creative writing classes. Notebooks stuffed with story ideas waiting for me to set them free from my mind were crammed in every purse and bag. But the need to make money won, pausing my dreams and leading me into a steadier career.

My writing has stalled and so has my life.

I sit staring at my apartment building, unsure how I got here. I don't remember a second of the drive. With a heavy sigh, I release the seatbelt, grabbing the trashcan from the passenger seat, and make my way up to my apartment. I press the button to call the elevator, and it does not light. I drop my head back in exasperation and make a mental note to cuss out the landlord as I start my hike up eight flights of stairs.

Sweat drips down my back, and I pant, pushing through my front door. I kick off my high heels unceremoniously, groaning in pleasure at being flatfooted after the unanticipated leg workout. The muscles in my quads shake from the exertion, and I silently promise to get myself a gym membership. My keys jingle as I drop them into the ceramic bowl on the entry table.

"Hey, babe? I'm home early." Making my way down the short hallway toward Scott's home office, I open the door, and the trashcan falls from my arms.

"Scott?"

The three monitors and a desk that lived in this room are missing. Quiet emptiness is all that remains. Confusion wraps around me. I make my way to the kitchen, calling out for him as I go, just in case he's hiding somewhere. Scott loves his pranks, though I find them hurtful most of the time. Silence echoes loudly as I turn into the kitchen.

Like the greatest cliché in the world, a note and his key sit on the counter.

Charlie,

I need space and to be with someone who has drive in their life. I'll let you keep my half of the rent this month.

Scott.

"Oh, you'll let me keep your half of the rent? What a fucking saint! Two years and not even a conversation?" I grab the vase of dead flowers from the counter and fling it against the cabinets.

This.

Fucking.

Day.

Moving to the cabinet above the refrigerator, I grab the tequila and take a long swig, picking up my phone as I go.

Courtney sits on my loveseat, her legs hanging over one arm as she screams at the television screen, supporting me as she has every day since we met in third grade.

"You're blowing this! You need to create a pyramid to reach the ring!" she yells at the TV.

"Remember that time in high school when the cheerleaders had to make that pyramid, but the bases had the flu and were too weak, causing the whole thing to come tumbling down?" I ask, lifting a glass to my mouth. The ice cubes clink around as I swallow the last dregs.

"I don't think the male population could have been more excited if some boobs had popped out," Courtney says, laughing.

My stomach grumbles, reminding me I have only consumed alcohol since coming home to Scott's note. I shimmy my way out of the depths of the couch, stumbling to the kitchen where the Chinese food we ordered sits. Stuffing an egg roll into my mouth, I grab the pitcher of margaritas out of the fridge. The condiment bottles knock together as the door slams shut.

Grabbing the egg roll from my mouth, I call out, "Do you need anything?"

"Bring me the cashew chicken!"

I shove the half-eaten egg roll back into my mouth and grab the white container with my empty hand.

The container smacks into Courtney's stomach as I drop it on her before shoving the rest of my egg roll into my mouth, chewing madly.

"What season are we on again?" I ask, settling back into my seat, covering my legs with a blanket.

"Two." Courtney says, holding up two fingers, for emphasis.

"How many are there?"

"Nine. But I'm pretty sure they are filming season ten. Or are about to." She pauses as two of the contestants yell at each other for a moment. "Did you hear that Jimmy and Jean got married? From season six?"

"How many couples does that make?"

"Seven, I want to say? More than most of the dating shows."

We continue watching the show, talking throughout. Critiquing the competitors' strategy, yelling suggestions, and wishing some of our favorite couples would kiss.

"What is a privilege that you would want to win?" Courtney asks.

On a weekly basis, the contestants split into teams, competing for a privilege while the losing team receives a week-long punishment.

"An ice cream sundae party. No question."

I can practically hear the eye roll in her response. "I should have known."

"Fine, what would you want?"

"A hot tub," she says

"They film in the summer!"

"So?"

"You would sweat just standing near it."

"That's neither here nor there," she says.

We watch in silence through another elimination challenge. Jacob Jacobson, the host, tells us to cast our votes to save one of the bottom two from elimination while a message flashes on the screen reminding us that voting has closed.

"How long can you live here before your savings run out?" Courtney asks as the credits roll, bringing me back to the reality of my situation.

"About two months. I just used some of my savings to pay off my car at Scott's suggestion, since we would be splitting bills. What a crock of shit."

"I hate to say this," she starts, a hiccup taking over, "but you might need to go back to work and apologize. At least until you can find another job."

"No."

"But—"

"No," I interrupt.

"Well, you have to make money somehow. Maybe you should sell pictures of your feet! I've heard that can be lucrative. Or people will pay you for your used underwear."

"You want me to sell my used underwear? Who the hell would buy my used underwear?" I ask, my tone incredulous.

"I bet many people would. There's quite a market."

"Okay, we need to talk about what you're looking at on the internet. Do I need to parent lock your phone?"

"Hey, I'm trying to be helpful. You're welcome," she replies, offended at my rejection of her idea.

"I'd rather apply to be on *House of Deceit* before I sold my underwear to people so they can jerk off into them."

Court sits up, turns, and puts her feet on the floor. Her eyes seem to look at two different points in the room, but she shakes her head and focuses.

"You should."

"What?"

"Apply."

"No."

"Why?"

"Because."

"Yes, great reason, Charles," Court says, using her favorite nickname for me as she rolls her eyes again. Sometimes I wonder if it makes her dizzy, how often she does that when we're together. "You could win a quarter of a million dollars! Just think of how long that would hold you over."

"That would only be if I won! I need money now. A job, Court. An actual job, not whatever those suggestions from you were."

"One, my suggestions are great ways to make money. And B, you can still apply. Who says you'd be picked?"

"I don't want to be on a TV show."

"Why?"

"Because I'm sure I'd be kicked out on week one, and I can't handle any more embarrassment in my life at the moment," I say, flinging my arms in the air dramatically.

"Or you could win the whole thing." She sucks down some more margarita as I drink straight from the pitcher.

The desire to throw up wakes me. Tripping over my laptop's charger cord and ripping it off the coffee table, I scramble off the floor, barely making it to the toilet before the contents of my stomach make another appearance. My nose throbs painfully as I lay down on the cool tile floor, breathing in and out. I twist my red hair up into a bun but refuse to move any more.

"Charles? Are you alive?" Courtney calls out. I groan from my new bed, trying not to move my body. A thud rings out from the living room. "Fuck. You need a bigger couch."

"I don't have a job to buy a bigger couch."

"When you have a new one, we are going shopping. I need to be able to roll over while still drunk and not fall off."

She crawls into the bathroom on her hands and knees, a bottle of water in one hand. Her glasses sit slightly crooked on her nose.

"Oh my God, bless you," I say, reaching for the sweet nectar.

"You are absolutely delusional if you think this is for you in any way, shape, or form. Fuck off and get your own."

"Pretty sure that is mine, since this is my apartment."

"Please stop yelling."

"I'm not yelling."

"It sounds like you're yelling."

She sits down and cracks open the bottle of water. Half of it promptly spills down her shirt as she tilts the bottle before it reaches her mouth.

I point at her. "That's karma for not sharing."

"I hate you."

"I hate you, too."

"I hate you more."

"That's not possible."

"Scoot over."

I wiggle to the left, opening more space between me and the vanity. She lies down, her sable hair spreading out around her head like a halo.

"Did we prank call my husband last night?"

"He was not thrilled. Do I have pants on?" I confirm.

"You do not. Thankfully, you have underwear on, though." She reaches out and slaps my thigh. "Don't you remember? You said that your knees were tired of being in straitjackets, so you took them off. Not before you fell on your face, but you got there eventually."

"Is that why my nose hurts?"

"Probably."

"So, no more tequila?" I raise my hand for her to shake.

She smacks it half-heartedly before replying, "For at least a week, yeah."

I doze lightly as we lay on my bathroom floor until Courtney's voice stirs me awake.

"What are you going to do today?"

"Die, hopefully," I tell her as my head pounds.

"And if you live?"

"Probably go see my parents, I guess. What about you?"

"Caleb has a birthday party to go to. Luckily, J.D. is going to take him. It'd be unfortunate if I threw up on a toddler."

"I feel like it would be payback, honestly."

"Still frowned upon," she reminds me.

"Yup. Okay, so up on three?"

"Ten."

"You got it."

I count to ten and we slowly hoist ourselves off the floor like arthritic octogenarians. Courtney leaves as I turn on the water for my shower.

I feel slightly more human once I'm clean and have brushed my teeth, but still need sunglasses in my apartment.

The taxi pulls up outside of my childhood home. My parents' house is a small shoe box. The green of the house is faded, the paint peeling off. The shutters are more gray than black, and the porch covered in flaking white paint. I don't believe my parents have done a single update in the almost twenty-nine years I have been alive.

"Mom? Dad?" I call out, as I let myself in, pushing my sunglasses on top of my head.

Wearing her favorite ruffle-edged floral apron, Mom steps into the entry between the living room and kitchen.

"Charlotte? What are you doing here?"

My mom is a soft woman. Both in stature and in voice. But her spine is straight steel, and when it comes to protecting her daughter, she is the fiercest person on the planet. I let her wrap her arms around me as I sink into her embrace. Sniffing the air, I ask, "Are you making cinnamon rolls?"

"Of course. It's the fifteenth of the month." My mom is as steady as the sun and lives her life by a book that only she knows. I could set my watch to her routine. Unfortunately, she didn't give me that trait, but she gave me her blue eyes, red hair, and sense of humor.

"I forgot. Is Dad here?"

"Oh, he's puttering around out in the garage. Why don't you go out there and get him for me? We can have cinnamon rolls and coffee. And maybe then your hangover will decrease enough you can stop squinting at the light."

The fact that my mother misses nothing is just as annoying now as it was when I was a teenager. I give her a sheepish smile as I make my way through the house and out the back door. The detached garage sits about twenty feet from the back door.

"Hey, Dad," I call out as I move into the garage. He rolls out from beneath the '67 Chevy Impala he's been tinkering with since I was a teenager, clad in faded blue overalls covered in various liquids and stains.

"Lottie Lou. Give me the five-eighths socket, will you?"

I move toward my dad's toolbox and grab the piece he needs. He slides back under the car and the tinkering sounds resume once more.

"Mom wanted me to tell you that the cinnamon rolls are ready."

"Sounds like it's time to go inside." He pulls himself out from under the car once more and sticks his hand out for me to help him to his feet. We are eye to eye as he stands, my height and lean frame coming from him.

"How's Courtney doing?" he asks, nudging me.

"She looks worse than I do," I smile. The little tufts of white hair circling my father's head are pulled out in every which way. The longer he's in the garage, the crazier his hair looks.

"I hope you girls had fun."

"Too much, probably."

He slips his hand around my elbow, and I let him lean on me.

"There's no such thing," he says.

CHAPTER TWO

MY DAD MOVES BEHIND my mother and slips his hands around her waist before pressing a kiss to her neck. They sway for a moment over the faded black and white checkered linoleum floor. When I was growing up, music would float upstairs from the living room after they put me to bed. Crooners crying out about how deeply they loved their soul mate. I would lie on my stomach at the top of the stairs and watch them dance in the living room, their eyes closed and smiles on their faces. Watching them created warmth in my heart. Like getting a glimpse of heaven this side of the veil.

I hope with all my heart that my parents will dance together for eternity, but the smallest twinge of jealousy flickers while watching them. I've searched for a love like theirs, but I haven't been able to find it for myself. Yet. Every time a relationship falls through the cracks, I wonder if I'll be alone forever. But I'd rather be alone than with the wrong person.

Still, I hope to find someone to dance with me in the kitchen.

"You're covered in dirt. Knock it off and get cleaned up," she says, swatting at him.

"Yes, dear." They share a smile, my mother blushing, making my stomach heave. And the sweet moment ends. I love that my parents are in love but choose to believe they have been celibate ever since they conceived me.

The pea green cabinet door squeaks as I grab plates while Dad washes up. As I set them next to my mother, the smell of coffee wafts up from the pot on the counter. I fill three mugs, adding cream and sugar to two, and take them to the table.

Silence reigns as we all tuck into our brunch until the last bit of icing has been licked from our plates.

"Are you ready to discuss why you're here?" Mom asks.

"I can't come visit my parents because I miss them?"

"You could, if you weren't sweating tequila." The annoyance in her voice makes me duck my head.

"Okay, that's fair," I concede.

"Are you a lesbian?" she blurts.

I almost choke on my tongue. "What? No, I'm not a lesbian. I would have told you by now."

"Well, Marjorie's son just came out to her this week, and he's about ten years older than you. And we'd hope you know we are completely supportive of whomever you love but weren't sure if you'd still be nervous to tell us." My mother pats my hand, her hands soft.

"Of course. I know you don't care who I love."

"So?"

"No, Mom!"

"Are you sure? Because you and Courtney would be so great together if she just kicked the husband to the curb."

"You love J.D.," I say with confusion.

"We do. We could never hate someone that won sweet Courtney's heart, but you two are such a good match," my mother says.

"Mom? Dad? I'm officially coming out to you as straight. I like men. Love them, in fact, even though they drive me crazy most days."

My mother's shoulders sag with disappointment and she releases a sigh. "All right then, I suppose."

I roll my eyes to the heavens and pray to anyone listening for strength.

"Now that we've gotten that out of the way, I wanted to tell you a few things. Scott broke up with me."

"Was he jealous of Courtney?"

I slam my head down on the table. "Oh. My. God. I'm not with Courtney! I don't have feelings for Courtney. I. Like. Dick. I can't believe I have to tell my parents that. I'm going to throw up."

"Okay, okay." My mother taps the table, her signal to calm down.

"Honey, what your mother is trying to say is that we never really liked Scott. He was so condescending. And the length of his pants was always weird. How much ankle do we really need to see? So, good riddance and all that," my dad says.

I lift my head and look at him. "Well, not entirely good riddance, because he was paying half the bills."

"But weren't you up for a promotion soon? I thought they had been promising you a senior writing position?" Mom asks. "Maybe that will help you bridge the gap while you look for a new roommate!"

"I'm almost thirty. The last thing I want right now is a roommate."

"Well, honey, there's nothing wrong with having a roommate."

"I lost my job."

My mother gasps and Dad's eyes go wide.

"Did that asshole boss of yours not want to give you the promotion? He can't just fire you!" Dad's indignation on my behalf makes me drop my face into my hands.

"To be honest, I quit. I quit my job without another one waiting and then Scott left me and now I have no income, no boyfriend, and my parents are disappointed I'm straight. I should just jump off a cliff."

"Now, I don't think there's any reason for dramatics," my mother says. "I'm sure you'll figure it out. And we can help you for a bit. Or you could move in here!"

"The cliff is sounding more and more appealing," I mumble under my breath. "I appreciate that offer, but I have some savings, so we'll see how it goes. I'm going to start sending out my resume tomorrow once I get it all cleaned up."

"Do you need another cinnamon roll, precious?" my dad asks, giving me sad puppy eyes.

"Yes, please," I mumble, hoping the sugar will somehow fix all my problems.

I grab my laptop from under the camel leather couch where it fell, praying that it starts up. The airplane landing sound is promising.

At least it's not completely silent. I check my email on my phone, search for used tablets that I could buy when my laptop explodes, and make myself some toast while I wait for the dinosaur to boot up.

Normally at this time on a Monday, I would be at the office wishing I would win the lottery so I could finally quit and write the book I've always wanted to write. After I recovered from my night of wallowing with Courtney, I decided to give myself the weekend to enjoy not worrying about anything. Not thinking about what I was going to do for money. Ignoring the fact that I live in an apartment that is bigger than I need, but I can't afford first and last month's rent to get into a smaller place. Blocking out that every time I look at my couch or the bed or the kitchen, I remember moments with Scott. Moments of happiness. Moments of passion.

Well, not quite passion. Scott was never a passionate guy. Never one to have sex outside of the bedroom or to try anything daring, passionate is definitely not a term I would attribute to him. Not that the sex was ever bad. It was really good. But a little variety is the spice of life! Or so I'm told.

The few days off to ignore any and all responsibilities were needed more than I realized. The time off gave me a chance to decompress and breathe through some of the anxiety that has been a constant companion since I walked out of my job. To accept where I am in life and that, while my plans are diverging from the expected path, there's no reason I won't be able to steer myself back on track.

I spend an hour updating my resume and reading every article I can find on how to optimize keywords and the available space. When I graduated college with my bachelor's in journalism, I found a company that I loved. I was able to move up and try many roles and expand my knowledge. It was a dream job. Except for Mark. We started on the same day. He was charming, if not a little awkward. We started dating quickly after we met.

He did all the right things. Gave me attention, bought me flowers, told me I was beautiful. All things I had never had before. Throughout my school years, I was a bit of a late bloomer. My first kiss didn't come until college from a guy I can barely remember. It was wet and, somehow, cold and not enjoyable at all. The lack of attention from the opposite sex made me believe that something was lacking within me and that drove me into Mark's arms.

But what I didn't realize was that he was undermining everything I did. Little barbs here and there. "Are you sure *that's* how you want to present that? Are you *sure* that's the angle to take this story?"

Until every molecule of my self-confidence eroded away.

But I was blind and thought myself in love. Enough to ask him to marry me and him laughing as he left.

His constant attack on my capabilities made me eventually doubt I was even capable at all. I avoided taking on more, harder work. I shied from the spotlight. And he stepped in where I stepped back. He kissed the right asses. Made the right contacts. And then he became my senior editor, where it all came crumbling down. I saw how his incompetence was hidden by the work of his team. How our pride in our jobs made him look good. How he stole our words and our work. We would edit each other's articles, sending them to him in perfect condition, and still he would claim they were unpublishable.

Mark took my dream job and morphed it into a nightmare.

Scott encouraged me to quit that job for over half of our relationship, but with the promise of a promotion and with a low demand for reporters in the area, I stayed.

The setting sun's rays march across my living room floor like soldiers in formation as I close my laptop. My fingers hurt from entering the same information over and over again. Over a hundred companies now have my resume. I lie down, letting the hard floor soothe my sore back and hope on every star that someone will call me.

I wake up with my face pressed against the floor. Three episodes of *House of Deceit* played while I was unconscious. The theme music loops while the screen asks me if I want to play another. I turn the TV off as Courtney texts asking me to babysit so she and J.D. can go on a date. I smile, knowing that's code for them to have sex in the car somewhere like randy teenagers. I send her a thumbs up and head out the door.

CHAPTER THREE

ALEC

*H*OUSE OF *DECEIT* SHOW creator, Bradley M. Johnson, stands at the front of the room. His charcoal gray suit is crisp with a blinding white button-down. He's gone crazy and included a raspberry pocket square instead of his normal blue one. Every outfit of his is some combination of gray, blue, and white.

His skin is artificially tan, making it seem like he just walked in off the beaches of Fiji instead of out of the spray tanning booth rumored to be set up in his basement. The new contestant specialists, or wranglers, as we are more typically called, jot down every word that comes out of his mouth. But I have this speech memorized.

This is my tenth year on the show. Ten years of wrangling contestants who all think they are smarter and sneakier than the last. For the past six years, my charge has made it to the final three. I have yet to find a winner, but I vow to make this my year.

"Season ten is going to be one of the best. We have a lot of surprises in store for our contestants," Bradley says, one hand in his pocket while he gestures with the other. "Now, because it's a major show milestone, the bigwigs have given us a prize budget of $500,000. Double the prize means a fiercer competition, so choose your contestant wisely because this also means that your bonus, if your contestant wins, will be greater."

This news moves through the crowd like a wave and I know people will be even more desperate when they go through the stack of applicants this year to find *the one*.

Wranglers on *House of Deceit* are in a unique position compared to other shows. Normally they manage multiple contestants, but that changed after season three when a guy snapped in week eight and almost killed the contestant he thought sabotaged him, leading to his elimination.

Not only do contestants suffer from physical stress of the competition, emotional stress of being cut off from friends and family for twelve weeks, but there is also the psychological warfare from the deceiver, the contestant tasked for the week to make their housemates' lives more miserable.

The wrangler that was managing him never recovered from the guilt of not giving him enough attention as the game continued and he grew more erratic.

Following that season, it went from three wranglers to twenty.

Initially, wranglers were assigned randomly until Sheila noticed that the women assigned to male wranglers were less likely to express when they needed something. From a new swimsuit if theirs broke, extra blankets at night, or even tampons if they ran out. They also weren't as forthcoming when being interviewed for their confessionals, eroding the entertainment value with the audience.

Our entire job boils down to making sure contestants have what they need to live and participate on the show and keeping them in the game mentally. With this objective in mind, it was determined that female wranglers would be assigned to the women; and male wranglers to the men.

That wasn't the only change, though. Now, as our contestants are eliminated, so are we. This elimination style of employment has led to a competition of our own between wranglers, leading the show runners to give us the ability to select the contestant we would like to be paired with.

It takes a few months to sort through the thousands of applications we receive and pick the one person we believe has the best shot at winning. We aren't allowed to help them with the game; we act more like their confidant. Sometimes, we'll tell them stories from our lives, real or not, about things that have happened to us. Maybe it's a way a sibling played a trick on us or something that really aggravated us. Little seeds to plant for them to work on breaking down their opponents. Small things to make them believe they are not alone in an environment that is unlike anything they've ever encountered before.

"Now, besides the cash bonus, this year there is an additional incentive," Bradley continues. "As you all know, we have a new show coming up in the fall called *If Ever There Was*. As a special bonus, the wrangler of the person who wins will have the opportunity to join the department of their choice on that show."

I look up at that, my interest piqued.

Being a wrangler offers you a chance to learn all about casting, managing talent, and so on, which is great for those who wish to go into the casting side. Or even those who have their eye on a producer track. But what it doesn't prepare you for is the hundreds of other jobs on a set. Jobs that can take years to get a foot in the door.

"I don't need to tell you how huge of an opportunity this is," Bradley continues, "but I will. In an industry where the best way to move up is to know someone who knows someone, this is a chance to go directly into the department you want. Now, I'm not saying that you'll be the lead sound person out of the gate, for example, but it can be a chance to broaden your horizons and learn from some of the best. It can be a way to gain some credits that mean the difference between making it in this town and going back to Hicksville, USA. Just like the winner of our show, it's a chance to change your life. So go out there and help us put on the best season this network has ever seen!"

The cheers are immediate and everyone's excitement is palpable. But they are going to have to get through me to win that opportunity.

"Now, here's your favorite boss, Sheila, with some updates." He cedes the floor to Sheila, who steps up and commands the room.

"Thanks, Brad. We are finalizing the contract with the new company for facial recognition software this week and will be doing training sessions next week on how to review clips in your queue. Please attend one. This will mean less footage for you to watch, so hopefully that will help with the late nights. Alec will be leading the trainings, so get with him.

"It has been determined that wranglers will not stay on property this year. There is a nearby motel that we have rented for the duration of the show. I will send out emails today with room assignments." I mentally send up a prayer for being high-ranking enough that Sheila determined I could have my own room. "There is a small wing that we will use for our offices. Whoever is your room partner will be your office partner, so get comfortable."

There is a chorus of groans, but she continues. They'll be fine once they get settled in.

"For those that are new, Alec has some tips. Alec?"

I stand from my chair and face the room, settling into my element.

"There is not a single applicant who can win me this competition," I say from my stool at the kitchen island. The higher stakes have made me irritable as I comb through application after application, sorting them into my various piles as I weigh each one.

My best friend, Tank, is watching tape and taking notes for football practice in the morning. Papers are spread out around him on the couch and on the coffee table. He is a six foot, eight inch bruiser of a man. In elementary school, he was tiny as can be and frequently picked on for his long hair and hand-me-down clothes, so I took pity on him and stood up for him. Until he hit his growth spurt in high school.

From the time we were fifteen, no one messed with him. He bulked up and began playing football. I think the coach cried at his tryout when he could outrun and bulldoze anyone in his path. Now, men wear their hair like his. He's since cut the long hair—too annoying inside the helmet, apparently—but it hasn't lessened his attractiveness. His three-day stubble, strong jaw, and light blue eyes would make him an immediate *yes* on any show in the country. I tried to get him to agree to a dating show in the off season for a few years, but he wouldn't have it. And now that he's dating my sister, I'm glad it never worked out.

"You say that every year," he says, writing something down in his notebook, "but your contestant always does well."

"Making it to the final three doesn't matter this year. If I don't find the winner, that's it for me. I can't keep wrangling. I'm losing my mind doing the same thing year after year. I thought I would do this for a season and then be able to move on." I sort another application into the "no" pile, which stands higher than the others by a landslide.

Sensing my uncharacteristic anxiety, he pauses the tape and gives me his full attention.

"Who are the ones that you keep thinking about? It might be small, but I see some in your possibles pile."

"Well, there's one named Cain Murphy. His personality test shows he has the killer drive needed to be a contender, but I wonder if he's not a bit too intense. Listen to this. When asked, 'What would you be willing to do to win?' he responded, 'Anything, so long as I wasn't caught.' If that doesn't sound like a serial killer in the making, I don't know what does."

"Yeah, that one seems a little iffy. Anyone else?"

"There's this guy, Charles Price. He had some interesting answers. At least, the ones that I could understand."

"Give me an example."

"Okay. When asked, 'How would you do with sleep or food deprivation?' he responded with 'Sounds like a normal Tuesday to me.'"

"Huh. Why would someone intentionally deprive themselves of food or sleep?"

"Maybe he's a parent?"

"I'm going to have Lore add that to the 'con' column for being a parent," Tank says.

"But you love kids," I point out, reading through the application again.

"Yeah, but I love sleep, too."

"There's another guy named Paul who sounds like he could be perfect. He's ex-military, so you know he can take any of the punishments we throw at him. And he's probably used to not being around his family for long stretches of time," I say, lifting the third application I'm seriously considering.

"In my experience, perfect rarely is. There's a reason you haven't picked him. Who is your gut telling you to pick?"

"I don't know." I fist my hands in my hair in frustration. This could be my only shot to get into directing.

My mother was a movie buff. We would watch any genre from the tent in the living room she would make for me, my sister, and her. As time passed, eventually it was just her and me, but I loved those tents. Her voice was a constant soundtrack explaining cinematography and sound mixing. But her favorite person of any movie was the director.

"They are the storytellers," she'd say while telling me about all the choices that had to be made for one scene.

She always said that many people can recite lines, evoke emotions from their audiences, but not everyone could be the creator of a story, making their vision reality.

Her passion lit the flame of my own, but my first time directing fanned it into an uncontrollable inferno. Knowing this might be my only shot at having an open door to such a competitive field has made me almost sick with indecision. I have applied for just about every job on set to get my foot in the door, but to no avail.

"Man, this indecisive thing isn't you. You've watched ten years of winners. Who is it?"

"Charles. There's something about his answers. He'll be able to win over the audience, which is what matters the most when it comes to avoiding elimination." I pick up the middle application again, a feeling in my gut pulling me toward the person.

"Sounds like you've made up your mind. Now, grab me a beer, will you?"

Rolling my eyes, I get up from my stool and grab beers for both of us. The sounds of a football game start back up. With my decision made, I pull out my phone and shoot a text off to Sheila confirming my choice, praying that someone else hasn't snapped him up during my deliberation. She responds almost immediately that she's got my choice locked and I unclench my jaw, trying to let the stress melt away. Easier said than done.

Slipping my phone back in my pocket, I hand Tank a beer as he moves some papers without taking his eyes off the game so I can sit down. I watch the game as he continues to take copious notes. Finally, it ends, and he turns off the TV.

"So, Lorelei wanted me to ask you a question," Tank says, serious.

"I feel like you're about to ask me for a kidney." My foot rests on the coffee table in front of me, my beer resting on my thigh.

"Close. She has a friend that she thinks you'd really get along with and she wants to go on a double date."

"Dude, I love you. I would jump in front of a car for you, but no. Also, why didn't my sister ask me herself?"

"Because she knows you'll say no and she also knows that I'll do anything to please her, and that includes kidnapping your dumb ass and forcing you to go on this date. You were just saying you'd jump in front of a car for me. Consider her a blonde, sexy car," he says.

I sigh dramatically, resigned to spending an evening on a date that I don't want to be on. I point at him with my beer bottle.

"You owe me so much more than you're thinking right now. I want suite tickets or some shit."

"You got it, brother."

Soap bubbles run down my abs as I wash myself off. Dread is all I feel at the prospect of the night. The only reason I agreed is because Tank would never let me be set up with someone that I couldn't get along with for a night. And sex.

I try to remember the last time I went on a date as I shut off the water, steam floating around me.

I'm not against dating, I just prefer to do it on my own timeline. Lorelei believes that I'm going to be an eternal bachelor, but by the end of the twelve-week shooting schedule, and dealing with all the emotions of my contestant, I am exhausted. Being attached to a single person day in and day out, always at their beck and call, drives me into the ground like nothing I've ever experienced. The last day of shooting is the last time I talk to my contestant. Some guilt will normally hit a week or two later when I can see the tired lines on their faces during their after-show press tour.

I've tried to date a few times during filming, but between my late nights and being away for months on end, it wears on the woman until she, inevitably, ends things.

I wipe the condensation from the mirror and begin putting product in my black hair, enhancing the slight wave before checking my stubble beard, confirming it's not too long. Many women have commented that the light dusting of hair enhances my sharp jawline. I'm not a conceited asshole, but I can definitely get most any woman, or a man if I was so inclined, that I want.

Tank's name lights up my phone as I whip my towel off and stride naked into my impressive closet.

"Hey, man. We are going to be leaving here in about fifteen minutes to pick up Georgia. Are you still down? Work hasn't locked you up, has it?"

"No, I'm good," I tell him. To keep things simple, I grab a black t-shirt, bomber jacket, and black jeans to wear tonight. "I should leave here around the same time you do."

"Awesome. We'll see you there. And don't bring the bike."

"I wasn't planning on it, but now that makes me want to."

"It scares Lorelei when she sees you riding it."

Lorelei, God bless her, took on the role of my mother when ours died, even though I am older. I let her do it because it makes her feel better and sometimes it's nice to have someone worry about me.

"Fine, I won't ride the bike. You're welcome."

"See you soon."

I end the call, grab some boxer briefs out of my drawer and get dressed. The all-black look can be boring, but during filming, this is my unofficial uniform. I spray on some cologne and head out the door, grabbing the keys to my SUV in deference to my sister's sensibilities.

I give myself a pep talk as I pull up in front of the restaurant. With Tank's celebrity status as the greatest tight end in the league, we can get into most places at the drop of a hat. I exit the car as the valet holds the door open for me, handing me a ticket as I walk by, and I thank him.

"Lore, beautiful as always," I say, as I join my sister and Tank in front of the restaurant, pressing a kiss to her cheek. I clap Tank on the back briefly before turning my attention to the stunner standing to the side. "And you must be Georgia. I'm Alec." I offer my hand and she takes it, looking me up and down hungrily.

"Charmed, I'm sure." She gives me a wink and adjusts her dress, making sure her ample breasts grab my attention. I wet my bottom lip, thinking about how her dress will look on my floor later. My sister takes Tank's arm and turns toward the restaurant. I put mine out for Georgia and she takes it eagerly.

"Dinner should be great. I've heard this place has amazing reviews," I say, trying to start some small talk.

"I'm sure it'll be fine. The after-dinner dessert, though, is much more important to me." I smile at her as she squeezes my arm and begin counting down the minutes until her mile long legs will be wrapped around my face.

CHAPTER FOUR

CHARLIE

"Last question. Why do you want this job?" Arnold asks. His red shirt and khakis are pressed to within an inch of their life.

"Well, to be completely honest with you, I need money." After two months of almost no responses to my job applications, desperation has taken hold. While I have managed to pay all my bills on time, I'm down to my last hundred dollars, with rent due in two weeks.

"Well, Charlotte—"

"You can call me Charlie," I repeat for the third time.

"—we like our associates to have a passion for retail and the customer experience." I wait, making sure he's finished as I remember a supermarket job I had in college where I watched two ladies get into a fistfight over some oat milk while an employee stood by and recorded the scene on their phone.

"I have a passion for paying my bills, so if that means I need to have a passion for retail and the customer experience, count me in."

"Right." He stands from his chair in the cramped office and extends his hand. "We'll review this and get back to you in a few days."

I grab his hand and thank him for his time. My heels click against the linoleum floor as I make my way to the front door. Flinging my purse into the passenger seat, I settle into my car as my phone rings.

"Hello?"

"Hi, Charlotte? This is Arnold at the Pop 'n Shop, and I wanted to let you know that while we are excited about your experience, we have chosen not to move forward with your candidacy at this time. We appreciate the time you put into meeting with us today and wish you the best of luck in your job hunt."

"Great, thanks for the call." I hang up the phone without waiting to hear if he has anything else to say. "You've got to be fucking kidding me," I say, slamming my head down to the steering wheel, accidentally honking the horn.

Dejected, I turn on my car and head straight for my parents'. I know Mom will finish dinner soon. They were always early eaters, and I can get away with a free meal.

"Who's there?" Mom calls out from the kitchen.

"It's your daughter."

She pokes her head out of the kitchen. "Charlotte? Were we expecting you?"

"No, I was nearby, so I thought I'd stop in. What smells so good?"

"I'm making roasted veggies and mashed potatoes while your dad cooks some steaks on the grill. Do you want to stay for dinner?"

"That'd be nice, thanks." I move into the kitchen and sit at the circular dining table off to the side. "I had an interview today."

"Oh? And?"

"They at least waited until I was in my car to call and reject me. It was for Pop 'n Shop. Just to get some money coming in. But even they don't want me. I might be the biggest loser on the face of the planet." I pick at a piece of skin next to my thumbnail absentmindedly.

Mom leaves the potato masher in the pot as she moves toward me, wiping her hands on the towel over her shoulder. She pulls the chair out next to me, grabbing my hands in hers.

"I know you feel that way right now because you've taken a few good lumps, but that's not the case. You'll find something, and it'll be exactly what you need in life. I just know it."

The stress I've been feeling weighs on my shoulders, bowing them in. My throat tightens with tears, forcing me to swallow past the lump.

"Thanks, Mom."

"Your dad and I love you. I'm sure it's not what you want to hear, but you always have a place here." I immediately try to pull back, but her grip is like iron.

"I understand that no one wants to move back in with their parents after so long on their own," she continues, "but sometimes, you need to make those hard decisions to get to something better. Just think about it, okay?"

I nod. "Okay." I wipe the single tear making its way down my cheek, pushing my emotions down once more. "Do you need any help?"

"Can you get the drinks together? Water for me and sweet tea for your dad." She stands and makes her way back to the oven, picking up the masher once more.

I push up from the table and grab three glasses from the cupboard beside the sink. The ice cubes clink into the glasses from the refrigerator door. Setting them all on the counter, I open the door and grab a Coke for me and the pitcher of sweet tea for my dad.

My dad walks through the back door, clicking the tongs absentmindedly in his hands.

"Pops. Mom said only ten more minutes on the sides," I say, grabbing up the glasses to take them to the table. He looks at me in happy surprise while blinding me with his headlamp. Without a free hand to block the light, my retinas burn.

"Lottie Lou! There's about half that on these steaks, but they'll need to rest."

"Can you turn your head or something? You're blinding me with the sun strapped to your face."

"Ope, sorry about that." He turns the light off as black spots dance in my vision.

"You look nice, Lottie Lou. What were you up to?"

"I had a job interview at Pop 'n Shop."

"Take mace if you get that job. Those shoppers can be vicious over a sale."

"Don't I know it, but they didn't hire me. I don't live for retail like they wanted."

"Their loss."

"Thanks." I sit in my chair and watch my parents dance around the kitchen as they finish cooking our meal.

My arms are overflowing with leftovers as I leave my parents' house. I dump the various containers in my front seat, thankful I won't have to resort to what would probably be my hundredth meal of canned chicken noodle soup to take the edge off my hunger. As I pull into the parking lot of my apartment, my gas light turns on. I stare at the mocking light for what feels like an eternity before I snap.

With my hands on the wheel in a death grip, I scream. I fling myself around like an angry octopus, unable to control my anxiety and stress for another moment. My emotions have been bottled up for the last few months while I've been limping along, trying to stay positive, and I just can't any longer. I pull my cell phone out of the cup holder, video call the only number I can, and rest my forehead on the wheel.

"So, how do I go about selling my used underwear?" I ask Courtney without preamble when she answers, raising my head to look at her.

"Ha! All right, attagirl. There are all sorts of websites. Maybe you should do both the underwear and feet. That way, if one is slow to get going, hopefully, the other will take off quicker." I watch her son run, squealing to the high heavens, as J.D. chases him around with a box on his head.

"What is J.D. wearing?"

"He's a dragon chasing the prince who came to save the princess." She grabs a spice from the counter next to her and adds it to whatever I hear sizzling in the pan.

"Sure, sure. Maybe I should just be a stripper. I feel like that will be a quicker way to make money." Courtney puts the lid on her pot, grabs her phone from where she has me leaning, and sits at her island while the dinner simmers.

"Babe, with love, you are one of the worst dancers I've ever seen in my entire life," Courtney tells me, sympathy in her voice.

"Maybe when my boobs are out, that won't matter."

"You would need boobs the size of Neptune to offset your complete and utter lack of rhythm."

"Rude. I think the size of Pluto would suffice," I try to joke.

"Pluto isn't a planet anymore."

"What does that matter, Court?"

"Well, I don't know! I just felt like it did," she says, exasperated.

"Can we get back on topic? My world is ending, and Pluto's lack of planetary status doesn't exactly rate high on my priority list."

"Right, yes. Do you have any nice underwear? People would probably want them faster if they have frills and things on them." She pulls the ponytail holder from her disheveled hair, fixing it as she ties it up once more.

"I don't exactly have the money to buy new underwear."

"I'll float you."

I sigh, looking up at the ceiling of my car. "This is, possibly, the rock bottom of my life."

"No way. This could be way worse. You could live with your parents."

"I sold my couch last week. I have been sitting on the floor of my apartment and my mom offered to let me move back in."

"If you don't want to do that, you could always move in with me." I knew she would offer at some point, but I could never take her up on the offer.

"Yes, because J.D. would love that. Where would I sleep?"

"I'll make him sleep on the couch, and you can sleep with me." She turns and looks toward the living room. "Hey, babe?"

"Yeah?" J.D. calls out from where he's being attacked with a cardboard sword wrapped in foil.

"Charles is going to move in with us, and you're gonna have to sleep on the couch so she can sleep with me."

"Sounds good," he responds.

"See?" she says, turning back to me. "He wouldn't care."

"That would thrill my mother. Sometimes I think she loves you more than me."

Courtney snorts. "Too bad she didn't have a son that I could have married."

"Court. Serious voice, serious moment. What do I do?"

"Serious answer. I don't know, babe. It's time to admit this isn't working and, I never thought I'd say this but, I think you need to move back home."

"No."

"I do not see *any* other option here. Your savings are gone. You don't have a roommate, and even if you did, finding one who would like to float you for the foreseeable future isn't going to happen. You could marry for money, you're hot, but we would have needed that to be plan A. I see no other option. I wish I did, but I don't." The pity in her voice tells me I can't avoid this any longer. I have to move back in with my parents.

"I could always step in front of a bus and hope they hit me just hard enough I could get a huge settlement, but not so hard that I'll die," I offer as a last-ditch attempt to save myself.

"That is too risky of a plan, and breaking in a new best friend is tedious. Do you realize how hard it is to find someone that understands sarcasm and dark humor? I have a toddler. I don't have time for that shit. Don't be selfish."

"You're right, you're right."

An incoming call from an unknown number pops up on my screen, covering the top half of Courtney's face. While I usually ignore those, the possibility of someone calling me about a job makes me giddy with excitement.

"Hey, babe, I have to let you go. Someone's calling. Maybe it's about a job."

"Okay, good luck! I hope it's not the AARP or a telemarketer. Hate you."

"Hate you more."

I click over to the call.

"Hello, this is Charlie."

"Hi, I'm looking for Charles Price?" a young female voice asks. I sit up in my chair and put a smile on my face, my mother's voice reminding me that your tone can reflect these things through the phone.

"Hi, this is Charlie Price."

"Oh, great. Hi! I'm Kayla with Cost Communications and I would like to congratulate you on being selected!"

Confusion grips me. Selected? I've sent out more resumes than I can count, but I don't remember applying for anything with a communications company. The state of my bank account reminds me not to be picky, even if I can't remember anything about the company.

"I'm so sorry, selected for what? Is this regarding a job I applied for?"

"A job? No, you've been selected to be a part of the tenth season of *House of Deceit*!" It seems like every sentence she says ends in an exclamation point. "We start filming soon and there is a long list of things that you'll need to get in order to prepare for your time in the mansion. What—"

"Sorry to interrupt and again, apologies, but I feel like I'm a thousand steps behind here."

"Maybe I'm not doing this right." Unease enters the girl's voice. "This is the first time I've had to make these calls. The normal person is out sick and yesterday was my first day. He said that everyone is always excited or they think it's a prank, but it's not a prank. I promise."

"I'm sure it's not." I take a deep breath and hold it for a few seconds. "Okay, let's take a pause. It's Kayla, right?"

"Yeah," she says in a dejected tone.

"So Kayla, you're with Cox Communications and you'd like me to be a contestant on *House of Deceit*?"

"Cost Communications," she says, emphasizing the first word, "and yes. We received your application back in April and we think you'd be a great addition."

"I didn't apply to be on *House of Deceit*."

"Well, if that's the case, someone applied for you, which is technically illegal and you wouldn't be eligible. It pays five thousand dollars just for agreeing to participate and then you can win the prize of half a million dollars, so maybe you did apply?"

A flash of Courtney and me lying on my floor with my computer between the two of us, Courtney typing furiously as I look on, bubbles up from the deep well of my memory.

"Did you say five thousand dollars?"

"Yes, with the opportunity to win five hundred thousand!"

"That's cool, but the five thousand. Do we get that before the show starts or at the end?"

"Oh! At the beginning. If you agree, we will forward the contracts to an attorney local to you. You'll sign them and then we will wire the money to your account after your first full day on the show. Of course, if anything were to happen and you don't appear on the show for at least twenty-four hours, you will have to repay the money."

Seeing no other viable options to my money woes, I agree.

"I'm in. I applied, I just forgot. I never thought I'd be picked and so I just pushed it from my brain," I tell the girl. She doesn't need to know all the specifics.

"Awesome! I'll send you an email to the address we have on file here and you'll be able to respond with the attorney's information that you'd like to use. You have a week from today to sign the contract and have them returned to us."

"Great, thank you so much." I hang up the phone, too stunned to move. "What. The fuck. Was that?"

I drop my smile and stiff posture as I quickly video call Courtney back and try not to pass out while I wait for her to pick up.

"Was it about a job?" She plates the finished food as J.D. and Caleb settle into the table behind her.

"Did I sign up for *House of Deceit*?"

"Random. How would I know?"

"Because the only night that I would have done such an idiotic thing like *signing up for a reality show*, would be when I was drunk with you two months ago and I vaguely remember you mentioning it. And she asked for *Charles* Price. You're the only one that calls me Charles, Court!" We sit in silence, unable to remember most of our tequila night.

"Are you going to do it?" she asks, breaking the silence.

"They are offering five grand just for signing up and being on the show for twenty-four hours. So, yeah."

"Okay, this has way more promise than selling your panties to people." J.D. chokes on his taco and she reaches over, absentmindedly patting him on the back.

"And way less embarrassing," I concede.

"Well, I wouldn't say that. Depends on how they edit the footage," Courtney reminds me.

"This is a nightmare, but the five thousand can keep me in my apartment for the next three months while I continue to job hunt. I'll just go, and then after the first few days, I'll say it's too stressful and drop out."

"Looking on the bright side, I love it. It's a nice change for you because I gotta tell ya, you've been a real bummer lately."

"I feel like I was entitled to a little self-pity."

"Fair point, but it's more than that. Mark destroyed the Charlie I knew, and you were getting better, more confident, and then Scott said that bullshit about needing someone with drive and it knocked you down again," her voice becomes hard, which is rare for her. "Have some faith in yourself that you can win and stay the entire time."

"I have to find a job. If I take the five thousand and stay, I'll be wasting the time I could job hunt while my expenses are covered."

"I hear you, I do, but you could win a quarter of a million dollars, dude," Court says.

"Half a million," I inform her.

"I'm sorry, my brain just glitched. What?"

"Half a million. They raised the prize this year, it seems."

"That seals it. You have to do it."

"But what if I went the entire way, lost, and then when I got home, I'd be in the same spot!" I say, lashing out at her.

"Okay, I'm coming over tonight and we are going to talk about this while we binge seasons, taking notes on the different types of competitions you should be ready for."

I roll my eyes but open my car door, making my way to my apartment, knowing she will not change her mind no matter what I say. "Okay, sounds good."

"And Charles?"

"Yeah?"

"You *can* win this."

CHAPTER FIVE

THE STRIP MALL THE attorney's office resides in is rundown and crumbling, more graffiti than paint on the face. Weeds grow through the cracks in the asphalt, potholes littering the parking lot. The "N" of a boarded-up nail salon hangs by a wire, spinning in the wind, while a stray cat sits on the sidewalk, a leg in the air as it cleans itself.

"Do you think this is right?" I ask Courtney.

"Only one way to find out, I guess. If someone jumps out at us, I am going to push you so they murder you first," she warns me.

"I thought you didn't have time to break in a new best friend?" I remind her.

She waves away my comment. "Sacrifices must be made."

We get out of the car and I look at the email for the suite number once more.

"I think it's on the left," I say.

"I'm going to haunt your ass when we get murdered," she says, following close behind me.

"I'll be murdered with you, so I won't have an ass to haunt."

"Then I'll haunt you in heaven," she hisses. "J.D. will get remarried 'cause he's a catch and I'll have to haunt him, too. This is going to be a very exhausting afterlife."

"Maybe you should save your energy and stop talking," I say, trying to suppress my smile at her fake outrage. Grabbing the handle, I push the door open.

The office is a fresh, serene blue. All the furniture and fixtures are up to date and beautiful, a stark difference from the outside. A sleek, well put together receptionist taps away at his keyboard behind a glossy marble desk.

"Hi, my name is —"

"Charlotte Price, yes, we've been expecting you. Hello. And your friend?"

"This is Courtney."

"Is she additional legal counsel?"

"No, just emotional support," I say, half joking, half not.

"She'll have to wait out here as there are things that must be discussed that require an NDA. In the meantime, may I offer either of you refreshment?"

"No, we are fine. Thank you," I answer for both of us.

We move to take our seats on the couch and wait. The plush seats swallow us. Courtney's feet don't touch the floor, and I fight against the giggle rising in my throat.

"Shut up. This couch is too deep!" She scoots back, her legs flailing a bit as she shifts backward. A snorting laugh escapes me as the attorney emerges from the hallway, wearing the exact same outfit as his online picture. He smiles at me.

"Sorry to interrupt the fun, but if you could follow me, Ms. Price?"

I smother the laughter still sitting in my chest as I get up to follow the man. He's shorter than my five-nine, but not terribly so. His suit is bland but fits him like a glove. The lights above us reflect as a soft glow off his bald spot. He stops outside an office, holding his hand out for me to lead the way.

"If I understand correctly, Ms. Price, you're here to sign a contract to appear on *House of Deceit*. Is that correct?" He flips through the papers in front of him, skimming them as he goes. "This seems like a straightforward agreement, but there are a few clauses I want to point out for your knowledge.

"The first is that you agree to take part in all competitions and any repercussions of losing said competitions. These punishments can include but are not limited to: deprivation of food, sleep, and clothing, loss of access to things in the mansion, manual labor, ice baths, and any other acts that do not include permanent physical harm or death. Do you have questions about that?"

"So, they can do anything they want but disable or kill me?"

"Basically, yes. And if you don't play, they will not be required to pay you any winnings."

"Okay, and the other clause?"

"Cost Communications will not be responsible for loss of employment or loss of any current or future income resulting from the show or its editing of any footage of you."

"What does that mean, exactly?"

"In layman's terms, if you get fired or have a hard time finding a job in the future due to any notoriety from the show, it's not their problem. With these shows, they edit them for the most entertainment value they can. Sometimes, that means something you say or do can be edited out of context and the audience could, very much, end up hating you. This could lead to people being fired or denied a job, as the cost to the company's reputation is not worth the risk of employing you. Someone who is recognizable by the public, good or bad, can become a liability to their employer."

I pick at the seam on the leg of my shorts, weighing my options. With my plan to only be on the show for a few days, it wouldn't be long enough to damage my reputation that badly. However, with my current desperation and lack of funds, the possibility of financial insecurity makes my stomach knot.

"Got it. I'm just going to be upfront with you. I don't have a job right now. And if I don't get that five grand sign-on bonus, I'll lose my apartment. So, I guess I'm okay with that."

"Understood. While you're on the show, you will have no contact with the outside world. I would suggest setting up a power of attorney so someone you trust can make decisions on your behalf. This also helps with things like paying your bills or talking to someone about your accounts. It's not typically a big deal nowadays with auto payment, but it's better to be safe than sorry."

He pulls another form from his desk and goes about explaining it. After over two hours, I have signed more paperwork than I care to ever again. I have a thick folder tucked under my arm as I make my way back to where Courtney is waiting. When I come out, she is lounging on the couch, her nose buried in a magazine. On the table next to her sits an empty mug and a candy wrapper.

"Hey," I call to her. She jumps from her spot, holding in the scream I can see she almost unleashed. She is the easiest person to scare in the world. "Are you ready?"

"Oh, yes." She puts the magazine on the coffee table and brings her mug up to the reception desk. "Just tell Susan she's right and you're wrong and you love her. Good luck," she says to him.

"Thanks, Court! Have a great day, ladies."

"What the hell was that?" I ask as we climb into Courtney's car. Mine did not have enough gas for the trip.

"What? He was having a very tense conversation and I could tell it was personal. I asked him if he wanted to talk. You were gone *a long time.*"

"I'm so sorry that signing my life away and agreeing to let someone torture me took so long. Next time, I'll just say 'fuck it' and sign."

"I'd appreciate that, thank you."

She backs out of the space, and I watch the crumbling building with the well-appointed office disappear into the distance, much like any thoughts about a pre-planned course for my life.

The sunlight is bright in my room, but I make no move to close the curtains. Sleep was scarce with the strange series of events over the past twenty-four hours. It feels like forever ago that I was considering moving in with my parents, and now I'm mere weeks from my bank account being flush. Still, my financial worries aren't completely wiped away.

I think about the half a million dollars. With that kind of money, I could buy myself a home in cash and not have to worry about paying rent ever again. The picture forms in my mind of me sipping coffee on my outdoor couch in early fall, my favorite cream sweater on, watching the sunrise over the lake. Birds would call as they woke and greeted the day. My elderly neighbors would invite me out on their boat on the weekends. Their handsome grandson would visit and we would fall in love with the wind in our hair as we cruise around the lake.

A horn honks, and my daydream dissipates like the mist on the lake I want to live beside. I roll over and look out my actual window and mentally prepare myself to tell my parents. Deciding to bite the bullet, I get out of bed and make my way to the bathroom.

My red hair is in absolute disarray. Half has fallen out of my ponytail and the crown is standing straight up. I take out the band that's barely holding on and try to brush my hair for a moment. Soon, it's nothing but a tangled rat's nest on top of my head, and I decide not to struggle further. Only washing will do. Turning on the water to warm, I strip out of my clothes, dumping them in the laundry hamper.

My one-woman concert brings the crowd to their feet and has erased my anxiety temporarily. Calls for encores convince me to give my fans what they want; I wouldn't have my career without them. I step off the stage and back into my bathroom. Cheers fade in my ears while I swipe the condensation from my mirror before brushing my formerly tangled hair as I move to my closet, throwing on the first clothes my hands touch.

My hallway is empty as I lock the door behind me. I punch the button, calling the elevator to my floor, ecstatic that I'll be able to fill my gas tank to the top on my way to my parents' house. My favorite song starts up on the radio as I turn on my car. With the smallest piece of hope blooming in my chest, I sing.

"Do you want some pie?" My mom bustles around the kitchen.

"What kind?"

"Apple with some vanilla ice cream."

"Oh, yeah. I need some of that, please," I say.

She nods and grabs a plate from the cabinet, moving to the counter and uncovering the pie. She sets the plate in front of me and kisses the top of my head.

"Thank you, Mommy," I tell her as I dig in.

Dad works on the Sunday crossword with his favorite pen.

"How's the crossword going, Pops?"

"This week is a little hard, Lottie Lou."

"Do you need any help?"

"Now, you know I don't take help." He winks at me and gets back to it. My mom sits down and kisses him on the cheek.

"So, I wanted to tell you about a real opportunity that has come up and it'll help me with my lack of income issue," I tell my parents.

"Oh, that's so great, Charlotte!" My mom reaches across the table. "What will you be doing? Did a newspaper hire you?"

"Not exactly."

"What are you going to be doing, sweetie?"

"See, here's the thing. Court and I, well, we were drinking after I quit and Scott left me—"

"We know, honey." My mom rolls her eyes.

I ignore that and continue. "What you don't know is that we signed me up for a game show. And I was picked."

"Oh, my goodness! That's so exciting! Which show?" My mom clasps her hands to her chest while I wonder if my dad heard me. I finish the pie and ice cream and push my plate to the side.

"What's a six-letter word for fraud? It has an 'I' in it." I look at my dad as he taps his pen to his lips.

"*House of Deceit.*"

"That's it!" Dad exclaims. He spells out deceit as he writes the word in the space. "That's so nice, Lottie. They'll be lucky to have you."

"You're going to meet *the* Jacob Jacobson?" my mother asks.

"Well, maybe not in person, but definitely over the screen in the mansion."

"Your mother really loves that man. He's on her pass list," Dad adds as he tries to solve the next clue. My mom blushes and swats at his arm.

"I didn't need to know that," I say, wishing I had more pie.

"Now, honey, I'm all for you doing what makes you happy, and not losing your apartment, but can I ask you a question?" Fearing the worst, I motion for her to ask. "What about your, you know, *issues*?"

"What issues are we talking about?"

"You know, your shy sphincter?" She whispers the last two words like someone might overhear us.

"What are you talking about?" My dad puts down his pen, a light smile on his face, knowing what's coming.

"I don't have a shy sphincter." I can't believe we are having this conversation, but then again, my mother holds the deep belief that no area of my life is off limits to her commentary.

"Well, honey, you're not being completely honest with yourself. You wouldn't even poop in the bathroom that was on your floor at your office."

"I figure it would be hard for people to take me seriously in a meeting if they hear my ass noises, mom."

"Don't be vulgar. What about that time you were seeing that nice boy, I forget his name, but he only had one bathroom and you left in the middle of the night to go to the gas station to relieve yourself and your car got stolen. Do you remember that?"

"Of course I remember that. My *car* got stolen."

"All I'm saying is that I've watched that show and they only have those communal toilet stalls," she says, trailing off.

"Deborah, leave the girl alone. You're not exactly pooping with the door open every night, yourself," my dad laughs.

"There should be some secrets between a husband and wife," my mother sniffs.

"I've been in there after you. I think we are past that." My mother's face flames red, almost as deep as our hair. Dad and I laugh at her discomfort until she's reluctantly laughing with us.

"Thank you for your concern, Mom," I tell her, "but this is an opportunity that will probably never come around again, and I have nothing keeping me from taking it. Plus, they are giving me five thousand dollars just to be on the show for a day."

"When do you leave?" my mom asks.

"In a few days. We have to be there a week early to record some introductions, promotional things, and stuff like that."

"My Lottie Lou Lou is going to be on *House of Deceit*. I hope you kick all their asses." Dad has a wicked gleam in his eye as he pats my hand. His smile unknots the nerves in my chest, and I smile with a lump in my throat. I'm going to miss my parents while I'm gone.

CHAPTER SIX

M Y EAR-BUDS DIE as the tires of the plane touch down on the ground in California. I take them out and sink into the sounds of the crying baby in the row behind me. The parent tries frantically to shush the kiddo, but nothing works. People around me grumble, but I let the wails wash over me.

My seat gets jostled, the baby squirming around in anger and the dad fighting to contain them within the small space, as the flight attendants announce we can get up. Accepting that it'll be a while before my row can deplane, I pop my head over the back of my seat. The baby stops flinging themselves around for a moment, looking at me. I duck back down before popping up again. The wails stop for a second before resuming. I pop over the chair again and this time, I get a watery smile.

By the time my row stands, I am in a deep game of peekaboo that has the baby squealing with laughter. People around us smile at the glee the baby is exhibiting, clapping its hands and gurgling happily.

"See ya later, kiddo." I stand to grab my things as the father thanks me. I give him a nod and smile before making my way down the aisle.

The baggage claim signs guide me like fairy lights through an enchanted forest. Waking up at four in the morning to catch my plane has made me tired, but my nervous excitement is winning out. Hordes of people wait, jostling for position in a race that is not happening. We all stand in a clump. The siren wails and the light flashes. Grabbing up our carry-ons, we move with a hive-like mind to get closer to the carousel. The spinning metal conveyor belt is the only thing standing between us and the sweet freedom of fresh air.

When I graduated high school, one of my gifts from some relative or another was a set of plain black suitcases. For someone who rarely traveled and only needed them to get to and from campus, I didn't much mind. But when you're in a creative major, which is pretty much any major that isn't STEM, you make even more creative friends.

Courtney and I had very different college experiences. Whereas she was in all the smart classes and absolutely smashed every one, my course load was lighter, not easier, but less demanding. While Court spent most of her days in the library, I spent mine with various people I'd met in some of my electives.

During one ill-fated semester, a painter took pity on me and my horrid attempts at surrealist art. He helped me pass, and I helped him learn where the clitoris is. We were both better for our time together. One night, after our rendezvous, he was bored. Getting out my paints that I had hardly touched once the class was over, he painted my boring black suitcases.

The flower designs are faded and chipped now, but they are still distinct enough that it takes me two seconds to find my bags. I shove through the unmoving wall of sweaty bodies before me and snatch my bags off the belt. Pretty much every piece of clothing that I own, and many that Courtney helped me shop for with a generous loan from my parents, is shoved in these two bags. The list of acceptable items was specific and limited. No visible brands or logos. No words. Evening attire was encouraged for the live eliminations. Shoes of various types, but they would provide any outfits needed for the competitions. And swimsuits. With the amount of downtime, swimsuits were a must.

Of course, we couldn't bring anything electronic. No smart watches or phones would be allowed in the house but were permitted up to the minute we left for the mansion. Mainly so production could coordinate with us. The only source of entertainment would be provided by the show. Board games, books, and cards. Anything else was prohibited. Thankfully, books were my haven. I just hoped they had some good titles.

The air is hot as I step out of the terminal, smacking me in the face as if I've opened an oven, but not smothering how North Carolina is. My skin starts sweating immediately but unlike back home, my normally frizzy hair isn't growing with each second that passes. I look around for the shuttle to the hotel I will stay at for the next week, counting down the moments until I can be alone in my room, the last place I'll have a moment alone for who knows how long.

The hotel is impressive. Giant chandeliers hang throughout the lobby, casting a soft, candle-like glow on the room below. Classic black-and-white checkered marble sweeps through the vast space. The bar is to my right. No TVs hang above it, encouraging the patrons to talk to one another. A woman in a red dress sits, lonely, sucking the olive off a stick before taking a drink.

"Hello, welcome to the Wagoner Hotel. How can I help you?" The receptionist has a hint of an accent I can't place. Her braids are long, and various gold and silver jewels hang from them. Red lips are set in a serene smile, and immediately I'm at ease.

"Hello, the last name is Price." Her long-nailed fingers start clacking away at the keys. "I'm not sure if it'll be under my name or not. Or maybe the company's name?" I'm more talking to myself; the woman's eyes haven't lifted from her screen since I first said my name.

"Charles Price?"

"That's me."

"Yes, Ms. Price, we have you right here. We have you for five nights. Is there anyone staying with you?" Still the serene smile, the beautiful eyes.

"No, just me, thank you."

She taps around again before feeding a card into a machine. She folds it into a little holder and then hands me a small piece of paper.

"Here's the Wi-Fi password. The dining room serves food twenty-four seven and there is room service. Per the booking, anything you would like is included. Just bill any food or services to your room. Now, if you'd like to enjoy the pool, it's right here." She points to a map she pulls from the counter by her computer. She shows me the various amenities, gym, pool, and bar, before telling me my room number. Before I know it, I'm on the elevator riding up to the tenth floor, my brain muddled from all the different directions.

I snap awake, hair plastered to my face. My legs are numb from passing out with them hanging over the edge of the bed. After dropping my bags right inside the door, I was devoid of enough energy to fully climb into bed before exhaustion beat me into submission. The sun is setting, a golden glow sliding down the wall. I move to stand up and immediately drop to the floor. I lay there for a moment like a starfish, giving my legs time to wake up. As sharp tingles run up my legs, I wonder if this is how Ariel felt when she received her land legs.

I get up and stumble to the bathroom. My skin feels covered in grime, so I quickly strip and hop into the shower. The water has great pressure and I groan in ecstasy, washing my hair so it has time to air dry before I meet my wrangler in the morning. A list of various activities that I have to complete sits in my inbox. After I climb out of the shower, the air cold against my warm skin, I brush my hair and put on a simple outfit. Keeping my face bare, I grab a copy of my favorite fantasy book. I slip the room key into my back pocket and make my way down to the bar.

The bartender stops wiping the bar and walks over to me. Flipping the white towel over the shoulder of his black vest, he sets a coaster in front of me and hands me a menu.

"Good evening, gorgeous. What can I get you to drink?" His dimples wink at me from the quintessential boy-next-door face.

I smile at him. "A glass of red wine would be great. Whatever you think is best."

"No problem," he says, moving away.

He comes back after a moment and sets a glass in front of me, the maroon liquid catching the last dying rays of sunlight through the window.

"Can I have the grilled chicken salad, please? With the dressing on the side?" I ask him.

"Anything for you." He winks at me, touching my hand slightly as he takes back the menu. My cheeks heat, causing him to smile. As the minutes tick on, the bar fills with people. The bartender is swept into the dinner rush while I sink down in my book. The cover and a good chunk of the pages are taped together.

At the top of my check, long after my two glasses of wine and dinner have disappeared, is a phone number and an imploring "Call me." I leave the receipt on the bar. After Scott, I have no intention of dating for a very long time. And that includes one-night stands. When I get back to my room, I immediately fall into the arms of sleep like a lover welcoming me home once more.

I hesitate outside the room, deep in the bowels of the hotel where my first interview will be. Seated right in the middle of a black, matte backdrop surrounded by many studio lights is a camera. Nerves hit my stomach like a battering ram. Questioning what the hell I got myself into, I move toward the closest person to me in a headset.

"Hello, I'm Charlie Price."

She looks at me from head to toe. "You're Charlie Price?"

"Yes?"

She presses a button on what looks like a battery pack on her hip. "Hey, get Alec down to the ballroom." A pause. "I don't care. Tell him it's an emergency."

Confusion and embarrassment creep in and I cross my arms over my stomach.

"Is there a problem? I signed the contract and everything."

"Let's get you into makeup," she says, pushing me toward the group of lighted mirrors. "We need you dressed and ready in ten minutes. Got it?"

"Yeah," I say, but I'm talking to her back. She's gone before I can get the entire word out.

I sit down and the makeup artist whips out a small bag of makeup. Without a word, she swipes some blush, mascara, and lipstick on me with a practiced hand. People in black rush in and out of the room, talking into their headsets, checking lists. The chaos seems organized. Every player is exactly where they should be, exactly when they should be there. They are the ballerinas in the day's dance and I'm the next principal who does not know what the routine is.

"You're done," she says as she starts cleaning her brushes. Standing from the chair, I'm unsure where to go. Stepping up to the woman I first talked to, I tapped her on the shoulder.

"Hi, sorry, but I'm ready. Where should I go?"

She looks me up and down again and a small fire of indignation flickers to life in me. I might not be a model, but I know that I'm a beautiful woman. Courtney and I are hit on any time we go out. I've caught men, and some women, checking me out as I move through the grocery store, giving me little smiles or winks. I open my mouth to ask what her problem is, but before I have the chance, the person I assume is the director calls me over to be seated in the blue chair in front of the camera. The lights are so much warmer than I ever thought they would be.

The camera-man steps behind the camera and soon a red light is on. A woman sits in the chair to the side and out of the camera's eye line. She smiles at me.

"Can you introduce yourself?"

It feels like the camera is moving closer to me by the second, the red light distracting me. Trying to push the nerves out, I smile, settling down into the calm that I reserve for when I conduct interviews. "Hello, my name is Charlie Price."

"What do you do for work, Charlie?"

"I am a, or, I *was* a journalist."

"Was? What happened?" She shifts in her seat. I see her working the angles, trying to fish out a good story for the first episode, so I give it to her.

"My boss was a jerk." I mentally smile at the thought of the indignation that Mark would feel if he saw this. "Actually, not only is he an asshole, he is an ex-boyfriend. One day, I couldn't take it anymore. I was tired of his shit and so I quit."

"Is that why you applied for *House of Deceit?*"

"The tequila I had been drinking made that decision. To be completely honest with you, I forgot I had applied until I received the phone call that I had been selected." I smile. "But I'm so thrilled to be here. It's such a great opportunity."

"The money prize must be pretty important to you."

"You could say that." I give her a full-watt smile. "But isn't it important to everyone? Why else would someone want to leave their life, come on this show, and possibly get torn to shreds?"

The back door opens and a man walks in, his imposing stature catching my attention. I can't peel my eyes from him as he strides across the room, and I miss my interviewer's response. He's in all black, like everyone, but he exudes power that makes my hair stand up like lightning is about to strike. Which may be the case, because he looks *pissed*.

CHAPTER SEVEN

ALEC

ALICE LOCKS EYES WITH me and doesn't blink as I stride toward her. I was in an important meeting, tying up last-minute details as the lead wrangler, when I was yanked out for this *emergency*. A stunning redhead sits in the interview chair. Her voice is low, smoky. Like a campfire on a fall day.

"What *the fuck* am I doing here? There was another forty minutes until I needed to be here to pick up Price."

I'm trying to rein in my temper, but it's quickly bubbling to the surface.

"Your contestant is here," Alice says.

I check my watch before looking around, not seeing him.

"Okay? Where is he? Does he need something and why couldn't you take care of it?"

"Well, *she* is right over there." She points behind me.

"She?"

"She."

I turn around and take in the woman that is apparently Charles. Red hair falls over her ample breasts in waves. Her long legs peek out beneath a short skirt. The black heels make them look even longer. When she smiles, laughing, pushing her hair over her shoulder as she answers a question, my lungs stop. My adoration of this beautiful woman sours with dread as I see this season going up in smoke along with my shot at directing.

My nails cut into my palms as I clench my fists. I can feel myself scowling. Unable to go back to my meeting, I watch the woman as she finishes up her interview. She's effervescent beneath the lights, but I seethe. I hate liars. Lies are what my ex-fiancé fed me for dinner every night.

"I love you."

Lie.

"He's just a work friend."

Lie.

"I would never cheat on you."

Lie.

Lies stole the dignity and respect I deserved from someone I had intended to spend my life with.

I send a text to Sheila, letting her know we are going to need to have a discussion. This mix-up will change the dynamics of the house. Every other season had an equal number of male and female participants to start with. While this changes after the first week, it will cause an issue with the way the rooms are situated. I shoot off a text to our attorneys that we'll need their input on the situation as well.

Without looking up from my phone, I ask Alice to please bring the woman to me as I hear her finishing up her interview. Sheila responds, telling me to meet her in twenty minutes and not to be late. I tap out a response, making a mental list of the other contestant applications I had read through, hoping one of my other top contenders is still available.

The woman's heels make a dull sound as she moves across the carpet. I look up into an alluring pair of sapphire eyes. Her smile is mesmerizing, but it does not lessen my scowl, her lies sticking in my craw. She holds out her hand as she stops in front of me.

"Hi, I'm Charlie Price." The smoky voice I noticed when I first walked in the room washes over me, but it does nothing to temper my anger. I grab her bicep and start pulling her from the room. "Hey, what the fuck is your problem?"

She struggles to rip her arm from my grip but is unable to do so, garnering the attention of a few of the newer staff, but no one stops us.

"Hey! Stop! Let go of me, you raging dick hole!" She continues hollering as I pull her from the room. I shove her into a small office across from the ballroom, releasing her when the door closes behind us.

I turn around, and I barely have a chance to inhale before her hand is connecting with my cheek. Fire rips through my face as my neck wrenches from one side to the next. I stretch my jaw, feeling where she slapped me. Her nostrils are flaring, and she's huffing and puffing like a freight train.

"Well, you definitely have a good arm on you," I tell her.

"You're lucky I didn't sucker punch you."

"Before you hit me again, maybe you'd like to explain why you lied on your application?"

"I didn't lie on my application, and even if I did, you have absolutely *no right* to manhandle me." She crosses her arms under her breasts, pushing them up. It takes everything in me to keep my eyes on hers, but I have a feeling if they stray for even a moment, I'm in for another physical altercation. I grit my teeth.

"I'm sorry about that. Now, let's discuss how I was expecting a man and you are most definitely"—I eye her up and down—"not."

"Why would I be a man?" she asks, moving to take a seat and I sit opposite her, pulling up her application on my phone.

"Your name is listed here as Charles Price. Charles tends to be a male name."

"My name is Charlotte. I go by Charlie and my best friend back home calls me Charles."

"So, you thought you'd use a name that's not yours to get around the equal starting numbers of men and women on the show?"

She rolls her eyes, and it lights my temper anew. "I just told you, it is my name. It's just not my government name." She crosses her long legs.

"I will be meeting with the executive producer of our show and the attorneys. Don't get too comfortable." I give her a sharp smile and stand, moving to leave the room, hoping I can get a new contestant here in time for the start of the show.

"Attorneys? Wait, hold on." She jogs, getting in front of me and throwing herself in front of the doors. "I can't be kicked off this show. At least, not before I fulfill the obligations to get the five grand I was promised just for making it to the mansion."

Her deep blue eyes are panicked, and for a moment the expression reminds me of Lorelei. Even though I'm fuming with the situation this woman has put us both in, I soften. But barely.

"I can't make any promises. The attorneys will have to make the call, but I'll do what I can to at least get you the five thousand, okay?"

"Okay. Thank you." She straightens, clearing her throat. "I never got your name."

"Alec. Alec King."

"Well, Alec King, it's nice to meet you." She sticks her hand at me again, and this time I take it. The air must be dry because I feel an electric shock as our skin meets. She gives me a tentative smile and I feel one side of my mouth kick up.

"I have to go. Continue with the rest of your schedule and I'll let you know what decision is made."

My footsteps echo against the marble floor of the hallway as I rush to Sheila's makeshift office.

I burst through the door exactly twenty minutes after Sheila texted me. She checks her watch, ever the stickler for punctuality. Chairs for twenty ring the oak table. Sheila is at the head of the table across from the doors while two attorneys sit on her left. The chair's wheels drag across the carpet as I pull it out from the table.

"Alec, you have us all here," Sheila says, linking her hands in front of her, "why don't you tell us what the issue is?"

"The contestant I picked completed the application using the name 'Charles Price.'" I hand out copies of the application to each person. "However, her *legal* name is Charlotte. We need to get one of the backups here in the next twenty-four hours."

"Her?" Sheila flips through the prints. "How did this happen?" She stops at the box asking for the person's gender and sees what I saw. "How did you miss this?"

I sigh, heavily. "Marshall thought it was an accident and, without confirming, he added it to the pile he sent out to the male wranglers. And to be transparent, it's not something I double check. After looking at the names, I move to their answers."

"Fucking Marshall. Okay, what's done is done. Now," she looks to the attorneys, "what are the actions we need to take? How can we avoid a lawsuit here?"

They take their own papers from the briefcases and give me and Sheila copies as well. The attorney on the right takes a deep breath and begins speaking.

"When we heard about there being an issue with Alec's contestant, we pulled the contract. Even though the application was filled out with the name Charles, she signed the contract to participate with her legal name. Using a nickname on the application doesn't make it invalid. The contract has been signed and notarized. She can only be removed from the competition if she breaks a rule."

"You've got to be kidding. We don't have the ability to remove someone for any reason?" Sheila asks.

The attorney on the right takes this question. He reaches up and pushes his glasses up his nose.

"The subsection that talks about falsifying anything does not include using a nickname. Everything about her is correct as far as we can tell and, as my partner said, she signed the contract with her legal name. It's binding."

Sheila taps her phone on the table. Her eyes are sightless as she calculates the options and makes a choice. "Obviously, we're not getting rid of this girl. Here's what we are going to do." She sits forward in her chair and I prepare to take notes to fulfill her wishes.

"The rooms. We are going to intermingle them this time around. Two women and two men in four of them. The other room will have three women and the last man. This could be a chance for more drama. Instead of the competitions for privileges being split based on gender, which was always stupid, it will be a random split. You will need to spread these changes to the others."

I nod, making notes.

"Now, you will need to talk to Charlotte and see if she would like a female wrangler." My heart freezes in my chest as I try not to let emotion take over. If she picks another wrangler, I'm out.

"I'm sorry, why would we need a new wrangler for her?"

"Alec, the role of the wrangler is to be this person's confidant, their best friend in the entire house. The one that keeps them from losing it when they don't know if they can trust anyone."

"I can be that for her. I'm the most senior wrangler. This isn't my first rodeo."

"The choice is hers. I'm not going to make her agree to having a man watch all of her footage, do her interviews, and all of that if she would feel more comfortable with a woman. I'm in the business of putting on the best show I can and that requires people to open up. Ask her. Now."

I pace outside of Charlie's hotel room after the concierge confirmed she hadn't come back down. Whispering to myself, I rehearse my speech. My hands fiddle with the edge of my jacket, pulling it down. Button. Unbutton. Button it again.

"Stop stalling." I lift my hand to knock as she pulls the door open.

"Oh, fuck me running!" She puts her hand to her chest and bends at the waist before standing straight and putting her hands on her hips. "You scared the shit out of me."

I smile at her, trying to be approachable. Polite. "Sorry. I was just coming to talk to you for a minute. Do you mind?"

"Oh, sure. I was going to grab some lunch, but I could have something brought up." She moves out of the way, ushering me in. "Would you like anything?" The kindness surprises me.

"I'll have whatever you're having. Thank you."

She nods, picking up the phone and dialing quickly.

"Hi there," she smiles, "yeah, it's Charlie Price in room 1015. Could I get two of the grilled chicken salads with the dressing on the side, please?" The voice on the other end of the phone is garbled. "And two of my normal dessert, please. Sure, sounds good. Thanks!"

"A salad sounds good."

"Their salads are really delicious and probably not at all healthy." She stands up from the bed and moves to sit on the edge, closer to where I'm leaning against the dresser. "So, what's up?"

Her thumb nail picks at the nail polish on one of her other fingers. After mom died, when Lore was particularly stressed, she'd pick at her fingers. Sometimes, she'd pick so much, they'd bleed. I hated watching her hurt herself, so every night I painted her nails. The next day, she'd pick off every fleck of polish.

Her hand is soft against my fingers as I bend forward, stopping the nervous tick. Sapphire blue eyes bore into mine with an intensity I feel move through my chest and clutch my lungs in a fist. Straightening, I cross my ankles and put my hands in my pockets. I give a small cough, getting my lungs working again.

She smiles and I know she's going to be a crowd favorite. Between her beauty and feisty personality, everyone is going to fall in love with her. I know it like I know the sound of my sister's laugh. It might not be enough to win, but I pray I'll be around to see how far she can take it.

CHAPTER EIGHT

CHARLIE

"ARE YOU GOING TO tell me what y'all came up with, or are we just spending quality time together?" I don't know why I say it. Flirting with the man who yanked me out of the ball-room like a toddler throwing a fit shouldn't happen. But between his genuine surprise when I asked him if he'd like lunch combined with his long, dark eyelashes fanning around bright, gray eyes, my hormones seem to be winning out.

"I wanted to share what we came up with, since we weren't ex-pecting you to be *you*," he says, his tone grating.

The desire to lock myself into the bathroom and sing while plug-ging my ears so I can't hear what's coming tries to take over me. It grabs hold of my legs, making them twitch, but I lock my body down. I will sit here and pretend my world will not crumble if I lose this chance. I will *not* give him a piece of any emotion I feel except vague disinterest.

"I'm going to need you to stop saying that like my existence is the equivalent of Armageddon bearing down on us," I tell him instead.

He stares at me for a moment. "Right, sorry," he clears his throat but says nothing.

"Any time now," I snark.

Maybe not so much as vague disinterest, then. His gray eyes flash, and the muscle in his jaw ticks.

"I'm here to offer you a choice. Typically, female contestants have a female wrangler but because of this mix-up, I picked you. For the next twelve weeks, if you'll have me, I'll be your wrangler. Sheila, the executive producer of the show and my manager, wanted to offer you the opportunity to switch to another wrangler."

"I'm not kicked off the show?" The terror at the thought of losing my apartment slowly dissipates.

"No. Per your contract, you've done nothing to warrant your early departure, so you get to stay."

Relief, cool and deep like a coursing river, washes my nerves away in its current.

"So, who would I be assigned to if I kick your ass to the curb? Which, P.S., you would totally deserve after the way you treated me." He fidgets. For a man who commands a room, he's been off center since the moment he walked in. This guy was an asshole, but the journalist in me rears her head, catching the whiff of a story.

"Um, unsure, actually. They'd have to pull in a new wrangler for you. There might be a veteran available, but if not, you'll be stuck with someone they pull out of a stack of applications for people that have never been on the show before."

"What do you get if you're my wrangler?"

"What makes you think wranglers get anything other than a pay-check?"

I open my mouth, but a knock at the door interrupts us.

"Room service!" the man calls out through the wood. I go to move from the bed, but Alec waves me down, pushing off the dresser. The cart wheel squeaks, a pitch that makes every hair on my body stand and my teeth clench as the attendant pushes it into the room.

Alec, the walking ad for men's suits, takes it and puts the cart right before me, signing the receipt in my place. After the server has left, he lifts the domes from our salads. His gray eyes sparkle with humor as he raises an admonishing eyebrow at me.

"Is that hot fudge on top of the ice cream?"

"Yes, yes, it is." I smile. I could eat my weight in hot fudge. I grab up the ice cream bowl and spoon and promptly dig in.

"Dessert before lunch?"

"Don't tell me you're a stickler for food consumption order? Let me tell you, your stomach doesn't understand the difference between eating ice cream at the end or beginning. Enjoy life. Maybe it'll get that stick out of your ass."

He stands up straight, affront etched on his face. It makes me want to sit on his mouth. I mentally slap myself. These smart comments might not be helpful to anyone in this room. Especially me, if I have to work with him daily.

Trying to keep myself from saying anything else snarky, or worse, flirtatious, I shove more ice cream into my mouth. The hot fudge melds with the vanilla ice cream, sliding down my throat in a dichotomy of temperatures. My smile is surprised when he grabs up his portion of dessert and digs in.

"If you want me to stick with you, and I can tell you do, you need to tell me why. What's in it for you?"

He sighs heavily and ignores my question as he takes a few more bites. I refuse to retract it. Either he answers, or I get assigned a new wrangler.

"I want to go into directing," he says.

I wait.

Nothing more comes.

"Okay? And?"

He scrapes the last bit of ice cream from his dish. We both set them down. As I start on my salad, he runs his hands through his lush hair.

"Fuck, okay. It's like this. This season, the wrangler of the winner gets the chance to be moved to the department of their choice for a new show with Cost Communications. I have tried to move to sit-coms for *years* and could never break in. This industry is a hierarchy and reality shows are at the bottom. It was the quickest way for me to get a foot in the door, but now it's biting me in the ass. Add to the nepotistic way the industry is run, and, well, this could be the only shot I have to make this change and get where I want to go."

My heart breaks for him. I think about how my job was supposed to be my big break but was a dead end. And then I think of all the things I would be willing to do for the break of getting my writing into the hands of someone who could make my novelist dreams come true, and the limit to those things would be minimal. How could I deny someone an opportunity to get what they want when it asks almost nothing of me?

I chew my salad, letting him stew in the uncertainty like I did this morning. Plus, he was an ass. He put his hands on me when I didn't consent to it; for that, he deserves to squirm. When he can tell I'm not going to answer immediately, he picks up his salad and digs in. Once the dishes are cleared and the cart is back in the hallway, I take pity on the man.

"You should know, I don't plan to stay on the show beyond the first week, at most," I inform him. Guilt racks me at the thought of my choice leading to his dream not being realized, but I'm sure he'll get another shot.

"All of my contestants in the past six years have made it to the final three. So long as you're athletic and can keep yourself out of the bottom two, I can help make you likable. I'll be watching all of your footage and choosing what parts are included in the show, as well as editing your interviews that we do together."

His confidence is enticing, but I notice a tightness around his eyes that divulges his nerves. Plus, my need for a job beats the slim possibility of winning. But I noticed the wording of his statement. He didn't say winners, he said top three, and only the winner receives a prize.

I scoot back onto the bed, arranging pillows to prop me up against the headboard.

"I'm sure you're competent at your job, but I have some money troubles I need to get back to."

"Half a million dollars could solve quite a few money problems," he says simply, crossing his ankle over his knee.

"It could, but only if I win it."

"It sounds like we both have a pretty good reason to make sure you're the last one standing, then."

My competitiveness rears its ugly head.

"What's in it for me? If I keep you as my wrangler?"

"I'll make you the fan favorite. The one everyone loves. The one the audience follows *after* the show. Brands give deals and endorsements to the contestants they feel like the audience clicks with. That could be money in your pocket, and you just said that's a draw for you. Do you know how much brands pay? Thousands. You'll barely have to do anything, and you'll be able to say goodbye to those money troubles."

I think of some of the contestants who have been on *House of Deceit* and how, after their season, I keep seeing them around. On other shows. With brands, like Alec mentioned. Even landing higher profile jobs. One is now a blockbuster actor.

The fame aspect doesn't attract me, but the thought of having some income on the side through brand deals is appealing in a way I can't ignore. And I'm sure I can convince Courtney to apply for jobs while I'm on the show. With the slowness of the hiring process, it could be weeks before I hear anything about the positions. I could very well be back home before anyone even wanted to interview me.

"Fine. I'll stick with you, but there are some conditions."

His smile morphs his face from simply stunning handsomeness to a complete work of art.

CHAPTER NINE

ALEC

S WEET RELIEF BLEEDS THE stress from my body. "What are the conditions?"

She throws up her arms. "Well, I don't know! Don't pressure me."

"If you come up with any, let me know. Until then, I have something to give you."

"I want to get to know you. I have to bare my soul to you, so I'm going to need the same from you."

Having a feeling she won't let this go, no matter how difficult this will be for me since I've never opened up to a contestant before, I agree.

"Fine, agreed."

From the inside of my jacket, I pull out a thick, dark blue notebook with the outline of a mansion on the front in gold leaf, along with an embroidered "Season Ten."

"This is for anything you want to write down during the season. Little things you're noticing around the house, your cast-mates, whatever. It's the only thing you'll get to study before the finale, so it's important to keep up with it."

Her fingers trace the cover.

"I can't believe this is real. I've seen the copies of these in ads on the internet, but I never realized how much better the real ones would be." She keeps tracing, not looking up. "How did I get here?" she asks, whispering to herself.

The air in the room changes, her mood seeming to drop. My professional side wars with the personal side. Unsure of how to support her, I hunt for anything to say.

"You're here because half a million dollars would be really nice," I say, floundering.

"I don't just mean here on the show, I mean *here*"—she motions to herself—"in life."

I understand what she means. I don't know when it happens exactly, but there's a point where it feels like you have all the time in the world and you're striving toward your dreams and what you think you're supposed to be doing.

And then one day, you look up. You look around.

Your life is nothing what you expected. The job that was taken as a stop-gap has somehow become a career. The relationship that doesn't really fit has become an engagement, or worse, a marriage.

"It seems like you've had a hard time of it lately, and I'm sure that has been stressful. From what I heard of your interview, it sounds like you had some pretty shitty boyfriends, as well. Maybe this show is going to be the thing you look back on in ten years and you say 'Man, if I hadn't taken that leap, I wouldn't have everything I've ever wanted.'"

She looks up at me with her dark blue eyes and smiles. "I'm normally not all over the place like this, emotionally. It's been a hard few months. Thank you for rolling with the punches."

"What's a wrangler for, after all?"

"I bet you're wishing I was an emotionally stunted man at this point," she says, trying to push humor into the slightly awkward moment.

"No. I didn't find anyone else in that stack who I thought could win."

She rolls her eyes. "That's right. You need to win just as much as me. I forgot."

Her words sting, like a snap of a rubber band to the arm. While true, I need to be a better wrangler for her. More in tune with what she needs. Before I can retort, she motions to the notebook in her hands that matches her eyes.

"Don't worry, I'll make sure to keep up with this. Is this the only one we get or can I get more if I fill it?" she asks. I can see the wheels turning in her head as she starts to think about the game once more.

"This is the only one you can have, so write small."

She nods, flipping through the empty pages until the words on the first few pages catch her eye.

"What are these?" she asks, reading them.

"Those are the rules of the game and the schedule for when things will be airing. The eliminations are live, but the contests are filmed earlier in the day, so we have time to edit the footage for the program in the evening."

She turns the notebook around and pushes it in my face.

"What about that one?"

Unsure which rule she means, I read through the list again. I proofed it before the books were printed, but maybe I missed something.

Rules for House of Deceit

Schedule:

Monday Mornings: Start of New Week
Tuesdays: Privilege Challenge
Fridays: Elimination Challenge
Sunday nights: Live Elimination

Rules:

1. The Deceiver may not inflict bodily harm to the other contestants in the house.

2. The Deceiver will be informed of their status by their wrangler Monday morning of their week.

3. The winner of the Elimination Challenge becomes the new Head Deceiver effective immediately after the Live Elimination on Sunday of the current week and holds this position until after the Live Elimination, one week later (e.g., the winner of week two's elimination challenge will be Head Deceiver during week three).

a. The Head Deceiver is exempt from participation in the Privilege Challenge unless participation is required to balance teams. They will be exempt from any punishment should they be on the losing team.

b. The Head Deceiver is exempt from participation in the Elimination Challenge and is safe from elimination.

c. The Head Deceiver will have access to their own private quarters and may invite whomever they wish into the room.

4. All house guests will wear the provided outfits during any and all challenges.

5. The punishment for the losing team on the Privilege Challenge will be effective immediately following the challenge and will last until the end of the Live Elimination of the same week.

6. No person will be exempt from the punishment of their team and cannot be assisted by any member within the house or production with said punishment.

"I'm confused, which one?" I ask.

"The outfits one? What type of clothes are y'all going to be putting us in?"

"That's really more for safety. A rock-climbing wall was involved one year, and one particular dumbass fought us tooth and nail to not have to wear the safety harness because he was a 'trained climber.': It's a liability thing," I say.

"What about number six? That's the only one that mentions production."

Fucking Madison.

"There was this wrangler, Madison. She was *way* too nice and when her contestant came crying to her about the fact she had to clean or something, Madison ended up helping. Needless to say, the next staff meeting was not fun. After that, they banned us from entering the house at all, except on rare occasions."

Charlie laughs slightly and I pass her back the notebook.

"I'm sure you have all sorts of good stories."

"There are quite a few, but I won't bore you with them all today." I check my watch. "Let's get you to your physical. It should be the last appointment you have."

CHAPTER TEN

CHARLIE

"ARE YOU READY?" COURTNEY asks. A ball sails past her head and smacks into the deep blue wall behind her. She doesn't flinch an inch. This is normal in her life.

"As ready as I'm going to be. I'm currently trying not to throw up." My legs are tucked under me on the bed and I try not to look at the clock every five seconds.

My packed bags wait by the door. This will be the last time I can talk to my best friend until who knows when. I've told her all about my conversation with Alec and begged her to keep my job hunt going.

"You're going to kill it, and when you come home, we are going to a beach somewhere with your winnings so hot men with palm fronds can fan us while others feed us skinless grapes. Just wait. It'll be the vacation of our lifetime."

I laugh. "Sounds perfect." I hear movement outside my door and pause. My heart skips a beat, but the person continues past me, and I relax.

"You're like a deer in the middle of the road staring into bright headlights."

"I want to peel my skin off to keep from freaking out. I have taken about five nervous shits already this morning."

Her eyes go big, sending off alarm bells in my head. "What?

"You have to poop," she whispers, "*in public.*"

I roll my eyes.

"It'll be fine."

"But remember the gas station—"

"Oh my *God*, that was *one* time. One." I hold up a finger to emphasize my point. "I've gotten better since then." She looks skeptical.

"Plus, it's not like they have microphones in there." She looks everywhere but at me. "Court?" I ask, pleading in my voice.

"Well, some of the later seasons have times when contestants have conversations in there. They don't show what's happening *in* the stall; I'm pretty sure that'd be illegal, but there are microphones."

I feel the blood drain from my face. "Holy. Fuck." As the panic sets in, a solid knock sounds at my door.

"Court, I gotta go. I'll miss you."

"I'll miss you, too. Stay strong in there. I know you can do this. I hate you."

My eyes go teary. There has not been a single day I have not talked to Courtney since I met her in third grade.

"I hate you, too." And just like that, she's gone.

It feels like I'm marching to my death as I open the door.

"Are you ready?" Alec asks.

Black dots appear in my vision as my breathing becomes ragged.

"I can't do this," I whisper, looking up at him.

"Whoa, what happened?" He steps forward and grabs my shoulders, squeezing them.

"I'm going to be on TV. I've never wanted to be on television. I'm going to make an absolute fool out of myself." Tears tighten my throat.

"Charlie, I need you to breathe." He takes a deep breath, and I try to match it. He repeats the motion a few more times until he can feel me relax. "I would never let you embarrass yourself. How else would I get you those brand deals you want?" He smirks. "We are in this together, okay? Me and you."

"Me and you," I repeat. "Okay. I can do this." I stand stock still as Alec and the nameless production assistant move back into the hallway. Seeing my hesitancy, Alec steps into the room.

"Give us just a moment. We'll be right out," he says, closing the door. "I don't want to rush you, Charlie, but we have a pretty tight timeline to stick to. I want to give you as much time as you need to collect yourself, but unfortunately, I can't."

He puts his arm around me and forcibly moves me to the bed, pushing me to sit down.

"You say this is you and me," I tell him, "but you're not the one in front of the camera. Wranglers aren't shown when they interview their contestants!" I get up and start walking around the room.

Stress typically leads to my fingers finding their way to my hair, running through the strands, but in deference to my imminent stardom, I crack my knuckles instead.

"You're right," Alec says, leaning against the dresser like he did the first time he was here. "I didn't really pay attention to how my other contestants were feeling on arrival day, so I'm not really sure how to help here."

"Of course you didn't notice anyone else's emotions, you robot."

"I'm sorry, I can't compute sarcasm. Please rephrase the statement." I give him a dead look in response to his horrible robot voice. "Charlie, you are a beautiful, funny woman and you're paired with me. This is going to be no problem. And I don't want to make this situation worse, but I'm going to remind you the five thousand dollars you desperately need will not be paid out if you don't make it to the mansion."

I stop my pacing and remind myself how much I do not want to be kicked out of my apartment.

"For the money, fine. But I swear if you pick some embarrassing clip of me, I will probably castrate you. And cry."

"Castrating me would really make my life less fun when I'm not shooting, Charlie."

I snort. "I'm sure the women of the world would be utterly devastated. I'm ready. Let's do this," I tell him.

He stands from the dresser. "That's my girl," he says, heading toward the door.

A small flutter at his words starts in my stomach, but the stress quickly runs it over once more. My bags feel like a thousand pounds, making each step require a monumental effort as I leave the room for the last time.

"Before we go, I need your phone," Alec says, holding out his hand. "I'll take care of it. Don't worry."

Reluctantly, I slap it down in his hand and head to meet my awaiting car. Each contestant is loaded into their own black car. There is no mingling before the cameras are rolling. Every moment of our days has been structured so we did not get a glimpse of one another.

An opaque divider is up between me and the driver and the windows in the back are blacked out, so I can't see where we are going. Every season, a different mansion is turned into the House of Deceit. The only consistency from one season to the next is each location has stunning views, from snowcapped mountains to scenic coastlines.

Minutes tick by and I try to keep track of them, but one dissolves into another as I fight the urge to pick at my nails.

I'm in my favorite green sun-dress. A sweetheart neckline cuts low as the bodice hugs me until it flares at my hips to hit mid-thigh. If not for its length, the skirt would be perfect for twirling. One of the few things from my closet that gives me confidence.

The car slows and then comes to a stop. I hear the driver's door open and I close my eyes, sending up one last prayer.

Sunlight blinds my vision as the car door is opened. The driver holds out his hand for me. Dry, warm skin meets my clammy hand and I want to apologize, but nerves trap my voice. My favorite gold wedges crunch against the rock as I stand from the car. As the door is closed, my mouth drops open. The mansion is gorgeous. A soaring structure of brick with ivy climbing the front. A gravel driveway circles a large stone fountain. Other than the driver, not a soul is around, but Alec prepared me for the solitary arrival. This is the last time I won't be recorded for the next, hopefully, twelve weeks.

"Good luck," the kind man says as he makes his way back to the driver's side.

I stare at the house, taking in the surreal view before me, as he puts the vehicle in drive and departs. When I can no longer hear the car, and I have my nerves somewhat controlled, I make my way up the lane.

The double doors are covered in wrought iron vines and flowers. I push them open and step into the cavernous entryway. I'm sure it's stunning, but I see nothing besides the tablet on the table before me. Pressing my thumb to the scanner, dots dance around while it analyzes my print. I wait. Green means I'm a regular player for the week. Red, the deceiver. At this moment, I'm not sure which I want to be more.

The screen flashes, and I smile—my body calms. I straighten my spine and walk into the game.

HOUSE OF DECEIT

WEEK ONE

CHAPTER ELEVEN

T HE ROOM IS DARK. I can't see any other competitors, but I sense other bodies in the room with me. The chair someone from production guided me to is deep, the edge of the cushion pushing into the back of my knees. The host, Jacob Jacobson's voice filters over the speakers, welcoming us to *House of Deceit*.

"The lights will come on in the mansion, and the games will begin in thirty seconds. Who's going to be the first Head Deceiver? Who will be the first eliminated? Will there be any alliances this season? Let's see what happens in ten, nine, eight..." The countdown hits zero, bright lights come on, and the game begins.

The blond man across from me is striking as he gives me a smile.

We all sit in a circle in the middle of a large living room. Two L-shaped couches are pushed to the side to make room for our first moments in the mansion. Directly in front of me, I see a hint of cabinets through a wide, arched doorway. To the left are floor to ceiling glass doors leading to the backyard.

No one makes a move and the awkwardness of the situation starts to settle in. I can feel the weight of all the cameras hiding in the room, watching us. One of the girls, who looks just over the twenty-one-year-old age requirement, is almost vibrating in her chair. Her bubblegum pink dress and pearls around her neck make her look like she's playing dress up in her mother's clothes.

"Hi, y'all. My name is Mary Ella. I'm from Alabama and the reigning Miss Pecan Pie. I am so excited to be here with y'all and get to know you! We are all going to be best friends. I can just tell. A little about me: I just graduated from 'Bama, roll tide! My daddy owns a chain of car dealerships, and I'm the manager there. I've tried out for the dating show *House of Desire*, twice, but I thought this would be more fun!" Her accent is thick but as precious as she is.

Her enthusiasm gets a few chuckles. I smile at her. Being an only child, I don't personally know how sibling dynamics feel, but something inside me wants to tuck in this little bundle of happiness and protect her from the big, bad world.

I continue to peek at the blond man out of the corner of my eye as we go around the room, introducing ourselves. I try to make mental notes for my journal later and become overwhelmed quickly after the fifth introduction, but a few stick out.

Cain smiles at the room, the gesture warm and welcoming. He is thin with thick, medium-brown hair. Most people would look over him, but there's something around the edges of his eyes that puts my hackles up.

Jaxon, a devout Christian, is here to spread the message. Harper, the atheist to his left, scoffs. That will be a fun pairing, I'm sure.

Every season seems to have at least two people on opposite sides of belief systems, and it tends to lead to heated interactions.

Lucas and Penelope are making eyes at each other, and I wonder how long it will take them to get physical. There are a few relationships that have come out of the house as the years have gone on. It's normal, really. You're locked up with people and have nothing to do but get to know each other.

Keith's salt and pepper hair—more salt than pepper—and the weathered look of his skin tell me he is the oldest one in the group. His pressed, checkered shirt, worn jeans, and cowboy boots paired with his gruff, no-nonsense demeanor endears him to me immediately.

"Hi, everyone. I'm Parker," the blond says. Besides Alec, Parker is one of the most beautiful men I've ever seen in person. His hair is thick, wavy, and past his shoulders. His beard is well-kept and accentuates his sharp jawline. A straight, strong nose and burning green eyes stare right at me. His broad shoulders press against the seams of his shirt, the material hugging his muscles nicely.

"Hi, Parker," we all intone. Very group therapy of us. I break the eye contact, but am quickly pulled back to his gaze.

"I am from Chicago. I own a construction company and like to play rugby on the weekends."

Short. Simple. To the point. I like it. My eyes have been drawn to Parker ever since the lights came on.

After they've all introduced themselves, I stand.

"Hi, I'm Charlie and I'm here because my best friend and I had too much tequila and a computer with internet access." A few give me soft laughs, but I don't want attention focused on me any longer. "I don't know about you all, but I'm ready to explore." It seems those are the exact words everyone was waiting to hear. Without further ado, everyone gets up and breaks off in different directions. Mary Ella looks around, her eyes big. She looks like a horse about to spook. I walk up to her.

"Hi, I'm Charlie," I remind her just in case, like me, she didn't catch everyone's name. "Would you like to explore with me?"

She smiles at me with relief, and I know I did the right thing, not leaving this girl to fend for herself. I couldn't imagine being dropped into a house of strangers as one of the youngest in the group.

"That would be so great. Thank you." She grabs my hand and links our fingers. I stare at it briefly before shrugging and going with it.

The house is full of twists and turns and long hallways. Some rooms are set up more formally than others. Leather couches that look like they belong in a distinguished professor's house. Heavy drapes that block the sun. Chandeliers dripping down from the ceiling. These rooms feel more like they belong in a palace, not a house being used in a reality TV competition.

Sounds of laughter and talking filter through the house as we continue on our way.

Other rooms are very casual. Deep, soft chairs and sofas. Eclectic collections of paintings and artwork line the various walls. Never having been in a home like this, I wonder if there were multiple designers or if the more relaxed vibes were added by the producers themselves to give us somewhere more comfortable. I almost feel sorry for the house with rooms that may not see a soul on a normal basis, but now has twenty people calling it home, sure to defile its perfection with their presence.

By the time Mary Ella and I walk back through the living room we all started in, our chairs have been removed and the couches are moved from the wall. The production team seems to work in a way that disturbs us as little as possible.

My subconscious can hear Mary Ella telling me all about her various family members, but the size of the kitchen is pulling my focus.

Large is an understatement for the room. There are two of each of the appliances. Two ovens. Two dishwashers. Two refrigerators. In one refrigerator there are bins with each person's name to hold the snacks they've requested or won. The dining room is off the kitchen with a long table. Each season varies. In some seasons, the contestants decide to have a nightly family dinner. Others, everyone fends for themselves. I wonder which kind we will be. As people leave the mansion, the table will get smaller and smaller.

There are multiple living rooms, one with the only TV in the house for the elimination meetings and any announcements Jacob Jacobson needs to make to us.

"—and that was when I really lost my virginity. Do you think the other time counted? I asked my best friend and she says no because he was thrusting between my leg and the bed, but I—"

We turn the corner and Mary Ella's jabbering drops away once more. The library is extensive and has a rolling ladder. I think I orgasm at the sight. Books line every shelf. There must be thousands. Making a mental note of its location, we carry on.

The bathroom is the size of my apartment. Showers and sinks in one room are communal. On each side, there are hallways that lead to the separate toilets. I breathe a deep sigh of relief that this season, the stalls are not in the bathroom themselves, lowering the likelihood any noises will be picked up, which will be a relief to everyone back home. Further down the hallways, I come to the joint dressing room.

Each person has their wardrobe. The faceless people behind the scenes have already unpacked our bags. There are circular tables with lighted mirrors and tons of electrical outlets for anyone wishing to style their hair.

In the back of the house, tucked away in a forgotten wing are three locked doors. One is labeled "Production," another "Interview," and the third is blank.

The interview room will be where my meetings with Alec are held. Each person meets there with their wrangler to discuss anything and everything. While there are specific times some of these conversations will happen, like after the competitions, the contestants can also call out in the house to meet with their wrangler. Whenever the wrangler is ready, they will request the contestant come to the interview room over the intercom system in the house.

During our time together after I decided to keep Alec as my wrangler, he made sure to give me the packet of all the ins and outs of filming.

Interviews with the wranglers, or the confessionals, are some of the best parts of the episodes. Courtney and I love what people tend to share when they finally have a moment where no other contestants are around. Their true feelings can really come out.

The best room of the entire house is locked, but it's the same every season. The elimination challenge comes with a special privilege. The winner of the challenge is not only safe from elimination, but they get their own bedroom. They enjoy privacy, an ensuite bathroom, and no chores. And I want to be in that room as much as possible.

I drop Mary Ella off at the room that has her and three other's names by the door, and let her get to know her new roommates. My finger traces the shell of my ear. I thought it had fallen off from how much she talked. Even with not giving her my full attention, much of Mary Ella's life story has taken root inside my brain. Against my will, I now know all about Mary Ella's cheerleading career, how she lost her virginity, the names of every family member she has, and how she had really wanted to go on *House of Desire.* She thought her boyfriend, Beau, would propose when they graduated college. That was always the plan. But he got cold feet and broke up with her in their senior year. I would have broken up with her as well. She's a sweet girl, if very naïve. But after she was rejected to participate in a competition for the heart of a random bachelor, this became her backup.

My roommates have all claimed their beds by the time I stroll in from my exploring, which means mine is closest to the door. It doesn't bother me. Courtney often says I can sleep through a tree falling on the house.

"Hey, girl. I'm Molly, fellow ginger." A towering, showstopper of a woman stands from her bed and moves over to me, flicking her copper red hair over her shoulder. Even with my taller-than-average height, I only come up to her chin. Her energy is warm and inviting. The freckles smattering her nose and cheeks are endearing. She wraps me in a hug, and I sink into it. "What do you think the best part of being a cat would be?"

The question takes me off guard, but only for a moment. Court often talks aloud about whatever thought flits through her mind.

"Probably napping in the sun. It's one of my favorite things as a human, so I would think that'd transfer over if I was a cat."

She nods. "That's a good one. I want to have the audacity to climb any surface." She moves out of the way so I can move further into the room. "This is Raven." Raven is laid out on her bed with an arm over her eyes. She throws me a peace sign but doesn't react to my presence. "Our other roommate is Jayden, the tall, lanky kid who looks like a stiff wind could blow him over."

I sit down on my bed and take a deep breath.

It's only been about an hour, but this doesn't seem so bad.

It's definitely better than sitting all alone on the floor of my apartment.

Our shortest house member, Ezra's, eyes dart around the table as he sucks up the spaghetti Molly volunteered to cook like a vacuum cleaner. The conversation has been stilted and devoid of overly personal topics as we all walk on eggshells trying to get to know each other. Penelope scowls down at the food, moving a meatball around with her fork but never takes a bite. I take a sip of my red wine, looking around the table.

"Who wants to address the elephant in the room?" Rebel says, with a snarky smile.

"What elephant?" the blue-eyed frat boy Carter asks. His blond hair is slicked back like a car salesman.

Parker sits to my right, his body heat warming me as I take a sip of water. Noticing there's almost none left in my glass, he grabs the pitcher from the middle of the table, refilling it for me when I put it back down on the table.

I smile at him in thanks, tuning back into the conversation I have a feeling is very much about me.

"The unevenness of our numbers," Keith says without looking up from his plate. The old man shovels in his food without seeming to taste it, but I appreciate his efficiency.

"There's twenty of us, though," Carter says, clueless.

"Normally, the starting numbers are ten men and ten women. There's a woman here that shouldn't be." Cain's sharp eyes flit around the room, taking everyone in.

Unease whirs within me. Alec and I were not sure how the audience would take the imbalance of contestants. Once eliminations start, the balance changes anyway, so he didn't believe it would be much of an issue. His boss decided the audience would not be informed of the mix-up, nor would the other wranglers. A picture of a bunch of people sitting around watching us all fighting about my presence at this table makes me sweat a bit.

Cain catches me squirming in my chair.

"Charlie, what do you think about this?" he asks.

All eyes turn to me. The weight of them added to the cameras I feel on me in this moment pushes me down in my chair and makes me wish I could melt into the floor.

"I'm sure the show handled whatever happened as best they could," I say, noncommittally.

"So, it's okay someone is taking up a position that should have been filled by someone else?" he asks, probing further.

"I think the people that are supposed to be here, are. Alec—"

"Alec King? He's your wrangler? It's you then. You shouldn't be here."

I mentally slap myself.

"Yes, Alec is my wrangler," I say, ignoring the other piece of his accusation. After my doctor's appointment, Alec and I decided what I would share and what I wouldn't but we both agreed honesty was incredibly important to keep the audience on my side.

"Well, well, well. Is he hot? My wrangler is *terrified* of him. She always mentions how she has to check with Alec any time I have a question," Penelope says, drinking her dirty martini.

"Why does it matter if he's attractive?" I ask, bewildered and unwilling to admit that out loud, knowing he'll hear it.

She shrugs a perfectly tan shoulder before shooting a wink at Lucas, our resident Olympian. Everyone goes back to their conversations, and I slump with relief at their general acceptance of me within the house.

"How did you get him to pick you?" Cain asks, making my stomach fall at his refusal to drop the subject.

"It's not like I was part of the process," I say, starting to get defensive.

Cain looks around at the other contestants. "Alec King's contestants always end up in the top three. Because this woman somehow got into this game, someone else lost their spot, most likely a spot in the final three. I'd be curious as to the legality of her being here."

I see it on their faces, he's starting to win some of them. He gives me a smirk as everyone focuses their attention on me once more, and I know he's the person I need to watch out for.

"How do you know that?" I ask.

"I studied," he says, simply.

Ever since the lights turned on, he has been incredibly pleasant and kind to everyone, but under the placid demeanor, there was something about him that made the hair on my neck stand up.

"There's nothing in the contract that states there must be ten men and ten women," Molly says, sticking up for me. "My father is an attorney, and we read every word of it together. There was nothing in it about the composition of the contestants. It's not like our wranglers participate in competitions for us or whatever. Charlie will have to stay out of the bottom two, just like everyone else."

I bump her knee under the table and smile. "Thanks, girl."

"Afraid you can't beat her?" Parker taunts.

"Well, I for one welcome the competition Charlie brings to the table. There's nothing my coach instilled in me more than strength in the face of adversity, and I encourage you all to take that advice to heart," Lucas says.

We all turn back to our spaghetti. Cain's shoulders tighten as he returns to his food, seemingly annoyed at his inability to turn everyone against me.

CHAPTER TWELVE

THE HOUSEHOLD MIGRATES OUTSIDE once we clear away the remnants of dinner. Pergolas cover multiple beds with gauzy curtains hanging on a track so they can be moved to enclose the bed or open it to the breeze. Molly and I have our curtains pushed open so the orange-tree-scented air can wrap around us. The lights in the pool make the water seem like it's dancing as people splash and play.

Ice clinks as I raise my habanero margarita to my lips. The mixture of salt from the rim and sweetness of the drink rolls across my tongue, the bite of the spice burning my throat. I notice Parker sitting on the pool's edge, his feet hanging in the water.

"So, why are you here?" Molly asks. Her straight-to-the-point questions thrill me. I look up at the stars through the slats above us.

"You first."

"On my birthday, I was sitting there, listening to everyone sing to me as twenty-six candles flickered on my cake, and I didn't recognize my life. I could feel myself changing, not fitting into the mold I had mindlessly fit myself into, and I didn't know what to do. Friends that didn't fit any longer. A job that couldn't pay my bills. A relationship that, well, saying it wasn't right is putting it nicely. I guess you could say I ran, hoping I could leave it all in the past."

It's nice knowing I'm not the only one trying to run from problems. We sit there in silence for a moment and watch the games in the pool. Teams have been created, one person on another's shoulders while they try to shove the other team off balance. The first team to fall loses.

"There's running to escape a situation and running toward the person you're supposed to become. And in my experience, those are very different things. The former, you end up in the same situation because wherever you run, there you are. But the latter," I pause, taking a drink, "the latter is more of a metamorphosis. Shedding who you were to become who you need to be. Better to run and be you than stay and hide from yourself."

Parker lifts his arms, his muscled back flexing as he ties up his hair before leaning back on his hands once more. His strong arms hold up his toned body as he watches the others having fun.

"So, why are you here?" Molly repeats.

I look at her bathed in the low light and give her my truth.

"Because I didn't have any other options."

It's Tuesday, privilege competition day, and the first full day when *House of Deceit* really begins. An air horn awakes us. I sit straight up in bed like Dracula from his coffin. Jayden gives a shout of surprise and tumbles to the floor, his leg tangled in his sheets. He sheepishly untangles himself, but remains there watching all of us. Raven is in a ball under the covers at the foot of her bed. She doesn't move. Molly rolls over and looks at me.

"Did you stick your finger in a light socket last night? You look like you've been electrocuted," she asks.

Mumbles come from Raven's cocoon.

"If you're gonna talk, babe, you gotta come out from under the covers," Molly tells her. Raven doesn't move, but slowly, her comforter inches down until her head is poking out.

"I said she was rolling around like a demented gymnast until about four in the morning. And you snore like a freight train, so I wouldn't be goin' and judgin' anyone else."

"Fair enough. My apologies my need for air ruined your night."

"I didn't notice," Jayden says shyly from the floor. He's so quiet and small I almost forgot he was there.

"Do your ears not work?" Raven sasses.

"Be nice," Molly tells her. I can't see Raven's eyes, but I know they rolled. Her obvious dislike of mornings is so reminiscent of Courtney, who will murder you with a single look if you speak to her before ten a.m., I have to keep myself from laughing.

"Attention everyone," the disembodied voice comes over the announcement system, interrupting our conversation, "the privilege competition will start in thirty minutes. Please be in the announcement room by that time, dressed in the provided attire."

I rub my eyes and throw back my blankets, climbing out.

"Why is it so freaking cold in this house?" I hiss. My thin cotton pajamas do nothing against the constant air conditioning. I haphazardly make my bed before making my way to the bathroom. Against one wall in the large room are racks of shower caddies filled with everyone's individual showering products. Next to the racks are two cabinets with drawers. Each drawer has a name and contains toothbrushes, toothpaste, floss, and various other requested necessities.

I wet my brush and pull it through my hair and pray Alec won't include this beautiful moment in the show this week. Molly had not been exaggerating the state of my appearance. People file in and out, everyone getting ready. The trough like sink has space for half of us at a time. I finish in the bathroom and make my way to the closet. Hanging from each wardrobe is the designated outfit for the day. I strip off my pajamas, accepting there will be no privacy, even when we need to change, and put on my blue tank top and matching shorts. Making my way out to the living room with the TV, I stop by the kitchen and grab a banana, unsure what we are in for.

Music blares through the surround sound; why it needs to be at the level of an outdoor concert, I'll never know. Jacob Jacobson's face comes on screen, the same smile he always wears plastered on his face.

"Good morning, contestants!" he says.

"Good morning, Jacob," we call back with less enthusiasm.

"Today marks the start of the games. Whichever team loses today will be in charge of making and cleaning up dinner for the entire house for the week! Now, you've been sorted into your teams already, blue and red. This game will be played in the backyard. Please, go there now and good luck!"

Looking around, I perk up, noticing Parker is in blue, too. The TV turns off and we all stand, shuffling outside.

Off to one side on the grass are two identical boards with the fifty state names running in five columns of ten. A red envelope hangs on the board and I grab it.

Turning to address everyone, I read the card.

"Hello, everyone, and welcome to your first challenge in the *House of Deceit*. Each team will have ten minutes to arrange the states by population. Each correct answer will be a point. The team with the most points wins. The time starts at the end of the reading of this card."

We scatter like a grenade was thrown in the middle of us. The blue team is made up of me, Angelica, Ava, Raven, Harper, Colyn, Carter, Cain, Parker, and Jayden.

"Does each person know the population of their home state?" Parker asks. Almost all of us shake our heads. "Alright, there goes that idea."

Cain shoves through the group and immediately starts putting states in an order. California, Florida, Texas, New York, Illinois, Pennsylvania, so on and so forth.

"Hey, what the hell, man?" Angelica asks.

Ava starts crying at the discourse. It's only the start of the second day and she's cried three times already.

"Texas and Florida are wrong," Jayden squeaks.

"No, they aren't, but I appreciate the help, bud," he says, placing three more states in quick succession. I can't tell if his tone is condescending or not, but it rubs me the wrong way. Courtney would hate this guy.

"Maybe Jayden's right. Let us help. We all have to bear the punishment if we lose," I say.

Cain looks at the group of us all staring as he holds Illinois in his hand. He smiles, his teeth perfect and white.

"Of course! Sorry, man," he says to Jayden, "my competitiveness took over. Where should this go?"

As a team, we continue the ranking.

A buzzer goes off and we all step back from our boards. I look at the red team's board. It seems like we have similar answers, but there are obvious discrepancies. A voice plays over the loudspeaker and announces each answer starting from the top. As they are announced, correct guesses light up green. In many of the cases, the correction to Cain's rankings were right. The red team ended up with thirty correct answers while the blue team had thirty-one.

I look at Raven and share a sigh of relief that we do not have to cook for the entire house. A monumental task with twenty different people here. With the game over, we all move back inside to start our first full day in the *House of Deceit*.

The interview room is an extremely pale green, but sparsely decorated so the contestants pouring out their deepest, darkest thoughts are the focal point. The chair in front of the camera is creamy leather and deep, welcoming, while the wrangler chair is an armless thing that looks egregiously uncomfortable.

Alec stands by a large camera, his hands tucked in the pockets of his black slacks. The top few buttons of his shirt are open, showing the beginnings of a firm chest I'm sure rests below the fabric. He smiles at me, and for a moment I forget he feels nothing for me other than detached professionalism.

"Hey," I say, clearing my throat when I hear the breathy quality of my voice.

"Hey, there. Good call on getting Cain to include you all in the challenge. He placed quite a few of those states wrong."

"I don't like that guy," I tell him simply as I make my way to my chair, tucking my feet under me as I sit. Pulling out my journal, I look at the few notes I've made. "I haven't noticed much with the deceiver, yet. Do you have any tips on how to look out for things?"

Alec sits on his chair, resting his ankle on top of the opposite knee.

"That's normal for the first few days. The first deceiver tends to have it the hardest. Between nerves and the fact no one has set a bar on what's going too far for the group, it can be hard to act. How are you feeling?"

His gray eyes are earnest, but his tone is the clipped, professional one I got used to when we met in the hotel. A part of me is sad at the loss of the more familiar tone we had by the end of our time together before the game started.

"I can feel the cameras on me at all times. My nerves are kind of shot, to be honest." I doodle flowers in the margins of my journal, keeping my eyes averted from the truth I just gave to Alec.

I hear him shift in his chair and look up at him, his gray eyes boring into me.

"Other than on the live shows, nothing is aired without me seeing it first. So just think of it like that. I'm the one watching you. Just me."

Butterflies launch in my stomach at his words. Maybe the cameras won't be so bad after all.

"Also, I just want you to know, I made sure your five thousand dollars was transferred into your account."

Relief, pure and sweet, sweeps through me as a weight is lifted from my shoulders.

CHAPTER THIRTEEN

ALEC

MY EYES ARE TIRED from watching hours of footage of Charlie. Although the new facial recognition software is greatly reducing the amount of time I have to spend combing through footage to find her, there are still twenty-four hours in a day. Luckily for my eyesight, she seems to enjoy going to bed early, although her early rising is a pain in my ass.

As the days pass, she's quickly asserting herself as a dark-humored, caring person and I foresee no issues selling her to our audiences. She does not seem to have any allegiance beyond her budding friendship with the striking, towering goddess that is Molly.

The other wranglers are seated in folding chairs placed around the makeshift viewing room when I walk in. Watching the immunity competitions together every week is a tradition. The cheering is enthusiastic. The trash talking is top-notch. Week one always has more of a party feel. The relief of getting through the first few days of filming and our charges settling into life in the mansion eases a lot of pressure.

Chinese food covers the buffet table this week. I grab a plate and load it down with the various options of lo mein, rice, and chicken dishes. This is the only night a week I eat whatever I want.

The singular empty chair is next to my buddy Frank.

"Who's yours this time?" he asks, as I sit down in my chair.

Frank scoops up some fried rice and shoves it in his face. He is an easygoing fellow, very different from me. But his affable nature tends to calm me from the stress filming can bring.

"Charlie Price."

His fork stops on the way to his mouth, and he puts it down on his plate, still full. "So you're the one who messed up the balance." His smile irritates me. "How did that happen, anyway? Some of the contestants are pretty pissed." He whispers this last bit, not wanting to be overheard by the others in the room.

"The interns put her application in the wrong pile. It's not like I was trying to cheat." The prospects of finally ending my stint with the show are too enticing to jeopardize.

"I know you weren't. You're way too much of a stick in the mud," he jokes, but when I simply cock an eyebrow at him, he continues. "But you have to admit, it can be hard to fight against someone who looks like that."

Defensiveness at the insinuation Charlie is nothing more than a pretty face instantly has my hackles up. "She's more than her looks, and she has to compete just like everyone else. Maybe instead of being jealous of how pretty she is, they should focus on making sure their contestants are prepared."

"Sorry, man, I didn't mean to bad-mouth her," Frank says, and I tamp down my anger, bringing the cool, professional demeanor I wear like armor to the forefront.

"It doesn't matter. I have the winner and that's all I care about," I say, a bit of snap lingering in my voice.

"I guess we'll see." His charge has made it to the final three a few times but, like me, he's never picked a winner. "I have Parker this year. I have a good feeling about him. So long as his crush on your girl doesn't distract him."

That catches my attention.

"He has a crush on Charlie?"

"Again, have you seen her? Of course he does."

I have seen Charlie. I know exactly what he means. But that doesn't make the spark of jealousy dissipate any faster.

"Well, keep him away from her. I need her focused and not getting emotionally attached to anyone."

"I'm right there with you, brother."

We watch the live feed of Jacob Jacobson standing in the studio in front of a monitor with the contestants bustling around in the house behind him. His raspberry suit makes my eyes burn while simultaneously making me realize how boring my closet is. His smile is glued to his face. I've only seen him without the smile once—when his spray tan application went wrong, and he was orange for a week. While the audience had a field day, the technician who applied the wrong color was left in tears.

"Welcome to the first immunity night at the *House of Deceit*! Season ten promises to have new twists and turns for our guests. Tonight, you'll watch them be put through an excruciating obstacle course that will challenge their mental and physical strength. The bottom two will be up for elimination on Sunday night. Earlier in the day, the contestants were randomly assigned the order they would tackle the course. Now, let's take a moment to say hello."

He turns toward the monitor on his right, the live stream of the competitors waiting for Jacob showing on the screen. He presses a button and appears on the TV in the house.

"Hello, Deceivers!"

"Hello, Jacob!" they intone.

"As you know, tonight is the immunity challenge. The bottom two *will* be eligible for elimination, while the winner will be Head Deceiver and immune from elimination next week. Not only that, they will also have a private bedroom to enjoy and will receive a special surprise! Your ranking will be determined by how quickly you finish the course. If no one finishes the course, it will be based on the last element completed, with any ties broken by time."

They clap as they have been told. Each wrangler coaches their player on the expected reactions at various announcements. While the goal is for everything to be authentic, there are a few instances where we want to ensure enthusiasm is shown. Their commitment to the show can wane when they are tired, hungry, and annoyed at being locked in.

Jacob reviews a few more rules and explanations, and the group moves to the backyard. During the day, all the windows are blocked so no one can see what the crew is setting up for them. There are exclamations as they see the course. The obstacles use every inch of the space, including the pool.

Lily pads, rope climbs, a rock wall, sandbag carry, and more are spread throughout the space. Ten total obstacles stand between them and possibly being eliminated.

Colyn is first to run. She stands at the starting line, nerves obvious in her stance, but when the bell goes off, she exposes herself as a threat. She's through four of the obstacles before I can blink. Pepper, her wrangler, shouts encouragement at the screen, her food completely abandoned.

Colyn pants as she tries to lift the sandbag onto her shoulders. Her arms are shot from the extended time it took her to complete the overhead bars portion of the course and before we know it, the gong rings out as she fails, three obstacles from the end.

Keith makes it a decent way through, taking his time, ending one obstacle short of Colyn, while Parker is the first person to complete the entire course.

Charlie is the last to run the course. Cain is solidly in the first position, and unless she learns how to fly, I don't believe she will beat him. Sharon and Ezra currently sit in the bottom two places. All Charlie must complete are four obstacles and she avoids being in the hot seat for the week. I watched her watch every competitor before her with sharp eyes, seeming to make note of the best way to beat each test.

She stands at the starting line, and I am hunched over, ignoring all jabs from my coworkers. Nothing matters beyond Charlie. The bell rings, and she's off, sprinting across the lily pads in the pool, barely causing a ripple. She hoists the sandbag across her shoulders and trudges a hundred feet through sand. Her slow and steady pace is smart. With the top spot out of reach, better to take her time and avoid putting a foot wrong. She looks up and studies the ten-foot rock wall, picking her path through the scarce holds. Almost to the top, she wipes sweat from her brow. Reaching up, she makes a grab for a hold, but she slips.

Time stops as she tumbles through the air, her hair blowing around her as the wind rushes by, and lands on the crash mat below her. She puts her hands on her head and stares in shock at the sky. I'm standing, my mouth hanging open. Eyes find me.

Charlie is in the bottom two.

She could be eliminated, and our time with *House of Deceit* could end a mere seven days from when it began. Charlie rolls off the mat and stands. Some people circle her, trying to comfort her, but she shakes them off and storms into the house.

The shot goes back to Jacob in the studio.

"Well, folks. We are almost done with our first week of season ten of House of Deceit. Cain will take over the winner's room Monday morning. He will also be exempt from elimination in week two. Charlie and Sharon are first on the chopping block. The polls are now open for you to cast your votes and will close one hour before the live elimination on Sunday! Now, let's look in on our contestants as they go on with their evening, some unsure if they will go home in a mere forty-eight hours."

He moves out of the way as the camera zooms in on the television behind him, showing the live feed of contestants milling about congratulating Cain on his win as the show ends.

On my phone, I switch through the various feeds inside the house until I find Charlie, sitting on the couch, holding her head in her hands. Her fire-red hair is all pulled over on one side and Parker lingers, his eyes not leaving my contestant.

I push the button to go over the announcement system. "Price, to the interview room. Now." I watch as she drops her head before pushing up from the couch. I pace my office, trying to get myself under control before I storm through the wrangler corridor.

The door to the interview room is at the end of the hallway and the closer I get, the more red I see. I burst through the door, slamming it behind me. Charlie sits on the chair looking dejected and sad, but that doesn't stop me.

"You're just trying to lose already, is that it? Can't wait to get back home to your life so you're just going to tank it?" I see my dreams going down the drain with Charlie.

My contestant hasn't been out in the first week *ever*. I sit on the chair, before immediately jumping up once more to pace the room, my anger riding me hard. "I could have picked anyone. The stack of applications was taller than me! But no, I decided on someone that used a nickname and was put *in the wrong fucking stack*! But I picked you! I picked you because I had a gut feeling you could win. You're the horse I bet my *entire career on*!"

A single tear falls down Charlie's cheek and the wind disappears from my sails. Guilt runs through me as she swipes angrily at the tears I've caused. I sit down on the chair, breathing to further calm myself.

After watching my sister cry herself to sleep every night for a year after our mom died, I have no place in me that can handle the tears of another. Ex-girlfriends thought it was weird I'd get up and leave at the hint of a tear, but they never understood I soaked up Lorelei's like a sponge and I'm too sodden to take any more.

"So much for 'me and you,' I guess," she says, and I feel like an asshole the size of Jupiter.

"Charlie—"

Her eyes are bright with hellfire when she looks up at me.

"You are such an asshole. My God. Did you think, even for a second, how maybe, just maybe, I was feeling pretty awful about myself? Do you know how *embarrassing* it is to be up for elimination on week one? I choked, I admit that, but you don't need to make me feel worse about it." Her ire with me puts steel in her words. "And, let's get one thing straight. Your career is not my problem. I will do the best I can in this competition for *me* and you can suck a big, furry dick if you think I'm not doing well enough for *your* benefit. But if you jump down my throat again, you're going to regret it. Consider it a condition of me keeping you around."

Her nostrils flare with anger, but the fire I see within her is what I saw on her application. What drew me to her.

What made me pick her.

"Listen, I'm sorry. That wasn't fair to you. It's not fair to put my career aspirations on your shoulders. Let's talk about how you're feeling right now." I have to draw myself back, break down the anger and put on the itchy clothes of the therapist. The thing I've never had to be for any other contestant.

"Why the fuck would I want to do that?" she asks, incredulously. "Before we move one step further in this competition, we are going to get on the same page about a few things." She perches on the edge of her chair and stares me down. "You might have picked me initially, but *I* am the only reason you're still working this season. *I* picked *you*, too."

She pauses, lets that sink in, and I realize she's right. I almost didn't get to participate in this season at all. But she decided to stick with me. While the half a million dollars is attractive, she has what she currently needs and could go home to search for a real job. She could tank this to spite me if I don't get my temper under control. Not only that, but she has taken an even bigger chance on me than I did on her.

All I can promise her is a maybe. I can't guarantee she'll get brand deals staying here, and she could lose her apartment if I'm wrong. It's sobering to realize someone could rest everything they have on your shoulders.

"Here's my first freaking condition," she continues, "if you want to remain my wrangler. This will be the *last* time you bring up this mix-up. If you throw it in my face again, I'm done.

"And guess what? You picked me. *Me*. No matter what stack it came out of, every single answer on that application was me. The only issue is you thought I had a dick swinging between my legs. What makes you think I'm any less capable? I've not been eliminated yet. You still have a shot at your dream and I still have a shot at winning."

"I'm sorry," I say. She's right. All of it. I picked her out of that stack for a reason. It doesn't matter that she's a woman. My gut told me the person sitting before me was the one. Now I need to back her.

"We need to get the audience to fall in love with me so they'll vote for me, which means you need to direct me," she says, her tone still not allowing for any bullshit.

"What?"

"Direct me. How do I need to come off to the audience in this interview?"

I pause for a moment. "You need to come off strong, like you're not worried about this hiccup. I want you to show them you still have fire and you'll do anything you can to win."

"What does that look like? Tell me what to do."

I'm intrigued and look at her with new eyes. The smattering of freckles across her nose and her big blue eyes read as the girl next door. Her lush body makes you want to touch her, kiss her, hear how she responds. And the fire within her makes you want to stand by her side against anything.

"Okay, first untuck your legs from under you. Sit on the edge of your seat like you can barely stand to be seated when all you want to do is compete again. Get another chance to prove yourself."

"Well, maybe it shouldn't be so cold in this house all the time!" She smiles as she does what I instruct. Her following my guidance sets off a different kind of warmth in my chest.

"You're going to have that same fire you came at me with. You're going to have the strong voice; you're going to tell everyone at home who wants you to go home to fuck off. Don't fidget and don't touch your hair. Are you ready?"

She straightens and I see the fire overtake her.

"Oh yeah, I'm ready. Let's do this."

I flip the camera on, the light giving her a glow.

"So, Charlie, how does it feel to be on the chopping block in the first week?" Her answering smile has a bite to it, daring anyone to come for her, and I know she wants this as much as I do.

CHAPTER FOURTEEN

CHARLIE

I FEEL LIKE A spotlight is on me as I sit in one of the black leather chairs designated for the bottom two. Every square inch of me is covered in sweat, and I'm grateful Courtney forced me to pack this black wrap dress. Trying to keep my mind off the fact I could go home in mere moments, I try to focus on not picking my nails. Alec was adamant the habit would deplete people's confidence in me.

My legs cross and uncross, my body calling to get up and expel this energy, but I'm locked down in this moment. In this blasted chair.

"Don't worry, sweetie, you're not going to go home tonight," Sharon says from beside me. Her roots show a hint of gray that seems to be completely covered by her chocolate hair dye.

Her dress is a pale yellow with a high neckline. She fiddles with the lace on her sleeves but gives me a reassuring smile.

"You could be the one who stays," I tell her, but I pray I'm wrong. I pray I'm here another day.

If it was me at home, I would vote for Sharon to stay. Courtney and I always loved to vote for who we thought of as the underdog in the weekly eliminations. Even though it was rare they would last, we always tried.

I tug at the sleeves of my dress, the fabric suddenly feeling like a burlap sack against my highly sensitive skin.

"We'll see," she says simply as the robotic voice starts counting down the last thirty seconds before we go live. Everyone still standing scrambles to their chairs, ready for Jacob Jacobson to come on the TV at any moment.

"Deceivers! Welcome to your first *live elimination*!" he exclaims.

He goes through the script, repeating Cain as the winner and Sharon and I as the bottom two up for elimination. The elimination episode, alone with his spiel, has been basically the same every week for the past nine seasons. I almost completely tune it out.

For the past half hour leading up to this moment, they've been airing various clips from the week that weren't included on the other episodes so audiences can see what we've been up to since the elimination competition.

"All throughout the week, our audience members have been voting. The votes are tallied and we are ready to say goodbye to the first person," Jacob continues.

Sharon grabs my hand and holds on to me as the lights darken and Jacob opens the white envelope he's been holding, reading it before focusing on us once more.

"Sharon..." He takes a dramatic pause.

Black dots dance in my vision.

This is my living nightmare. I'm about to be embarrassed on national television by being eliminated first. My chest feels like a hippopotamus is sitting on it, keeping oxygen from reaching my lungs.

"I'm sorry, but you will not be continuing into week two. Charlie, you've been saved by the audience," Jacob continues.

Relief droops my shoulders. While I hoped for this outcome, I would be lying if I said I hadn't been a ball of nerves for the past two days, worried I would never get a chance to appeal to brands.

Sitting in this chair made me realize how much I want to prove to myself I can do this. That I deserve to be here, no matter that it was a mix-up that changed the entire course of my life.

I want to prove I was worth the bet for Alec.

Jacob disappears and we are set free from the live show. Parker stands up from the couch and walks over to me. His charcoal suit is tailored perfectly, and I watch him with hungry eyes.

"Close call, huh?" he asks.

"Too close for my comfort, that's for sure."

He reaches a hand out to me and helps me stand. My black dress brushes against my legs as he pulls me up.

"Next week will be better."

"I'll make sure of it. Especially after the ass-chewing my wrangler gave me."

Parker's face darkens. "He yelled at you?" he asks, seeming to get annoyed on my behalf. "He shouldn't talk to you like that."

"Don't worry about it," I say waving away his concern. "I yelled at him right back."

He chuckles, his face brightening immediately. "If you need me to kick his ass, let me know."

I snort. Alec's angry face flashes in my mind at Parker's offer. I know his hackles are raised like an angry cat. I rub my thumb back and forth over his hand, which I still hold.

"We've come to an understanding. And I can kick his ass on my own." My smile seems to calm him.

I stand on my tiptoes and press a light kiss on his cheek. His face turns pink and the effect is so cute, I feel butterflies in my stomach. This imposing man blushes over a chaste cheek kiss.

"Thanks for the offer, though."

He opens his mouth to respond, but we are interrupted.

"I was very worried I would have to make a different friend in this house. You can't leave your fellow ginger sister. It's in the code." Molly comes bounding over, wrapping me in a hug and breaking the moment between Parker and me. I mouth sorry to Parker, but he waves off my apology and moves off to talk to some of the others.

"I'm going to help Sharon pack. Do you want to come with me?"

"Sure, let's do that."

Molly links her arm with mine and leads me back to the dressing room.

Sharon cries silently, kneeling beside her suitcase as she folds her clothes.

"Hey, Sharon, do you need some help?" Molly approaches her like she would a wounded animal. A quiet voice, no sudden movements.

"That'd be really nice, thank you." She runs the back of her hand against her wet eyes and sniffles. Her eyes are rimmed red when she looks up at me. "I'm happy it's me instead of you. I miss my daughter. I don't know if I could have lasted another week."

I smile, dropping to my knees and grabbing a shirt from the pile.

"Thank you. I'm glad you get to go home to her then, but we'll be sorry to see you go."

Once Sharon has her things together, we help her to the front door, where the remainder of the group waits. Cain makes an effort to help Sharon with her bags and, while everyone else sees it as a nice gesture, I find him as transparent as glass, the calculation behind his moves obvious after working with Mark for years. There are tears from most of us, more from the reality of the game sinking in than any particular attachment to Sharon.

With a last wave, she climbs into the limo and just like that, there's only nineteen of us left.

WEEK TWO

CHAPTER FIFTEEN

MONDAY IS MY FAVORITE day of the week. It's basically a day in limbo. There are no punishments or competitions. No wake-up calls. We just get to relax. Fortunately, I'm an early riser and I like to take advantage of the fact a lot of people sleep in on these days. But after the stress of possibly going home, exhaustion took over and dragged me deep into sleep.

When I finally roll out of bed, I see Raven is still buried in her ball of blankets while the other two beds are already empty. Jayden's sits neat as a pin while Molly's is more haphazardly made. Padding to the bathroom, I undo my braid I've taken to putting my hair in at night so as not to have a repeat of the first morning's Einstein look.

By the time I get to the bathroom, I practically waddle, I need to pee so badly.

"Hey girl. Want to eat breakfast together?" Molly asks from her place in front of the mirror as I walk by her, going to the women's side of the toilets.

"Sure thing," I call out without stopping.

Pulling down my shorts, I sleepily take a seat.

Water starts dripping onto the bathroom floor, wetting my feet.

"What the fuck?" I say, looking down. But it's not water on the ground. "What the fuck!"

I spread my legs, looking between them, and that's when I notice it.

Saran wrap.

With a shriek, I stand from the toilet and sprint to the shower. Without a care, I strip as I run, leaving my clothes where they fall.

"What's wrong?" Molly asks, but I ignore her.

"Get it off, get it off, get it off," I say as I jump into the cold water, not wanting to wait for it to warm.

"What's going on?" I hear Mateo ask. "I heard screaming."

"Someone put saran wrap on the toilets!" I shriek from the shower as we hear a few shouts from the men's side.

Soon all the showers are full as people are washing themselves from the misadventure.

"Fucking deceiver," I yell as I wash myself from head to toe again. Just to be safe.

I know it's Carter that's to blame this week. Who else would put *saran wrap* on the fucking toilets but a frat boy, no more mature than a prepubescent boy.

He better sleep with one eye open whenever it's my week to be the deceiver.

The sun is warm through the pergola over the daybed I'm dozing on. Jaxon is praying somewhere while Rebel chants on her yoga mat. Lucas yells out commands to the people who have joined him in his daily exercise routine.

"Good job, Ezra! Push it harder, Angelica!" he calls out.

I hear someone swimming laps, rhythmic slaps of arms against the water. The swimming stops, and I hear the person heave themselves out of the pool. A shadow and a few drops of water fall across my face, causing me to crack an eye. Parker's abs are a work of art, especially as water runs down them. Each dip and divot makes me want to run my tongue over them, chasing each drop. He cocks an eyebrow at me with a slight smirk, and I realize I've been staring at him for a long time.

"Your light snoring is very cute."

"Were you just sitting there listening to me sleep?" I ask, a little put off.

He laughs and it's a nice sound. "No, there were a few snores that weren't so delicate."

"Oh God," I say, embarrassment making me wish there was a cliff nearby I could jump from. I push myself up and lean against the bed's headboard. "I will stay awake for the rest of my time in this mansion. What's up, Parker?" I grab the pillow and put it on my lap, slapping it a few times, giving my hands something to do.

"I was bored and figured I'd come see what you were doing. Can I sit?" I bend my legs and wave at him to take a seat. He lies on his side, resting his head against his hand. "So, tell me about yourself." I laugh, and he smiles at me. His smile is beautiful and makes my heart clench. My traitorous brain brings a picture of Alec to the forefront and I feel annoyingly guilty for being attracted to this man.

I berate myself with a reminder there is no need to feel guilty over the taciturn wrangler.

"What do you want to know?"

"What's the worst thing you ever lied to your parents about?"

I groan, covering my face with my hands for a split second and think about the likely dozen cameras that are currently recording this moment.

"You realize this conversation will probably be aired, and then I'm going to end up grounded after the fact, right?"

"How old are you?" he questions with a raised eyebrow and a slightly mocking smile.

"Twenty-eight, almost twenty-nine."

"The statute of limitations has passed with a minimum of a decade between this moment and the crime."

"You've never met my mother."

"That's a good point."

Having Parker's full attention is like being pressed against a wall with a hand at your throat, holding you there, but not choking. I love everything about it and I have to remind myself I don't want to start anything with a competitor.

"Back when I was fifteen, my best friend Courtney convinced me we should sneak out of our houses, go to a party being held at a popular senior's house, and try alcohol for the first time."

I fall over, hiding my face with the pillow. He laughs as he fights with me to pull the pillow from my face.

"Wow, what a rebel you are! Did you successfully try some alcohol?"

"We had exactly one sip of beer before someone realized the *uncool underclassmen* were in their midst and kicked us out. We walked home and climbed back in through my window. My dad was waiting and asked where we were. We told him we went to the park around the corner from our house. I don't think he believed us, but he didn't tell my mom, so we got away with it."

A strand of blond hair falls in front of Parker's face with the kiss of the wind. My hand itches to tuck it back, but instead I sit up and hold my hands out palms up. He looks at me quizzically before I wiggle my fingers, wanting to play a simple game as we talk. Catching on, he shifts, sitting up and placing his hands on top of mine, palm to palm.

"Tell me something about you, now." I flinch my hands, making him pull his back.

"What do you want to know?" he parrots my question back to me.

"How did you lose your virginity?" I move like a striking snake trying to slap the top of his hands but he's just a second faster and pulls his away before I can connect.

"Oh, that's a fun story. There was a cheerleader, she was the most popular girl in school. She was cheering for our rugby game. Now, normally, I was a bench rider, but this game was a blowout, so I was finally allowed to play."

I flip my hands over and successfully smack him while his reflexes are a little slower due to the story. We switch positions so mine are on top of his now.

"My first catch," he continues, "I was tackled but they couldn't bring me down until we were well into the sideline. We took out the cheerleaders' pyramid and she landed on top of me. We went out on a few dates and then one thing led to another, and we christened the back seat of her mother's car."

"How romantic," I laugh. "No candles and rose petals?"

"Not that time, but I've stepped up my game now that I can invite women back to my apartment."

"I can only imagine how many take you up on that," I say, a small kernel of jealousy sliding in my tone. Parker takes this moment to make his move and slap the backs of my hands, my skin stinging.

"Ouch!"

Locking his eyes with mine, he takes both hands and presses a perfect kiss against each. I run my tongue against my bottom lip, wishing he would kiss me like that. For some reason, guilt over Alec worms its way into my gut once more, causing me to gently take back my hands.

"I haven't brought any back in a long time, but that's a story for a different day." He runs a finger up the side of my thigh before rolling onto his back. I lie down next to him, the edge of my hand touching his. I wrap my pinky around his and we both lay there staring up at the sky through the pergola above us.

I'm obviously attracted to Parker, but even though I typically want to smack Alec, I can't seem to get him out of my head.

CHAPTER SIXTEEN

ALEC

MY FINGER SLAMS DOWN on the space bar, pausing the footage. Frank emailed me the clip of Charlie and Parker's time on the daybed, letting me know he'd like to add it as part of the clips for the week. It's a good angle. A great angle, really. Not only will it feed into the audience's love of a good "will they, won't they" story, it will pretty much guarantee that shows will want to interview them together if they can make it far enough.

But why does the thought of an on-screen romance make me want to keep Charlie as far away from Parker as possible?

The minutes tick by and I get closer and closer to the deadline to submit clips for today's privilege show. Since there are so many contestants right now, each wrangler must provide up to three clips excluding entire cast activities like the competitions. Sheila and Bradley take care of picking out what will be shown from those bits as they are the main part of the show, whereas the clips we provide are more supplemental stories. I always pick clips based on the image I'm trying to sell for my contestant and I weigh the pros and cons of the clip Frank sent, ignoring my annoyance at their obvious flirting.

The twinge of irrational jealousy makes the decision for me. I type out an email telling Frank to submit the clip and hit send. Instant regret grips me, worried the romance will distract her, and I try to recall the message, but a loud voice pulls my attention.

"Joshua, what's the problem?" I ask as he stomps past my office door. He stops at my hard tone.

"Nothing, don't worry about it. My contestant is just an asshole," he says.

"Who's your contestant?"

"Cain," he says, puffing his chest.

"You pick a contestant that says he's willing to do anything to win, they tend to be assholes. I understand you're new, but you need to get your emotions under control. Twelve weeks is a long time after all, and if he's already getting under your skin, it's going to be an issue."

"Actually, bud, Cain has an issue with *your girl* being here, which is a pretty fair issue to have. Maybe I should go talk to Sheila about the dissatisfaction of a promising contestant." His eyes flash with the threat and it takes everything in me not to physically slap the little pissant down.

"Watch your fucking tone, Josh. Sheila might be our boss, but I'm still the head wrangler and *my* opinion influences who is brought back next year. If you think for one moment Sheila and the whole host of attorneys for Cost Communications weren't consulted to make sure Charlie could still compete once we realized the mix-up, you are sorely mistaken.

"Now, why don't you stop your infantile crying, tell your contestant to win on his own merits, and scurry along to whatever closet they've designated as your office."

A rebuttal presses against his lips but he holds it in. The best choice he could make, really. He storms off down the hallway, but as I move back into my office, I have to ask myself if I would have stood up for the reputation of my contestant on any other season.

No, no, you wouldn't, bubbles up from the back of my mind, but I silence the voice, shutting the door behind me.

My contestant's reputation is my reputation. It's as simple as that.

The viewing room is crowded for our Wednesday morning team meeting. Everyone mingles around the table laden with various breakfast foods. Cutting in the line, I grab a simple croissant before shuffling further into the room, my usual breakfast tea in my hand. Sheila stands at the front of the room, notes in front of her on a table while her fingers fly, texting on her phone.

"Alec, get up here, please," she says, not looking up from her phone. I never should have doubted if she noticed my entrance.

"What do you need?" Many people find my brusque demeanor rude, but Sheila loves the no-nonsense approach.

"Status on the items I gave you," she says.

"The outfits for the elimination challenge on Friday are good to go and Cain refused a reward as Head Deceiver this week. Apparently, he didn't like any of the options," I say, providing Sheila an update on all the items she had left in my care, in addition to my wrangler duties with Charlie.

As head wrangler, I act as Sheila's right hand. The promotion five years ago was appreciated but expected. Every year I have done my best to take on any additional responsibility I could, trying to bolster my resume.

"Great. Now sit."

Without another word, I take my usual chair in the front row.

"Let's get started," Sheila says, and the room immediately goes quiet. "The privilege episode aired last night to eight million viewers, slightly up from the elimination episode, as we expected. Viewership will normally drop some in the middle weeks as people are weeded out. Encourage drama where you can. That is always a big draw. Also, I received some requests this week about new notebooks for a few contestants because they lost theirs. These requests are denied. As previously informed, they only receive one."

"But they don't have anything to write in!" one of the newer wranglers adds.

"Not my problem. Alec, come up and give the reminders, please."

I stand from my chair, brushing the crumbs from my pastry off my pants. All the eyes settle on me. This doesn't bother me in the slightest, but it makes me think of Charlie and how she sometimes feels the viewers' eyes on her, and my gut twists with sympathy as I go through my list.

I catch my name in the credits as the end of the episode runs on the left of the screen while the next show starts on the right. Watching the rerun is important to me so I can see how the audience's viewing experience of my participant is.

Charlie playing Marco Polo in the pool with Keith and a few others seems to have been a light-hearted moment the audience enjoyed and I mentally pat myself on the back. Their friendship makes no sense, but their connection is there. Keith doesn't seem to be attached to anyone beyond my red-headed smart ass.

The crowd loves her humor, but what they love even more is her budding romance with Parker. As much as I wanted to keep the talk on the daybed out for selfish reasons, the director in me knew it was good television.

There are few things audiences love more than love.

My butt is numb from sitting on the lumpy bed of my hotel room for three hours, scrolling various message boards, articles, and daytime shows for any hint of the feeling the public holds for Charlie. My notebook is full of various feedback they don't know they are giving me so we can adjust our approach.

We're only in week two, and she's standing out exactly like I knew she would.

The song "Barbie Girl" blares from somewhere deep in the covers and I mentally curse out my sister.

"How many times have I told you to stop adding a ringtone to your contact?" I ask without preamble when her face fills my screen.

"About as many times as I told you to stop kissing my friends under the bleachers in high school. We aren't even yet. You need to talk to your best friend. He's pissing me off," Lorelei says.

Part of the agreement between the three of us when they started dating was they would not put me in the middle of any relationship drama. I open my mouth to remind her of this, but she cuts me off.

"I told him I didn't want him to propose when you weren't here to celebrate, and what does that lug head do?"

"Tank proposed?" I sit up straight on my bed. "When?"

"Today!" She lifts her hand in front of the camera, banishing her fake anger. "Isn't it gorgeous?"

Happiness fills every molecule of my body. My sister is my favorite person on the entire planet, and I never thought she would find someone I felt deserved her. But then again, Tank has taken care of her in a way she would be lucky to have for the rest of her life.

"He didn't ask my permission," I say, fake angry.

She rolls her eyes. The job of a brother annoying his sister is never done.

"I'm not a prize-winning cow. You have no say in the matter."

"You're way too snarky to win any prizes. As a human or a cow," I tell her.

"Congratulate me or so help me God, I will slap your photo on a billboard on the main drag announcing you have chlamydia."

I smile at the threat, a favorite of hers. "Congratulations. I'm glad you'll be making Tank's life hell until the end of time. We'll celebrate when I get done filming. Deal?"

"Deal. Speaking of filming, your girl is a stunner. If I liked women, I'd make you introduce me."

"Why does everyone keep telling me how beautiful she is like I'm blind?" I ask, exasperated.

"Knowing how you get during the season, I doubt you've noticed. Then again, you've not had to spend quality time with a knockout during a season either. But who the fuck is this Parker guy and why is he encroaching on your girl?"

"She's not my girl in the way you mean, and he's not encroaching. Frank is Parker's wrangler. He picked that clip this week and I approved."

She scowls as she studies my face for any hint of my underlying feelings and, in that moment, she looks more like Mom than I've ever seen her.

Grief envelopes me suddenly, my eyes going misty. My thumb hovers over the hang-up button but Lore and I made a pact we wouldn't hide our sadness from each other.

The world, yes, if we must. But each other? Never.

"Are you okay?" she asks, sensing the change in me.

"I just wish Mom was here. To help you plan the wedding. The sound of her voice is fading in my head and then you gave me that look and for a moment, I heard it. Clear as a bell."

Her mouth downturns as she tries to fight her own tears. Knowing I don't want to delve any deeper into my emotions, she shows me her love by changing the subject.

"Have you kissed her yet?"

If I was at my desk, I'd probably bang my head against it at the question.

"I'm a professional, Lorelei, for fuck's sake. I'm too busy trying to figure out how to make sure the audience loves her so they don't vote her out if she's in the bottom two again to try and make moves. Plus, for the *third* time, I'm not interested in her like that."

"I'll let you go with that answer for now, but just know, I have fifty bucks on you kissing her before the end of week four. Tank thinks you'll hold out until six."

"I hate you both," I tell her, and her laugh fills my room.

CHAPTER SEVENTEEN

CHARLIE

ALEC BURSTS THROUGH THE interview room door. His hair looks like hands ran through the strands multiple times.

"You look like you just came from a good snog in the backseat of a car," I say.

"You're not British," he retorts, but doesn't refute my accusation and for some reason, a small flash of anger that anyone would touch him goes through me.

"Did you want me to sing you the kissing song? I'd have to have the name of the other person to do it."

"I wasn't kissing anyone. Don't be ridiculous." He rolls his eyes at me as he sits in his chair, running his hands over his hair. While it doesn't set it to his usual perfect style, it does tame some of the crazier bits. "The audience is really enjoying your antics with Keith. They find the grumpy sunshine dynamic hilarious. They are also thoroughly enjoying that both deceivers so far have messed with the sizing of Ezra's clothes, and I have to agree it's pretty funny." He ticks things off in his notebook as he shares them with me. He promised to report back after every episode on what seems to be working.

"He has such a height complex, it's crazy. If anyone even hints at the fact he's on the shorter side, he blows a gasket."

His gray eyes seem annoyed today when he looks at me, but instead of taking it personally, I decide to chalk it up to his asshole tendencies coming out to play.

"Viewers are also absolutely starved for more flirting between you and Parker," he says, his annoyance solidifying in a voice of stone.

"We aren't flirting."

His eyebrows go up so fast, I'm sure they are going to disappear into his hairline. Embarrassment makes me start sweating. I don't want this formidable man to think I'm just here for a hookup. Parker is attractive, but there's something holding me back.

If I met him before the game, before Alec, I absolutely would have been interested in dating him, but no matter how much I'm loath to admit it, the man in front of me has captured my attention and I can't seem to shake it.

"Well, whatever you want to call your interactions, they are eating it up. I think you should really lean into it and give them what they want."

"What are you saying? I should kiss him or something?"

While I'm sure the experience would be extremely pleasant, I can't bring myself to kiss someone just because the audience would enjoy it.

Alec's face goes stormy and I feel like I messed up on a test I didn't know I was taking.

"I wouldn't pull a Penelope and Lucas by any means, but if you want to kiss him, then you should."

"I never said I want to kiss him." I pull my feet up into the chair and tuck them under me, trying to make myself a little smaller against the outright anger that's starting to pump off my wrangler.

"It's not like I care. Kiss him if you want. Our goal is to get you to the end of the game. He's not an ogre."

I perk up at this. A molecule of hope.

"You're jealous."

"What?"

"You heard me."

"I'm not jealous. Don't flatter yourself."

I want to smack him like I did on our first meeting, but I hold back, sure that would get me booted from the show.

"You can admit it. I won't judge you for it. It makes sense, after all. We spend all this time together talking. You can admit you have a little crush on me."

All I want is for him to say I'm right. Would I do anything about it? No. But it would make me feel less crazy for the crush I seem to have on him.

"It would be the height of unprofessionalism for me to have a crush on my contestant. I just want you to win so I can become a director. Other than that, I have no interest in you."

My heart squeezes for a fraction of a second, but the last thing I want to do is show him his words affected me. He sits there in his usual all black outfit, perfectly tailored, and I do what any insulted, hurt person would do.

I change the subject.

"How do you keep your clothes so black?" I ask him. "Do you have someone do your laundry? All of your clothes look brand new and it's pissing me off. Mine are all faded to various shades of gray."

He looks down at his shirt, awkwardly holding his arms out from his body. "No, I just wash it all inside out on gentle."

"No special soap?"

"I'm very confused about this line of questioning," he says.

His anger seems to be dissipating rapidly at my off-the-wall line of questioning, but at least I got him away from telling me in no uncertain terms he could never be attracted to me.

"Well, I'm very confused by how you look like you only own one outfit and yet it looks brand new every day. We've been here what, almost three weeks if you include the time we were at the hotel? I have yet to see you in a different outfit. How many of that shirt do you own?"

He shrugs, nonplussed. "I don't know, quite a few. It makes getting ready for the day easier."

"Do you own any other clothes?"

"Why wouldn't I own other clothes?"

"What are they? Footie pajamas? I bet you have some footie pajamas with the little butt flap."

A bark of laughter breaks out of him. Seeing his happy side makes my insides feel fuzzy like a freshly popped bottle of champagne.

"I don't have footie pajamas with a butt flap," he says, laugh lines by his eyes.

"Do you have some without a butt flap?"

"No, I don't have any footie pajamas, period. I sleep in boxer briefs."

I feel my cheeks turn pink and I want nothing more than to see these boxer briefs.

"They are black, though. And I have silk sheets," he adds. He looks almost shocked with himself at the level of personal details he just shared with me.

"What a cliché," I laugh, not shocked this stunningly hot man is the epitome of a playboy.

"Which part?" he asks with what seems to be genuine curiosity.

"The sheets and the all black."

"I don't only decorate in or only own black. I'm not a funeral director. Or a vampire."

"I never thought you were a vampire. Your teeth aren't sharp enough," I joke again.

He rolls his eyes. "Just wanted to make sure."

"I notice you didn't say you're not Batman, though." I tap my lips with my finger, giving him fake consideration.

"Do you think I'd do this job if I was a billionaire vigilante?"

"Maybe you want to stay humble?" I offer.

"I'm not Batman."

"Prove it," I demand.

"What?" His tone tells me he's giving me a chance to change what I said, but I decide to double down.

"Prove. It."

My gaze locks with his. As his eyes harden again and he sits up straight, I worry I crossed a line I didn't see.

"You do not give the commands here. I do."

I lick my lips. The cold man before me doesn't turn me off; just the opposite.

"Yes, sir."

I don't know why I say it. He's hardly older than me, but in this moment, it's the only thing I can think to say.

Hungry pleasure seems to light his eyes.

"That's a good girl. Let's get started. Untuck your legs."

Praise has never been a big deal to me, but each nerve ending in me is on fire.

Following his direction, I put my feet on the ground as he flips the camera on to record with zero acknowledgment that I have melted into a puddle of desire in front of him.

I've never been one for dirty talk. Mark and Scott sounded more like they were trying to reenact a bad porn but couldn't deliver the lines well.

But I think I'd do almost anything to have Alec King tell me I was a good girl again.

He crosses his ankle over his leg, the default pose he takes with me.

"Tell me about your week so far," he says, and that's our cue for me to be *Charlie Price, contestant on House of Deceit.*

"This week has been so great. Getting to know everyone has been a lot of fun. Keith has been really surprising me with his friendship, but I love talking to him about his farm back home. I have a list of about fifty movies to watch when I get back home." I laugh.

It sounds breathy and fake to me, but it doesn't matter. The people at home don't know the real me and they never really will. What's a fake laugh between us.

I lock eyes with Alec, putting a sly smile on my face.

"But the person I've enjoyed getting to know the most has been Parker."

WEEK THREE

CHAPTER EIGHTEEN

I T HAS BEEN SEVENTY hours since my team lost the privilege challenge this week. Seventy-two hours since the last time I tasted the sweet nectar of a French roast as it slid down my throat, the caffeine thrumming through my veins, and nothing makes me more vengeful than a lack of caffeine.

The smell of Keith's coffee makes me want to launch myself over the table and tackle him to the ground. As the Head Deceiver this week, he didn't have to participate in the challenge, which just adds to my hostility. Luckily for Carter, he was eliminated before I could execute my vendetta against him, while I settled in the middle of the pack.

For the past few days, my head has been throbbing to the point where I can hardly think. My caffeine headaches have been debilitating with the inadvertent cold turkey approach to not drinking as many cups of coffee in the morning.

But not only have we been denied coffee, we have also been relegated to oatmeal, unseasoned chicken, and broccoli for every meal until the week resets on Sunday night. The only drink we can have is water.

I miss my food having taste.

And salt.

Molly sings as she cooks in the kitchen. One of the winning team members, she's allowed to eat whatever she wants. Penelope and Lucas make out at the other end of the table, but I'm so starved for delicious food they don't register in my mind.

The handle of my spoon cuts into the palm of my hand, I'm squeezing it so hard.

"I feel like you're about to stab me in the throat with your spoon, girl," Keith says in his no-nonsense way.

"It might be worth it for a sip of your coffee."

He smiles at me from beneath his big, bushy mustache.

"I could take you."

"I'm in a caffeineless rage, it might give me super strength. I have something to fight for."

"The preservation of my coffee gives me something to fight for."

"Don't worry, if she tries to kill you, I'm your witness," Rebel says from beside me, toying with her oatmeal as well. "That and the probably fifty cameras pointing at us right now."

Neither Keith nor I acknowledge her, locked into a demented staring contest over his breakfast. Despite my threats, he continues shoveling food in his mouth before taking a slow bite of his crispy bacon.

He chews, moaning in pleasure.

"Keith, you're walking a thin line, my friend." I try to take another bite of my oatmeal, but it gets stuck in my throat. I push my bowl away from me. Food is devoid of all joy right now. I barely ate yesterday. After three days of bland food, I'm ready to commit murder for a piece of crispy bacon.

Courtney would come and visit me in jail if I snapped.

Keith has a giant smile on his face as he swirls a bite of pancake in front of my face. The soup spoon holds a pool of syrup beneath the pancake, making my mouth water. Not only can I not have seasoned food, but the stupid deceiver has also taken to hiding all the cutlery in the house except the spoons, adding to my frustration.

I feel someone walk in, but I'm focused on the buttery bite in front of me.

"What's going on here?" Parker asks.

"A test of wills," Keith says, popping the pancake in his mouth, smiling as he chews.

"You're an ass," I tell him, turning to Parker. He's dressed in workout gear, a towel hooked over his shoulder. "Where have you been?"

"The gym."

"We have a gym? Where is it?"

"Red, maybe you should stop looking at my food with goo-goo eyes and pay attention to your surroundings a bit more."

I turn back to Keith and flip him off. "Did you know we had a gym, Grandpa?"

"I guess you'll never know." He mops up every last drop of syrup before popping the final bite of his breakfast in his mouth. He winks at me as he picks up his empty plate and takes a slurping sip from his coffee mug on his way back to the kitchen.

"Hey, sorry. I can't seem to focus when people are waving pancakes in my face. But seriously, where's the gym?"

"Can't say I blame you there, babe, and I'll show you the gym sometime. Are you ready for the competition today?" Parker asks, his smile not reaching his eyes.

"About as ready as I can be. Are you okay?"

"What?"

"Something just feels off," I say, touching his forearm lightly.

"Oh, yeah. Today's just a hard day for me. Don't worry about it. I'll talk to you later, okay?"

"Sure."

Parker turns to leave, but I reach out and stop him. "I'm here, if you need anything." He nods, rubbing my hand, and continues on his way out of the kitchen.

"Price, to the interview room," the disembodied voice says.

My curiosity beats my hunger for a second. Alec never calls me to interview this close to a competition.

"Run along to your handler," Keith says, popping his head around the corner. I flip him off again and make my way out of the dining room.

"Bite me."

Bursting through the door marked "Interview," I see Alec standing there, hands tucked into his pockets.

"What's up?" I ask immediately.

"I'll give you a sip of my coffee if you win today."

I stop midstride, temporarily looking like the person on a pedestrian walking signal.

"I'm sorry, I just hallucinated the ever-professional Alec King offering to break a rule," I say, not wanting him to know I'd do a lot of things in this moment for a sip of coffee.

"Don't be a smart ass. We don't have time. I'll give you one," he holds up his finger emphasizing his point, "sip of coffee if you win Head Deceiver today. We need the audience to see you win some challenges."

I stick my hand out. "Shake on it."

His hand is warm and soft, threatening to distract me. I drop it quickly.

"Deal," I say.

The elimination contest seemed simple when Jacob Jacobson laid out the parameters, but as I stand here staring at the math problem, I'm not so sure.

Each round, a question for a fifth-grade placement test is asked. The first person to answer correctly gets to pick a chair. After that, a game of musical chairs ensues.

I fight with the fractions until Mary Ella smacks her buzzer, yelling out her answer. Keith confirms the answer and she skips over, picking her chair. The rest of us move to a dot on the ground and ready for the music.

Adrenaline courses through me as Keith presses play on the boombox and the music starts. Repetitive notes quickly embed themselves in my brain and I know I'll be playing this song over and over again in my head. The music cuts, and I pounce. Raven looks at me as she runs to the same chair and I ready myself to fight for it.

She falls to the ground with an "oof" as I push against her with my full weight.

Everyone is playing to win but what they don't know is, I'm not only playing for exemption from elimination, I'm playing for a sip of coffee.

All the seats are taken, and Angelica stomps her foot in anger at being the first one out and up for elimination. She moves over to the bench to wait out the rest of the game as we all return to our podiums for the next question.

We are all ready as Keith reads off the next question.

"How far is the Earth from the sun?"

Molly smacks her buzzer.

"94 million miles," she says.

"Correct!" Keith tells her.

Molly gives a whoop of excitement and moves to take her seat. Musical notes permeate the air as we all walk in a circle, preparing for the music to stop. As silence descends, anarchy reins.

I slam my shoulder into Mateo without a hint of remorse as he goes to sit in the chair I've decided is mine. He sprawls on the ground as I get my ass on the seat, wrapping my hands around the edges and holding on for dear life.

Penelope scrambles up from the dirt where she landed as Raven won the seat they were both scrambling for. Digging her feet into the ground, she sprints for another of the open chairs. Penelope wins a seat by slipping underneath Parker as he goes to sit down. I cackle at the shock on the Viking's face as he is knocked to the ground. Pushing off the ground, he all but tackles the last open chair from Jayden. The last one left, Jayden will join Angelica and will be up for elimination.

As the rounds progress, the fight for the remaining chairs becomes more and more feral. My arms are covered in scratches and one of my sleeves has been completely ripped off. Colyn holds an ice pack to her cheek; a rogue elbow having caught her across the face. Round after round we play until it's down to the final two.

Me and Cain.

Keith flips the card over and starts reading.

"What is the longest river in the United States?"

Hope. The smallest strand of hope runs through my veins. I know this answer.

Cain and I both go to press our buttons. A second passes. Two. My button lights up showing I hit it first.

"The Missouri River," I say.

"That is"—Keith takes a pause. Safe from elimination, he's eating up our anxiety—"correct! Congratulations, Charlie! Please take the remaining seat."

Everyone claps as I turn around and head toward the throne behind me. Whooping with excitement and giddy with relief, I go to sit and look upon my subjects.

Parker moves to kneel before me. "My queen, I will be loyal to your rule for all days. Long live the queen!" he says.

I stand and move toward him, preparing to knight him with my imaginary sword. I don't care it's silly. I'm so happy about the fact I just guaranteed my place into week five and a sip of coffee, I'm all in the acting. As I get close, he lunges forward, throwing me over his shoulder. Bouncing against his back, I notice Cain scowling through the others that are following us.

"Pool party!" Parker calls out, his previous sadness vanished, and cheers go up.

He launches me high into the air and I laugh with glee as I splash into the water. I am soaked.

But I won. And that is all that matters.

CHAPTER NINETEEN

M Y SHOES SQUELCH AS I sprint to the interview room. Alec hasn't called me, but I don't care. I know he'll be there. I burst through the door and am greeted with his smiling face. Without missing a beat, I launch myself into Alec's arms, wrapping my legs around his waist.

I don't care if I'm dripping wet.

I don't care if he's clean as a whistle.

And in this moment, I don't think he does either. He catches me, his arms wrapping tightly around me.

"You did it," he whispers in my ear.

"I did."

We stand there, holding each other, exuberant happiness leaking from both of us before, slowly, the energy changes. I pull back and look at him as he lets me go. I slide down his body and become heated, feeling every ridge of him. His gray eyes hold mine. His hands are heavy on my hips.

"You owe me coffee," I say, trying to defuse the tension but my voice betrays what our closeness is doing to me.

"I do, yes."

Clearing his throat, he moves away from me toward a to-go coffee cup sitting on the table next to his chair. He holds the cup out to me and I take it, careful not to touch him. Not to push him any more than I already have.

"Thanks," I say.

Taking a moment, I pop the lid off the cup, taking a deep inhale of its contents. With the reverence of an archaeologist with an artifact, I cherish the cup in my hands.

I take one deep sip.

It explodes over my taste buds and I swear to any deity listening to not take coffee for granted ever again. As I put the lid back on, I pause.

"This is my order."

"No, it's not." He rocks back on his heels.

"Yes, it is. Unless you also drink a piccolo."

I watch him, and for the first time he fidgets.

"I didn't want to get you something you didn't like, considering you were only going to get one drink of it."

"Are you going to finish it? I don't want it to go to waste. I would have taken whatever your usual is. That was the deal."

"I, uh, I don't actually," he stutters. "I don't drink coffee. I only drink tea."

"Oh. Then why did you offer—"

"I was just trying to be nice."

My chest warms like I gulped down the entire cup of scalding liquid.

"Thank you," I say, suddenly shy.

"You're welcome."

Unsure what to do, I hand him back the cup and move to sit in my chair. He sits in his, resting his ankle on his knee like always.

"Proud of me?" I ask, needing to know he thinks I did a good job.

The heart-stopping smile appears once more, this time a dimple catching my attention.

"More than you could imagine," he says.

"You should come with me when I see the room for the first time. You're my wrangler. This is your win, too!" I shouldn't have said it, but my mouth ran away with me. Ever since he offered me a sip of coffee if I won, it felt like things had changed. Like maybe we were becoming friends and I can't help but wanting to keep that feeling.

"I can't, I'm sorry. We're not allowed into the mansion except when told by our higher ups. I could get fired."

My shoulders slump with disappointment. "That's right. I forgot. Sorry I asked."

"I'll make sure to watch you on the live feed when you go in for the first time. How about that? You can talk to me like I'm in the room," he says, his voice soft. A good wrangler taking care of his contestant.

"That'd be great," I say but my voice lacks enthusiasm.

"Are you ready to get started?"

I close my eyes and take a deep breath, holding it in. Pushing down the sadness because there can't be a single normal moment in this house, I let my mansion persona come to the surface. When I open my eyes, I'm ready.

"Charlie, how does it feel to win the elimination challenge and immunity going into week four?"

"It feels euphoric. The weight that has lifted knowing I'll be here for at least two more weeks is so freeing. These people are starting to become my family. It's so funny because, when I watched *House of Deceit* at home, I always thought how silly it was when everyone talked about becoming family with strangers. But you do. You spend every moment with them. The bonding process is different. No one else will ever understand your experience with your fellow housemates. Knowing I get to spend more time with them is fantastic." I lock eyes with Alec, hoping he can read between my words. With every day that passes, I'm desperate to make sure he knows where I stand. That I want to spend more time with *him*.

He shifts in his seat, clearing his throat. I think I see pink rising in his cheeks but brush it off as the glow from the red light of the camera next to him.

"And let's not forget to mention I am allowed to eat seasoned food again!" I continue. "That's been the hardest part this week. You don't realize how, stripped of any form of entertainment, food *becomes* your entertainment. On days where there's no competitions or game nights or whatever, who cares if you spend three hours cooking? There's nothing else requiring your time. It's really been enlightening. But that might just be the hunger talking."

We laugh and talk until Alec finally determines he has the footage he needs for this.

"You get one question."

"Question about what?" I ask.

"About me. I'll answer anything you ask. Consider it an additional reward."

Part of my requirements to stay my wrangler was I wanted to get to know Alec as a person. He's done better about opening up, yet I can tell he still holds himself back. Keeps the professional distance.

A part of me wants to ask something frivolous and fun but I want to know every fiber of this man. A serious question then.

"Who's your favorite person?"

His gray eyes stare at me for a moment and then he takes a deep breath.

"Lorelei, my sister. She is my everything." I'm worried that's all he's going to give me and then he continues.

"Our mother died when I was seventeen. While I am the older brother and should have been taking care of Lore, she took it on herself to raise me. Even before that we were really close. I went to every one of her soccer games and dance recitals. She came to every one of my best friend's football games with me.

"We went to the same college and shared an apartment together. I would die for her without a moment's hesitation or regret. She's incredibly caring. She's engaged to that same best friend, Tank, now. He proposed last week."

He takes a beat, his fingers messing with the hem of his pant leg, while I digest everything he told me. As I open my mouth to respond, or maybe thank him for telling me, he keeps going, surprising me.

"There were no bright spots in my mother's death. I became an angry kid. It took a lot of time to dig myself out. But Lorelei never judged me. Never gave up on me when I snapped at her or kissed her friends under the bleachers to distract myself. Sure, I loved her and we became inseparable, but I can only imagine how hard it was for her as well.

"There were a lot of years, and still some random moments, where I wish I could exchange myself for our mother so Lore can have her mom back."

His voice cracks, the smallest fissure in his control, and it's all I can take.

I get up from my chair and kneel in front of him. As he talked, his eyes turned toward the ground and there's nothing I need more than to see the man I know in them. The cantankerous pain in my ass. I grab his hands in mine and he looks at me.

"I'm sure she wouldn't want to exchange you. I'm sorry you went through that."

He smiles at me, a small one. "Thanks. I hope you're right."

The sadness I see eats away at me and I want nothing more than to erase it.

"I don't have any siblings, but I can tell you, I would be obliterated if something happened to Courtney. I would not be able to survive. I'm not saying losing either of my parents wouldn't rip the heart from my body and leave me with nothing, but I know, deep down I *know*, I would never be able to face life without her. I am so deeply sorry for every moment you've had to spend without your mother. For every time you've wanted to call her and realized you couldn't. My heart breaks for you." I dab quickly at the tears trying to fall. "But I can't tell you how glad I am you're here with me."

Alec unclenches his death grip and turns one hand, lacing our fingers together. We sit there for a while, deep within our own thoughts, but tethered to the moment together.

The door to the interview room closes behind me, but I stop. Cain stands, back pressed against the wall, arms crossed over his chest.

"Do you know what percentage of people that win the elimination challenge during week three make it into the final three?" he asks cryptically.

"Um, no?" My gut tells me he's not going to let me leave until he's had his say and nerves threaten to overtake me.

"Sixty-six percent."

"Thanks for the fun fact. I'll make sure to write it down in my notebook in case it's on the final trivia game." I go to walk past him but he quickly pushes off the wall, stepping in front of me.

"It should have been me." His voice is menacing, all vestiges of the nice guy he pretends to be, gone.

"Dude, I was just faster to the buzzer. It's not a big deal. Be faster next time."

He walks into my space and I move back, pressing myself against the door. I think about screaming, hoping Alec is watching the live feed, but I'm sure he's catching up on other things after our long time in the interview room.

"Alec King is your wrangler."

"Thanks for the update. Now get out of my way." I lace my words with anger to hide the fear I am feeling being cornered by this man, hoping he buys the act.

"Eight of the last nine years, Alec's contestant has won immunity going into week four. The last six years, that person has made it to the final three. You were never supposed to be here. You shouldn't have him as your wrangler. He should be mine. I'm the better choice." His eyes are crazy, and spittle is showering over me. "I've studied every season. I've run every possibility. But now I'm stuck with a brand-new wrangler who doesn't know anything. Alec King should be my wrangler."

All sanity leaves my body as I decide to egg him on.

"And yet, he still passed on you."

His face turns red and a very real fear he is going to hurt me crystallizes. I put my hand on the doorknob, praying it's still unlocked, ready to try and open it to throw us off balance should he attempt anything. But he doesn't. He steps back, giving me more space. Gathering the pieces of his affable guy next door persona, ready to put the mask back on.

"I know he's cheating. How else has he gotten such consistent results?"

"He would never, and more importantly, neither would I." The accusation against Alec sears through me, burning away all the fear.

"I'm watching you," he says, moving back to lean against the wall once more.

"Great, watch away," I say, moving down the hallway, back to where there are other people, afraid to be alone.

WEEK FOUR

CHAPTER TWENTY

HEAD THROBBING FROM OUR impromptu party celebrating the know-it-all Angelica's departure, I stare at the door hiding the bedroom that will be mine for the next week. The metal handle bites my skin with its coldness as I push the door open to my sanctuary. Bedside lamps provide soft light. Fake candles sit on the various shelves and the dresser top, giving the room a romantic and relaxed feeling. The room is painted a deep emerald, including the ceiling. Every tense muscle relaxes.

Going from living alone for the past two months to being around people constantly has been a hard adjustment. It's not that I don't appreciate getting to know my fellow competitors, but sometimes I'd like to be able to read without interruption. I close the door softly behind me, not wanting to disturb the silence, pocketing the key sitting in the lock for when I want to leave later.

On the bed, in the very center of the black comforter, sits a white box with a red ribbon. Plush gray carpet pads my footsteps as I make my way over to the bed. I climb up and kneel next to my box. Giddy with anticipation, I undo the bow and raise the lid. Inside sits a pair of footie pajamas in a deep golden color.

Butt flap included.

A delighted laugh escapes me and I quickly whip off my top and shorts and slip into the pajamas. Neither Cain nor Keith came out of the Head Deceiver room with new pajamas, so I know this present is from Alec to me. That he thought of me.

For being such a hard-ass, he has a very caring side as well.

"Thank you for this," I say, knowing Alec's watching. When this man says he's going to do something, you can count on that. "I love them." Touched, I blow a kiss into the room, not sure where the cameras are here. But I am certain there are some. They are everywhere.

Scott never bought me little presents because he thought I'd enjoy them. Even for my birthdays, the gift was practical. A blender, a treadmill, and a paper shredder. He never once brought home flowers on a random Tuesday because he thought they'd make me happy. Never my favorite candy because he was at the store and saw it and knew I had a bad day. He would never buy me something we had once joked about.

I crawl back onto the bed and sit with my legs crossed. Closing my eyes, I count my breaths. Emptying my mind of all thoughts, I center myself for the first time in weeks. Silence brushes its fingers across my cheek. It wraps its arms around me and pulls me tightly to its chest. It consumes me. I open my eyes and know I will fight to be back in this room again.

A low bell interrupts my sacred silence, but I don't mind. A screen drops down from the ceiling, the motor whirring. I was so engrossed in the quiet and being alone I didn't take full stock of my surroundings. A black projector blends into the dark room. It flicks on once the screen has fully descended. Jacob Jacobson's fake smile sits before me on the screen.

"Hello, Charlie. Welcome to your oasis for the week. Please enjoy all the comforts offered to you during this time. As a special surprise, you will be able to enjoy a movie night! You're welcome to have others join you, up to five guests."

I gasp with excitement. A night of entertainment and the people in the mansion I've become closest to sounds as close to heaven as I will get here.

"The movie night will be on Thursday night. Please let your wrangler know by Wednesday what movies and snacks you'd like to enjoy during this special time. If you have any questions, please let your wrangler know."

The screen goes dark and begins its return journey up the wall. The list of who I should invite starts making itself in my head. Molly, of course. Keith, without a doubt. I think of Parker and his searing gaze. Parker, yes. He should come. Maybe Mateo? My brain spins a wheel of the remaining names, trying to land on a few more but unable to do so. Choosing not to let the indecisiveness bother me, I let it be a game-time decision. One thing I know for sure, I won't tell the others about this surprise. Instead, I'll surprise them with the perk. A small smile graces my mouth as I think of their reactions.

After some time, I leave the room to go hang out with the rest of the house. The past few weeks, all I've wanted is peace, but now that

I have it, I miss the others. Plus, I can almost hear Alec telling me the audience will like it more if I'm social.

"Could you get me some construction paper in various colors?" I ask Alec after our chat for the show.

He thought it would be good to talk about my family some and how I miss them. Apparently, the audience is really sinking their teeth into the girl next door image we are trying to portray with my interviews. A doting daughter. A loving aunt in the life of her best friend's kid. Single. Attainable.

"What are you wanting to make?" he asks, bringing out his ever-present phone to take notes.

"Some invitations for the movie night," I tell him. He smiles at my giddiness about surprising my friends.

"I'll bring it to you tomorrow."

"Perfect, thank you. Did we have anything else to talk about today?"

"Did you want to talk about anything else today?" He cuffs his shirt sleeves just below his elbows, revealing his forearms. Suddenly, I am very aware I've never seen him in anything but full sleeves because I would remember the tattoos covering his sculpted arms.

"Charlie?"

"Hm?" I look up at him.

He cocks an eyebrow at me, lacing his hands together and resting them on his knee.

"Did you want to continue staring at me or would you like to answer my question?" His smug tone makes me want to prove to him I wasn't staring, just lost in thought. Then again, I've always been a terrible liar.

"What was your question?"

"What were you thinking about?"

My cheeks warm. "How I was surprised you have tattoos." I try to appear unconcerned, but his face tells me I'm failing.

"Oh? And why's that?"

"Because you're tight-laced."

He scoffs. "I'm not tight-laced."

"You're so tightly laced, you're basically a corset. But it's okay, I still like you," I tell him.

His eyes sparkle with humor.

"That was an interesting turn of phrase, the corset thing. Do you realize how often you do that?"

"Do what?"

"Turn boring observations into pithy little statements. It's part of why you're so good in interviews. Because you don't say the same thing everyone else would."

"Maybe I'm just playing with the audience. Making them overlook me. Or maybe it's just my journalism background."

"No, I don't think that's it. It's the same humor I saw on your application."

"You picked me because you were attracted to my drunk jokes?" I ask with a tinge of humor. He rolls his eyes.

"Not *attracted* attracted, just I saw the benefit of humor in winning the audience's sympathies."

"Sure, sure. It's okay to say you liked me on paper when you thought I was a man."

"It wasn't like that and you know it, but let's go back for a moment. You like me, huh? You think I'm sexy?"

"I don't know what you're talking about. I didn't say that." My entire body flashes hot like I just climbed into a bathtub full of magma.

At least I don't think I've ever said it out loud.

He snorts. "Fine, we'll shelve that. But you most definitely did say you like me. Don't make me replay the tape. And the other thing I inferred because I'm not only sexy, I'm also intuitive."

This joking, soft man is endearing. He's the one who makes my heart squeeze. But the stern, domineering man I met initially, the one who directs me and makes my pussy squeeze, is equally attractive.

"You're awfully full of yourself, sir," I joke.

"That might be true, but I don't hear you denying it."

Emboldened, I stand up and move toward him. With one finger, I trace the lines of his tattoos and a trail of goosebumps follows. I might be attracted to this man, he's one of the most gorgeous men I've laid eyes on, but I'm hoping I'm not the only one affected.

"I'll let you pick the movie, but make it a romantic comedy. They are my favorite." I walk to the door with significantly more confidence than I feel. Looking back, I smirk at the heated look he's giving me.

"Don't forget the construction paper, please."

CHAPTER TWENTY-ONE

I PEEK INTO MY actual bedroom and watch as Molly finds the movie ticket I stuck under her pillow. Her squealing glee is infectious and I go running into the room, bouncing on her bed.

"What movie are we going to watch?" she asks.

"I told Alec to surprise me. I thought that would be more fun. It should be a romcom, though."

She fans herself with her ticket. The red face states "Admit One" in large, bold letters. My mother always thought I should use my beautiful penmanship to write wedding invitations for people and make lots of money, but I always found myself getting bored writing the same thing over and over and *over*. So now I use my skills primarily for fun.

At nine p.m. the next day, my invitees begin to stream in. Molly is the first, carrying her pillow and blanket.

"Those are cute pajamas. Are they new?" she asks of my onesie as she gives me a hug.

"No, I just haven't worn them yet," I lie.

She looks around the bedroom, letting out a low whistle before turning back to me.

"I've never been so excited to watch a movie in my entire life. You could show me graphically violent driver's education films and I'd froth at the mouth to watch them," she tells me with no preamble.

"I have dreams about lying on my couch for a Saturday, not moving, binge-watching shows and movies."

Television never enticed me before being in the mansion. It was more something I had on in the background versus actively watching. But the moment I was told I couldn't watch anything, it has been all I've wanted to do.

Mateo walks in. His pajamas are shiny leopard print. Molly and I share a look but quickly tamp down the giggles that want to come out.

"Thanks for inviting me, Charlie! It's so nice to be included," he says, hugging me. I can feel my ribs crack beneath his arms.

"We love hanging out with you! Those are some fun pajamas," I say with my last breath.

As he releases me, I try to suck air deep into my lungs as discreetly as possible.

He hugs Molly, air kissing each cheek.

"My boyfriend likes to say I'm an animal in the bedroom. He bought me these." He puts his hands in his pockets and moves about, showing the different angles of the gaudy fabric.

"That's very nice of him. Help yourself to a drink," I say, indicating the dresser behind me.

"Can I get you ladies anything?" he asks, grabbing a plastic cup.

"A spicy margarita would be great," Molly says. "Charlie has gotten me addicted."

I smile at her. "Make that two, please, Mateo."

"Will do, my lovelies."

Ice clinks in the shaker as he takes care of us. Rebel comes strutting in, her tight midriff on display in her yoga gear.

"Hey, Rebel. Do you want a drink?" I ask her, giving her a one-armed hug.

The yogi has quickly become one of my favorite people. With all of our free time, she has taught me a lot about her spirituality while helping me become more flexible through yoga. Nothing bonds two people together like accidentally farting in downward dog.

"Normally, I'd say no, but since it's a special occasion." She hugs Mateo from behind, who pauses his drink making to pat her hands around his waist. "Can you make me one of those, as well, Mateo?"

"Of course, darling."

Keith is dressed in plain pajamas, a white undershirt and shorts, but I'm impressed he adhered to the dress code all the same.

"Hey, Grandpa," I say to him, hugging him around the middle.

"Hi there, Red. Thanks for the invite. What movie are we going to watch?"

"Oh, you're going to hate it. It's going to be sappy, love city," I tell him. "My wrangler picked the 2005 version of *Pride and Prejudice*."

Keith scoffs. He enjoys westerns almost exclusively, he's told me before, but I knew he'd be here if for no reason other than I invited him. He goes around the room, greeting each person. He doesn't hug anyone but me, but no one's offended by the lack of physical affection. I'm the exception that proves the rule. As we all get settled in, enjoying our drinks, Parker walks in.

His gray sweatpants hang low on his hips and I am all but drooling. The white shirt is tight, showing the ridges of his abs. Maybe it wouldn't be so difficult to play up a romance between us as Alec suggested, but the thought of using Parker makes me want to quit the show and damn the consequences.

"Hey, beautiful," he says, kissing my cheek. Everyone hoots at us, mocking Parker's greeting, but he's not fazed.

Molly gives me a wink as I burn from embarrassment.

"Does anyone need their drink refreshed?" Parker asks, making his way to the drink station. A chorus of no's reaches him, but it's nice he thought to ask.

Once everyone is settled with their snacks and drinks again, we start the movie. Parker stands next to the bed, holding his drink, and motions for me to scoot over. I'm sandwiched between Molly and Parker and every nerve on my body is alive with his proximity. The opening credits scroll as Parker drags his finger up and down my leg.

The movie plays, but I see none of it while Parker's hand rests within mine.

There are light snores all around. I'm almost hanging off the bed with Molly all but starfished on my side. Parker moved to the ground as she started falling asleep, giving me more space.

Sitting up on the bed, I consider going to sleep out on the couch. Sadness would consume me at the loss of a night in the room alone if I hadn't had so much fun with everyone.

"Charlie?"

My name is so faint, I almost think I'm hearing things, but then a feather light touch runs down my forearm. Leaning over the bed, I look in Parker's eyes, lit by the dim light from the TV.

He yanks his head to the side, indicating the door, and I nod. The lights in the house are dimmed, all the main spaces empty, as we make our way outside.

The night air is cooler but still humid from the day. Soft lights illuminate the daybeds around the pool and I follow Parker to the closest one. We both lean against the low headboard watching the pool.

"Last week, before the elimination challenge, you were having a bad day. I wanted to check on you now that I finally have you alone. Did you want to talk about it?" I ask, breaking the silence.

I feel him looking at me, but I keep my gaze forward. Sometimes it's easier to give your truth when there's not another's gaze probing you.

"I don't want to ruin the evening," he says, turning back to the pool.

"You won't, but I also am not going to make you."

We sit in silence awhile. Sinking into the pillow propped behind my back, the concert given by the insects of the evening starts to lull me into a doze, as the refreshing wind caresses my face.

"It was the anniversary of my divorce. It's been five years. Not my favorite day." Parker's voice jolts me from my sleeping twilight into wakefulness once more. "One day she was there and then she wasn't," he says, sadness in his voice.

"You make it sound like she died."

"She might as well have. We went to bed one night and then in the morning, she was gone. I haven't seen her since."

I sit there, digesting that information. I couldn't imagine running from someone I loved enough to marry, but I also know I don't have the entire story so I try not to judge.

"Can I ask you something that might seem like it's deflecting?"

"Always," he says.

"Why are you here?" I ask, repeating the question Molly asked me on the first night.

This time I'm the one looking at him while his gaze holds onto the pool.

His strong chest rises and pauses at the top. When I think he's going to hold his breath until he passes out, avoiding this conversation, he releases it.

"There was a day I was driving home from work and I realized the entire drive I was hoping someone would run a red light or something and crash into my car. I knew I had to change something.

"She *loved* this show. Loved it. We watched every episode live and even after she left, I watched. We turned down plans to be able to watch it. I didn't care. It made her happy. I would have locked the world away to watch an episode with her. When I got home that day, I signed up. Maybe a small part of me hoped she'd see me. Miss me."

I wait. I would wait as many minutes as needed for him to tell this story and not consider a single one a waste.

"She was my best friend and the cheerleader in the story I told you about my virginity. I loved her more than anything. I think I loved her before I knew she existed."

My heart is crushed into pieces so small you'd have to look at them under a microscope to see them.

"I'm not going to pretend like I have any idea what you've been through over the past five years. What you've survived. Just by you sitting here, you're stronger than you give yourself credit for."

"Thanks," he says, bumping my shoulder. "I'm just tired of missing her. I still live in our house and it's like everything has just stopped. Including me," he admits.

"Have you considered talking to a therapist? It's not a miracle cure, but it could help you to let go. Let you move on because you deserve to have someone choose you, every day."

We sink into silence again, but this time it is crushing like we are beneath miles of dirt and soil.

"Parker," I say, interrupting his thoughts.

"Charlie?"

I feel like I'm seeing this Viking of a man before me for the first time. The fine lines and heaviness around his eyes.

The sadness.

"I don't know if you were told, but our wranglers are pushing clips of us together, making it seem like there's *something* here," I say, feeling a little silly. He flirts with me, calls me beautiful, but in light of the new information, I don't know what to make of all of it.

"I know. Frank told me. He wanted to make sure I was good with it before he aired it. I should have talked to you, I'm sorry I didn't."

His huge hand takes up half of my thigh where he places it. I set mine on top, wrapping my fingers around his.

"I wouldn't want to be tied to anyone else in this house, but..." I trail off.

"Charlie," he turns his entire body toward me, crossing his legs. I match his position. "You're the first woman I have been attracted to since I met Brittany, but I'm not so delusional to believe I can offer you anything of substance. At least not right now."

His candor is refreshing and I find myself smiling.

"That's very flattering. For the record, you're gorgeous. I'm just going to get that out there, but we could help each other."

"I'm listening."

"What if we lean into this a bit, now with both parties knowing about it, and we play it up. Alec, my wrangler—"

"I remember," he says, his voice a little angry, not forgiving him for hurting my feelings earlier in the game.

"Right, so he says the audience is eating it up and we are more likely to continue moving forward if people are interested in us. As a couple." I look at him and decide to lay all of my cards on the table. "My financial situation back home is not ideal." I twist my frizzy red hair into a low knot, getting it off my neck. "I'm hoping to make it long enough brands will want to work with me when I get out of here so I can have some income while I look for a new job."

"That's a really good plan. I'm in. Should we kiss on it?" he asks with a smirk.

I stick my hand out. "What about a shake?"

And just like that, I've made my first alliance of the game.

WEEK FIVE

CHAPTER TWENTY-TWO

ALEC

"Y OU'LL RECEIVE YOUR LAST paycheck next week. Alec has your flight information if it's not already in your email," Sheila says to the brand-new wrangler crying in her office. "You've not been fired, this isn't a big deal. Your contestant is just going home and we don't need extra people here."

Normally, I would make the arrangements for the ousted wrangler without a meeting, but Sheila tries to make it a little more personal for the newer ones.

"Your flight is in a few hours. There's an appointment set for you tomorrow morning at nine at the main Cost Communications building. They'll let you know what show you'll be going to assist on next," I tell the girl.

Her name didn't stick in my head as her contestant, Harper, was relatively low maintenance as far as production was concerned.

The tears have me mentally adding her to the list of wranglers who will not be invited back in the future.

After she's been dismissed, I take her seat.

"Charlie is the deceiver this week. Please make sure to notify her," Sheila tells me.

I make a note in my phone and start thinking of the various tricks she can play on the others.

"I'll make sure to do that."

She finishes typing and then focuses on me fully.

"I've been notified some of our episodes are ranking low in the ratings. Lower than we would expect at this time. Communicate to the other wranglers to make sure they are putting forward their most compelling clips. There seems to be less drama this season than normal and the audience is picking up on that. It's not to leave this room, but we are going to throw something big at them next week."

I nod, making more notes in my phone.

"Anything in particular?" I ask.

"We are still kicking around some ideas. How's your contestant doing?"

"Charlie and Parker have agreed to play up the romance aspect of their relationship. I have a feeling that is really going to help ratings."

When Charlie told me about their agreement, I knew it would be great for the show, but a part of me just wanted to tie her to the interview chair and not let Parker near her.

Trying to push the jealousy down and remind myself I was the one that suggested this angle in the first place, I grind my teeth.

"That'll definitely help. People really seem to love Charlie, and Parker is hot," Sheila says.

This conversation is doing great things for my temper, but I can't let Sheila see my feelings for Charlie are starting to progress past the professionalism I should be holding tightly to.

But the tighter I try to hold to the rigidity I've relied on most of my life, it seems the faster it slips away. Charlie has a way of getting into people and taking root there. There's not been a single episode or interview where a contestant didn't like her. Even Cain is keeping any negative feelings he might have to himself. Playing the good guy.

"If that's all, get out."

I smirk at her dismissal, pushing myself out of my chair, checking my watch, counting down to my interview with Charlie.

Charlie walks into the room, her long legs clad in cutoff shorts and a shirt with a deep v displaying her perfect cleavage and suddenly my mouth waters at the sight. Her skin looks so soft, begging me to run my finger along the neckline of her shirt. I feel my dick starting to stiffen in my pants. After watching Parker touch her so freely, all I can think about is how much I want to feel her skin.

The intensity of my attraction takes me by surprise. I've always known she was lovely in a logical way, but the knowledge going from analytical to physical catches me off guard.

"Hey, I need to win another elimination challenge. I already miss the Head Deceiver room and being able to sit in complete silence," she says, unaware of the effect she's having on my dick.

"Yeah, I'm sure it's nice," I say.

"Are you okay? You're sweating. I've never seen you sweat before. Did another stick get shoved up your ass?"

"Nope, still just the one up there, nestled against my prostate."

All the blood in my head moving its way down to my dick can be the only explanation for the fact that sentence came out of my mouth. I have never joked around with a contestant before. I have barely joked around with ex-girlfriends and yet here I am, using words like "prostate" in casual conversation.

Charlie's face is completely shocked until, suddenly, she's bent over laughing.

Her laugh is beautiful. Carefree and unrestrained. I feel my cheeks lift in an answering smile and the distinct desire to make her laugh again comes over me.

"What do we have to talk about today?" she asks, settling down in her chair.

Moving toward mine, I tell her the good news.

"You're the deceiver this week."

"Oh, fuck yes!" she exclaims, pumping her fist in the air. "I've been waiting for this."

"Do you have some plans for what you want to do?" I ask.

"Not a one, but I figure since I've got you on my team, we'll come up with something good."

Her trust in me is comforting and I want to give her an idea great enough to deserve that confidence.

"I definitely think we should have a tailor mess with more of Ezra's clothes. People have really been enjoying that as a running joke. But the real question is, how mean do you want to get?"

I cross my leg, resting my ankle on my knee, thankful my crotch has finally calmed down.

She closes her eyes, hiding their sapphire color from me.

"The person cutting up the photos everyone brought from home last week was really harsh. I'm glad I was in the private room for that one, I would have cried. So, nothing that bad. Courtney and I did watch *The Parent Trap,* studying in case I was the deceiver," she says.

I agree about the pictures. Copies of the pictures were made and replaced the real ones so something irreplaceable wasn't damaged. Each wrangler found their contestant's original picture on their desk the next day. Luckily, they couldn't get to Charlie's with her being in the Head Deceiver room, because it would have killed me to keep it from her.

In situations like this where the prank is actually a ruse, the contestants are never told until after they are eliminated so as to keep tensions high in the house. I want to tell Charlie after watching her console Molly about the picture of her grandparents for an hour, but I don't.

"Anything out of the movie sound good?"

"I was thinking about the honey on the floor in front of the beds thing would be good."

I pull out my phone and open my notes app.

"That's a good one. I can get you the honey you need. Any others? I tend to suggest two or three things. So that makes two, including Ezra's clothes."

"Is it too childish to freeze people's underwear?"

I snort. "No, that's a great idea. My sister did that to some girls in high school. There was this group of bullies and my sister was really popular so she invited them all over.

"In the middle of the night, she woke me up and made me help her freeze everyone's bras. In the morning, when they found out what she did, she threatened to do worse if they didn't stop being assholes."

Sharing has started to come more naturally to our interactions and it has made me enjoy our time together more and more.

"I'm sure you were thrilled to get to touch all those bras. I have a feeling you were a horny little bastard of a teenager," she says, laughing.

"Joke's on you, I had already touched three bras by that point," I say, putting a smug look on my face.

"Silly me, I should have known. I bet all the girls wanted you to touch their bras." She winks at me and the desire to kiss her takes over.

"I don't know about all of that," I say, feeling my walls crumble around me.

This woman is going to be my undoing.

CHAPTER TWENTY-THREE

CHARLIE

Penelope is posing in front of the mirror in her bra and underwear when I walk into the dressing room. Checking every angle, she bends around, pouting her thick lips. Ava comes in on my heels, sniffling. I ignore the sound, unwilling to engage in whatever has led to tears this time. As she wipes them again, I watch her with Alec's skepticism, wondering if the tears are genuine or not.

"Oh my *God*. Would you stop *crying*? You're basically on a free vacation. Relax." Penelope's snotty tone makes Ava start crying anew.

"There's no need to be a dick to the girl, Pen," Rebel says. "Just because Lucas hasn't fucked you this week doesn't mean you need to take it out on her."

"I don't know what you're talking about," Penelope sniffs. I laugh to myself. Almost everyone has walked in on them hooking up somewhere in this house.

"Sure you don't. Your ass prints are basically etched into the shower glass, but we can pretend like that was someone else."

I snort and Mary Ella laughs.

Penelope doesn't answer. She rips her robe off the mirror, puts it on without tying it, and angrily sashays from the room. We all break out into laughter once she's out of the room.

"Thank you," Ava tells Rebel.

"No problem. But she's not wrong, kid. The water works are getting old. Charlie, don't forget our yoga session later. Your chakras are out of whack and it's giving me a migraine." She grabs her outfit for the upcoming competition and leaves the room as well.

"Sure thing, Rebel!" I call out as she leaves.

I inch the padded pants up my legs, jumping to get the tight fabric over my ass, having given up long ago on trying to guess our competitions. We received notice the privilege game would be in an hour. While everyone finished up their activities, I took advantage to change without the crush of bodies. For how big the room is, when everyone is getting changed at the same time, it feels like the size of a jewelry box. I pull on my padded shirt as Cain walks into the room.

"The honey was a real nice touch," he says.

Taking a page out of Alec's book, I put on a face of professional indifference.

"What are you talking about, Cain?"

"Alec King's contestants are almost always the deceiver in week five. You're his contestant, so it was you. Don't worry, I'll make note of everything you do this week for the final challenge." Cain's obsession with the game, and specifically Alec, is starting to creep me out.

"Yes, because they couldn't possibly change things around this season," I say, trying to throw him off my trail. "Get a life, Cain."

Not wanting to engage with him further, I move to the living room to await further instruction.

The chairs the bottom two sit in are my favorite after my experience week one. I sat in them as a sort of immersion therapy after the stress of almost being eliminated. One is now my normal seat. Sitting down, I turn around until I can hang my head down toward the ground. My feet bounce as I sing silently to myself.

Suddenly, my legs are pushed over and I'm doing an impromptu somersault, landing in a heap on the floor.

"Would you rather be a toothless dragon or the strongest squirrel?" Molly's random questions no longer shock me. Small talk is not her preferred communication style.

"Toothless dragon, duh," I say, setting my back against the now empty chair.

"Same. I want to be able to fly, even if I have to drink dragon smoothies every day since I wouldn't be able to chew."

Ezra walks in. His outfit is slightly too long, and I try to smother my laugh.

"Who keeps fucking with my clothes?" he screams at no one in particular this time. My self-control goes out the window and a small laugh escapes.

I make a mental note to hug Alec for pulling off the pant switch.

"Ezra, good. Toothless dragon or strongest squirrel?" Molly asks, her head lying on my outstretched legs.

"Oh, because I'm short you think I'd pick a squirrel, right? Is that it?"

Awkward silence settles on the room while Ezra's angry, beady eyes jump between us.

"You would benefit from some pot, my friend. Mellow out a bit." I let this laugh out fully as I run my fingers through Molly's hair, making sure to use my nails on her scalp. She purrs like a cat as she closes her eyes.

Ezra stomps over to one of the couches and flings himself down, pouting.

"What do you think we are doing today?" I ask, unable to fully let go of trying to guess our competitions.

"Hopefully something that gets you and Parker wet and climbing all over each other. I miss porn and y'all are the closest thing I have. The sexual tension is *thick*."

"There is no sexual tension between me and Parker," I say, trying to pretend like I'm just being shy, even though there really isn't any tension.

Ever since making our agreement, Parker and I have done a pretty good job of playing up a romance. Holding hands, spending time talking. Luckily, Parker is fun to talk to and his friendship has become important to me.

"I mean, Christ himself is probably yelling at the TV screen for you two to do it already, but sure." Her grin is evil and I pull her hair. "Ow! Brat."

If not Christ, I'm sure Courtney is yelling at the TV for the same reason.

"You will burn in Hell if you take the Lord's name in vain, Molly," Jaxon says, coming into the room. We ignore him as we normally do.

"There's nothing between me and Parker," I whisper as the room continues to fill.

"Girl, you need to climb that man like a tree, take whatever he gives you, thank him, and beg for more." I flick her on the nose.

I consider telling her about the agreement we have, but decide against it, wanting to keep it believable with everyone in the house.

We stand outside with our face masks on top of our heads and paintball guns in our hands as we listen to Head Deceiver, Molly, read from the instruction card.

Sweat rolls down my back despite the short amount of time we've been outside. Inflatable blocks dot the backyard. Parker stands at my side, bumping into my arm when he notices my attention wavering.

"The blue team will start on the right side, the red on the left. The last player standing wins it for their team," Molly finishes.

Parker is on the blue team today while I'm on red.

"What were the consequences for the losers?" I ask him in a whisper.

"A five a.m. wake up time to do various cleaning jobs as well as only being able to take cold showers for the week."

"Cold showers? I hate to tell you this, but your ass is going down. I will shoot you straight in the face to avoid a cold shower."

"The feeling is mutual, babe. I'll send you warm vibes when I'm in my lava level hot showers." His smile is beautiful and makes my heart squeeze at the sadness that tinges it.

Knowing this part will probably be shown in this week's episode, I give him a wink before separating to our sides. Molly steps up to me before I can go to my side.

"Must be nice not to have skin in the game," I joke. We would have an odd number without her, so she gets to participate this week. But she doesn't have to suffer the ramifications like the rest of us.

"A cold shower is good for the soul. Cleansing." She gets into a quick tree pose, imitating Rebel.

"In that case, I want my soul as black as tar." I blow her a kiss before strolling away, feeling Parker's eyes follow me across the yard.

The red team huddles up with Penelope taking lead.

"All right, team, what we want—"

"Don't get shot. Let's do this," Lucas interrupts. "Break." He claps his hands and we disperse.

"You are such a douche!" Penelope yells at him.

"Now's not the time for a lover's quarrel," Keith says in his no-bullshit tone. "Red," he says to me, presenting his closed fist.

"Grandpa," I say, tapping my knuckles to his.

"You got my back, I got yours?" he asks.

"Deal," I respond, pulling my mask down, centering myself.

The buzzer sounds and we are off. Keith and I get low behind one of the inflatables. I look around the left side right as a paintball hits the inflatable. I barely pull myself back in time. Keith sits next to me. Paintballs are hitting all around us. Strikes against the barriers and people.

"They've got us pinned down," Keith says.

"How long have you been wanting to say that?" I tease, temporarily forgetting the game.

"A while." He smiles behind his mask.

"Glad we could make that happen for you."

"Me too, Red, me too."

"We're going to get to the big "X" in the middle. There are a few in there for us to hit. On three."

Keith counts us down and we sprint to our new location. Paintballs fly around us. I hear Molly laughing maniacally. Ava is crying in the distance, probably got hit or a butterfly flapped its wings.

The battle is intense. We dip, dive, and dodge. Slowly, people are eliminated as they peek around barriers. On a particularly daring ambush, Keith and I were able to come around and take out three blue team members at once, including Cain.

Parker is the last blue team member. Keith, Jayden, and I are all that remains of the stalwart red team.

"Here's the plan. We are going to send you and the kid out," Keith says to me. "He won't shoot you, at least, not initially. While he's picking the two of you off, I'll take him down and we won't have to polar bear plunge every time we want to be clean."

We both look at Jayden.

"Are you good with that?" I ask. He always seems so frail to me. His sickly pallor paired with his skeletal physique makes me want to wrap him in a bubble and give him a warm blanket.

"I'll do anything if it means we win this one. I will *not* shower if it's not warm."

In deference to the collective olfactory senses of the household, Keith and I know winning is the only option. Jayden and I count to five and then head out on opposite sides and try to flank Parker where he's hiding behind an inflatable.

A hand pinches my side, causing me to yelp and turn, ready to shoot, but Parker knocks my gun out of the way sending my paintball wide.

"Did you just pinch me?" I ask, slightly outraged.

"Hey, babe," he smiles behind his mask. "Just couldn't keep my hands off you."

He has been so good selling our fake relationship for the audience, sometimes I almost believe it myself.

"You can't shoot me," I tell him.

"And why not?"

"Because I'll cry every day if I have to take a cold shower. And Jayden won't shower at all."

As he thinks, I see a small movement out of the corner of my eye, but I'm determined to keep his attention.

"If you let me shoot you, I'll kiss you," I offer, thinking about how the audience would love that. Courtney, specifically. Not that it would be a burden to me.

"You think your kiss is worth *me* having to freeze my balls off every day? I'll get frostbite on my dick."

"I'm sure you can come up with a way to keep it warm," I smirk.

The paintball smacks into my chest, a sharp sting. My jaw drops.

"You shot me!" I exclaim.

"I hate cold showers," he says with a wide grin.

But Keith pops up behind him and shoots him in the back, ending the game. The red team is ecstatic. The celebration is like that of a team that just won a championship game. Parker smiles at me with his mask on his head.

Putting my hand on his shoulder, I stand on my tiptoes, pressing a kiss to his cheek.

"A consolation prize," I tell him.

"You're never a consolation prize," he says, winking at me and I know the audience is going to eat this up.

CHAPTER TWENTY-FOUR

O UR PLATES ARE EMPTY but we all sit around chatting until Molly stands at the head of the dinner table and clinks her wine glass with her knife, cutting through the din of family dinner. Every night, the house has taken to eating together. If any team is on a food restriction, one member of that team will fix their food while someone cooks a meal for everyone else. There have been a few big misses like when Lucas made his normal training meal for the house. While an Olympic volleyball player may need to eat grilled chicken and enough veggies to feed three, not everyone was as thrilled about the meal. Mary Ella, on the other hand, made the best fried chicken I have ever had. The outside was crispy and flavorful, with a hint of spice.

"I would like to take a moment to tell you all how much this experience has been one of a kind. The support and love in this house, in the midst of a competition, has been nourishing. And while I love you all, it's time for," she pauses dramatically, "Girls' Night!"

We hoot and holler, stomping our feet as we toast to spending a night having fun together.

"Ladies, meet me in the winner's room in five minutes!"

Chairs scrape as we all clamor to put our dishes away, the guys watching us with indulgent smiles on most of their faces, as we head off to get changed. Molly announced the dress code is pajamas only, taking a page from my book. Anyone not meeting these criteria would not be let in. This rule was put into place for one person specifically.

Penelope has had the hardest time relaxing in the house. Always aware of being recorded, she dresses to the nines no matter what we are doing. While I fully support people doing what makes them comfortable, little comments have let us all know she does it because her family demands perfection in everything, including her looks, at all times. Her mother would stand her in front of the mirror and circle the fat on her body, she told us all one night when she was deep in a bottle of wine. Because of her family's status, having regular employment was hard for her so she turned to social media, which further exacerbated the drive for perfection.

Molly has left a hole in our room this week being in the winner's room. I'm happy for her, but I miss our time whispering together in the night. The pajamas Alec gave me have become a favorite. Not only do they keep me warm, but that he thought of me enough to get them makes hummingbirds flutter in my stomach. I slip on the golden pajamas and make my way to the winner's room.

Bottles of champagne lie around the floor. We relax with green hydrating masks on our faces as we wait for our nails to dry, music playing from the karaoke machine as Penelope sings along, finally relaxed. The intricate designs she painted on her nails astound me as I blow on mine.

Black is always my favorite nail color. To spice up my boring fingers, Molly's words, not mine, she added some swirling designs with a glossy black on top of the matte black I had painted.

I lie on the ground, my feet on the bed, listening to everyone talk and have fun when Mary Ella decides to shock the room.

"I kissed Jayden," she admits, and we all erupt.

"When?" Rebel asks, excitedly.

"Where?" Penelope demands.

"In the kitchen," she says, blushing.

"That's not what I meant." Pen snickers as Rebel smacks her arm.

"How was it?" I throw into the fray.

We all squeal and gossip for hours. Rebel does tarot readings for everyone. I'm not sure she knows how to really give a reading, but it is fun all the same.

Molly goes first.

"What's your birthday?" Rebel asks, getting out her various charts.

"May 20th, 1996."

I try to make mental notes of everyone's birthdays to add to my notebook later, but the drinks start making my brain fuzzy and I'm not sure they'll stick.

Deep into the night, people start dropping to the pull of the Sandman, but instead of going back to their rooms, they all sleep on the floor.

Molly and I are lying in her bed, somewhere between tipsy and drunk.

"I need you to not judge me when I say this." Her head is on my shoulder, one arm wrapped around her.

"You got it," I say before giving a hearty hiccup.

"I have a crush on my wrangler. She's just so funny and beautiful."

I pause a moment, trying to keep my loose tongue from blurting out that not thinking about my wrangler is becoming almost impossible.

Especially in the shower.

Or at night.

"You should do something about it," I tell her, but I feel like I'm talking to myself.

"I can't," she says dejectedly. "She has a girlfriend."

"Ugh, of course she does. Not that I want to add pain to this moment, but you know she will probably watch this footage and know this information, right?" I ask.

She sits up straight, almost cracking her head against my nose.

"Sometimes I actually forget we are being recorded all the time. Does that ever happen to you?" she asks, looking down at me in the dim light.

"Not really, no. It gets exhausting, always being aware, but what can you do?" I shrug.

What I don't share is I try to think about Alec being the only one watching me. That it's just me and him.

"I think she's my soul mate," Molly continues.

"Your wrangler?" I ask, my mind having drifted to Alec.

"Danielle, yeah."

"Life is too short. Tell her. At least then you'll know," I suggest, yet unable to take my own advice.

Pushing Molly off my arm, I'm thankful she's only one small step above a corpse when she's asleep. Calf muscles burning, I walk on tiptoes to the giant dressing room, trying not to stumble as I'm still a little tipsy.

The honey prank worked like a charm earlier this week.

Deep in the middle of a sex dream where Alec had me bent over the arm of the couch in the living room while everyone was asleep, I was woken up by shrieks from an angry Keith.

"What on God's green Earth!" he hollered, waking up more people.

More squeals echoed through the house as more feet met sticky honey.

"There's fucking honey on the floor!" Colyn yelled out from the room next to mine.

Alec and I agreed I would have to prank myself as well this week so as not to raise any suspicions of my involvement. What I didn't anticipate was how hard it would be to clean the honey off my feet and the floor. Production ended up bringing in a set of professional cleaners to help us out.

I would have felt guilty for creating this work for them had Alec not convinced me they are being compensated very well for the work.

The house is dark, but there are dim lights illuminating the hallways so we can move around without hurting ourselves. I think about Alec having to watch my lackluster James Bond impression as I sneak through the house in my gold pajamas, thankful these segments are never aired based on previous seasons.

"Oh, hey Charlie. How's the sleepover going?" Jayden asks, as I run into him in the bathroom.

"Hey, Jayden, it's good. Someone's asleep in the Head Deceiver bathroom from too much champagne."

I add a little dance to my stance, trying to sell that I have to go to the bathroom.

"I'll let you get to it. Good night," he says, making his way out of the bathroom and presumably back to the bedroom.

His steps fade as he shuffles away. I stand in the bathroom, waiting to see if anyone else comes in. After no one does, I make my way into the dressing room.

Without turning on the light, I find one of the hampers, emptying it in a dark corner. Moving from one dresser to another, I search for each person's undergarments, dropping them into the hamper in a large pile.

At my dresser, I pull open the top drawer.

"I should have picked things I didn't have to include myself in," I say, pocketing a clean pair of underwear so I can still shower in the morning before dumping the rest of the pairs I brought with me into the hamper.

The wheel of the hamper squeaks as I move toward the kitchen.

"Shush," I hiss at the wheel, but it doesn't listen.

I check around the corner before making my way into the kitchen. Moving quickly, I turn on the faucet, dumping the contents of the hamper into the massive sink.

The freezers are full of food, but I tuck underwear into every nook and crevice I can find. Filled with evil glee, I shove the last handful of underwear into the last open space in the freezer door.

WEEK SIX

CHAPTER TWENTY-FIVE

MOLLY IS SHOVING A breakfast burrito into her mouth, trying to finish eating as Jacob Johnson comes on the screen in the primary living room. His suit today is a teal that looks nice against his skin. His ultra-white teeth are slightly off-center.

"Hello, housemates!" His consistency in the enthusiasm of his greeting always surprises me. It's like when the camera is on, nothing else exists. Although, it must be much easier for him since he's not on camera all day, every day, maintaining a steady demeanor every second.

"As you all know, the weekly elimination is in two days, making today an elimination challenge day! The competition set for today will be done in pairs, which have been randomly assigned, and you will be informed of after this message. Cain, because you won the exemption earlier this week, you can sit this challenge out, but it excludes you from winning the prize."

He smiles in a way that tries to come off as humble happiness but all I see is the jerk behind the mask.

"Now, the top team this week will receive an extraordinary surprise. Instead of winning the private bedroom this week, each person on the winning team will receive a thirty-minute private phone call from home," he finishes.

The announcement is met with twitters of excitement around the room. It has been hard for many people to be cut off so completely from their families and friends, including me. Being unable to text or call Courtney whenever I want has been eating away at me week after week.

Even with connections in the house, they aren't Court.

"Yes, very exciting. The not-so-fun part is this. This week, the elimination will be slightly different. There will be no audience vote this week." He pauses dramatically. "Instead of voting to eliminate a house guest, you will vote for who you want to stay! One person from the bottom four teams will continue to week seven. The top three teams will make this decision, and if there is a tie in the voting, Cain will be the tiebreaker. This singular person will be the one to continue in the game, all others will be eliminated."

My jaw drops as shouts of outrage rise from the majority of the players.

"That's not fair!"

"We're getting rid of half?"

"What's the competition?"

"Please, everyone, let's calm down. This does mean seven people will go home in forty-eight hours. Good luck!"

And with that, the TV flips off once more. A moment of stunned silence echoes loudly before everyone explodes. I try to maintain a cool demeanor, sure it'll help me with the audience if they see I'm not easily shaken, if I make it past this week.

A production worker I do not recognize walks into the room and attempts to call for silence, but panic has taken control of the group, and no one hears him. I wait while he continues to try before I roll my eyes, stick two fingers in my mouth, and issue a sharp, loud whistle.

"Thank you, Charlie. Hello, everyone! I'm Derek, and I have your team assignments." He begins going down the list on the clipboard in his hand, calling out names one by one. "Parker, you're with Charlie."

That is the best news I could have hoped for. I know we will do anything necessary to make it into week seven. He continues reading the pairings as Parker and I stare at each other, a silent promise running between us.

"Hello, everyone. The outfits you need are in the changing room. You have ten minutes to change, and then please come out to the backyard." And with that, Derek leaves.

Parker's blue shorts are tight and hide nothing, not that my matching blue bikini hides much more. The triangle top barely contains my heavy chest, while the blue bottoms hardly protect me. In a moment of calm before the competition that is more likely to send us home than not, I take a second to appreciate the perfection of the man standing before me.

"This should be fun," I say. He smiles at me as we move toward the backyard, grabbing my hand to offer me comfort as well as sell our relationship to the audience.

I couldn't have asked for a better partner to be in a fake TV romance with.

These competitions have been mentally and physically exhausting, but this one is weighing all of us down in a way none of the others have up until this point. There is a resounding silence as everyone makes their way outside with us. The threat of half the house going home looms over all of our actions.

Cain is sitting in the royalty chair, in a pair of the same bottoms as the other guys except his are black. Each team is a different color that corresponds with a platform in the middle of the pool. Each platform has a walkway from the pool's edge to a small circle. We take a moment, looking around to determine what we will be doing.

"Everyone, please gather over here!" Cain calls out, his tone perfectly pitched with empathy for us. He pulls out a card as we gather at the foot of the throne. I wish I had immunity this week with such a large number leaving, but I wouldn't want anyone else to possibly be the reason Parker goes home, either.

"This week, the competition is simple. Everyone will dip themselves in the pool of baby oil over there"—he lifts his arm and points—"then you and your teammate will walk to your platform in the pool. You will *not* touch this platform until the horn sounds. Once it sounds, you both will climb on and everyone has thirty seconds to get situated."

Everyone looks over at the platforms, noting the lack of room for two people. "After the thirty seconds," Cain continues, "the competition begins. Each team must stay on their platform for the duration of the event. If either of you touch the water, you are both disqualified. Good luck."

I turn to Parker. "I need that phone call," I tell him, matter-of-factly.

He nods. "Then you'll get it."

We all make our way to the kiddie pool of oil where we lie down and roll around so every inch of us is covered. My skin feels gross and I can't wait to get the goop off of me, but I push it to the side and sink into the calm. Parker and I hold hands as we make our way down the plank to our platform, and we study it while we wait.

"The best way is for me to stand with my back to your front," I whisper. "That way we take up as little space as possible. You'll have to put your arms around me."

"What a burden," he jokes.

The air is uncharacteristically cool and goosebumps raise on my arms. Seeing my discomfort, he chafes my arms, trying to warm them with friction, but the oil makes it impossible. In the final seconds, I grab one of his hands, squeezing.

The horn blows and we step onto the platform. I move into more of the middle of the circle while Parker settles behind me, his feet closer to the edges. My ass nestles perfectly against his dick as he wraps his arms around me.

"Perfect, this is going to be excruciating," he says very quietly into my ear, hoping our microphones don't pick up the inappropriate comment. I giggle and press my ass into him ever so slightly. "Stop, you devil woman."

The clock counts down our last few seconds to get situated before the horn goes off again.

I settle into the stance, making sure not to lock my knees as I look at the other pairs. Some decided to be front to front while others mirrored me and Parker. I watch as the comfort level of each pairing slowly becomes apparent. Instead of settling into the position, they try to touch as little as possible, standing rigidly.

"Guess they couldn't have picked an indoor activity today, huh?" I ask, shivering.

"No, I suppose not. Tell me. Who are you going to call when we win this?"

I smile as I rest my head against his chest.

"My best friend, Courtney. I need her advice on a few things."

"Anything I can help you with?" he asks.

"No, but thank you. What about you?"

"Honestly, I'm not sure, but it'll just be nice to get to talk to *someone*."

We settle into silence, periodically talking but generally just spending time in our thoughts. Minutes tick by as we continue to stand in the chilly day, my body aching to move.

"Tell me a joke," Parker demands.

After falling into the pool, Lucas, Raven, Ezra, and Ava sit on the bench watching us struggle to stay on. Parker and I are only two teams away from being safe and we are doing everything we can to stay in this mentally.

"What did the green grape say to the purple grape?" I ask him.

"I dunno, what?"

"Breathe, stupid."

He snorts as I chuckle at the stupid joke that has always been my favorite. Soon, we are descending into delirious giggles, our bodies tired from standing on these platforms for over an hour but in the moment, I feel no pain.

"Mateo, please. I have to move," Mary Ella whines in her southern accent.

"Okay," Mateo concedes, "but slowly."

As she spins, her elbow smacks into Mateo, throwing him off balance and into the water with a large splash. Waves move across the pool shaking all the platforms, causing Keith and Colyn to fall too.

Relief floods through me.

We are safe.

Noticing the same thing, Rebel and Penelope separate, give matching whoops and cannonball into the pool. The resulting waves shake the platforms, but Molly and Jayden fall in first, coming in second. With a giant splash, she and Jayden fall into the pool, crowning me and Parker the winners.

Already off balance from all the waves, we let the momentum take us into the pool.

The water runs off my oiled body as I break the surface. Parker's smile is bright and beautiful, and I know it matches my own. Grabbing ahold of me, Parker yanks me through the water toward him.

Bending toward me, he brushes his lips against mine. I'm surprised, but the relief we made it when so many will go home overwhelms me. As he begins to back away, I pull his body against mine. Standing on my tiptoes, I let our tongues tangle.

His lips are soft.

So soft.

And he tastes so good as I explore his mouth.

He pulls me tighter against him, his hand fisting in my hair.

The kiss is the best I've had.

And as we pull apart, both gasping for air, I notice the lack of heat running through my body.

Once production was able to get us all out of the pool, they told us to meet our wranglers in the living room. Sounds of people making their way through the house reach us as we all sit patiently, if not a little confused.

The first wrangler into the living room heads straight to Molly, and for a moment I enjoy watching her and Danielle interact. Molly is giggly and starry-eyed in a way I have never seen before, her heart on her sleeve.

But what I wasn't anticipating is seeing the same look on Danielle's face. How Molly could think Danielle isn't into her is crazy. Smiling to myself, I give Danielle's relationship mere weeks before it ends once Molly leaves the mansion while a quiet part of me wishes it could be the same way with me and Alec.

Looking through the crowd, my heart skips a beat. Alec's face is placid, his professional wrangler face, but my ability to read him has improved and now I can see the simmering rage.

"Was it the best kiss you ever had?" Alec asks quietly, smirking at me.

"Be careful, you're going to seem jealous," I taunt him, matching his volume, knowing they won't be airing this footage.

I think I can hear his teeth grind as his jaw clenches, the muscle twitching causing me to smile. His face darkens further as he crosses his arms over his chest, lighting a fire down in my belly.

"Why are y'all out here? I thought wranglers weren't allowed in the house," I ask, trying to get him to relax.

"Avoiding my question," he asserts.

"Fine, yes, okay? My previous boyfriends weren't exactly great kissers and Parker *definitely* knows what he's doing. But it being a good kiss and feeling something from it are two different things."

Taking a chance, I pull on his arm until he uncrosses them, aware we are in a room full of people.

"It felt good, but it was just a kiss."

His fingers touch my hand for a fraction of a second before he tucks his hands into his pants.

"Good." His gray eyes search mine and the desire to stroke his cheek is almost overwhelming, the crowd and cameras keeping me in line. "We are out here because the show runners sent us in to make sure everyone is okay. Normally, this only happens if someone quits the game early, but with the large amount of people on the chopping block, they thought it would be good to send us in."

I smile at him. "But I won," I say.

When he smiles, the room and everyone in it falls away.

"I didn't have a doubt. They are going to pick the person you talk to based on the list of important people you provided us in your application. Since I'm head wrangler, I might have some sway."

"If there's any way, I need to talk to Courtney. Please. I need my best friend." I don't want to seem desperate, but I'm willing to beg if I have to. Not being able to talk to the one person in the world who knows me the best has worn on me every day.

"I'll do my best. Also, watch out for Cain," he whispers so quietly I can barely hear him. "I don't like the way he was looking at you when you and Parker won."

"He has a weird obsession with you and the show. He's convinced the reason you're not his wrangler is because of me. I'm pretty much avoiding him, but I'll keep a better eye out," I say.

"If you weren't in the pile, I still wouldn't have picked him," he tells me.

"I wish someone would tell *him* that!" I say, annoyed, making Alec laugh as warmth spreads through me.

The house is quiet. Molly's gentle snores echo around our room. I've long since gotten used to the sounds of other people in the mansion. The first week here left me exhausted. Sounds of people sleeping and moving about compounded with the knowledge we were being watched kept my mind racing into the wee hours of the night. Even as a deep sleeper, it has been hard. But I don't have that issue any longer.

I toss and turn, thinking about Alec's small touches today. Six weeks without an orgasm has made the simplest of contact drive me wild. Between kissing Parker today and Alec's obvious jealousy, I'm already a few touches away from completion. I flip on my back and rub my legs together.

Arousal heats my skin and I can feel my wetness gathering between my thighs. I look at my roommates, passed out. But I'm worried they'll hear me. I get up from my bed and tiptoe out into the hallway, shutting the door behind me. On the same silent feet I would use to sneak an extra piece of pie after my parents went to bed, I make my way to my favorite daybed outside.

The desire to touch myself is so strong. At home, I have a vibrator I would turn on quickly and bring myself to climax. But I didn't bring old faithful with me. I never imagined I would be able to do that with other people and cameras in the room. But in this moment, it doesn't seem to matter.

At the thought of cameras, an image of Alec invades my mind and the numerous times he has told me he watches everything I do. That I'm his so long as I am in this mansion. And if I'm his, I know he won't air this. It'll just be ours.

My control snaps.

Lying against the pillows, I rip open the snaps on my golden pajamas. I'm breathing heavy and the wind is cool against my overheated skin, my tits bared to the night sky. Sliding my hand between my legs, I'm glad for my lack of panties. I think about the cameras that can probably see me right now and pray Alec is watching the live feed.

I slide my fingers through my wetness before moving to my clit. I'm so revved up, the simple touch sends a jolt through me and I moan. I sink my fingers deep inside and curve them, hitting the spot I need immediately. I can feel Alec's eyes on me as I finger myself, my breasts heaving with my breath. With each thrust, the sounds of my dripping pussy echo in the air.

I move faster, aware anyone could come out here, but it doesn't stop me. I'm too close.

Moaning, I twist my tight nipple to the point of pain.

I think about his hands on me while his mouth devours me. I pause a moment, trying to delay the delicious feeling. The cool air tightens my nipples painfully. In my mind, Alec's gray eyes devour me as I continue to work myself until he's so turned on, he takes out his big, thick cock.

He strokes himself as my orgasm builds until I fall over the edge with the thought of Alec jerking himself ruthlessly at the same time.

I'm panting as I pull my fingers out of my pussy. That was the most intense orgasm I've ever had. I pray no other wranglers were watching the feed as I catch movement out of the corner of my eye. I stop dead in my tracks. Parker steps in from the shadows and stalks over to me.

His movements are cat like, smooth, but he can't hide his throbbing cock in those sinful sweatpants. As he reaches me, he tosses me a damp washcloth before turning his back and giving me privacy.

With practiced efficiency, I clean myself up before buttoning myself back into my pajamas.

"You can turn around now," I say. "What are you doing out here?"

"I couldn't sleep and I was coming out here to look at the stars. You seemed to really be enjoying yourself and honestly, it was really hot so I didn't want to interrupt. Sorry, for watching."

He sits down on the bed next to me, making sure to give me space.

"That's okay. If our positions were reversed, I wouldn't have walked away either," I admit to him.

"So, Alec, huh? Someone is crushing hard on their wrangler." He waggles his eyebrows at me and I laugh as embarrassment courses through me.

"Oh, did I say his name?" I would be embarrassed but I'm still high from my first orgasm in over a month.

"No, but I saw the two of you together today and then this? I put two and two together," he says with a kind smile. "Our 'relationship' is for the sake of the game, so you don't owe me any explanations. Besides, I'm not ready for anything real. But flirting with such a beautiful woman has been nice." He winks at me and I can see the smallest tinder of happiness lighting in him.

"It's been nice flirting with you, too," I admit. "It's been a long time since I've had any sort of attention, and this low-stakes thing has been nice."

"I just want to make sure we can be friends? I really have enjoyed spending time with you and when we leave this house, I'm hoping that'll continue."

Relief floods through me that we are on the same page.

"I would really love that," I say, grabbing his hand and giving it a quick squeeze.

He stands from the bed and pulls me to my feet, putting his hands on my shoulders.

"Time for ice cream?"

"With hot fudge?" I ask.

"You read my mind." He takes my hand, and we head to the kitchen.

CHAPTER TWENTY-SIX

E VERYONE IS GETTING DRESSED at the same time. Emotions are running high, with six people deciding the fate of eight. Everyone is running around, trying to secure last-minute votes of safety. Everyone except Keith has come to talk to me over the past few days and it's been difficult since I can only save one person. Molly and I whisper back and forth, trying to be respectful that we are safe. Parker knots his tie and looks at me from head to toe before winking at me as he walks out.

"No sexual tension, my ass," Molly mocks, shooting me an exaggerated wink and sauntering away as well. When I told Alec I'd agree to a fake relationship with Parker, we decided I would keep the arrangement secret until I get out of the mansion. I hope Molly can forgive me for lying to her once we are out of here.

My hands smooth down my green dress from the day I arrived. This is my favorite dress, and I chose it on purpose. My nerves are making me nauseous, wanting everyone to be able to stay but knowing that's impossible. However, the confidence from my dress helps keep me steady. I crack my knuckles absentmindedly as I file toward the primary living room. We sit in tense silence, waiting.

"Deceivers! Welcome to elimination night!" Jacob Jacobson is his usual chipper self. It grates on a day when half of us will be departing. "Before we start, Charlie and Parker, congratulations on your win. You can expect your phone calls after next week's privilege competition."

"Thank you, Jacob," Parker says.

"We can't wait," I respond.

"A reminder of what will happen this elimination cycle. The three winning teams will go into the interview room individually and cast their vote for who to save. Whoever wins the vote will be able to continue to week seven," Jacob continues. "First up is Charlie."

I stand from my chair, look at those on the chopping block, and know who I will save. Each step toward the interview room sounds like a death knell. These people have become my family; luckily, two of my favorites are already safe.

The room is empty except for the regular chair and a camera. A small part of me had hoped to find Alec waiting for me, but he is not. This is live. I sit down in the chair and clear my throat.

"I vote to save Keith," I tell the audience at home. I went through everyone with Alec making pros and cons for each person, but at the end of the meeting, I knew I wouldn't be able to bring myself to save anyone but my favorite grandpa.

Task complete, I stand and exit the room once more. When I get back, Jacob Jacobson calls Parker's name.

"I've got your back. Don't worry," he whispers in my ear before making his way back to the room.

One by one, we make our way back to the interview room and cast our votes. Once Penelope sits back down, Jacob Jacobson pulls our attention back to him.

"Voting is now complete, and we have a tie. If I announce your name, please stand."

We all wait on the edges of our seats.

"Keith."

Keith stands in his dark wash jeans, black button-down shirt, and worn cowboy boots.

"Lucas."

Lucas stands in his khakis and boat shoes, the All-American Olympian.

"You both received two votes to save you." He turns. "Cain, you will be the deciding vote. Please make your way to the interview room."

He stands and turns to us, putting on a sad mask.

"I want to say something before I cast my vote. If I had the ability, I would save you all. This is a family and I want my family to stay together. But I hope you understand, if I don't save you, it's not from a lack of love." He walks off toward the interview room and I want to vomit at both his fake speech and the fact the fate of one of my favorite people in the house is left up to my least favorite.

None of us talk while we wait for Cain to return. Once he takes his seat, my back muscles tighten.

"Lucas, will you please step forward," Jacob Jacobson instructs. "Cain has cast his vote and you will"—he pauses, dragging out the suspense for the home audience—"*not* be continuing on. Keith, Cain voted to save you.

"Lucas, Raven, Mary Ella, Ava, Colyn, Ezra, Mateo, I'm sorry, but you have been eliminated from the *House of Deceit*."

Relief floods me and I don't care what Cain thinks he can accomplish by keeping Keith in the house. I take three steps and fling my arms around my grandpa, happy tears wetting my eyes.

I stand outside the interview room door, debating running away and ignoring Alec's summons. Maybe he didn't see me on camera and I'm just being silly, but I can't seem to make myself reach for the door handle. Wasting a few more seconds, I hear Courtney's voice in my head telling me to suck it up and face him.

The door is ripped open, Alec standing there, looking down on me.

"Don't just stand there," he says, "get in here."

As he turns his back on me, moving into the room once more, I wonder if maybe he didn't see my little show. The door clicks shut and I decide to pretend like nothing is different. As we settle into our respective chairs, I relax at how normal he seems. He reaches up and flips on the camera, launching us into the interview.

We do take after take until I'm afraid I'm going to cry from exhaustion and all the emotions I was forced to go through, Alec wanting to make sure we had the exact right shot.

"Okay, enough of that," he says, shutting off the camera and I slump in my chair with relief.

Finally.

"Charlie, you are mine for the duration of this show. I watch everything you do. Every moment, I see it. You and me, remember?"

"Yes, I remember."

He leans forward, resting his elbows on his knees, making sure I'm looking straight into his gray eyes. Alec quirks an eyebrow at me, an evil smile starting to light his face.

Embarrassment tries to take over, but I don't allow it. I'm not embarrassed. I know he enjoyed watching and I'm not going to let him shame me for enjoying my body.

"Were you thinking of me?" he whispers, his voice deeper than usual.

I was wondering if he was going to ever bring up what happened out on the daybed. I was starting to think he never would and our connection was all in my head.

Lust fills me as he lets his professionalism slide away. The lights in the room are bright and a bead of sweat rolls between my breasts. Alec's smug reaction emboldens me and I know this is the make-or-break moment. I arrange my face in a mask of satisfaction and lie with everything I have in me.

"I was thinking of Parker. His skin was so slick the other day. Feeling his abs, having his cock pressed against my ass. Any time I moved, it would jump. His fingers dug into my skin and I just knew that it was taking everything in him not to sink into me. Did you see him watching me? Did it make you jealous he got to be there with me?"

His face darkens.

"I thought so," I say into the silence. "Did you wish it were your fingers in my pussy? Tell me you came watching me." I stand up, moving toward him. Nervous butterflies attack my stomach, but I don't stop. I'm tired of this dance. He leans back in his chair, tilting his head back so he can see me.

"Did you come watching me while I touched myself to another man?" I straddle his lap, rubbing myself against his hard cock, and run my fingers through his soft hair like I've been dreaming of since day one. He leans into my hand briefly before surging up, grabbing onto my thighs.

The chair crashes to the ground. I give a startled gasp as he pushes me against the wall, his body holding me up, as his strong grasp encircles my throat like a necklace. I shamelessly grind against him for only a moment.

"You're lying and I *hate* liars. Now tell the truth."

"Okay, okay. I confess. It was me who forgot to feed the class pet in third—"

He cuts me off. "Were you. Thinking. About. Me?"

"It was you. I was thinking about you," I rasp.

He tilts my head up before smashing his mouth on mine. It's a battle of tongues and teeth as we fight for dominance. My hands go back to his lush hair, roughly pulling it. Alec's spicy scent envelops me as he grabs one of my hands and pins it to the wall above my head, linking our fingers. We break apart, panting. His gray eyes lock on my lips and I lick his taste off.

He runs his thumb over my bottom lip, pulling it down.

"Don't forget you're mine," he says, circling his hips, causing me to moan.

"Whoever said I was yours?" I ask him, but the desire in my voice undermines the dig.

He smirks at me.

"I did," he whispers back, giving me a searing, chaste kiss.

"We'll see," I tell him as we break apart once more. "Someone could come in."

His entire body locks up before he unhooks my legs from around him, dropping me down to the ground. Once my legs are beneath me again, he paces around the small room, running his hands through his hair. He points a stern finger at me, anger etched on every pane of his body.

"This was a mistake that will never happen again. Keep your *fucking* hands and lips and everything else to yourself. Don't finger fuck yourself anymore. Don't entice Parker into kissing you to get a rise out of me." His chest heaves as he stares me down, daring me to push back.

As his words register, piping hot magma-like rage erupts.

"You think I'm trying to use Parker to get to you? Are you fucking insane? You were the one who suggested we lean into a relationship for the audience! And guess what, you giant prick? I'm doing it because I want to win this, not just for the money, but so you get a shot at your dream! My stupid crush on you makes me want to do anything I can to help you. I thought you *finally* were going to admit you have a crush on me too, but here you are, pushing me away. Again!"

I straighten and look into his face, regret at his words etched there, but I ignore it. "But fuck this. I'm done. I'm going to win this game and it's going to have *nothing* to do with you. You're welcome, for being the one that will make it so you can finally realize your dream, you absolute asshole. And when you're at your dream job, you'll think about me every day and how I made that happen, but I'll never think of you again once I'm free from this mansion."

I storm out of the room as angry tears prick my eyes. The last thing I want is for that insensitive man to see any emotion from me. I immediately go to the shower and climb in, fully clothed. As the water soaks into my clothes, I let my tears out.

CHAPTER TWENTY-SEVEN

ALEC

INSTANT REGRET GRIPS ME because she's right. I do like her. I think I've liked her since she slapped me across the face. I want to run after her, but the rules against going into the mansion make me pace like a caged animal.

"Oh, hey man," Parker says, walking into the interview room I should have vacated five minutes ago. "How's it going? Charlie looked pretty upset." His green eyes search my face, looking for the answer.

"Hey, *man*," I seethe, "keep your fucking hands to yourself."

"I haven't touched you."

"But you touched her."

The smirk that lights his face makes a red mist creep into my vision.

"You fucked it up, didn't you?" The laid-back demeanor leaves him and standing before me is the man chosen for this competition. "The only reason I touched her is because *you* suggested we play this up for the camera. Next time, don't suggest that when you like the girl. And she would kill me if she knew I was saying this, but hurt her again, I'll beat the shit out of you for her."

"She'd probably do it on her own," I tell him.

Frank, Parker's wrangler walks in, and we make eye contact, the tension in the room obvious. He looks to his charge, the person who will own his loyalty for the time being.

"You okay, Parker?" he asks.

"Yeah, man. I'm good. I was just talking to Alec here." He turns to me. "We good?" he asks me.

"Of course. Have a great interview, Parker. Frank." I slip my wrangler persona back on and smile, clapping Parker on the back before exiting the room, but I shed it once more as I walk through the hallway and back to my office. Anger still sits within my stomach, but so does something else.

I've seen the thoughtful things she does for Parker. Bringing him a glass of water when she notices his is empty while they work out. Touching his arm when he seems out of sorts. Just little things. And then I think of our times together. The little things between us are there, but different. The way she lets me direct her. Own her. How she allows me to be myself, the fact she cares about who I really am. Our interactions are limited to this room, but maybe that's better. Maybe it has allowed us the freedom to focus on each other.

Or maybe, this woman I'm falling for is not meant to be mine outside of this room. I know one thing, though.

I would be lucky to have her.

My phone vibrates in my pocket as I shut my office door behind me. Fishing it from my pocket I accept the video call, Lore's face filling my screen.

"I saw that kiss between her and Parker. That was *hot* and on behalf of all the viewing audience, I thank you," Lorelei says, jumping straight into the conversation.

The dragon of jealousy within me roars to life at the thought of Parker's hands on my girl.

"I don't want to talk about that," I say through gritted teeth. "Is this really why you called me?"

"I was calling to see if Tank won our bet." She looks at me with a critical eye as I remember the bet her and my best friend made weeks ago. Shock takes over her face as her eyes go wide, mouth dropping open. "Oh my God! You kissed Charlie, didn't you?"

Dragging a hand down my face, I blow a raspberry.

"Yes."

"Babe! He did it!" she calls out to Tank. She turns back to me. "It doesn't matter that you just cost me fifty bucks, that's how excited I am."

My mountain of a best friend pops his head out of the hallway, wet hair half styled.

"I told you he wouldn't be able to resist once Parker kissed her. Way to go, buddy! I can't wait to meet her at Christmas." He disappears once more and Lorelei looks at me.

"You're not going to meet her!" I call out but he's already gone.

Groaning, I drop my head down to my desk.

"I fucked it up, Lore."

"You got jealous, didn't you? She's not that cheating twat, Alec."

"You don't think I know that?" I snap.

"Don't you take that tone with me, buster." In that moment, she sounds just like my father yelling at me from his recliner in the living room.

"Sorry," I mumble. "And yes, I yelled at her for kissing Parker."

"Is she dating him for real?"

"No, it's all for the show."

I've never told Lorelei about the strategy I was using with my contestant before the end of the season, but if I want her help, I have to put it all out on the table. She listens intently as I tell her everything that has happened from the moment I walked into the ballroom at the hotel.

"You need to take her on an apology date," she says.

"You're supposed to be helping me out, Lore. She can't leave the mansion!"

"So do it in the mansion!" she says, mocking my outraged tone. "Show her you care, Alec. I can tell you really care about this girl. Now show her."

I sit watching Charlie read in the library, thinking about how I would take her on a date. Reading is her favorite thing to pass the time. Sometimes the words make her throw her head back and laugh. I laugh, too, watching her. Other times, I see tears streaming down her face. Those are the ones I mark down the title and read at night in the hotel.

My phone vibrates, pulling my attention away from Charlie. With a heavy sigh, I drop my legs off my desk and stand. The hallways are empty due to the late hour as I go to Sheila's office. I knock.

"Come in." I hear through the door, causing me to push open the door and move into the room. "Oh, Alec. Sit down."

Sheila sits behind a simple desk with two folding chairs in front. She doesn't have time for people to come and gossip, so her seating arrangements are uncomfortable. Her long nails clack against the keyboard as I sit on the cold metal. She folds her hands in front of her and focuses on me.

"So, I know you have been looking to get onto a different show for a while now," she says.

"I would like to direct," I tell her.

"Tom Cochran called me," she says watching me for my reaction to her mention of one of the most prestigious directors in the business. "After nearly thirty years of making blockbusters, he's ready to slow down and move to made-for-TV movies. He'd like to talk to you."

Excitement puts an uncharacteristic smile on my face.

"Really? That's great."

"So then you're serious about leaving *House of Deceit*?"

I take a deep breath. This industry is extremely small. Any perceived slight could come back and bite me in the ass years later and damage a career I've fought to build tooth and nail.

"I've loved my time here as a wrangler, but I've been here for ten years, and I am ready to try my hand at something different."

She leans back and crosses her legs.

"I agree. It's time. I don't want to lose you, but I want to help you take this step. He only had one opening on his calendar for the week after next. I went ahead and accepted it on your behalf. Here's the address and his PA's phone number." She pushes a piece of paper across the desk. I pick it up and stare at it, unseeing.

"Thank you for this, Sheila. I really appreciate it."

"I know you do. I also know you will do me proud. Now get out."

She waves me away and focuses on her computer once more. The door clicks shut behind me as I return to my office. The paper is stark white against the dark brown desktop. The handwriting is crisp. The opportunity of my life could be sitting in this specific combination of letters and numbers.

Movement catches my attention and I see Charlie getting up from her chair and doing a quick forward fold. I send a quick thank you to Rebel for getting her into yoga. I look back at the address again and feel the slightest bit of hesitation.

"What the fuck am I doing?" I ask the empty office. I run my hands through my hair and stare at Charlie as she moves about the mansion.

My fingers trace my lips like I can still feel her kiss.

With only eight people left, the game is going to start getting real. If I leave now, will I hurt Charlie's chances of winning?

But this might be the only chance I have. She's not guaranteed to win and if she doesn't, this could be my only shot. But what if she gets paired with a shitty wrangler? She could go home and have to move in with her parents.

"Why am I hesitating? She's going to go home after she's done with the show, and it won't matter."

But I know why I'm hesitating. No matter how much I want to ignore it.

I don't want to leave her.

That firecracker of a woman has wormed her way into my heart when I wasn't paying attention. I pick up my phone and type in the number from the paper before shooting off a quick text.

WEEK SEVEN

CHAPTER TWENTY-EIGHT

CHARLIE

THIS WEEK HAS BEEN one of the worst in the mansion. Everyone seems to have moved out of the honeymoon stage and tensions are running high, tempers are running short, and it feels like we are all walking on eggshells.

On top of that, Alec has been trying to talk to me about our blowup last week in our few interview moments, but I don't think I can take him telling me, for what feels like the millionth time, he's not interested in me outside of our professional arrangement. Even though I'm pretty sure it's bullshit, it still stings.

Grumpy from not being able to sleep with all the thoughts in my head, I change into a sundress for the day, adding a few swipes of mascara to my lashes. I want to look nice for my video call home despite my sour disposition.

"What the hell are you talking about?" Rebel asks, exasperation deep in her voice.

"You used my special face mask. I told you I had to get it from Korea, and I have to make it last until the end of the show!" Penelope yells at her.

"If you think you're going to make it to the final, you're delusional," Rebel retorts.

"You're not going to deny using my face mask?"

"It's a stupid accusation, and I wasn't giving it enough credence to deny it. I didn't use your stupid face goop. Lord knows the chemicals that are probably in that stuff. Now leave me alone."

Out of patience, I snap. "Can you two please, for the love of fuck, bicker somewhere else? It was probably the deceiver. Hello? We are in the House of freaking Deceit!"

The deceiver this week seems to be going for the things people have either brought into the house or requested specifically for their use.

"There's no need to be fucking rude, Charlie," Penelope sniffs at me.

"You two fight almost every single day. Can we not have one day of peace?" I ask her.

"You want peace? Okay. How about you and Molly stop the giggling in the middle of the night?"

Keith walks into the dressing room.

"What's going on ladies?" he asks, but we ignore him.

"Oh, yes, how dare we have any freaking fun in this stupid house," I shoot back.

"Having fun is fine when everyone's awake!"

"Oh, stop being a stupid cow, Penelope," Molly says and that seems to be the lit match on the tinder box of our emotions.

All hell breaks loose.

We all begin yelling over each other, not caring what anyone else is saying. The guys slowly filter into the room, trying to figure out the cause of the noise, and then Rebel pulls my hair. I slap her arm as pain shoots through my scalp. I see a flash of red hair out of the corner of my eye as Penelope is tackled; however, since her hand is tangled in my hair, we all go down in a clump.

Limbs fly and the screaming continues. Hands reach in and try to separate us. I bite someone on the arm and a manly yell echoes around the room. Suddenly, strong arms band around me and rip me from the melee.

"Calm down," Parker says into my ear as he holds me away from the others.

My hair hangs in my face as I puff like a freight train. Keith has a hold of Penelope in one hand and Rebel in the other.

"Knock it off," he says, shaking them. "What the hell happened here?"

"Why don't you ask your *precious Red*?" Rebel spits, looking at me, venom dripping from Keith's nickname for me.

"Me? Ask her!" I say, indicating Penelope.

"Nothing. It was just a misunderstanding." She tries to look nonplussed but her ripped shirt and the slap mark across her cheek undercut her statement.

The guys let us go and everyone gradually files out of the room. Molly looks at me and smiles.

"Well, I guess we can all guess what clips are going to be included for the audience this week," she says, and we dissolve into a fit of giggles.

"I'm going to get in trouble with Alec for that one," I say, and we giggle more.

The interview room is empty except a tablet that sits on a table in the middle. My hands are sweating as my lungs work overtime to draw in air. Parker took his phone call an hour ago, seeming lighter at the end, which made me happy. But now I sit here like I'm about to be interrogated by the police.

The screen lights up, and I see Courtney's face for the first time in over seven weeks. My eyes immediately prick with tears as I swipe to answer.

"Charles, finally. Please tell me you've let Mr. Tall Blond tie you to a bed." She's sitting on her bed, and although I can't see all of her, I know she has her legs crossed and is wearing mismatched socks and pants with dried paint on them.

I laugh as a tear escapes. I dash it away quickly.

"No, but he did kiss me."

"They aired that, and I have to say, that was *some kiss*."

"Oh right. That makes sense."

"Did you think they wouldn't?" She cocks her eyebrow at me, taking a drink of her wine.

"I don't want to talk about the show yet. How are you? How's the family? How are my parents? Have you checked on them? I can only imagine what they think about all of this." Worry over their reactions of my time here invades my thoughts for the first time.

"Girl, relax. My family is fine and so are your parents. They think it's fantastic you're on the show. And they love this whole girl next door thing you've got going on. They are completely oblivious to the sexual undertone, but that's for the best."

"Oh, God," I say dropping my head in my hands.

"Hey, the good news is you're going to get a *lot* of dates after this show."

"That's probably good. It will help me get over my giant crush on my wrangler." I roll my eyes.

"As if I didn't already know. I can see the glow on you." Court bounces around in giddy excitement. "Why the wrangler, though? Parker seems like an amazing guy." She rests her chin on her fists.

"He called me a good girl," I tell her.

She blinks a few times as she processes.

"I'm sorry, did you come on the spot? Why would he do that to you? Did you report him to HR? Who can work in that sort of sexual environment? Please tell me you've ridden him."

"Why are you being so horny? Are you and J.D. in a rut?"

She points a finger at me as she quickly sips her wine.

"J.D. and I could be having hot, raucous sex, and I would still be frothing at the mouth for these details, and you know it. Don't be stingy. Give momma the details."

"Parker is all a ruse for the audience. My wrangler suggested it to help me win favor and get people to want us to stay in the house together. But every time Parker and I do something, it seems like he gets jealous. I don't know. I'm probably just seeing things I want to see."

I tell her every detail possible in the short time we have together. Every second lasts a year but also less than a flap of a hummingbird's wing. But in no time at all, a countdown pops up at the top of the tablet screen, counting down the last minute of our talk.

"Court, we only have a bit longer. I know you don't do emotion, but I miss you and I hate you. Go ahead and tell J.D. you'll be coming to stay with me for a weekend when I come home so we can catch up. For real."

"Deal. You're going to figure it out, Charles. Take pictures of both their dicks. Preferably with a ruler next to them for ref—"

The call cuts off and the screen goes black.

Silence hugs me as I breathe a non-recorded breath. Knowing there's not a camera on me makes me want to dance or scream. Or sit here and be me. But nothing in this mansion is permanent. Definitely not silence. A knock shatters the moment like a baseball through a glass window. Alec pops his head inside the door.

"Hey," he says, a bit shyly. "How did it go?" He pushes into the room, shutting the door behind him.

"Well. She wants pictures of yours and Parker's dicks," I tell him, mainly to see his reaction.

Courtney will never censor herself for someone else. If that type of statement shocks him, this would never work. My brain immediately berates my heart for wishing there could be something to make work at the end of this. But my conversation with Court reminded me, outside these walls, there's a whole life waiting for me to return. Sure, it doesn't include a job or a couch, but there are people waiting for me. There are things I want to do. And I realized how much I want to do them even if I have to do them alone.

"I'll send one to her when I get back to my office. She doesn't need one of Parker's," he jokes.

I laugh as the tears I didn't realize were threatening fall down my cheeks. In the blink of an eye, my face is pressed into Alec's shoulder, and I'm wrapped in his arms. Picking me up, he settles me onto his lap as he takes my seat. My cries echo around us while he pets my hair. I lose time as he rocks me. As I calm down, he rearranges me so my back is pressed against his front. I melt like butter on hot bread against his chest. He reaches up and tucks my hair behind my ear, trailing his thumb down my cheek.

"I'm so sorry about our fight, Charlie. I fucked up," Alec whispers.

"You can trust me, you know," I say.

And I hope he does. Because I want to know him, if he would just let me in. I learned long ago you can't turn from someone's shadows. Not if you care about them. Not if you want to know them. The real *them*. I could look at the blackest pieces of Alec's heart and not flinch in fear, if he would just let me.

Because I'm falling for this man and I pray he's falling for me too.

"Do you want to tell me what happened?" he asks.

"I didn't realize how much I missed being home. How much this entire situation is so surreal and crazy. You can't do anything without someone seeing it. No matter how much someone acts like your friend, it could all be a lie. It could all be for the game. And that is exhausting in a way I never anticipated. I miss Courtney. I miss my parents. I miss sleeping without the thought that the country will hear me snore."

"You don't snore," he jokes. "I should know." He huffs out a breath as I elbow him in the ribs.

"You know what I mean."

"I can only imagine the amount of stress you are under. I always thought I did a pretty good job empathizing with my contestants, but I realize how little I know what it feels like to be going through this experience. I'm sorry it's been so hard on you." He runs his fingers up and down my arm, and my attention focuses on every touch.

He continues. "You're so close to the end. You're over halfway and you're doing a fucking *killer* job. You have to keep at it for a few more weeks. And I'm here for you when you need someone to talk to. Even if it's not about the show."

I nod.

"People were going crazy for you two. Half of the articles about the show are about you and Parker. After reading them and my sister talking about how hot you two are together, I got jealous. And then, to make matters worse, the thought of being hurt again makes me act crazy," he admits.

I try not to breathe too deeply or move for fear of breaking the bubble of honesty we are trapped in.

"It's just a ruse, Alec."

I run my fingers over his tattooed forearm, his sleeves cuffed to the elbow. My favorite.

"I know. I *know* that, logically, but my heart just doesn't," he pauses, seeming unable to continue.

"It triggers you," I finish for him.

"Yes. I hate to admit it and I'd like to think I'm over it, but the thought of losing you, or ruining this before it can get off the ground, makes me want to not even try." I feel his lips press against the side of my head and I smile.

"My ex-girlfriend cheated on me. For a long time," he admits.

"Ah, that's why you hate liars." I feel him nod.

I feel his lips press against my shoulder.

"I don't know what to do about any of these feelings," he says, the words imprinting on my skin. "I shouldn't want you. You're my contestant. It's unprofessional."

His lips continue tattooing my skin, making my heart skip a beat.

"I don't either, but I don't want to pretend they aren't there."

He reaches up, firm fingers on my jaw, and pulls my face to the side. His lips are warm at the corner of my mouth. As he presses kisses against my jaw, his hand moves to my hair.

"Alec," I whisper. I feel myself getting wet as he kisses my neck, his tongue swirling over the skin.

His hand leaves my hair and begins traveling down my body. Pulling the strap of my dress, he frees my breast. He swirls a finger over my taut nipple, and wetness gathers between my thighs.

"I've been thinking about sucking on these nipples since you pulled them out on the daybed."

He twists it, just as I did, causing me to moan with the bite of pain.

"I'm going to make you come, okay?"

Words escape me as he continues kissing my neck, pulling down the other strap, freeing my whole chest, so I nod my consent. Letting go of my face, both hands begin exploring my body. My head settles onto his shoulder and I soak in every touch.

Roaming over my pussy, he continues to my inner thighs, dragging his nails against the sensitive skin on the way back up, making me shiver.

He slips one hand up my dress and touches me.

"No panties, Charlie?"

"No," I moan. His hand moves further down, slipping over my clit before teasing my opening. "Alec, that feels good."

"You're so wet for me, baby." Fingers swirling, he gathers my wetness and moves back to my clit, giving it attention.

"Oh, fuck, Alec," I say into the room.

My legs spread, giving him better access. My breathing hitches as he dips down again, slipping the tip of his finger inside me before removing it again.

"Tell me what you want, baby," he says, his voice dripping with lust.

His cock is hard against my back and I grind against him, making him moan in my ear.

"Fuck me with your fingers. Please? I need it," I say, too turned on to be embarrassed.

He groans at my words.

"That's it. I'll give you anything you ask for," he says, his heart rate picking up against my back. Without hesitation, he sinks two fingers deep inside me. "You feel so good. Your pussy is so tight."

He moves his fingers, curving them, hitting the perfect spot. His other hand travels back up my body before settling around my neck, adding pressure.

"Tell me you're mine."

I resist, wanting to see what he'll do. As his hand tightens around my throat, my orgasm nears.

"Say it," he growls in my ear, biting my earlobe.

"I'm yours," I call out, grinding myself against his hand, chasing my orgasm. "You and me. Don't stop. Please, don't stop."

Every muscle in my body clenches as he continues fucking me with his fingers, whispering dirty things in my ear.

"Your pussy is squeezing my fingers. You're so close. Come for me, Charlie. Come for me now."

His words push me over the cliff and my entire body pulses with my orgasm. My moans are unrestrained as he keeps moving his fingers, letting me ride out my pleasure.

I melt against him, trying to catch my breath.

As I lie there coming down from my high, he raises his fingers to his mouth, sucking them clean.

"You need to go back into the house," he says, pressing chaste kisses to my neck.

Without a word I nod, moving my body slowly until I'm standing. He pulls me to him as he stands and places a hard kiss on my lips. The taste of myself on him makes me want to get him naked, but I know he's right, I have to go.

"I'll see you tomorrow?" I ask, my arms around his neck.

"Count on it," he says, kissing me before releasing me.

I turn toward the door, opening it and going into the one place he can't follow. Into the *House of Deceit*.

This was not how I meant for our first real moment after our kiss to go, but then again, I never intended to fall for my keeper, either.

CHAPTER TWENTY-NINE

M Y HANDS ARE PRUNING in the warm, soapy water as the stack of breakfast dishes is dwindling at a slow, steady pace, while an apron with strawberries on it protects my dress. The dishwashers have been out for a few days. Production has tried fixing them, to no avail. We've been promised a service technician should be here tomorrow. Until then, it's up to us.

"Do you have any idea who the deceiver is this week? Because they need to pay for this one. I'm tired of washing dishes," I complain to Keith.

"Just be glad we are on the breakfast shift. Dinner has way more dishes."

The sponge slips out of my hand and into the water. I reach in, searching for it. I scream. Water flings all over me, and Keith grabs me and pulls me back from the sink. He grabs my hand roughly and checks both sides.

"What the hell happened, Red?" he asks once he's confirmed I'm uninjured.

"Something touched my hand," I tell him.

"Something touched your hand? You acted like you stuck your hand in a live garbage disposal. 'Bout gave me a damn heart attack."

"I'm scared of sharks swimming through the pipes and chomping on me." Watching scary movies with Courtney when we were young was a bad idea.

"Christ's sake," he says gruffly, dragging his hand down his face.

I move back toward the sink, but he stops me with a hand.

"I'll wash." He holds out the towel he's been drying with, and I snatch it out of his hand.

"You think one little shark is in the sink, and you're relegated to drying. This is some horseshit," I mumble under my breath.

"Maybe next time you don't take ten years off my life, and I'll let you do the washing."

I open my mouth to snark back at him, but I'm interrupted by the announcement horn. Keith and I look at each other and stop what we are doing.

"What do you think that's for?" he asks.

"I don't know, but it had better end in ice cream or something fun."

He offers me his arm, which I take, as we walk to the living room.

"Hello, deceivers!" Jacob Jacobson calls. His suit is sunshine yellow and similarly burns my retinas.

"Hey, J.J.," someone responds.

"What's up, J squared," another says.

"Today, we have a special surprise for you, house guests. We are over halfway through the competition. In celebration, we would like to offer you a chance to work together as a house! The prize? A DJ will be brought in to host a party!"

Molly and I cheer the loudest. Anything that is outside of the norm is a welcome distraction.

We all stand in a circle beside the pool, vaguely looking from one to another. The countdown on the screen sits there ominously. We shift from one foot to another. I look at Parker, who winks at me. His commitment to our farce has been perfect and, while we haven't kissed since last week, we make sure to exchange little touches to show intimacy the audience might be missing out on. I think of Alec as I trace a finger down his forearm, wishing it was him before focusing back on the group.

"We just need to pick someone to start," I say.

"You do it, then," Penelope says.

"Fine."

I grab the Lifesaver off the table in front of me and open the wrapper. Molly snatches up the box of toothpicks, taking one and passing them around. We all open them, putting them in our mouths. I put the Lifesaver on the end of mine and check to make sure everyone is ready. I tuck my hands behind my back and turn to Parker. The clock starts counting down and we begin.

He bends his knees and goes cross-eyed trying to stick his toothpick through the hole of the Lifesaver. I would laugh if not for the game. Parker lunges a bit and I give a mumbled yelp as he sticks me in the cheek. After a few shallow stabs, he finally gets it through the hole. I tip my head down as he tips his head back and the Lifesaver transfers to his toothpick. With a whole minute taken off the clock.

"Nine minutes left," I tell everyone as Parker turns toward Keith.

With their hands behind their backs, they lean toward each other like they are going to share a passionate kiss. I giggle as they lean in and the Lifesaver drops to the floor. Everyone groans. I grab the circle candy and put the toothpick back in my mouth. We have eight and a half minutes left to transfer the candy from one toothpick to another without dropping it.

Everyone waits in anticipation for their turn.

"Act like you're in one of Charlie's slutty novels and you're about to kiss the man you've had a crush on for months," Molly directs Pen as she tries to get the candy from the unenthusiastic Cain.

The clock counts down the last few seconds as the candy moves and we all wait with bated breath.

My mouth is dry, and my head pounds like my brain is being mined for gold. I pull the blanket over my head, blocking out as much of the sun as I can. There is a foot under the blanket with me, and it must be Courtney's. The weirdest dream mixed with the desire to throw up woke me up. I try to make a mental note to never drink tequila again, but the miners must be chiseling away at that piece of my brain right now because as soon as I have the thought, it's gone.

"Court? Are you alive?"

The blankets start groaning and the foot kicks me in the nose.

"Cock sucking son of a bitch!" I sit up in bed before immediately flopping back down with a groan, holding my nose. My eyes water from the pain and the brightness as I realize this is not my room. I would never paint a wall white.

"It wasn't a dream," I whisper to myself. "Hey, Molly, you twat! You kicked me in the nose!"

"What do?" she asks.

"Huh?"

"What?"

She moves again, this time kicking me in the stomach.

"I am going to cunt punch you if you kick me one more time," I tell her as I rip the blankets off her face. "Molly!"

Hissing like a cat being baptized, she sits up in bed. Her copper hair sticks out in many different directions. She has one earring dangling from her ear, a smear of red lipstick on her cheek, and her bra wrapped around one shoulder. Her naked boobs are hanging out of the arm holes of the tank top she has on.

"I hate you," she tells me, reminding me of Courtney.

"Whoa, there," I say, covering my eyes. "Put the girls back in their assigned seats."

"Whoops," she says. "It's safe now."

I drop my hand. "You look very pretty this morning."

"You have mascara down one cheek and a '90s side ponytail. I wouldn't be casting stones anytime soon."

"Fair enough. Why do my thighs hurt?"

"You made us have a twerking competition. Takes a surprising amount of thigh strength."

"That tracks. Did I win?"

"You did, yes. Out of pity."

"I'll take it."

"I gotta tell you, girl, you're probably the worst dancer I've ever seen."

"Yeah," I say, "I've heard that before." I rub one of my eyes, and it comes away with a black ring. I'm sure I just made my raccoon eyes worse, but maybe not, based on Molly's breakdown of my looks.

"Some party," she comments. "A good way to go out if I get eliminated tonight."

"You're not going home tonight," I tell her, grabbing her hand and squeezing it. The thought of my towering goddess leaving me makes me want to cry and throw up. Probably at the same time. But I have no control over the audience. Worry filters through the haze of yesterday's alcohol.

"Do you want help packing?" I ask.

"Yes, please."

I nod, but we don't move. It has been a long forty-eight hours being unsure if my grumpy grandpa or Molly will be eliminated. The realness of the fact we are over halfway done is starting to sink in.

I could win this.

The light at the end of the tunnel is starting to show.

But to get there, I have to lose one of my friends.

As the day wears on, we don't leave each other's side. We talk of nothing and everything. Make plans to meet up in the real world. Exchange phone numbers. I reassure her over and over again her time in this mansion isn't done. I keep a brave face and convince her it would make no sense to send her home over Keith.

But still, we pack all of her things. We track down every lost sock, and every loaned shirt. Every hair tie and makeup brush. I zip her bag, and I know, deep in my gut, we won't be unzipping it.

Not here.

Not tonight.

Molly clings to my hand as we walk down the hallway to the living room. I hug her before moving to the couch to take my seat. The chopping block chairs, as we so lovingly call them, sit slightly apart from the rest of us. Parker sits next to me, his thigh pressed against mine in silent companionship. He's given us our space today and it made my heart squeeze at the consideration.

The room is silent tonight. No side conversations or banter. One week ago, we lost half of our number, and we are all a little traumatized. I keep my eyes on Molly, offering her a reassuring smile any time she meets mine. Her copper hair is slicked to one side like a noir movie star.

Jacob Jacobson comes on the screen and we go through the normal drama. He reminds us what is at stake, like we could ever forget half a million dollars is on the line, and who is on the chopping block.

"Now that we are halfway through the season, there will be a new rule. Those who are not on the chopping block will be voting to eliminate one contestant. The audience's vote will count as one vote for elimination and be added to the house votes."

I feel my mouth drop open as I look at Molly, an equally shocked expression on her face. Unlike last week when the room erupted into a full-blown panic, this change is met with devastated acceptance.

Our family has to be broken apart week by week, but now we are the ones causing the fissure.

"Parker, as one of our Head Deceivers, you're first."

He stands from his chair and makes his way to the interview room.

"Psst, Red."

I look to Keith leaning around Molly, his cowboy hat perched on his head.

"What's up, Grandpa?" I ask, trying not to cry. Or worse, vomit from stress.

"You can vote to eliminate me. It's okay. I see the panic on your face."

"But I don't want you to leave either," I say, tears blurring my vision. I reach a hand out across the space, and he takes it. Squeezes. His hand is warm and dry.

"You have to vote for someone, Red. Vote for me." Molly pretends she can't hear us, but her eyes water and I know she's touched.

Our hands release as Parker comes back into the room. He gives me a sympathetic smile as Jacob calls my name.

The walk back to the interview room feels endless. No matter what, someone I love is going home. I think about my time with each of them. The deep talks I've had with Molly. The silly moments I've had with Keith.

There is no wrangler in the room this time. Only the camera with the red light, letting me know I'm being recorded as I sit down in the seat.

I try to cast my vote, but my voice is lost, choked with tears and sorrow. Clearing it, I look into the camera, at the people sitting at home and show them my devastation.

"I vote to eliminate Keith," I tell the viewers. Wiping away the tear rolling down my cheek, I make my way back out to the living room.

Jayden stands and makes his way to cast his vote as I move back into the room.

Leaving my chair empty, I decide to sit on the floor between the two chairs and hold up my hands, one for each of them to hold on to. We sit like that, in silence as person after person files from the room. When the final vote is cast, there's a momentary pause before Jacob is handed an envelope.

"Molly, Keith. Let's find out which one of you will be continuing on the hunt for half a million dollars, and which will go home."

The lights in the studio and our house dim, the music compelling. He pulls out the white envelope and opens it before reading, "Molly. I'm sorry, you will not be joining us next week. Keith, congratulations, your hunt continues." He continues talking to the audience, but I don't hear any of the words. No matter who went home, I was going to be broken by the loss, but that doesn't stop my heart from cracking in two.

I stand and crush her to me, as she bends down to hug me.

"It's okay. You're okay. Don't let them see you cry," I tell her. She nods into my shoulder before standing up and putting a broken smile on her face.

"You have to win the money so you can come visit me. Promise?"

"I promise," I tell her.

Without another word, she hugs everyone and makes her way to the front door. With a backward glance, she blows us all a kiss, and she's gone. Crushed, I stand in the entryway long after she's gone, my tears streaming down my face.

Eventually, Parker comes and ushers me to bed, tucking me into his sheets.

As I fall asleep, his body dipping the bed on his side, all I can do is wish Alec was the one in bed next to me.

WEEK EIGHT

CHAPTER THIRTY

ALEC

I PACE THE INTERVIEW room while I wait for Charlie to get dressed. Normally I don't call her to the interview room this early, but watching her cry herself to sleep last night made me feel like I was seventeen again, only this time, hopefully, I can make her feel better. I might have failed Lorelei, but I won't fail Charlie.

The door cracks and I all but tackle her to the ground.

Her soft body is pressed against every inch of mine, and my mind quickly goes from wanting to support her to wrapping her legs around my hips and pinning her against the wall.

Pulling back before she can feel what my thoughts are doing to my body, I look into her blue eyes, my thumbs stroking her cheeks.

"Are you okay?" I ask.

Eyes filling with tears, she simply nods.

"Did I ever tell you about the time I made Lorelei mad and she put laxatives in my water?" I blurt out, needing to stop the tears and hear her laugh.

She gives me a watery laugh. "No, but now you have to."

With my arm around her shoulders, I lead her over to her chair before taking mine. She tucks her legs under her and settles in.

"When I was sixteen, my dad had to get a colonoscopy and he had some leftover laxatives from the prep. At this point, I had my driver's license and our parents let us have one of their older cars so I could drive us to and from school and our various activities.

"One thing you have to understand about Lorelei is she always loved messing with me. For fun, she decided to spread a rumor around the school I was afraid of the dark. She'd make an amazing deceiver," I add as an aside.

"I'm sure that went over well," she jokes, getting into the story.

"So well," I say, rolling my eyes. "By the end of the day, it had morphed into me sleeping with a glow in the dark clock for toddlers."

"Courtney has one of those for my nephew!" she says, laughing.

A chuckle comes out. I'll sacrifice my dignity for her happiness.

"Anyway, by the end of the day, I was pretty tired of being mocked and was in a deep rage. When the last bell rang, I left the school without her. She thought I was just playing a prank on her and moved the car. Once she figured it out, the buses had already left and she walked home, my parents thinking I dropped her off at a friend's.

"About a week later, she put some laxatives in my drink. It was a very humbling experience," I say, finishing my story.

"I think I would like your sister," she says, the sadness gone from her face.

"She's already told me she wants to meet you. She really enjoys watching you on the show, thinks you seem cool."

"Whenever I get kicked out of the mansion, maybe she should have a girl's weekend with me and Courtney. Anyone who doses you with laxatives is a good person in my book."

"Thanks for that," I say, chuckling. "Do you want to talk about the change in the rules?"

"It hurts more to vote people out ourselves," she admits.

"It's not your fault Molly went home," I reassure her.

"I know, but I still couldn't save her either. Do I need to start making alliances with people now? It's not really something we focused on before, but now things are changing and maybe we should switch up our plan."

I think back to other seasons when a few times the contestants would vote someone out midweek. Those years were the ones with the most drama, as people would try to secure votes but be stabbed in the back.

"That's definitely something we might want to address on a weekly basis based on who's on the block. You do already have a partner in Parker and Keith, so that's good.

"But we want to continue with the angle we've gone with as far as the audience is concerned. Brands will start reaching out to production about contacting their favorites soon, so we don't want to suddenly turn you into another person."

"We are really close to the end, aren't we?" she asks.

Sadness starts to take over at the thought of only having a few more weeks with Charlie and I panic.

"Will you go on a date with me?" I ask, wanting more time with this beautiful woman and heeding Lorelei's advice to show her I care.

She blinks at me for a moment, and I wonder if I fucked it up. It seemed like we were getting closer, considering she was sitting on my lap and orgasmed from my touch, but maybe I misread the situation.

"Like, when I leave the mansion?"

"No, tomorrow."

"Where?" she asks, and rightfully so.

I scramble, not having a plan, but I don't want to back out now. Realizing how much I want this, I come up with a plan on the spot.

"In here. It'll be nice, I promise."

"What are we going to do?"

"It's a surprise," I say. So, maybe I only have a part of the plan. "Charlie, will you go on a date with me?" I ask her again.

Her smile is beautiful and warms my heart.

"I'd love to."

CHAPTER THIRTY-ONE

CHARLIE

"THE LOSING TEAM WILL be without their kitchen privileges until Sunday. Everything you eat or drink will be provided by the production team." Penelope reads from the card as Head Deceiver for the week.

I look at the blue team and size us up. Parker, Cain, and me against Keith, Jayden, and Rebel.

"If I end up on food restriction again, I'm going to smother someone in their sleep. Just be aware," I tell them both. Cain stares me down and I turn back, my skin crawling from the anger in his eyes, and catch Parker shifting his weight.

The sun hangs low in the sky, giving him a golden halo. His hair is tied back into a low bun while his muscles are, as always, on display. The Romans would have chiseled his likeness into stone and worshiped him as a god. He's beautiful, but Alec calls to me in a way no one else ever has.

"The winner will be determined by the best of three in water volleyball games," Penelope finishes.

We all jump into the pool and get ready to play. Our team won the game of rock, paper, scissors so we get to serve first. Cain sends the ball flying over the net and smacks Jayden in the face.

"Ah!" he screams, as blood gushes from his nose.

I turn to Cain. "Seriously?" I ask him. "It's not been two seconds."

My dislike for Cain has deepened as the weeks have gone by. His nice guy routine has started to falter the more I catch him watching me, holding true to his promise. It's creepy and starting to piss me off. His hatred for me seems to grow the higher I finish in elimination competitions. The attention is antagonistic. In fact, I bet he voted for Molly to be eliminated last week, knowing it would piss me off.

"It was an accident. It's not like I meant to hurt him," Cain says, giving me an evil smile no one else notices as they attend to Jayden.

The medical team comes out and helps get Jayden squared away. Once he's good, we go back to our game.

Rebel serves the ball over the net and I go to return it. Water rushes up my nose and into my mouth as a large body crashes down on top of me. I keep my eyes closed tight and put my feet against the bottom to push myself up, but as the body moves off me, the person's hand pushes down on my head.

I fight against it, but instead of moving when I slap at the person, their fingers coil into my hair, actively holding me down. I open my eyes, the chlorine immediately making them burn but I don't care.

I was unable to take a deep breath, unprepared to go under for an extended amount of time.

I grab onto the forearm, clawing my nails into their skin and use my feet to try and push against them, but their strength overpowers me. As my lungs start to burn as much as my eyes, the pressure is removed from my head and I shoot like a rocket to break the surface. Standing there, I hack and cough, trying to bring up the water I swallowed as I was pushed under.

I look at Cain who smiles.

"You asshole!"

I leap at him, but I'm caught before I can sink my nails or teeth into his flesh.

"Whoa! What happened?" Parker asks.

"You didn't see that dick try to drown me? Are you serious right now?" I ask him.

He takes his hands off me and holds them up in a placating gesture. "I'm sorry, I didn't see it. I saw him struggling to get up. You both went down pretty hard," Parker defends himself.

"I wasn't trying to drown you! You're so dramatic, Charlie. We were tangled up. That's a pretty serious accusation to throw around." His smile makes me murderous, but I know he's just wanting a reaction from me.

As everyone shuffles around, readying themselves to get back to the game, I vow to do anything I can to keep Cain from winning this season.

Kitchen restriction is keeping me from my favorite rainy-day tea, but the sound of raindrops keeps me from minding too much. The

clouds turned gray and heavy as the day progressed before finally releasing their pent-up tears upon the world. Mother nature's sadness
soaks into the ground. The air becomes thick with the smell of wet
grass and rainwater. I listen to the pitter patter of the drops against
the pavement, my feet tucked up under me as I drink my water.

The day has taken forever as I wait for my date with Alec tonight.

The sound of the sliding glass door opening and shutting behind
me breaks the silence, but I try to ignore the person. Rebel settles
into the patio chair next to me, mimicking how I'm seated.

"Rain is one of my favorite sounds. I'm a water sign. It's the song
of my soul," she says, watching the water pound the pool. The pool
where I almost died today.

"Back when I was younger," I start, "my dad would open the front
door of the house to let the moisture in the house. He would sit out
on the front porch. We had these rocking chairs with chipping paint
and the porch would creak as you rocked. But every time it rained,
he'd sit outside and rock. Slow and steady.

"Then one day, I was maybe four or five, he realized I was afraid
of the storms. And he said 'Lottie Lou, there's nothing to be afraid
of. Everyone cries, Mother Nature included. You can't be afraid of
someone letting sadness out. Keeping it in rots but letting it out
cleanses.'

"He pulled me up on his knee out in that creaking rocking chair
and we rocked for hours. The screen door would slap against the
door frame sometimes when the wind would pick up, but I never
felt safer and more loved than I did sitting on the porch. Eventually,
my dad got me my own rocking chair."

"I love that he sees it as her having a healing cry instead of anger."

We sit there and let the moment wash over us. The memory of my dad holding me close is so vivid, I can almost feel my body rocking. Eventually the sky darkens enough we can no longer see. Without saying a word, Rebel stands and reaches out her hand, pulling me to my feet. We walk back into the house, share a smile, and go our separate ways.

The kitchen is beautiful. Dark, timeless cabinets. A white stone countertop. The appliances gleam beneath the overhead lights. My feet itch to go in there and open the refrigerator, looking for a snack.

"Do you think the food will float out of there and push itself into your waiting hands?" Parker asks.

Ever since Molly left, I've been sleeping in his bed. Not for any sexual reason, but because I just need to know I'm not completely alone in the house. No one has brought up the arrangement. Not even Alec, but I hope he knows we never cross any lines.

Plus, I'm sure the audience will be happy to see our relationship progressing as the weeks move on, especially now that I can't bring myself to kiss Parker in deference to Alec.

"I'm trying to use my mind powers to summon it, but you're distracting me."

"I'm the reason you can't levitate food?"

"Yes. Duh." I bump my arm against him. "I miss food already," I sigh.

"It's not even been a day," he tells me.

"Shush, you. You don't understand our relationship. Any time apart is hard."

"It's not like you can never eat. You just can only have what production gives you."

I cross my arms over my chest and look at him.

"Did you taste the bologna sandwich we were given for dinner? The other team had freaking filet! They were rubbing it in our faces. I bet it was Keith's suggestion. He's a brat. He knows what it would do to me," I mumble more to myself than Parker.

His fingers are warm as he gently grabs my chin, turning my head toward him.

"Trying to get your attention away from food is quite the task," he jokes, his hand dropping away. "Do you want to hang out? I feel like I haven't gotten you alone in a long time."

I shift my focus wholly to him.

"I'd love that, but—"

"Price to the interview room," floats from the speakers, interrupting me.

I try not to let my giddiness show, but Parker must see it on my face no matter how hard I try to stifle my excitement for my date with Alec.

"I'll come find you later?"

"Sure," he says, smiling softly. "Have fun." He gives me a soft kiss on the cheek.

Trying not to draw attention to myself, I make my way to the interview room, trying to guess what Alec could have planned for me.

Vanilla and honey intermingle in the air as I cross the threshold into the interview room. Candles warm the air and throw a gentle glow on the walls. Alec stands in the middle of a checkered blanket. His black slacks hug his thick thighs while his black shirt shows his smooth chest behind the open buttons.

The men I dated were never this gorgeous. They were always attractive, but Alec is a man that turns heads. They never smiled at me the way Alec does. They never really cared about who I was as a person, but more so what I could give them.

They also never had abs that make me want to burn all their shirts, either.

I push the thoughts from my mind and follow the trail of rose petals from the door to Alec.

"You look absolutely stunning," he says, giving me a soft kiss.

My white sun dress is simple but hugs all of my curves. The sweetheart neckline enhances my cleavage and I know I made the right choice when his eyes get stuck there for a moment.

Rebel helped me do my hair, adding soft waves. Luckily, she was bored and didn't ask many questions. With few ways to entertain ourselves, some of us girls have enjoyed giving each other makeovers whenever we want something to do.

He grabs my hand and pulls me down to the blanket. A small stack of books sits next to a plate of steak, mashed potatoes, and asparagus. A bottle of wine sits uncorked and breathing.

"That smells amazing," I moan, my mouth watering.

"I know you've already had dinner, so I hope you're still hungry."

"By dinner, do you mean my gourmet bologna sandwich? That was barely food. You won't get in trouble for giving me this, will you?" I ask, worried about him.

We already pushed the boundaries of the wrangler/contestant relationship the last time we were in this room.

"You're allowed to eat whatever production makes you. I'm a part of production. Don't worry," he says, touching my hand.

"You made this yourself? I'm impressed."

"If you consider dialing the phone and placing the order to be 'making it.'"

Laughing, butterflies settle in my stomach at the soft look he gives me. I've thought Alec was hot from the first moment I saw him, but bathed in candlelight, he's a showstopper and all I want to do is kiss him.

Giving my hands something to do, I grab the bottle and pour a swallow into my glass. The flavors roll over my taste buds.

"This is amazing," I say.

He takes the bottle from me and pours us both glasses. My eyes drink him in as thirstily as I drank the sip of wine.

"A toast," he says, raising his glass. "To every second that led to this moment."

Our glasses clink and I take another small sip, wanting to savor the only chance I'll have to taste something exquisite this week.

"What are the books for?" I ask as I cut into my steak.

The meat is perfectly tender and seasoned. I try to remind myself of the manners my mother drilled into me so I don't eat every bite of food within two minutes.

"Well, there's very few options as far as activities go and I know you love to read so, I thought I would read one to you. Whichever one you want."

I take another bite and grab up the first book. The title makes me raise my eyebrows as I read the synopsis on the back.

"Will Paige be able to resist the call of Damion? Will Damion be able to resist the call of Paige's blood? Will either of them be able to resist the lust coursing through their veins?"

I look up at him and smile.

"You're going to read me smut?" I take another drink of wine before reading the back of another.

"I thought it would be fun. I'll even do different voices for you," he jokes, cutting his steak.

"Well, aren't I lucky?" I grab the other books and read them.

Alec has provided me with some great options. A pirate and a barmaid. A baseball player and a reporter. A second chance romance between a divorcée and her high school love. I read the backs a few times as I finish my meal before picking.

"I'm going to have to go for the pirate," I say, tapping the cover. "I always had a thing for Captain Hook when I was growing up."

"I always had a thing for Wendy," he says. "But maybe by the end of this I'll have a thing for a barmaid."

I smack his stomach and I move to sit by him, handing him the book I've chosen.

"Start reading, mister."

CHAPTER THIRTY-TWO

ALEC

I LOOK AT THE outfit for my interview I have hanging on the back of the door throughout the day. Last night with Charlie was amazing. After reading to her for an hour, we ended up making out in a slow, sensual way, letting our hands wander but never crossing a line.

In my real life, I never take the time just for romance. The only reason I kiss women is because they need it. But I think I would be content to only kiss Charlie forever, if that was all she was willing to give me.

Part of me wonders if I shouldn't have asked her out on a date when I haven't told her about my interview. All morning, I have been going crazy with the thought of leaving her. Tapping out a message to cancel the interview, deleting it, tapping it out again. Over and over. My guilt and hesitation are maddening. I watch as Charlie gets ready for today's elimination competition, a test of endurance to see who can last the longest in a box filled with bugs. Hoots and hollers come from the wrangler watching room. A knock on the door sounds as I start to take off my shirt. Pulling it back down, I move across the room.

"Hey, Alec. Just wanted to see if you were going to join us. I feel like I've hardly seen you this season," Frank says.

"Yeah, I've just been needing some alone time. You know how it gets on these shoots. Lots of late nights."

"This one has definitely been more tiring, that's for sure." He leans against the door jamb. "Our contestants have been getting awfully friendly," he says, wiggling his eyebrows at me.

Unsure if Parker told him about Charlie's and his arrangement, I decide to err on the side of caution and not mention it. What a contestant does or does not share with their wrangler is none of my business, and he might not have had time to watch the clip where they made the agreement.

"They have. The audience is loving it, but I hope he's not really getting attached. I don't need her distracted."

"I guess we will see." He pushes off the jamb. "See you in there."

Shutting the door, I don't bother to remind him I'm leaving for the evening, and begin shucking my clothes, throwing on the light gray suit without a care, only thinking how shocked Charlie would be to see me in something that's not black.

Making my way out back, whirring cuts through the late afternoon calm as a speck of a helicopter pulls closer, landing on the mansion's landing pad. I button my suit jacket as I walk toward it. Once settled, the pilot lifts us into the air, ferrying me off to an interview I don't really want to go to.

One that could change my life.

That could give me everything I've ever wanted.

"The flight should only be about forty-five minutes. Mr. Cochran is at his beach house this evening," the pilot tells me through the headset.

"Sounds great. Thank you."

The rest of our flight passes in silence. I focus on mentally preparing for this meeting, but my thoughts keep turning back to Charlie. A tiny bit of her shine has worn off since Molly was eliminated. Like she's retreated into herself a bit. I wish I could fix it and make her feel better. She is still sleeping with Parker every night. Sure, it's nothing more than sleeping, but the jealousy still makes me want to tear my hair out.

However, I refuse to let my jealousy of their fake relationship ruin what might be happening with us.

Outdoor lanterns become visible as we crest a hill. The sunset would be dizzying with its fiery reds and warm oranges, but I barely notice it now. As we descend, I shove Charlie and the mansion into the back of my mind and turn on my dominating personality she has slowly made me wear less and less.

The silence is deafening as the helicopter motor cuts off. I take off my headset and exit. A beautiful blonde in a skintight white dress stands, waiting for me with a leather-bound notebook in her hands. Her makeup is perfect. Not a single brush mark is out of place. Everything about this woman is what I would chase when Tank and I went out to the bars.

"Mr. King, please follow me."

Her accent is posh and, before Charlie, would have been the final nail in the coffin, cementing my desire to sleep with her. But all I can think about now is getting back to the mansion and watching Charlie read in her favorite chair while the sun sets through the stained glass.

The pool glows into the dimming light of the day. A large, perfectly appointed table sits beneath the shelter of the house above it.

"Mr. Cochran desires dinner out tonight. Please take a seat and he'll be with you shortly."

I nod in her direction and move to pull out the chair next to the head of the table. I sit, looking out at the paradise that Tom Cochran has made with his storied career. Over the stone wall is the ocean crashing against it, battering to get to the land beyond. The sound of the waves puts me in something of a trance that is snapped when Tom comes walking out, looking more like he's ready for sunbathing in Tuscany than a job interview.

He's squat, with a bit of a belly. His shock of white hair contrasts against his deeply tanned skin. A man that loves the sun. I stand to meet him, holding my hand out for him to shake, unprepared for the bear hug he wraps me into.

"Mr. Cochran, it's so nice to meet you," I say as I straighten my jacket once he releases me.

"Tom, please. Sit, sit," he instructs, waving me down. No longer than half a second passes before someone steps up to us.

"Sir, today the chef has prepared a delicious Wagyu steak with—"

"Yes, please. Whatever he has prepared is fine. Please serve the wine," he interrupts.

"Yes, sir. Excuse me, sir."

Each bite of the exquisite meal sits like lead in my stomach as the thought rises of Charlie eating a peanut butter and jelly sandwich, or something equally as pitiful that I know production has planned.

Cochran's staff invisibly bustle around us. Never once do we want for anything; you'd think our plates and cups were self-filling. The food is delicious and yet it tastes like dirt in my mouth, the steak from last night infinitely better. But that might have more to do with the company I had.

My suit feels like sandpaper against my body as I chafe at the desire to hop back in the helicopter and sprint away. Tom regales me with stories of directing Hollywood blockbusters, leading actor squabbles, and the joys of watching the product of your blood, sweat, and tears win awards.

"Let's talk about how you want to be a director. Where did the desire come from?" he asks, the first real question of the interview.

I sit up. "My mom. She showed me the world of storytelling and I've been in love ever since. To have a vision and to make something *exactly* as imagined..." I trail off. "It's art. It's moving art and I just want a chance to be the artist."

"My boy, I couldn't have put it better myself. It'll be a lot of long days. Time away. Are you ready for that? It can make life difficult."

Charlie's smile enters my mind, but still, I say, "I'm positive."

I feel each grain of sand as it falls in the hourglass of my life. Each moment, excruciating. Every rotation of the blades above my head, I change my mind on whether I should tell Charlie about my interview. I promised her it was us in this together, but I don't want her to think I'm using her.

After an eternity, the mansion comes into view and my heart squeezes at being so close to her once again. The second I'm given the signal, I jump out and hustle into the mansion, my red tie flapping in the wind.

My jacket hits the ground as I walk into my office. This job is the chance I've been looking for and yet, I'm not as excited as I thought I'd be now that it's here.

Loosening my tie, I toe off my shoes, my only thought on catching a glimpse of the woman that consumes my every thought, even when my dream might become a reality. Before I can log onto my computer to check on Charlie, my phone vibrates with Sheila's name popping up on the screen. Opening the message, I see Charlie will have to wait.

Answering the summons, I make my way to Sheila's office, taking a moment to put my shoes back on. She wouldn't find my shoeless state funny. Her door is open, so I walk in without bothering to knock.

"You're here late," I say to her, sitting down in my usual chair.

"I had a few things to finish up and I wanted to talk to you about your meeting with Tom. How did it go?"

"It went well. He offered me the job."

"I knew he would. He would be a fool not to, though it's a loss for us. When do you start?"

"He starts casting meetings in two weeks, but I mentioned to him my contract with *House of Deceit* isn't complete for another few weeks. I told him I'd need to check with you before committing. He said I can take the weekend."

"Don't worry about that," she says, waving away my concern. "We'll find someone to replace you with Price, if that's what you're worried about. She would still be taken care of. Getting in on the ground level, from the first moment, is a big deal," she tells me. "I can give her to the wrangler of the person that leaves this week."

"She and I are in a good rhythm. I would hate to mess up her chances."

For the first time in the ten years I've known Sheila, her voice softens.

"Alec," she says, clasping her hands on her desk in front of her. "I have talked to every contact I have. Raved about you to anyone who would listen. This is your shot. I know you take your job seriously, it's why you're so important to me and losing you will be a huge pain in my ass, but you may never get another chance like this.

"Take the few days, but Alec, you will hate yourself if you don't take it. I promise."

I nod, knowing she's right. But maybe this dream isn't the thing that matters anymore.

"I understand. I'll let you know what I decide. And I just want to say thank you, for being my mentor for all these years," I say, feeling oddly emotional that she cares so much about my career progression.

"All right, well, sounds good. Now get out of my office."

Without further prompting, I leave and head back to my signifi-cantly smaller office and pull up the live feed. Charlie is reading in the library, a robe loosely tied around her. I'm surprised she's not asleep, but glad I get a moment to watch her relax.

Cain comes in on a tear. They begin shouting at each other, seeming to be resuming a previous fight. Confused, I try to pull up footage from earlier in the day to determine what the issue was, but Charlie stands from her chair, her book falling to the ground. Both fuming, they stand there staring at each other, until they aren't.

Cain grabs her arms roughly and Charlie's panicked face is all I need to see to get my feet flying.

"Oh, fuck no," I say.

Rage takes the driver's seat in my brain, coursing through my veins, as I almost rip the door off. I move through the maze of producer offices and storm into the house, all regard for the rules melted from my brain. I fly to the library where they are.

"You think you can keep me from winning this thing? You're like a kid trying to play chess with a grandmaster."

"Listen here, you stupid bitch, I *will* win this. I will get you disqualified if I have to. Leave this fucking house."

Their yelling drives me faster, the need to reach her fierce. Charlie's eyes lock on mine and widen at the anger pulsing off me.

"Alec, don't!" she yells, but her warning falls on deaf ears.

I grab a handful of Cain's shirt and pull him off her.

"What the hell!?" he exclaims as I throw him down on the ground wanting to launch myself at him, but I restrain myself. Standing above him, I glare down and let all of my hate and anger show.

"Keep your hands off her. Get the fuck out of here."

He stands up from the floor, regaining his composure and cockiness I've seen throughout the game. I should worry about what he has planned, but I want to get him away from Charlie so I can check on her as quickly as possible.

"Interesting that you're here, Alec King. Aren't wranglers supposed to stay out of the mansion?"

Warning bells go off in my head, but I ignore them.

"You were hurting her," I say simply.

"Simple misunderstanding. But she's not supposed to be here, is she?"

"Cain, if she had ended up in the right pile, she still would have been chosen. You're here. Why does it matter who your wrangler is?"

"Because I deserve the best," he hisses before straightening out his features once more. "But you're right. It doesn't matter anymore. I'm going to win and your girl won't make it to the final three."

He puts his hands in his pockets and walks toward the door. I shift, keeping myself between him and Charlie in case I need to protect her.

"Have a good night," he calls over his shoulder.

I turn to Charlie. She stands half-perched on the table, her hand clutching her robe closed. Her red, lush mouth hangs open as she stares at me with wide eyes. My tongue flicks out, wetting my bottom lip. Without another thought, I go to her.

CHAPTER THIRTY-THREE

CHARLIE

"ARE YOU OKAY?" He grabs my arms, checking where Cain grabbed me. Anger turns to worry in his eyes as he checks me over.

"I'm fine, don't worry about it," I say. "But you have to get out of here." I push at him, worried he's already been in the mansion too long.

"What the hell was happening in here?" he demands, ignoring my concern.

"You know, if a red tie and white shirt is the only thing of color you own besides black, that's not much better," I say, but he won't be distracted.

My core clenches in anticipation while nerves rack my body.

"He was claiming I sabotaged him during the elimination competition today because I *almost* won Head Deceiver instead of him."

"You need to stay away from him. He's got it out for you."

"Don't I know it," I say, waving away his words. "Keith and Parker are in the bottom two. Supposedly something bit Keith and did you know Parker is afraid of bugs? Because I gotta tell you, I wasn't expecting that," I ramble trying to get the worried look in his eyes to recede.

The table edge presses into me as Alec crowds me, his eyes heating.

"What are you wearing under the robe?" he asks, running his fingers over my silk-covered breast.

"Nothing," I whisper.

"You're walking around here basically naked?"

"Yes?" His fingers feel amazing, but the barrier between us is too much. I ache to touch him, but I don't want to make him retreat to his wrangler persona.

"Were you just hoping for someone to untie this robe? Run their hands all over you?"

Striking like a snake, he grabs a handful of my hair, pulling a yelp from my throat. A few strands tear free under his grip and I don't care. All I want is for him to own me, mark me as his.

"Didn't I tell you while you're in this house you're mine?"

My heart starts racing as I grab his hips, pulling him tighter against me.

"Yes," I whisper.

"Say it."

"I'm yours," I tell him.

My thighs are drenched from my arousal. Never in my life have I been this turned on.

His gray eyes hold my gaze as he unties my robe with reverent hands. The material pools around my hips as he pushes the sleeves down my arms.

"You're the most beautiful creature I've ever seen," he tells me, cradling my breasts in his hands. His thumbs rub over my taut nipples, teasing me. "I haven't been able to stop thinking about you coming on my cock since you came on my hand."

"Me either. You're all I can think about."

He sucks a nipple into his mouth, swirling his tongue around. I stare down at him as he lavishes my breasts with attention. The peak of his tongue as he nibbles his way to the other side makes me wish his face was between my legs.

Kissing his way up my body, he tilts my head away, giving himself greater access to my neck. Desperate for more friction, I try to rub myself against him, but he has me pinned and unable to move.

"Alec," I say, asking for something, but I'm not sure what.

"Yes?"

"Please."

He pulls away from my neck and wraps my hair around his hand, adding tension.

"Use your words," he commands.

"I need you to taste me."

He swipes his tongue along my collarbone slowly.

"Like that?" he asks, his eyes sparkling with challenge.

"I need you to eat my pussy," I say, grabbing his hair and gently pushing him down to his knees before me.

Feeling powerful as he looks up at me from his knees, I'm forced to lean back on the table as he hooks my leg up and over his shoulder. His fingers grip my thighs so hard, there will be bruises tomorrow.

I moan as he peppers kisses up the soft skin of my inner thigh.

He runs his thumb over my slit, gathering my arousal.

"You're so wet for me, baby. Do you want my mouth on you?"

"Yes. Taste me. Taste me right now," I beg, ending on a moan as he licks me with the flat of his tongue.

"Delicious," he says.

"Alec, please."

A sharp slap lands on the outside of my thigh, followed immediately by his tongue thrusting inside me. The pain sharpens the pleasure as he devours me. My legs start to shake as he works me over.

His tongue drives me to the edge faster than I've ever been, my hand fisting in his hair and holding him to me.

"I'm going to come," I moan. "Don't stop."

One swipe of his tongue away from cresting into white hot pleasure, he pulls back.

"You asshole," I say, pissed off and horny.

He smiles, peppering my inner thighs with kisses once more.

"You're going to come on my cock like the good girl I know you are."

As I melt at his words, Alec stands before kissing me hard. My taste mingled with his drives me insane and I want to get on my knees for him.

He spins me around and presses my chest down on the table before kicking my legs wide. My pussy clenches as he grabs my ass, spreading me apart. One sharp slap and I'm already dancing on the edge of orgasm again as he manhandles me.

"I need you inside me," I say, as I hear him undo his pants.

Twisting around, I watch as he reaches his hand in and pulls out his hard length. My mouth waters as he lazily strokes himself, his gaze so heated, I'm surprised the room hasn't combusted into flames around us.

"I don't have—" he starts.

"IUD," I say, panting.

With a strong hand, he pushes me back down. Grabbing a handful of my hair, he thrusts deep into me and I bow off the table.

I cry out from the invasion, but meet every punishing thrust he gives me. He's so deep in me it's almost too much, but every stroke builds my pleasure.

"You feel so good, baby," He croons, rubbing his free hand down my spine. "You take me so good, don't you?"

I clench around him as he withdraws, his deep moan spurring me on.

"Harder. Give it to me harder," I whisper, but he hears me and knows just what I need.

He grunts with each thrust, pounding into me. I'll feel this every time I sit tomorrow, but it'll be worth it. The orgasm I feel building threatens to overtake me.

"I'm so close. Don't stop, please, don't stop."

I meet him thrust for thrust, sweat breaking out over my skin as all of my nerves come alive. Our hips slap together, our pleasure echoing around us.

Without missing a thrust, he slaps my ass and I break.

"I'm coming," I cry out as waves of pleasure crash over me, spinning me around in their wake.

"Good girl," he says, pressing his hard chest into my back as he hikes up my leg.

The change of angle drives me wild as he presses into me. His thrusts become erratic.

"Come inside me, Alec. Fill me up," I say, chasing another orgasm.

With just a few more strokes, he comes with a shout, his dick twitching within me as he spends himself.

We lay there panting, his full weight on me, as he lets my leg down. Slowly, he pulls out of me, and I immediately miss him being inside me.

He pulls me to standing before gently pressing me back to sit on the table. I smile at him.

"That was totally better than I imagined," I joke and he bursts out laughing before kissing me roughly.

"Agreed," he says, tucking my hair behind my ear.

His next kiss is gentle and my heart tugs.

"I would normally get something to clean you up with, but I need to get going before I get both of us in trouble," he says as he pulls my robe back on me, tying a nice little bow in front.

Now more than ever, I wish we had met under other circumstances. I want nothing more than to curl up with this man under the covers until we recover and could do it all over again.

"I'll see you tomorrow," I say.

The smile he gives me is like the sun breaking through the clouds after multiple rainy days.

"I can hardly wait," he says, tucking himself away.

Leaning in, he kisses me again before resting his forehead against mine.

"See you tomorrow," he says, pressing one last kiss to my lips before hurrying from the room.

CHAPTER THIRTY-FOUR

TRYING TO KEEP MYSELF from running to the interview room every five seconds to climb on top of Alec, my brain shifts through the events of the week. While my time in the library was amazing, I keep coming back to the fact Parker is on the chopping block. After losing Molly last week, the thought of losing Parker as well almost puts me into a tailspin. Almost. I stand at the back doors, staring out at the pool. If I was home, I would scroll on social media trying to keep my thoughts at bay, but here, there are no phones. No social media. No television. And I can only read so many books.

Considering going for a swim, I wonder idly if Courtney has taken Caleb to the pool yet this summer. As kids, we always loved diving for rings, pretending like we were dolphins or mermaids, and lived in the water.

As I'm thinking of Courtney, an idea to distract myself from thinking of Alec and the chopping block situation comes to me. One thing I love about my best friend is she is an amazing baker. It's one of her talents. Over the years, she has taught me various decorating techniques along with her best recipes.

I think through the people who are left in the house to help me set it up and my choice is easy. Keith had three rambunctious sons and now has seven equally rambunctious grandkids he would sacrifice himself for without a moment's hesitation. I know from stories he loved setting up fun activities for them. Turning toward the interior of the house, I go to find my soon-to-be partner in crime.

Keith is asleep on the couch in the library. As I walk in, I pause at the table for a moment, remembering Alec's hands on me. Shaking myself from the memory before I become overwhelmed, I look at Keith.

His arms are crossed over his chest like he's giving someone in his dream a light dressing down. Probably one of his sons or a new ranch hand. His light snores move around the room. On sneaking feet, I inch to one of the chairs and grab the pillow. I tiptoe until I'm standing over him. Winding up the pillow, I bring it down, smacking it right on Keith's chest. He comes to life with a growl and wild eyes until he sees it's me.

"What the fuck, Red?"

"I'm bored. Wanna have a cookie decorating contest? We need to do something for your birthday," I tell him, pillow dangling from my hand.

"Don't go saying the 'b' word! Plus, I can't. I'm dead from the heart attack you just gave me." He puts his hand on his chest and drapes himself on the couch, sticking his tongue out. He only does that when he wants to pretend to be extremely dead. Normally when I wake him up, he just lies like a vampire in a coffin with his hands crossed on his chest, a normal amount of dead.

"You can't be dead. I need your help, Grandpa. Plus, I have it on good authority you're too stubborn to have a heart attack."

He cracks one eye open but doesn't move out of his position. "Maybe not, but I might smack you around a little."

"Oooooh, I'm very scared. Plus, you use the heart attack too much. It's lost its efficacy. Up and at 'em!"

"You're an asshole." He sits up and looks at me.

"Do you need help getting up so you don't break a hip?"

He looks at me, cocking his eyebrow. His stern looks do nothing but make me laugh. He might be a hard-ass cowboy back home, but here, with me, he's nothing but a giant softy. While I've always gravitated toward Molly and Parker, Keith has been a steady presence for me in the house.

"Didn't your parents teach you to respect your elders?" He shoos me back and stands up, giving a big stretch.

"If you saw my mom talk to my grandma, you'd understand where I get it from. It's all from a place of love."

"I know it is, Red." He puts his arm around my shoulders and gives me a squeeze before dropping it.

"Let's go round everyone up," he says, leading me out of the room.

Making my way around the house I announce there is a fun activity in the kitchen for anyone who would like to take part while Keith goes to ask his wrangler about an exception for those of us on restriction. Cain, of course, completely ignores me, but I prefer that to his normal glare. Plus, he hasn't participated in a singular house event since we got here that was not contractually obligated.

Penelope, Jayden, Parker, and Rebel crowd around the island waiting to find out what we are going to do.

"So, Keith and I thought we should have a cookie decorating contest," I announce.

"Production said anyone on restriction can decorate them but not eat them. Sorry about it. There will be a lot for those of us who aren't on restriction," he says, smiling at me.

"I hate you," I tell him before turning back to the others. "Everyone will get six cookies. The decorations will be graded on creativity, cohesiveness, and execution."

Jayden raises his hand.

"You don't have to raise your hand," I tell him.

"Oh, sorry. Could I help bake the cookies?" he asks, his face earnest.

"Sure! I'd love the help while the others make some buttercream and royal icings."

We split off into teams after a few instructions on how to make the various icings. I grab aprons for me and Jayden while he grabs the stand mixer and brings it over to the island.

"Do you know how to make sugar cookies?" I ask him.

"My grandma and I used to make cookies for all of our neighbors every Christmas," he tells me, grabbing various ingredients from the pantry and fridge.

"So, you're totally going to kick our asses," I joke.

His face looks even younger when he smiles, but the joy is so evident, I'm already glad we decided to do this activity.

"Hopefully," he says, tying the apron around his waist.

The kitchen is an utter disaster as we all move to the dining room where the cookies have been cooling as Jayden and I pulled them from the oven. The icing team is covered in powdered sugar after a small tussle over the bag.

Penelope spoons icing into different bowls with makeshift piping bags available, everyone getting the same options. We all sit at our various decorating stations.

"Everyone has one hour," Keith says. "Three, two, one!"

We all scramble to decorate our cookies. I decide to go with a dinosaur theme including a comet, two different dinosaurs, a dinosaur egg, a volcano, and Earth.

Grabbing the food dyes in the middle of the table, I mix various colors into my buttercream on the plate in front of me.

"Who does everyone think will end up on another television show?" Rebel asks.

"What do you mean?" Parker asks, hunched over his cookies.

"There's always one person from each season who seems to end up making reality shows their job. Who will it be for us?"

"Lucas," Penelope responds, sucking a drop of icing from her thumb. While she and the Olympian were fighting toward the end, I wonder if she misses him more than she lets on.

"Oh, that's a good one," I say. "I think it'll be Parker."

He looks up at me, an eyebrow raised. "What? Why?"

"I just have a feeling you're going to end up on a dating show or something. Can you imagine the stack of applications to get a piece of the towering Viking man?" I tease.

Rebel and Penelope smile and look at Parker.

"They would have to hide the filming location to get people not to show up," Rebel says.

"Wait, I thought you guys were dating?" Jayden says, looking between us.

"We are just having fun. We'll figure it out once we leave the mansion. Until then, it's casual," Parker says, saving me from having to come up with a lie.

It's not like I can tell everyone I want to give a relationship with my wrangler a go.

When time is called, we all stand around the table looking at everyone's cookies.

"Is that an egg?" I ask Grandpa, pointing to one of his cookies.

"It was supposed to be the sun," he says sheepishly.

I move down the table, laughing at the various decorations. Jayden went with a Christmas theme and I smile, hoping his grandma is touched at the display.

"Holy crap," Parker says, standing in front of Rebel's cookies. I move over there and my mouth drops.

Sitting in front of me is a perfect replica of a cartoon princess I recognize from being at Courtney's house. Another cookie has the horse sidekick, a cityscape across the remaining four.

"Wow," I whisper.

"Did I forget to mention baking is one of my hobbies?" Rebel checks her nails, trying to smother the smile but I catch it. "Oops."

"Well, I think we know who's going to win," Jayden whispers.

"All those for Rebel to be the winner?" I ask, and all hands go up.

She lets out an excited whoop and does a little shimmy as we all congratulate her. Everyone cleans up, some eating their cookies, while those of us on restriction pack them away in storage containers for the others. I pack up my cookies, intending to take them to Alec as a treat. With a soft smile at the thought of his gentle goodbye kiss, I make my way to the interview room.

Alec is waiting for me, which tells me he was watching the live feed.

"The dinosaur cookies were my favorite," he says when I open the door.

"You can't be trusted, you're a little biased."

He takes the bag of cookies from me and puts them in the seat of his chair before he moves to me, wrapping his arms around me and lifting me from my feet.

"I missed you," he whispers in my ear, surprising me.

He sets me back down and I press a kiss to his lips. I want to pretend like I'm not as affected as I am, but every time I see him, my entire body lights up.

"I missed you, too," I admit, an equally large smile on my face.

"And don't worry, I deleted the footage."

I feel the smile drop from my face as I realize what he's saying.

"The cameras," I whisper. "I forgot about the cameras."

Black dots blink in my vision as the blood rushes from my head. My body feels heavy as the dots grow.

"Charlotte, hey, look at me," Alec demands, grabbing my shoulders and shaking me a touch.

"We made a sex tape," I say, horrified.

"Only a little," he tries to joke as tears fill my eyes.

Other people might have seen that footage before it was deleted. My stomach tries to revolt, but I force it into submission.

Alec pushes me down into my chair before pushing a glass of water into my hands and telling me to drink. There's no ice, but the cool liquid is nice, getting me to focus on my body.

"I went to my office the second I left and deleted the footage. There aren't any copies. I was very thorough. Trust me."

He talks to me like he's talking to a spooked animal, while stroking my hair.

"I trust you," I say, realizing I do.

Even outside of the mansion, I know if he promised he took care of something, it would be taken care of.

"Tell me a story while I try to calm down?"

"Lore and Tank had a bet on when we would kiss," he tells me, shocking me again.

"Why would they bet on that?"

He sighs heavily before sitting down on the ground. I smile at his relaxed posture, something I never thought would happen with the man I first met who had a stick wedged so far up his ass he could have coughed out splinters.

"Apparently, my sister saw you on the first episode and had no faith in my professionalism."

The disdain in his voice makes me laugh.

"You weren't exactly being professional when you licked my pussy, were you?" I ask him, heating. Suddenly I want nothing more than to have this man between my thighs again.

I drop out of my chair and crawl to him. His eyes darken as he watches my hips sway as I make my way to him. He licks his bottom lip, cocking his head slightly to the side and I feel myself melt.

I sit back on my heels as I reach him, my hands traveling up his thighs slowly as I straddle his lap. His hard length presses into me as I rub on him.

"Are you feeling very professional right now?"

"Not even a little," he says, pulling my face down to his, giving me a searing kiss.

"Keith, I'm sorry, but this will be the end of your stay in the *House of Deceit*," Jacob Jacobson says. My stomach falls at losing Keith, but when I look at Parker, all I feel is happiness I have at least another week with him. We all stand and say our goodbyes.

My eyes tear up as I hug him. "You kick all their asses, Red. You better win this thing, for me," he whispers in my ear. I nod and step back. We shared numbers earlier and when I'm on the outside of this house, I'll call him. We have a date with his whole family and some of his favorite movies to share. The door shuts behind him and I turn back into the house.

The beads of my borrowed black dress clink together as I make my way through the remaining people. My stomach somersaults at how close I was to losing Parker. We make eye contact over everyone's heads. I indicate I'm going to the dressing room and turn before I see if he acknowledges me.

Keith's wardrobe stands empty. After Sharon's tear-filled packing when she was eliminated in week one, the two contestants on the chopping block have packed before the live show. I go to my wardrobe and put a pair of soft sleep shorts on before unzipping the dress. I pull on a zip-up hoodie Alec had gotten for me last week after

I wished I had something light to throw on in the evenings as Cain walks in.

I try to ignore the asshole, but my nerves light up every time I'm in a room alone with him. I toss Rebel's dress in her wardrobe, having borrowed it when I suddenly hated every dress I brought with me, noting to apologize for the way I returned it.

"Sounded like you had an interesting night the other night," Cain comments, stopping me.

"What are you talking about?" I ask, trying not to show any emotion.

He moves to block my exit, causing the hair on my arms to rise and my pulse pick up.

"Someone is quite the little whore, isn't she? Fucking her wrangler." The derogatory term makes me bristle.

"Fuck you," I try to shove around him.

"You think just because no one came into the room no one heard? You were moaning like a bitch in heat. I'm surprised you didn't wake the entire house begging him not to stop. Tsk. Tsk. Tsk. You must not care about his job. All you care about is having everyone panting for a piece of that ass like that'll keep you in this house. How will Parker feel about this?"

His lack of participation in group activities will be his downfall, if he really believes Parker and I are together. He moves toward me and suddenly I'm on alert. I pray the cameras are being monitored or if I'm delayed enough, Parker will come to find me.

"Don't you fucking touch me," I warn.

"Or what?"

"There are hundreds of cameras around here. Someone will see it and come." I send up prayers that I'm correct.

"Those cameras didn't stop you, did they?"

"He took care of the recordings. He told me."

"You sure about that? That's a lot of trust in someone that didn't tell you about his job interview."

"He told me about it. Why wouldn't he? I'm sure he'll get it," I lie, sure he's trying to get under my skin.

He studies me and the smile he gives is more predator showing his teeth. "You're a terrible liar."

My insides are jelly. I try to shift my weight to one leg, readying myself to knee him in the groin as hard as I can.

"I wouldn't be so trusting of everything he says if I were you. His goal is to get you to win. What would he tell you to get you there? Or maybe, what wouldn't he?"

He stalks from the room and I slide down to the floor. Tears gather in my eyes for the second time today as adrenaline makes me shake.

WEEK NINE

CHAPTER THIRTY-FIVE

ALEC

THE MOTEL'S PARKING LOT is empty when I'm dropped off. With eyes like sandpaper from lack of sleep, I flip on the bedside table lamp, a 1970s orange and brown monstrosity. Most nights I have been staying at the mansion far longer than normal seasons, watching Charlie on the live feed until she goes to sleep.

Books sit by the door of my room, reminding me I need to take them back to the mansion. As Charlie tears through them, she has taken to giving me her favorites so I can read them as well. Unsure if it's allowed, I've been keeping them squirreled away from my office until I can finish them.

Lacking any sort of standout amenities, the one thing this motel has is shower pressure. The jet stream of water power-washes my skin, as I wash the previous day from my body.

It has been a few days since Charlie's and my time in the library. As the sounds of her moans and the taste of her come to mind, I harden. While I've had good sex before, with Charlie, it was better than anything before it. Unlike my other partners, I was able to read her so well.

Her responsiveness was as addicting as the deep, guttural moans she released as she came on my cock.

Knowing I won't be able to focus all day with a raging hard-on, I take matters into my own hands. Closing my eyes, I picture what it would be like to have Charlie in my bedroom with me.

On her knees, bathed in the soft lighting of the room, her pale skin glows. Her breasts are heavy and beg for my mouth, which I'll give her, but not yet.

Beautiful deep blue eyes look at me as I tilt her chin up. Need, deep and unrelenting, is in her eyes. For me. For what I can give her.

"Open," I say, my voice already husky with lust.

She follows instructions so well, my good girl. Lining up my hips with her mouth, I grab her hair and thrust in until she gags, pulling a moan from my throat. Easing back, I let her recover, but not for long.

Her mouth is warm, wet. Perfect.

"Suck my *cock*," I moan as she swirls her tongue around my length before flicking the underside of the head.

Her smart mouth is talented as I begin to thrust, shallowly at first. Cheeks hollowing, she sucks me with the perfect pressure as I withdraw.

She drives me wild as my hands find her hair, guiding her bobbing head into the perfect rhythm. Grabbing onto the back of my thighs, she relaxes, letting me use her for my pleasure.

Grunting, I thrust over and over.

"That's right, baby. You're so good at this. You're perfect."

She looks up at me from her knees and I'm only a few moments away from coming.

"Do you want me to come down your throat? Are you going to drink me down like the good girl you are?" I ask.

She nods and I feel my orgasm climb. Grunting as I keep moving, one of her hands moves to my balls, fondling them. As with her mouth, her movements have the perfect amount of pressure and before I know it, I'm coming so hard, I see stars.

My orgasm splashes against the shower wall as I call out for Charlie, wishing she was really here, her name on my tongue every morning since week five when she invaded my brain for the first time as I pleasured myself.

Breathing heavily, I finish my shower before turning off the water, feeling spent but invigorated. I can hardly wait until Charlie wins this whole thing so I can truly have my way with her every morning.

Running behind, I throw clothes on, thankful for my unofficial uniform.

A car idles for me outside as I pull the door closed behind me, tucking my key into a pocket on my backpack.

"Good morning, George," I say to my driver as I pull open the back door and climb in.

While a large man, George is one of the most unimposing people I've ever met. Always with a soft, kind word, he cares for the people around him. After meeting him for the first time on season four when our normal driver couldn't join us, I told Sheila we would be bringing him back from now on.

"Good morning, Mr. King. Would you like to make a stop for tea this morning?" he asks.

He doesn't only drive me around, as I typically just need to go between the motel and the filming location, but every morning of shooting, he is waiting for me as steady as the sun.

"That would be great, thank you. How's your wife doing?" I ask.

"Oh, she's doing fine. She's started nesting. We have about a month left, so her mother has moved in to help her until I can come home. She sends me pictures every day of whatever she's put together for the baby," he says, in his thick New Orleans accent.

His wife, a California native, convinced him to move there once they found out they were pregnant.

"That sounds nice. As I've told you before, please let Sheila or myself know if you need to leave to go be with her. You'll be compensated regardless."

"Thank you, Sir," he says before fading away into silence.

"Hey George, we are going to make one other pit stop this morning," I tell him, a small smile on my face.

My tea is perfect this morning as I walk into the wranglers' quarters, a book tucked away for Charlie in my bag, making my way to my office. Sheila's assistant, Peggy, cuts me off in the hallway telling me I'm needed.

Turning on my heel, I head to Sheila's space, wrapping a knuckle on the open door.

Barely taking a second to look at me before returning her attention to her screen, she says, "Seven different brands have reached out about their interest in Charlie as a spokesperson this week."

Putting my backpack next to the chair in front of her desk, I take a sip from my cup, trying to hide my smile.

"That's great. Which ones, specifically?"

"The usual, but there's one in there I have a feeling she'll take a particular interest in," she says before finishing her task and turning to me. "Have you talked to Tom Cochran yet?" she asks.

I knew this was coming and I still don't know exactly what my answer is going to be. If this were any other season, or hell, just a few weeks ago, I would have taken this job without a moment's hesitation. But that's all I seem to be doing now. Hesitating.

"Not yet, but it's on my list for the day."

"Good. Make sure it happens. Now, get out and take those with you." She indicates to a stack of papers.

Snatching them up, I make my way to my office.

Each company that is interested in Charlie has provided a breakdown of what they would like to partner with her for and the various different things based on how far she makes it for the last few weeks. As a winner, she stands to gain a substantial uptick in money for each of these deals. I look through them until I come to the second to last one, a large smile taking over my face.

While Charlie can take a combination of any of these deals or none at all, I know of at least one she will be signing on for.

Charlie has the papers laid out around her on the floor of the interview room with my gift tucked in her lap. She gave me a deep kiss for the new pirate book I found for her. It's one Lorelei had told me about from her book club and I thought Charlie would enjoy it.

Various notes are scribbled in the margins of all the different deals as she weighs the pros and cons of each brand based on when she leaves the game.

"You don't have to choose right now," I remind her. "You'll want to talk to your attorney about them before you sign anything." After an hour of muttering to herself, she doesn't seem any closer to a decision.

She twists her hair up, sticking my pen through the strands, pinning them in place.

"I think I have them ranked from most enticing to least," she says, a slightly deranged look in her eyes.

For a moment, I take her in and I see the weight of worry she is carrying. Tucking my phone away in my pocket I squat down in front of her, moving her papers so I don't mess them up.

"Hey," I say, lifting her chin so she looks at me, "all of these are good deals. But I have one you're going to like even better. I wanted you to give the other ones a fair shot before I showed you."

Reaching over, I pull the final offer out from my back pocket. She snatches it from my hands and I watch her read it.

She tucks a stray strand of hair behind her ear and suddenly I'm in my house. She sits on the couch engrossed in a book as the sun is setting through the windows, the ocean glinting like diamonds. I come home, but she doesn't notice, so ensnared by the world within the pages. We would talk about our days, cook dinner together, and then make love unhurriedly before finally drifting off to sleep.

The vision is so vivid I'm disoriented coming back to the current moment as she squeals.

"They would pay me to sample their coffee and try to get people to buy it? What a dream."

She hugs the offer to her chest, seeming much lighter than she was only moments ago.

"Basically." My fingers twitch as I try to ignore the impulse to touch her. "Can I kiss you?"

Her arms drop and she looks at me, a sexy little smirk on her mouth.

"You never need to ask," she says, reaching out to me.

Her lips are soft, intoxicating, and I sink deeper, willing to drown in this woman.

CHAPTER THIRTY-SIX

CHARLIE

THE DRESSING ROOM IS quiet as I struggle with the tight purple spandex. I jump, trying to pull the material up over my ass. Slipping my arms through the straps, I notice the giant "C" in the middle of my chest. Less physical challenges allow for production to dress us up in more fun outfits and this one is definitely my favorite. Grabbing the cape off my wardrobe and affixing it to the Velcro on the straps of my suit, I look in the mirror and laugh.

Everyone turns to me, checking out my outfit before shifting their attention back to their own wardrobe.

There's less friendly ribbing now as we get ready for the competition. With only three more elimination challenges, including this one, we are starting to see the light at the end of the tunnel. The half million dollars is becoming much more real. Half of those of us remaining will be in the finale. No one will admit it, but we all watch the others wondering who it'll be.

I'm spending more and more time taking notes of the various things I see and hear from other contestants in my notebook. Each night, I also open to a random page and try to memorize everything on the page for the last competition.

One day, at the very beginning, we all talked about what we would do if we won the game as we got dressed.

"I would pay off my student loans," Jayden says, uncharacteristically going first.

"That's so boring," Penelope says, rolling her eyes.

"Most people would probably do something similar. I would take myself and my Byron on a nice little vacation and then set the grandbabies up for their future," Sharon says.

"Is Byron your husband?" Mary Ella asks, holding her hand over her heart. If she was any more earnest, I'd think it was a farce. But I believe she really is just naive.

"Byron is my Schnauzer."

"Oh," Mary Ella responds, her face falling with disappointment, causing us all to laugh.

"I would finally get started on my car collection. A 1969 Ford Mustang Mach. 1 would be first on that list," Lucas says, jumping in. Everyone just looks around like we know what that means.

Keith speaks up in the silence. "I'm going to build my wife her dream home. She has always wanted a greenhouse with a view of our land and I would want to give that to her. I'll build her that and fill it with every plant she could want."

"Well, I want a vaginal rejuvenation," Penelope says.

"What the hell is a vaginal rejuvenation?" Keith asks.

My eyes glaze over after about twenty minutes of talking about vaginas and the various ways they can be rejuvenated. I was never self-conscious about my vagina before, but now I'm reconsidering.

"Have you heard of any of this?" I ask Raven, who is sitting next to me as we pull on our socks and shoes.

"Oh, yeah, hasn't everyone?" she asks, sarcastically.

"I have never once thought about the length of my pussy lips, but what if every partner I've had has noticed it? What if they are abnormally long? Maybe I should make an appointment when I get home."

"I'd be happy to take a look for you later, if you want," Lucas says, leaning over from my other side. He gives me what I believe he thinks of as a devilish smile but looks more like he's trying not to be sick after taking a shot with his friends.

"I'm gonna pass on that."

"Why don't you try Penelope? Apparently, she has a lot of thoughts on the status of her vagina," Raven says to him.

"I have a lot of thoughts on the status of your vagina," he replies.

"What about the status of my fist in your face?"

"You can't punch an Olympic athlete," he says, affronted.

"Twenty bucks says you're wrong," Raven says, and I know she will do it if she senses a microsecond's hesitation.

My attention is called back to the group as Colyn, sweet, shy Colyn says, "I am going to buy a monster truck and run over my car. I'll probably have an orgasm while doing it, too. That stupid POS has broken down on me for the last time."

The murderous look in her eye lets us know she's not joking.

A large screen has been moved into the living room for today's challenge. Currently, we only see the back of large playing cards. At the beginning of the game, I used to wonder about what was in store, but there have been so many things production has come up with I never would have thought of, I quickly gave up.

"Welcome to the week nine elimination challenge!" Jacob Jacobson calls out. His suit today is sky blue with a bright red tie and white shirt. It gives me a headache, but it's tame in comparison to his normal wear.

I wonder idly if he learned the inflections he uses every time he talks to us from some acting class and never took the time to make them more believable. It's like a robot was told what feelings are, but since it has never actually felt them, they can only make hollow mimicries.

One of our favorite pastimes in the house is to use our best Jacob voices.

"This week our theme is superpowers! You have all been dressed as superheroes to match your superhero comic!"

The cards on the screen turn over and there we are, forever memorialized on what look to be covers for six different comics. While Cain doesn't have to play due to his immunity from last week, they still drew him.

The faces of the cards are all relatively busy and it's difficult to distinguish one from another. I search for mine and there I am, a purple suit and mask hiding my identity. I'm flying above a city with my red hair fluttering behind me. I smile. No wonder Alec randomly asked me what kind of superpower I wanted last week.

"My dearest deceivers, this game is a challenge to your memory. The person to match all the cards the fastest will win"—the light changes and Jacob puts on his ominous tone—"while the bottom two will be on the chopping block.

"Earlier in the day, the remaining house guests drew the order they would go in this challenge. Parker, you're first."

Parker steps up to the screen and waits for the bell. His blue suit is almost indecent and I have no doubt the viewers at home are going crazy. He hears the sound and leaps into action, flipping the top card on both rows making note of the cards displayed. He moves on to the second card in the top row, realizes they don't match either of the others and flips the second on the bottom row next. He moves down the rows methodically, matching the cards quickly.

I was never particularly good at matching games when I was younger. For some reason, my eyes don't pick up patterns without taking my time.

Rebel steps up in her orange suit and readies for her turn. This time, when the cards flip, the scenes depicted are the same, but who is in what pose has changed. She moves through the rows of cards but with less of a plan and makes her matches. Parker remains in the lead with Rebel a good ten seconds behind. Red-suited Penelope follows and easily beats Rebel.

With sweaty palms and weak knees, I step up to the screen and follow Parker's lead, however, I can feel I'm not moving fast enough. The changing poses are messing me up as I try to determine my matches. I make a few quickly, but I know I've not beaten Penelope or Parker. I make my last match and step back. Only two seconds before Rebel with Jayden to go.

My eyes don't leave Jayden as he moves with startling efficiency through the board. Without missing a trick, every match he makes, I can feel the possibility of going home creeping up in my chest. As he finishes his round, I look at the flashing time. One tenth of a second secures Parker's win.

But I'm in the bottom two. On the chopping block. In less than forty-eight hours, I could go home.

Ending all the hard work Alec and I have put in to get me here.

Two mugs steam in my hands as I make my way out to the pool deck where Parker sits beneath the dawn sky. The breeze caresses my skin as I set the coffee on the table beside him.

He looks up at me, shutting the book he was reading.

"Can I sit?" I ask.

"Always. You know you have my vote, right?"

Alec and I assumed his vote was in the bag, but having confirmation is always nice, and I tell him as much. We sit in silence, letting the sun rise as we drink our coffee. Unwilling to take the liquid for granted ever again, I sip slowly, savoring every drop.

"Cain is definitely never going to vote for me, same with Penelope, so my only hope is the audience wants to keep me more than Rebel."

"I believe in you," he says, as he gathers his blond hair and ties it up off his neck.

I fiddle with the edge of my shorts, pulling at loose strings. Thoughts of my family swirl in my mind now that I might be seeing them within a few days. If I'm being honest with myself, I never expected to last this long.

"Do you ever want to quit?" I ask, voicing something I haven't told Alec has crossed my mind.

"Not really, no." He sits and waits, letting me choose if I want to go deeper into this conversation or not.

"It's a lot, the competitions and being recorded all the time. All of it. It's a lot and we've been here two and a half months. I'm just ready to go home. I miss my parents and Courtney." I pause, weighing the options. "But I like spending time with my wrangler," I tell him.

Searching my face, I see the moment when he catches my meaning.

"Yeah, it's definitely hard. The relationships we've built in this house are unlike anything we'll ever find again. But you'll stay connected when you leave." He nudges my knee with his foot, making me recoil. He laughs at my disgusted facial expression, feet being my least favorite part of the body. "Guess we should go talk to Jayden, try to deepen some bonds."

The past two days have been mentally exhausting trying to secure enough votes to make it into week ten, but the relief of making it through the elimination makes me all but skip to the interview room for my standing Sunday night interview. I need to unpack my clothes, but it can wait until I've had a chance to let the hyperactivity from surviving for another week wear off. All the energy is also keeping the sadness of Rebel going home at bay. For now.

Plus, my lips are dying to be on Alec's once more.

Alec and I have been cautious; worried someone would find out about us. We kept our interviews over the past few days short and to the point. There was some kissing and touching, but nothing like in the library.

Alec is sitting in his chair with a dark smile on his face. I walk to him, kissing him hello.

"We will do something a little different for our interview today."

"Oh, okay," I say. The anticipation of what's coming makes my hands shake. "What are we going to do?"

"Come over here," he demands.

"Why?"

His eyes are dark. No humor. Nothing of the soft man I've found beneath the hard exterior.

"Don't make me tell you again, Charlotte." His stern tone makes my pussy pulse with lust. I stand up and move toward him slowly, kicking off my shoes as I move. I stay standing, waiting for him to instruct me.

"Straddle me." That's a command I'm happy to follow. Putting my legs on either side of his, I settle onto his lap.

I want to push, to ask questions, but I want to see where this is going to go. Scott was never a demanding lover. We always had sex, in our bed, and only before we were both turned in for the night.

There was no spontaneity. No *need* to be on each other.

With Alec there is nothing but need.

He pushes the skirt of my dress up, holding it at my hips.

"Take my dick out," he says, his eyes fixed on the growing wet spot between my legs, my arousal soaking the fabric. "You're such a good girl."

Pride lights my chest. I love being his good girl. I love his filthy mouth. I was never one for dirty talk. It always felt so artificial and took me out of the moment. But with Alec, it sounds natural. Alluring. I want to be his. For him to own me and make me beg for his cock. I want *him* and everything he is.

Rubbing the bead of pre-cum on his tip, I slide my hand up and down his length as soon as I have him free. Taking his finger, he traces the edge of my lace panties, before yanking them to the side.

"Take me, Charlotte," he demands.

Desire coursing through me, I rub myself up his length, swallowing his moan as I fuse our lips together. My patience disappears like morning mist being burned away by the sun and I take control.

With no build up, I slam myself down on his cock.

"Fuck, Charlie," he moans as I take his lips in a rough kiss.

I ride him hard and fast, chasing my climax. I'm mindless, riding him desperately until I come with a shout. The orgasm barely takes the edge off my need. I climb off of him and pull him out of the chair before pushing him down to the ground.

"Little desperate, are we?" he says, cocky as all hell, but I don't care.

All I can think about is how much I need him again.

"This is your fault."

I mount him again, this time backward. He slaps my ass, driving me harder. As I slam myself on his cock over and over again, his grunts below me are delicious and I eat them up.

"Charlie, I'm going to come," he says seconds before I feel him spill his seed inside me. I ride him through his orgasm until I find my own.

Rolling off of him, I lie panting on the ground beside him.

"Wow," he says simply and we both laugh. "We should probably talk about how to keep you from the bottom two going forward."

We both sit up and arrange our clothes, once more back in the game.

WEEK TEN

CHAPTER THIRTY-SEVEN

ALEC

I watch as Parker and Charlie run on the treadmills. Sweat rolls down her back, her sports bra doing nothing to cover her glistening skin. My mouth waters at the thought of her riding me with equal fervor. My pants tighten as I consider releasing the pressure. My phone dings as I unbuckle my belt. Pausing, I grab it up off my desk.

My office. Now.

Shoving my chair back, I leave my office, my lust dying as my heart starts galloping on my way to Sheila's office. Her assistant is standing beside her closed door, tapping away on the tablet in her hands.

"Hey, I was summoned?" I ask, the formality kicking off alarm bells in my head.

She nods before knocking as she opens the door. "Mr. King is here to see you."

"Send him in."

She moves out of my way and I walk into the room, my stride stuttering as I see one of the attorneys from when we had to determine if Charlie was going to stay in the competition or not. He pushes his glasses up his nose.

"Alec, take a seat."

"What's going on, Sheila?" I start sweating as I try not to squirm under her stern gaze.

"This is a yes or no question. I expect to hear nothing beyond one of those words come out of your mouth. Do you understand me?"

"Yes."

"Did you enter the house?"

"Yes."

"Did you have sex with Charlie Price?"

My heart stops beating. I consider lying but know it will do me no good. She wouldn't be asking this question if she didn't know the answer.

"Yes."

Sheila looks toward the attorney and I see the death of the career I've always wanted.

"Larry, what are the repercussions? Could we be sued? Does she need to be expelled from the competition?"

He pushes his glasses up his nose again, scooting to the front of his chair. Horror that my actions could ruin everything Charlie has worked for takes over. She is mere days from the finale and my inability to remain professional might make her lose this show.

"There is no rule in the contract that a contestant can't have sexual relations with someone on the show. It does not specify that would exclude members of production. As such, Ms. Price has done nothing wrong and can stay on the show. The goal is to keep this under wraps since it was obvious the"—he clears his throat and straightens his tie—"*activities* were consensual."

Relief that she is safe washes over me as my brain catches on one of Larry's words.

"What does he mean 'obvious'?" I ask Sheila.

"Alec, you couldn't think we wouldn't show the event to the attorneys who are charged with protecting not just your ass, but this show's!"

"That was a private moment—"

"That was in front of at least three different cameras!" she says, slamming her hand down on her desk. Flames of anger flicker in her eyes as she stares me down, daring me to speak again. "If you wanted to keep it private, you never should have done it." She turns back to Larry. "Do I need to fire Alec?"

Until this moment, I was more worried about what our actions would mean for Charlie, but now I go cold as if plunged into the ice-covered waters of the Arctic. Sheila says it with no emotion, yet I feel every emotion in the matter of seconds before my brain shuts down. Larry's response sounds far away.

"We reviewed the employment contract Alec, and all the wranglers, signed at the beginning of production. While you can fire any of them for no reason at all, there is not an explicit rule stating they are not allowed to have a relationship with a contestant."

I begin counting, something I started doing in moments of stress when I was a teenager at the suggestion of the therapist from freshman year of college.

One.

Two.

Three.

"There is a clause," he starts. *Four. Five. Six.* "About professional conduct and we believe any judge would agree sexual misconduct, even consensual, would not be considered professional. It's our opinion that legally, you can fire Mr. King and he would not be able to sue for wrongful termination."

Sheila raises her hand as Larry goes to continue, but he quickly snaps his mouth shut.

"I've already heard all of that. I knew I could fire you before I called you in here. Do you know why I wanted you to hear that?"

"No," I say, sticking with her original direction of sticking to yes or no answers.

"I wanted you to hear that so you will accept the deal I'm about to offer you."

"Price, to the interview room," I say over the in-house speakers.

I pace the room as I wait for her to join me. My fingers run through my hair multiple times, messing it up. Footsteps echo outside the room right before the door bursts open. Charlie smiles and launches herself in my arms. I hold her up for longer than necessary, relishing the feel of her against me.

My hands tangle in her hair as I press my lips to hers, drinking down her taste like a man in the desert getting a drink of water for the first time. Her hands fall to my hips as she pulls me flush against her. She runs her hands up my chest, warmth trailing behind her path, reaching up to unbutton my shirt.

Reluctantly, I pull away from her and stop her hands from their task.

"Charlie, wait."

I grab her wrists and push her off me. Inside, my heart cracks open as I see the hesitation in her eyes.

"We need to talk," I tell her.

"I assumed since you called me in here, but we can talk in a minute," she says standing on her tiptoes, closing her eyes to kiss me again. I pull back until she opens them and looks at me.

"No, we need to talk first."

"Is everything okay?" I can see her nerves in her movements as she goes to sit in her normal chair.

I slide into the wrangler personality I have worn every other season with every other contestant I've been in charge of.

"It's time to end this. It's not you, it's me." I hear the void of emotion in my voice. "It wouldn't be beneficial if our relationship got out. There's more at stake here. People will think we cheated, and I don't need my reputation tarnished. Plus, brands wouldn't want to work with someone embroiled in scandal." Part of me prays she can read me well enough to know every piece of me is fighting to be with her even as I purposely break her heart.

She scoffs. "You did not, seriously, just say that to me. Don't act like this is to protect me. You've been using me this entire time. You just wanted your shot at directing."

"I was offered an incredible opportunity and I don't need you anymore," I continue.

I cross my arms over my chest, creating space between us, silently begging her to fight me. To call me on my bullshit and see I'm trying to protect her. That everything I'm doing is for her. But her face falls and I know that's not the case.

CHAPTER THIRTY-EIGHT

CHARLIE

M Y CONFRONTATION WITH CAIN comes back to my mind, and I realize it now.

He was right.

Alec was hiding this from me, and I never bothered to ask him if it was true when Cain told me about it.

I berate myself for ever believing what Alec was saying. He has always been honest about needing me to make his career dreams come true. Why would I ever think anything would change? That he wouldn't jump on a chance if it was presented to him?

That I mattered to him.

"I'm sorry. It was fun while it lasted," he adds, another stab to my heart.

As he crushes my soul, I realize I love this man.

"Stop," I whisper.

My shoulders collapse inward as I hug myself. I look at his cold, gray eyes as he stares me down without a hint of emotion. The Alec I met during my promotional photo shoot is the Alec sitting before me right now. Not the man who has a sister he's crazy about. Not the one who had his mom kiss his scraped knee when he fell out of his tree house. Not the one who built that tree house with his dad and split a root beer with him over a job well done.

As my heart breaks, I choose to feel numb. Alec King has gotten my smiles and my laughs. He's gotten my love, but he'll not get to see a single tear. He won't get a single moment of my sadness.

I sit up straight and look him dead on.

"So, what happens now? Do I get a new wrangler? We only have two weeks left at this point. Will I just share a wrangler with someone?"

Alec seems a bit taken aback by my straightforward questions.

"You'll be assigned the wrangler of whomever is eliminated this week. Jayden and Penelope's wranglers are both great at their jobs. You will hardly realize I'm gone."

"No problem," I say, waving away his words. He could not be more wrong.

I will know every second he's not here with me.

"This is for the best, Charlie. It's better to end it now, before anyone finds out. I'm doing this for you."

My body moves without a conscious choice from me and I stand from my chair.

"All right, well, if that's all, I'm going to get back to Parker."

I see the sting of my words landing, his jealousy over our closeness never fully put to rest, but I don't care.

"Charlie," he calls out as my hand touches the doorknob. "I really am sorry. I'll—," he cuts himself off. My brain imagines his voice breaking.

"Sure. Good luck, by the way. You deserve it." I pull the door open and walk out of the room, proud my voice never shook with the emotion flowing through me.

My feet carry me back down to the gym where I throw myself into the rest of my workout. Seeing that Parker left all the equipment set with the appropriate weight for me, I settle myself onto the bench, taking the barbell into my hands. Pushing out the various repetitions, tears leak from my eyes. Racking the weights, I sit up, shoving my fist against my lips, silencing the sobs my broken heart is crying.

Hurt threatens to crush me as I yell silently into the void. The knife of Alec's words has cut my heart into bloody ribbons. But why would he stay? Scott's words in his letter come back to me.

"I need someone that has drive."

Alec has drive. He wants something from his life. He has dreams and goals. What do I want? To make my rent. That's not passion. He needs someone who understands, who can push him to be better, support him. And what do I have to offer?

Nothing.

When I'm done with the routine and my muscles are jelly, I make my way to the showers, stripping out of my sweaty clothes and climbing in to wash everything away.

Moving into the closet, I rip the top drawer open of my assigned dresser. The first thing I see is the onesie Alec gave me. Snatching it up, I throw it behind me before I grab up the next set that touches my hands.

Crawling into my own bed, I pull the covers up above my head, shivering without the added warmth of my gifted pajamas, and let tears silently run down my face. This will be the only time I allow myself to cry so freely about all the promises he gave me. All the hopes and dreams.

Tonight is for wallowing. Tomorrow will be for getting my head back into the game.

CHAPTER THIRTY-NINE

ALEC

IGNORING EVERYONE WHO TRIES to stop me for some inane thing or another, I make my way to my office, grabbing my few personal belongings and shoving them into my bag.

Pulling my phone from my pocket, I text George, asking him to pull the car around. Reliable as the phases of the moon, he's there waiting as I step from the mansion.

"Hello, sir. Where to?" George asks, ever the professional.

"Back to the motel, please." I can hear the lack of emotion in my voice, but there's nothing I can do about it. As Charlie walked out the door, it felt like Death itself stopped my heart in my chest.

"It's great you're getting an early start to your evening. You've been working like crazy this season, Mr. King."

I was working crazy hours because I wanted to be near her. In case she needed me. So I could see her.

He continues talking about small things, but I don't respond. It's as if I'm frozen in the back of this car, unable to move. My phone vibrates in my pocket and I consider throwing the device from the car but my finger swipes, answering the call of its own volition.

"Tom, how are you?" I say, putting on my wrangler voice, the only thing I can fall back on to appear calm.

"Alec, my boy, good to talk to you. Sheila rang me last night that you'd be joining my production and you were able to get your schedule worked out. I wanted to call you myself and welcome you to the production! My assistant is working on the details of how to get you out here. She should have them for you in about an hour."

Realization that she knew she was going to fire me for longer than she let on sets in but I don't let it take over. Settling into emotionlessness.

"That's perfect, thank you so much for being flexible. I really appreciate the opportunity."

"Of course! I've worked my entire career to be able to be flexible. See you on set tomorrow."

He hangs up the phone and my hand drops back down to my lap.

I want to be excited. I want to be happy. I want to feel triumphant for finally beating the odds and getting the shot I've always wanted.

But Charlie's face as I broke her heart, the shattered pieces of what we could have been littering the interview room floor, smothers every other feeling.

WEEK ELEVEN

CHAPTER FORTY

CHARLIE

THE MANSION FEELS CAVERNOUS with only four people.

"Charlie Price, to the interview room, please."

I put my coffee cup down and make my way through the house. The idea of going to the interview without Alec waiting inside for me rips my heart to shreds. Penelope always mentioned she enjoyed her wrangler, but it will never be the same.

As I weave through the labyrinth of the mansion, I wonder how many contestants are still close with their wrangler. Or do they all have to cut the cord to be there for their new charge? To not take work home, so to speak. Alec had mentioned previously he was not in contact with any of his previous charges. I always felt a glow of smugness when he'd tell me this. I knew I would be different. I knew he wouldn't be able to leave me behind.

I was stupid for thinking it ever meant anything at all.

The woman sitting inside the room is tiny, with gray hair and sharp eyes. Her face is welcoming, but I know it won't make a difference. This woman didn't choose me. She was assigned. And that makes all the difference.

"Hi Charlie, I'm Martha. It's a pleasure to meet you in person. Penelope only ever had good things to say about you."

I sit down on the comfortable chair and stare her down as she tries to become my friend.

"No, she didn't. Why would she? We weren't particularly close and she started drama all the time," I contest.

She smiles at me sheepishly. "I didn't want to hurt your feelings."

"So, you lied to me? Not a very good first impression, Martha." I tsk.

Her expression changes from affable grandma to savvy wrangler.

"Oh, I'm sure Alec liked you very much. No one would have ever been brave enough to give him shit, but I have a feeling you did."

"Why did you call me in here?"

I wasn't going to talk about Alec with this woman. I wasn't going to talk about Alec with anyone. He was mine. Everything that was aired from this room was made for the audience. We had worked hard at cultivating my image. I trusted him, with more than just how I was being portrayed to the people at home. But I don't trust her.

"I just wanted to introduce myself and say hi. I have skimmed through your released footage and I see the angle Alec was taking and I figure I'll continue with it. Everyone loves a girl next door they think they have a chance with. No need to change anything in the eleventh hour."

"If that's all," I stand.

"It's not." I don't sit back down and just stare at her, hoping she'll balk. "Sit." She points a finger at the chair.

I don't take commands from anyone but Alec.

My stubbornness must be written on my face because she quickly changes tactics, softening.

"Charlie, please. We have to work together. We are going to have to see each other every single day for, hopefully, another week beyond this one. Please, sit?"

"What is it? I would like to get back to the house."

"Sure thing. I'll make this quick." She gives up and stands, tucking her hands in her pockets. "I don't care that you'd prefer Alec, a lot of women would. From now until you leave this house, I am your wrangler and even though I didn't pick you, I want you to understand I support you a hundred percent. Anything you need, I'm here to help. You don't have to be my friend. You don't have to like me, but it would do you some good to have someone to talk to. That's what I'm offering here."

"I'm good. See you at our next interview."

I don't need Alec.

I *certainly* don't need Martha.

All I'll ever need, all I've ever needed, I realize, is me.

I walk to the door to make my way back into the house as Martha calls out once more.

"Snuggle with Parker some today! Everyone is eating it up!"

That's the last thing I want to do, but I still have a game to play.

The happiness that permeated my days of the past few weeks has taken a nosedive. Parker has noticed, and I'm sure he has a guess, but he hasn't forced me to talk. I know he's here for me if I need him, but this is something I want to process on my own.

Parker and I are sitting in the living room with my feet on his lap. His strong fingers rub my arches and I try not to moan out loud. Cain stomps through the room as he makes his way to the kitchen. He seems even more furious every time he sees me the past few days. I would care, since he never seems entirely stable to me, but with a broken heart, I just don't have it in me.

"Do you realize this time next week, we could be walking out of this house for the last time?" I ask Parker.

"How does that make you feel?" He holds his thumb against a pressure point before moving up to my ankles.

"It feels surreal. And surprisingly, a little sad. Obviously, I'm going to miss seeing you every day, but everything is easier here. I don't have to think about bills or work. Or how I don't own a couch. I'm going to miss that simplicity."

"What's the first thing you're going to do when you leave here? Other than buy a couch, because we've talked about that every week," he jokes.

"I am going to go home and dance around the living room naked. Or just sit in complete silence and enjoy being the only person in my living space for the first time in three months. What are you going to do?"

"I'm going to sell my company and all of my stuff and move somewhere that isn't saturated in memories. Maybe a new state entirely."

"Well, you'll always have a friend in North Carolina if you choose to move there."

"I'll keep that in mind," he says, smiling.

I take my feet out of his grip and turn to hang my head off of the couch, my legs in the air where my head should be. Molly and I would sit like this most days. There's something about looking at the world upside down that we enjoyed.

"Are you ready for the final competition?" I ask. "Court and I were always impressed with how much people could remember."

"My journal is full to the brim." Jayden stands up from the chair in the corner.

I jump as he startles me, throwing off my weight. My legs fall into Parker's head and I kick him in the face. I try to get my feet to the ground and they land in Parker's lap as I slide to the ground. He gasps as my feet connect with what feels like his balls. He grabs his junk and pushes my legs off him as he curls into a loose ball.

I untangle myself from the heap I landed in on the floor.

"When did you get in here?" I ask Jayden. "Are you okay?" I say, turning to Parker who flashes me a thumbs up but retches.

"I've been here the entire time. I was sitting here when you two walked in." He looks at me with observant eyes and for the first time I feel like I see him. "You'd be surprised at how easily you're overlooked if you don't appear confident and capable. But I made it here. And I'm going to win."

He closes his book and leaves the room. I look back at Parker who is finally breathing evenly again.

"This is going to be interesting," Parker says.

I never viewed Jayden as a real threat, but he's right. I can only imagine the things he's privy to.

"To say the least."

We stand outside in all-black outfits as Jacob Jacobson explains the final elimination challenge we have to survive to make it into the final three. There is no immunity here. We all must compete. The top two will move on to week twelve. The bottom two will have to pray for salvation with votes.

Black cloths cover the four tables, one for each of us, while ropes hang down from above. The ropes are on pulleys, one for our left hand and one for the right.

The goal is to get our ball through the maze, avoiding the holes throughout that can drop our balls, forcing us to start over. The covers whoosh as they are pulled from the boxes. We have twenty seconds to look at the mazes and plot our course before the timer begins.

I make a mental map. While speed is important in this game, control is going to be the difference between winning and losing.

"Contestants, step onto your podiums." We follow Jacob's instruction and I block out everything.

No one else is here.

There are no cameras on me.

Alec does not exist.

The last one is harder, but I do it. This is for me. This entire game, I've worked to prove I could get to this point. That I deserved to be here despite the mix-up.

That I'm capable on my own.

As I ready myself, I can almost hear Courtney saying, "*You got this, Charles,*" to the TV.

Airhorn sounding, I grab onto the ropes and test them as we were not told how to control the board.

Pulling both ropes down at the same time tilts the board away from me. Releasing them both tilts it toward me. And then, of course, pulling one side only pulls that side up.

Cain's ball has already fallen out of one of the holes and he has started over. Always quick to bull rush ahead in games of finesse or patience, he typically doesn't do as well.

I pull both of my ropes, tilting the box away from me and pushing my ball into the maze.

Left.

Right.

Straight.

Back just a little.

Left.

Left again.

On and on it carves its way through as I move with slow, purposeful movements.

Cain's ball drops through again and the string of curses will require a lot of bleeping for it to be shown to the audience.

I hit a long, straight stretch, but the hole in the middle only allows for the ball to skirt along one side and bypass it. Not wanting to start over, I pull and release my ropes inch by inch, my ball crawling down the path.

Parker curses, pulling my attention for a moment, as his ball drops from the bottom.

As I go to turn back to my table, Jayden's lights up in green.

He's finished.

He made it to the final three. The boy that has been in the middle of the pack or just above the bottom two the entire game, is the first into the finale.

I block everything out once more.

Making the final few turns, my ball slides over the finish line, the table lighting up green milliseconds before Cain's.

I did it.

My hands come up covering my face as tears start streaming down it.

I'm in the finale.

Cain explodes from his chair, snapping. "You've got to be fucking kidding me!"

"I'm sorry, Cain, but the votes have been tallied. Parker will be continuing on into the finale. I'm sure the disappointment you're feeling is intense right now, but you have been eliminated from *House of Deceit*. Please exit the mansion," Jacob Jacobson says.

The TV he was on goes black as, I assume, they have moved on to other announcements for the show.

"You shouldn't be here!" he says pointing at me. "I thought you'd get tossed with the tape!"

"What t—"

I don't get to finish my sentence as he lunges at me, grabbing my arms and shaking me.

"You should have been eliminated, you stupid bitch! I should be in the final three!"

My teeth rattle as it feels like my brain is being slammed around inside my skull. I'm shoved down to the ground, my shoulder slamming down.

I hear the sound of flesh on flesh as Parker punches Cain in the face. The room is flooded with production assistants helping him to secure the incensed Cain. Parker comes over to me and tucks my hair behind my ear.

"Are you hurt? We can get medical in here."

"No," I say, brushing his hand off my face. "I'm fine. Thanks for having my back, even though I wish it could have been me to punch him."

He laughs as Jayden, Parker, and I are ushered to the kitchen so everyone can focus on Cain.

Cain is watched the entire time while he packs his things to leave the mansion. He yells from the dressing room, outrage and insult dripping off every word, but we ignore him.

"Look at us," Jayden says, smiling. "We are the final three."

Parker and I smile at each other. "Holy shit." I say and we all start giggling.

Production ushers Cain out of the mansion. "You shouldn't be here, bitch! They said you'd be disqualified. You shouldn't be here!" He tries lunging at me again, but this time the assistants are ready and block him.

"What the hell is he talking about? Why would you be disqualified?" Parker asks.

"Hell if I know," I lie, not wanting the story of my heartbreak to be headline fodder, "but thankfully I'm still here."

WEEK TWELVE
THE FINALE

CHAPTER FORTY-ONE

ALEC

"WHICH ONE DID YOU like?" Tom asks, stabbing his salad.

The sun is warm against my skin, but I feel cold. Every time I think of Charlie, which is every second of every day, I miss her. I can hardly sleep at the thought of her in the mansion without me. Of never seeing her again.

"The one with black hair has the most on-camera potential. If you get her a few acting classes to tighten up that thing with her voice when she has to do serious lines, crowds will love her. She has that spark," I tell him, without any feeling.

"Hmm, I was thinking the blonde had a bit more of a camera presence," he says.

The birds chirp around us. Our table is secluded from the remainder of the alfresco diners. I take a bite of my perfectly prepared chicken and mull over his comment. Washing it down with a sip of the wine Tom had insisted on, I look out at the park.

"She does, but she only has one facet and eventually the audience will be bored with that."

"We'll bring them both back for a second round of auditions. Make a note, will you?"

His words register through the haze in my brain and I pull out my phone, immediately typing into my ever-present list.

"You've got it."

"I will say, you have an amazing eye for talent. I never would have looked twice at that kid, the one you picked for the male lead, but he really is perfect."

"Part of picking a contestant to back for *House of Deceit* is knowing when someone can not only win the competition, but do the infinitely harder job of winning the audience. It takes a specific type of person." I tuck my phone away once I have all the notes he needs typed out.

He continues eating his salad and we both sit in our own thoughts. I look at my watch and think through where Charlie will be on the last day of the game. I've watched every episode since my departure, unable to go without seeing her if I have the opportunity. The tortured look in her eyes breaks my heart, but I know I did the right thing for her. And for my career, if not for my heart.

On the last day in the mansion, the final three contestants are separated and won't see each other until they complete the final challenge, live. The last episode is around three hours long with various interviews of eliminated contests and clips of the final three leading into the challenge. And ends with the crowning of the winner.

In my mind's eye, I can see Charlie pacing her room as she waits for the final challenge.

"I'm glad you were able to come on board, my boy. Sheila was right about everything she said," Cochran says, breaking me out of my thoughts of Charlie. "I was a little surprised when she called to tell me your availability changed."

"Yes, finding someone to take over that I thought could do a great job for my contestant was important, but I would have been crazy to turn this opportunity down. Changing a wrangler so late in the game could derail someone. I had to weigh my commitment to the person I chose against my career. I'm glad it worked out."

"Who did you pick?"

"Charlie Price."

"Oh, yes, she's great. Very charismatic and quite easy on the eyes," he wiggles his bushy eyebrows at me.

"Yes, she is," I chuckle.

"Her loss is my gain. But I hope she wins. My sister and I love the show. We always watch *House of Deceit*. My wife hates reality television, but we seemed to bond over it immediately when my Bonnie introduced us. Every year it feels like we have a new show to watch."

"That must be why you were so willing to interview me. I've found my resume gives people pause when it comes to 'real' shows and movies."

He waves his hand in the air.

"Bah. I never believe in any of that. If you have the instincts, that's what really matters. You can't teach that. Sheila said you're the best wrangler she's ever had. How your contestants always go to the final. She told me your last few and I watched some of their seasons and they always seemed to be the best on camera. I saw how their storylines always highlighted their strengths even if they were a little lackluster. I thought, 'If he can pick someone like that out of a stack of applications, he has the eye to bring a vision to life.'"

"I appreciate you taking the chance on me," I tell him sincerely. I might be upset I had to leave Charlie, but I am getting a chance at my dream. One that I can't let my heartache ruin.

"You should go," he says.

"Go? Go where?"

"Go back to the hotel. Watch the show. We don't have much else happening today now that these auditions are done. And here soon I'll be calling my sister-in-law to watch the finale together. You should go. Get settled in early and see if your horse wins the race."

"I would hate to leave you without help for the day," I tell him, but my heart isn't in it. I want to watch Charlie. I want to soak in every second of the last time I'll get to see her live.

"You think you're the only person who can help me? Please," he jokes. "Plus, if I have to see you mope any more, *I* might jump off a cliff. Go watch your girl."

"How did—"

"I can see love when it's right in front of my face. You look how I felt when I was stupid enough to let Bonnie walk away from me for all of a week. I'll tell you this for free. Nothing in my life would mean anything if Bonnie wasn't waiting for me at home. Now get out of here. I'll see you in the morning."

"Thank you, Tom," I say, putting my napkin on the table and standing.

"And kid? Don't wait too long to go back to her. A girl like that? She won't be around forever."

Lorelei is folding the laundry on our video call while I hear Tank scrubbing the bathroom, singing along to his favorite song from the '90s. They could hire help, but they enjoy taking care of their home together.

My TV is on, but muted while we talk, as I wait for the finale to start.

"When's the next time you're going to be home?" she asks.

In a regular year of filming, I would be going home tomorrow. The wranglers party just as hard at the finale as the contestants do. Lorelei and Tank take me out to dinner for a job well done, and then I enjoy six weeks without talking to anyone. Sometimes I'd go to another country and just spend time at the beach.

"There's a break in our schedule in a little under a month. I'll be home then."

"I have someone I want you to meet while you're here since you and Charlie didn't work out. She's smart and funny. A little quirky. Beautiful, of course."

"Lore, I don't want to meet anyone right now. I'm busy with this new job and learning everything I can from Tom."

Her gray eyes get large and a little wet. She knows I'll say yes to anything to keep her from crying. "Well, yeah, I get that. But even when you're busy, you have time to meet people."

I roll my eyes. That's true. I rarely would turn down someone my sister wanted me to meet if for no other reason than to get laid. But since I've met Charlie, I have no desire for anyone else.

"I don't want to just mess around anymore. I want something more, something real. But for right now, can you drop it?" I drag my hand through my rapidly drying hair.

"You fell in love with her, didn't you?" She watches me with knowing eyes.

"I wouldn't say *love*," I hedge.

"I knew it!" She slaps the table she's sitting at. "I fucking told Tank you were in love with Charlie and he swore up, down, and sideways you would never fall for her, but you did! When can I meet her? Even though you fucked it up, do you think she'll go on girls' trips with me? Is she as amazing in real life as she is on the show?" She runs out of breath before I can get a word in edgewise.

Annoyed at the direction of this conversation, I give in so it ends as quickly as possible.

"What makes you think I fucked it up? And she mentioned wanting you to go on a girls' weekend with her and her best friend. And she's even better in real life."

"Because I've met you and sometimes, and I love you, but sometimes you can be an asshole."

"I'm not an asshole!" I smile at the accusation, remembering when Charlie called me the same thing as I worshiped her.

"Remember that time Mom and Dad were out on a date and you were in charge and you threw shoes at me any time I moved from the couch? I almost peed my pants! Only assholes throw their shoes at their precious angel baby little sisters."

"Angel? The girl who let the air out of my tires every week for a month? You wish."

"Pah," she says, swiping a hand through the air. "How about the time I had to tell Dad I was the one that dented his car so he wouldn't kill you?"

"I feel like we are even on that one," I tell her.

"Fine, fine. But seriously, no jokes. Do you want to fix it?"

Charlie's face flashes in my mind, her head resting in my lap as I read to her. My fingers run through her hair as I read the pirate book she selected. She giggles as I try to give the characters different voices. I would feel humiliated if not for her laugh.

Looking down at her, she smiles up at me and the last piece clicks into place.

"I love her. I don't really know when it started, but through our time in the interview room, I fell in love with her. I'm not sure I could want anyone the way I want her. But if it gets out that we are together, with what happened...I had to..." I trail off."I had to. I can't tarnish her reputation. She has brands begging for her to be their spokesperson. If anything came out, and we were together, it could hurt her ability to distance herself from me to save face. I did it for her, Lore."

My voice catches in my throat at the end and I'm afraid I'm going to cry in front of my sister. I don't want her to worry about me and the second she sees tears, she'll be banging down the door of my hotel. I have to keep it together while I'm here.

"Are you going to watch the show tonight?" she asks.

"Yeah, I want to see if she wins," I say, as the opening credits start.

I got to unmute my TV but an unsaved but memorized number pops up on my screen and my heart starts racing.

"Lore, someone's calling me and I have to take this. I'll call you tomorrow. Love you."

I hang up on her before she can respond and accept the new call.

"Did you make it?" I ask, my fingers holding my phone so tightly I'm afraid it'll crack.

CHAPTER FORTY-TWO

CHARLIE

THE SUN IS STARTING to set on the mansion, turning everything to gold like Midas's touch. My green sequin dress glints in the dying light. I try to keep my fidgeting hands away from my 1940s soft waves, much like Molly would wear hers. I feel the heaviness of the eyes of the cameras covering me from every angle. As it's the finale, there are numerous visible cameras set up around us.

Alec's voice comes into my mind and I can almost feel his fingers caressing my cheek.

"*Just you and me,*" he says, the memory of his voice making my heart break all over again.

But I put on the persona he crafted for me. The woman standing here looks calm and poised and not at all like the one of twelve weeks ago who stood in front of this mansion, probably looking nervous and a little nauseated.

But now, I know I can do this.

Jacob Jacobson stands at the host podium beside a giant board with various categories and dollar values. A makeup crew touches up his face with powder in the summer heat.

"We are live in thirty seconds!" a member of production announces over the house's PA system.

Jayden, Parker, and I wait to be called down to our podiums to begin the final trivia competition.

"How are you both feeling?" Parker asks.

His suit is perfectly tailored. The deep blue is beautiful against the crisp white shirt. His hair sits in surfer boy waves.

"I'm ready. This should be easy," Jayden says, smiling at us. The confident man before us is so unlike the one we've spent the last twelve weeks with, I feel like I'm participating in the finale with a stranger.

"I'm excited," I say, but I know he can see the pain in my eyes.

Reaching out, he squeezes my hand as the voice starts counting down the last ten seconds. We get set up, prepped in advance for what to expect tonight.

Lights that were strategically placed around the yard flip on and Jacob is talking into a camera welcoming the audience to the final competition of season ten.

"Charlie Price, welcome to the finale of *House of Deceit*," Jacob Jacobson says over the speakers in the house.

With a deep breath, I plaster a smile on my face and walk down the red carpet to my podium in the middle.

"Thank you, Jacob. It's great to be here."

"It's been a long road for you."

"It's been a long road for all of us. As much as I've loved my time here, I'm ready to see my family."

Turning his attention back to the camera, he calls down Parker and then Jayden in succession.

"Charlie, you won the poll from the audience this week, so you will go first. Please choose a category."

Our final game begins.

I tap my matte black nails on the edges of the podium, take a centering breath, and call out the first category.

"Winners of the Week for two thousand," I say.

"From the team of privilege winners in week two, who said 'If I was them, I would suck whatever I needed to avoid that punishment'?" Jacob reads out.

Parker buzzes first, but Jayden and I are fast on his heels. "Angelica," he says.

I can picture the page of my journal this exchange was written on, while the first points of the game flash under Parker's name.

"Vices for one thousand," he says, calling the next category.

"Which contestant was notorious for putting gum on the underside of things?"

I buzz first this time, with Jayden just seconds behind.

"Harper."

"That's correct," Jacob tells me, and being on the board helps my stomach settle.

"Charlie, another category, please."

"Game nights for three thousand."

"How many different colors of card decks were there on the night the house played Rummy?"

All three of us press our buttons at the exact same time, but Jayden's podium lights up.

"Four. Head Deceivers, three thousand," he says, not waiting for Jacob to confirm his guess.

"Which Head Deceiver was Penelope talking to when she said 'I hate this stupid game. You all suck and I don't know why I came here'?" Jacob reads.

I buzz and provide the correct answer, furthering my lead.

"With Charlie in the lead, who's going to come out on top? Find out after we hear a word from our sponsors," Jacob Jacobson tells the camera.

Production starts moving around, touching up our faces as we go to commercial.

"You're doing a great job," Parker says, whispering into my ear, ignoring his makeup person.

"Thanks. I'm sorry you're in the bottom right now," I say, blotting my new layer of lipstick.

"Hey, this is every person for themselves. Kick my ass, if you must."

His eyes crinkle as he smiles.

"No matter what happens, thank you for being my friend," I tell him, emotion tightening my voice.

"Thanks for bringing me back to life," he says.

I nod, unable to say anything for fear of crying. Production is counting down our return from commercial and we look forward, competitors once more.

"Charlie, next category, please," Jacob says.

"Deceivers, two thousand."

"Who was the deceiver that Saran wrapped the toilets?"

Parker gets this one. And then Jayden goes on a run, getting four questions in a row, including one about Ezra's socks during a game night that is so random, I had no chance. What I felt was a solid lead is quickly overcome by Jayden.

"Weeks for fifteen hundred," Jayden says.

"What week did Colyn learn how to do a handstand?"

I buzz, my podium lighting up. "Three," I say.

"Incorrect," Jacob says, calling Jayden's name as he buzzes next, unaware the points falling off my board has stunned me like a blow to the head.

"Week four," he says, his points going up as he calls for the next category.

Sweat starts to roll down my back despite the night air cooling down now the sun has sunk beneath the horizon.

"Competitions for a thousand," Jayden says as I try to bring my attention back to the task at hand.

"Which round of musical chairs did Mateo lose in?"

I buzz, beating out both guys. "Five."

"Oh, no, I'm sorry Charlie. Yes, Jayden?" He directs his gaze away from me as Jayden gives the correct answer of round four.

I start picking at my nail polish as nerves threaten to overtake me. Heading into another quick break, I picture Alec sitting in his chair in the interview room.

"*You know this stuff, Price. You're really going to give up on me? After everything we've done to get you here? Where's the girl I picked from her application?*"

As we come back, I settle down and ready myself for a comeback.

Commercial breaks come and go and suddenly, we are on the final question.

"Jayden, you lead by five hundred points with 20,500. Charlie, you are currently in second with twenty thousand, and Parker, you are in third with ninety-five hundred," Jacob says, still looking powder dry.

Dramatic music plays over the speakers and the lights all come down. "Last question, Deceivers, and this one is for all of you. As a reminder, you will wager up to the amount of points you currently have. If you get the answer correct, you will win that amount. If you answer incorrectly, you will lose that amount. Understood?" We all give verbal consent per the attorney's instruction.

Jacob readies to ask the final question of the season.

"What is the combined age of all the house guests at the time they left the house?"

I begin writing furiously on the tablet that has been provided for the purpose of this last question.

Jacob turns to the camera and speaks to the audience. "As our contestants answer this final question that stands between them and half a million dollars, let's take one final break. Make sure to stick around to find out who will win season ten of *House of Deceit* and half a million dollars, live!"

As we go to commercial once more, we lock in our answers, but when I go to write down my wager, I hesitate. Looking at my board, I try to decide the number of points I want to wager. Jayden will probably assume I'd bet everything. If Jayden and I both get the answer wrong, but I wager under a thousand points, I would still beat Parker, no matter what he puts down. And if Jayden wagered enough, I could still win. But if I do that, and we both get the answer correct, he will win.

I wish Alec was here to tell me what to do. To go with the safe answer or bet everything and pray. We are told to lock in our wagers as we are counted down to the end of the commercial break.

With my heart in my throat, I put down my life-changing number.

Jacob Jacobson welcomes the viewers back as my stomach knots and I mentally chant, *I will not pass out from nerves.* I try to think through all the birth dates of the contestants once more. There were a few birthdays during the production schedule, but I'm wracking my brain to remember if they happened before or after the specific person left. I check my answer one more time, even though it's too late to change.

This money could make my life easier for the foreseeable future. It's more than I needed to avoid living with my parents when I came into this house. Combined with the product partnerships that will hopefully be waiting for me, I could walk out of here without a care in the world.

But even being so close to solving all of my problems, all I want to do right now is see Alec.

Before I'm ready, the lights come back on and Jacob holds our fate in his hands.

"Hello, deceivers. Congratulations on getting this far. Your answers have been reviewed and the final points totaled. In my hands, I have the results of the competition." He shows us a heavy, dark blue envelope. "In just a moment, you all will exit this house for the first time in twelve weeks, one of you half a million dollars richer! Are you ready to see who has won?"

"Yes!" all of us chorus together.

"Please, make your way to the entryway."

I take a moment and look around the backyard for the last time. Turning from my podium, I hold my hands out to the guys, wanting us to walk out of here together.

Walking through the mansion that has become home, my eyes get misty as I take it in once more.

Two production assistants dressed as butlers open the doors.

"Jayden, Parker, Charlie," Jacob Jacobson says, his voice filtering over the speakers as he's moved to the front of the house for the post-game interview, "the winner of *House of Deceit* season ten is—" he takes a pause that lasts a year.

My heart races a mile a minute while a bead of sweat inches its way down my spine.

I bite my lip as the front doors to the mansion open for the first time in three months.

And then Jacob is saying, "Charlie Price!"

I'm speechless as I look to Parker who is smiling at me like he won himself.

Both of the guys drop my hands and clap for me as I make my way through the foyer. I cross the threshold and my face breaks into a smile as tears gather in my eyes.

Fireworks explode from behind the mansion while confetti rains down along the front doorway as I step out of the *House of Deceit* as the winner.

Jayden and Parker trail behind as we leave for the first time in three months. The booms of fireworks rattle in my chest. All the past contestants swarm us as we have our first breaths of free air, Molly and Keith wrapping me in their arms first. Everyone is cheering and hugging me but all I can do is wish Alec was here to watch this. To celebrate my win. *Our* win. Because I couldn't have done this without him. I would have gone crazy long before the end of the game. Parker steps in front of me once we are on the driveway, and sweeps me into a hard, spinning hug.

"I knew you could do it, Charlie. I knew you were going to win it from day one." He sets me back down on my feet and softly kisses me. He takes a second and searches my face. "What's wrong?"

"I—" A blur of a wrangler comes up to my side and grabs my arm, walking me over to a lighted set with Jacob Jacobson standing in the middle having his makeup touched up. I look back at him and mouth sorry but he waves me off.

"Charlie, we need you. You have to interview with Jacob right now. He's ready and we will go live in two minutes." I trail behind her, trying not to fall over. "I've got her!" she calls out, shoving me toward the lifted platform.

Hair and makeup attack me, quickly adjusting everything that has been mussed in the congratulations I received. Someone with a clipboard and a headset comes up to me and starts talking at a rapid pace.

"Okay, Charlie, when we come back from commercial, Jacob is going to give a quick speech and then he's going to invite you onto the stage. You have three minutes and then we'll be taking you to the after-party. There will be more cameras there, but no further interviews."

"No problem," I say. Not a single ounce of enthusiasm lives in my body at the thought of more cameras. The camera person counts down before indicating to Jacob we are live. It's odd watching him introduce me after knowing him behind a screen for so many weeks.

"—our winner, Charlie Price!" Everyone cheers and I step onto the stage. As I feel lights against my back, I paste a smile onto my face. Jacob holds his arms open to me and I step in. He air kisses each cheek before indicating I should take the chair across from him.

My green sparkle dress irritates me but I fight against fidgeting with it, my mother's voice in my head to be demure.

"Charlie, Charlie, Charlie. First of all, I want to wish you my deepest congratulations! It has been a long twelve weeks, but it must have been so satisfying to come out of it the winner!"

"Yes, it's been the most surreal experience of my entire life. I feel like I'm in a dream right now. It just hasn't sunk in!" A giddy voice I don't recognize comes from me and I try to make myself relax.

"I'm sure you are so excited to finally be out of the mansion..." he trails off, expectantly.

"Honestly, I kind of miss the mansion right now. It's been my home for twelve weeks and while that's not a long time, it's enough time to completely change your life. To make lifelong friendships."

"You and Parker seemed closer than some. How was it to form such a close relationship?"

"Parker is an amazing man and I've had the time of my life with him, with everyone. Our friendship is something I will cherish for the rest of my life."

"After Molly was eliminated, it seemed he was a spot of comfort for you," he pressures.

"I missed being home with my friends and family. I was broken up with only a few months prior after a couple years with the person. Losing someone I was close to was really hard. Having a friend in that house was the difference between my ability to last the entirety of the game and going home early. Parker was happy to fulfill that role for me and I him."

"Charlie, thank you for your time and congratulations again."

"Of course, thank you."

Jacob Jacobson turns toward the camera, dismissing me now that our time together is over. He thanks the audience for watching the season and promises an even better one next year. I smile benignly until the red light of the camera blinks out.

I stand from the chair and see movement out of the corner of my eye. Courtney stands there, hands clasped in front of her chest, the largest smile I have ever seen in my life plastered on her face. With no thoughts in my brain, I launch myself at her, wrap her tightly in my arms, and cry.

CHAPTER FORTY-THREE

I HAVE COURTNEY'S HAND grasped tightly in mine as I fight through the throngs of well-wishers and show people. All the contestants, the wranglers, production crew, and anyone else involved with our season plus many others are dancing and drinking to their heart's content. After twelve weeks of work and competitions, everyone is thrilled to be done.

Parker walks up to me and smiles at Courtney.

"Parker, I want you to meet my best friend, Courtney. Courtney, Parker."

"Courtney, it is truly a pleasure to meet you. I've heard so much about you." He kisses the back of her hand, making her swoon.

"The pleasure is all mine. I haven't been told anything about you, but I promise that will change." He chuckles before turning back to me.

"Courtney, if you wouldn't mind, I'm going to steal Charlie for just a moment, but I'll bring her back to you soon. If you'd like to grab a drink, I can deposit her at the bar when we're done."

Like the traitor she is, Courtney waves goodbye to me without another word and makes her way to the bar.

"The family wants to celebrate your win with you," he says, steering me toward the group of season ten contestants.

Every molecule of my body wants to crawl into my bed and not talk to another human besides Courtney for a year, but I suck it up because this will be the last time we all stand in this place together.

"Red, I am so damn proud of you," Keith says, his voice gruffer than normal. "The wife can't wait to meet you."

"I can't wait either. I've missed you, Grandpa."

He pats me on the back before letting me go, allowing Molly to step in. Her copper dress matches her hair perfectly.

"You're definitely going to pay for the girls' trip we will be planning once you're settled in back home."

"You've got it," I say, the smile splitting my face. "Courtney's over at the bar. Will you go make sure she's okay?" I ask. Other than Parker or Alec, I wouldn't trust my best friend with anyone else.

Molly scurries away as Jayden walks up to me.

"What was the answer?" he asks.

"Six hundred thirty-eight," I tell him.

He looks at me quizzically. "Who else had a birthday before they left?"

I cock an eyebrow at him.

"I'm a little surprised you don't know," I tease. "Keith's birthday was the day of the cookie decorating. He made me promise not to tell anyone under threat of sharing my most embarrassing story with everyone."

"That deal definitely worked out in more ways than one," he says. "Congratulations, no hard feelings." He wraps me in a quick hug before starting to head back to the party. He pauses.

"What did you bet?" he asks, turning back around.

"Does it matter?"

He shrugs. "I just want to know if I would have won if I had gotten the answer correct."

With a light heart, I tell him. "I bet it all."

"Sounds like you had more faith than I thought you would. I had you pegged for the safe bet to beat Parker even if you guessed wrong."

"I had nothing left to lose," I say, waving and turning back to the group as he walks off.

An hour passes as we all hang out and talk. Each person makes their way over to me to offer congratulations except for Cain, who's missing. Not that I care.

We all exchange numbers with anyone we wish to stay in contact with and eventually everyone makes their way to the bar and then the dance floor.

I turn to head toward Courtney, but a large hand stops me.

"Can we talk for a second?" Parker says.

He helps me stay steady on the uneven ground as we distance ourselves from the party raging on the side lawn.

"How are you doing?" he asks.

"I'm exhausted, honestly. I keep thinking about my bed and how much I just want to disappear."

"That's not what I'm talking about."

"I know," I say. "I'm feeling a lot of things. Alec is gone. He should be here. I'm only here because of him and it feels wrong he's not here to celebrate with me," I tell him, honestly. We are long past the point of holding anything back from each other.

"Where did he go?" he asks, frowning down at me.

Choking back tears, my emotions all over the place tonight, I tell him everything.

"Okay," he says wrapping me in his arms. "I'm not going to ask about it anymore because there's still a lot of night left before you can leave, but just know, the offer to kick his ass is still on the table."

"Parker," I pull back, looking up at him, "I just want you to know I'm so glad I met you. I'm always here, anything you need."

"I thought this show would change me, but really it was you," he tucks my hair behind my ear and the touch is nice. "I'm ready to take a step forward in my life and I couldn't do it without your friendship."

With a final hug, he leads me back to where Courtney leans against the bar, talking to a member of production.

I feel eyes on me as I make my way through the crowd. I guess being watched doesn't stop at the threshold of the mansion.

The hotel room door has barely closed before Courtney is on me.

"Tell me," she demands, but I take my time.

On the desk is the itinerary for my day of interviews following my win. Skimming over it, I notice I have to be awake in two hours for my cross-country flight. I strip out of the sparkle dress, buying myself time, excited to get the itchy fabric away from my skin.

"Tell you what?" I pause at the footie pajamas in my bag, my hand hovering in the air, before I grab the pajamas I wore at the beginning of the competition.

"Don't play dumb with me. What happened in that house, Charles?"

"More than I have the time or desire to tell you right now."

"Okay, answer me this then. Did he hurt you?"

"There was definitely some spanking involved, if that's what you mean," I say, trying to avoid the real question.

She snorts a laugh and levels a finger at me.

"You're not diverting my attention with your sexcapades. What happened?"

I roll my eyes at my best friend who will never let this go. "I fell in love with him, Court, and he used me."

Her eyes soften. Out of everything in the past forty-eight hours, this is what causes the damn to break. Tears come out in a flood, even after I swore not to cry over this man again.

"The wrangler? What did he get out of it?"

"His dream."

"Okay. Charlotte, serious voice, serious moment." She moves me to the bed, sitting us down without removing her arm from around my shoulders. "I am telling you, with a hundred percent certainty, he did not do it for the game. That man is so desperately in love with you, he probably didn't know what to do about it with the game coming to an end."

"No, he has been working toward that goal for ten years. I was just his ticket in."

"Charles, did you notice neither Parker nor Jayden had friends or family here?"

I dry my eyes looking at her.

"What?

"I wasn't supposed to tell you this, but Alec called me. He told me that he had to leave, but he didn't want you to not have someone here to celebrate with in case you won. Or lost, really. He bought my plane ticket. He arranged everything."

I feel my mouth drop open at this revelation.

"He called you?"

"I've had a ticket since the end of week ten. I'm telling you, that man *loves* you. I don't care what else he's done, he loves you."

I would cry more, but my tear ducts have nothing left as confusion runs through me. Did he just feel bad for abandoning me? Or is Courtney right and he loves me? Without his phone number, I don't have any way to get in contact with him. And I know I can't handle it if she's wrong. Courtney shifts on the bed, pulling me into her side.

"All right then. Okay." She hugs me again as I sniffle. "I love you, Charles. We'll figure this out. You deserve all the happiness in the world."

I snuggle, ready to fall asleep beside my best friend.

"I love you, too, Court."

AFTER

CHAPTER FORTY-FOUR

I WATCH THE TARMAC come closer to the plane as we land. A deep breath escapes me as my body relaxes for the first time in the two weeks since I won *House of Deceit*. I was on every morning show, talk show, and radio show that wanted to talk to me. The punishing schedule was exhausting, but it was a part of my contract.

Every day I missed Alec. The pain of being separated from him continues to tear my heart from my chest every second.

The escalator takes me down to baggage claim, where my parents are waiting with signs, flowers, and balloons. Happy embarrassment brings my first genuine smile since the day Alec ended things with me. I drop my purse and carry-on before letting them engulf me in hugs. My mom kisses my cheek, and my dad pats me on the back as he swallows back his tears.

"We missed you, Lottie Lou."

"I missed you too, Pops."

"You did so well on the show, honey. We watched every episode. People would ask us questions, but we didn't have anything to tell them! But you and that Parker boy looked so sweet together."

"Parker and I had an agreement, Mom. We're just friends," I tell her.

"Well, that's unfortunate. He was quite stunning." She fans herself as my dad grabs up my carry-on while I grab my purse.

"She has quite the crush on him. She was hoping you'd be bringing him around." My dad waggles his eyebrows while my mom blushes so deeply it looks like she laid in the sun for ten hours with no sunscreen.

"We parked in hourly parking. Let's get going before our bill is insane," my mother says, walking away with a sniff.

My dad and I laugh as we finish collecting all of my luggage from the baggage claim and make the drive home. My mother natters about all the gossip and goings on I missed in the past fifteen weeks, since I first left for the show. We pull up in front of my building, where my dad helps me get my suitcases into the lobby before hugging me again and heading back to my waiting mother.

Elevator doors close behind me and a tiny sliver of excitement to be back in my space takes hold. As the doors open on my floor, I remember how I sold my couch before I left and make a mental note to buy another one tomorrow now that my winnings have cleared. I stick the key in the lock, and the sound of soft music greets me.

I slam the door behind me and drop my keys into the bowl, the smell of something cooking wafting from the kitchen. There are wine glasses on the coffee table, candles lit everywhere, and a "welcome home" sign taped across the doorway.

My heartbeat quickens with hope. Maybe Alec changed his mind. I know all he'd have to do is call Court and she's let him in my apartment.

Hope builds as I put my suitcases at the entrance of the hallway and drop my backpack along with them. Grabbing up a wine glass, I take a deep drink. Tears prick my eyes as I move through the apartment. I have been so lost without him.

"What the fuck?" I whisper to myself. I watch Scott shifting through the cabinets trying to find whatever it is he's looking for. He turns around and spots me.

"Babe! You're home!" Scott wraps me into a hug, that I do not return as complete and utter shock takes hold of me. When he steps back, he has a giant smile on his face.

"What, in the absolute *fuck,* are you doing here?" I ask him. His face falls slightly, but he recovers.

"I've missed you and I just wanted us to take another shot," Scott says.

I stand there, staring. The pot on the stove boils over, causing him to jump and start cooking once more.

"Um, hey, I'm going to go take a shower really quick. Get the airplane smell off me."

"Okay, sugar. Dinner will be ready in about fifteen minutes," he calls out as I move woodenly to my bedroom.

Shutting the door behind me, I slide down it while pulling out my phone. Courtney answers on the first ring, putting a bookmark into her book, various kid noises in the background.

"I see you're finally home," she says.

"Scott is here."

She gets up from her couch and scurries to the bedroom, locking the door. "What the hell do you mean Scott is there?"

"I mean, he's moved back in and is acting like he didn't walk out on me and leave a note. And how the hell did he get in here? He left his key."

"Did you ever remove him from the lease? If not, the super probably gave it to him or something. What are you going to do?"

"I don't know, dude. I want him out of my house, but he's all moved in and making dinner! I can't just kick him out, can I?"

She sighs and shifts on the bed. "Listen, I will support you in whatever you want to do, but you're hurting from the situation in the mansion and sometimes, it's easier to slip back into something that doesn't hurt. But the distraction won't mean you're over it and what I think you need right now is time to heal and figure out what you want to do with your life.

"You are in a unique position. You didn't win never-work-again money, but you did win money that will give you time to figure out what your next step is and I don't think backsliding is it."

"I hear you. He can't be back for anything good, right? Either way, this is going to be a tomorrow Charlie's problem. I just can't deal with it right now."

"That's fair. Go take a shower, eat, go to bed early and figure it all out once you're settled back in."

"Do you want to go couch shopping tomorrow?" I ask. "The freeloader didn't seem to bring one with him."

She snorts. "I already took the day off. In the meantime, what are you going to do about Scott for tonight?"

"Kick him in the shin?"

"That's definitely one way to handle it."

"I'll put him in the guestroom and figure it out." The person he left is no longer the person I am. But there's still a part of me that remembers what it was like to be with him. While our love was never an inferno that my attraction to Alec was, he was a kind, steady man I loved spending time with.

"I have no idea. It's been weeks and I've not heard from Alec," I continue. "It might be nice to split the rent with someone for the moment. Maybe we could just be roommates?"

"Girl, you just won half a million dollars! You don't need a roommate. You're not the poor Charlie who was moments away from having to move in with your parents. What do you *want*?"

"I want a new couch," I say, avoiding her question.

"I'm going to slap you first thing when I see you tomorrow," she promises.

"I want Alec."

"Okay, then how are you going to get him?"

"I don't know!"

"Well, figure it out," she says and hangs up.

CHAPTER FORTY-FIVE

ALEC

MY PHONE IS PROPPED up on my dresser, a clip of my favorite interview of Charlie playing as I button my shirt. Lorelei made sure to plan her engagement party when I had a weekend free. As a public figure, Tank was able to secure a highly sought after hotel's rooftop restaurant for the shindig with very little notice. I go to grab a pair of cufflinks from the drawer when sounds of a fist on my front door stop me. Moving through the house, the pounding becomes insistent. Rude, almost.

Pissed, I rip the door open.

"What—" A fist connects with my face and I sprawl on the floor of my entryway as the person makes their way into my house, shutting the door behind them. Fear at the thought of a home invasion grips me as I look up at the intruder.

"The fuck was that for?" I scream at Parker. "Holy shit, that hurt, you damn asshole!"

"*That* was for hurting her, which I warned you *not* to do."

"So, you figured you'd come and punch me in the face?"

"You deserved it and you know it. In fact, I wouldn't be surprised if that didn't feel a little good. Pain you deserve." He reaches a hand out to me. Unsure if he's going to pull me up just to punch me again, I hesitate before finally taking it.

Clapping me on the back, he says, "Let's get you some ice, buddy."

As we move through my house, I ask, "Did you come across the country just to punch me in the face?"

Ignoring me, he looks around as we make our way to the kitchen.

"This is really nice. Surprisingly warm and inviting," he says, pulling out a stool at the island and I can feel him watching me as I create an ice pack and press it to my eye. "Did you decorate in here? It's nice. I might have to hire you."

"No, my sister Lorelei took care of that. She was convinced my bachelor pad was the reason I was single."

"I'm assuming that wasn't the reason."

"No. I was single because I hadn't met Charlie." He nods like he understands and just sits, watching me. For a second, I think I understand what it felt like to be Charlie in the house. Monitored.

"For the hundredth time, would you like to share with me why you're here?" I ask him.

"I figured I would help you stop standing in your own way," he says simply.

"I don't know what that's supposed to mean. What am I standing in my own way of?"

"Charlie, dumbass. She got home from her tour a few days ago. I called to check. We are going to go visit and either get you back in her good graces or give you both a chance to talk about whatever shit happened and then move on."

My heart skips a beat. I've considered showing up on her doorstep begging her on bended knee to forgive me. But the thought of her telling me I lost any chance I had with her kept me in place, missing her and not knowing what to do about it.

"She doesn't want me back, man. I was an ass," I say.

"You didn't see her after whatever happened between the two of you. I'm telling you, she misses you. Stop being a baby, suck it up, and go apologize."

I dump my ice pack into the sink, moving to the fridge and yanking it open.

"Do you want a drink?" I ask.

"I wouldn't be upset with a beer, if you have one."

Grabbing two, I hand one to the man who might end up saving me from myself.

Twisting off the top, I take a deep drink.

"So, before we come up with a plan for me to get my girl back, how the hell did you find out where I live?"

It takes me twenty-four hours to get everything lined up and then we are on a red-eye to North Carolina. I let Tom know where I was going and he was more than thrilled to give me a few days to get my life in order. "Go get her, son," he said with enthusiasm before hanging up on me.

Lorelei could tell I was a bundle of nerves at her party and kicked me out after an hour. Plus, the black eye was ruining her pictures. The airplane is loaded down with passengers trying to get to the East Coast. Soon, we are taxiing and in the air. Unable to sleep, I watch a movie while Parker reads.

The sounds of passengers moving around interrupt the quiet. Rays of sunlight crest the horizon outside the window as we circle Atlanta. Our connection takes off in an hour. While I chafe at the delay, I'm thankful for the chance to stretch my legs.

"Do you think she's going to go for this?" I ask.

"For the seventh time, yes. I'm going to need you to trust me. Just a little."

He leans his head back and closes his eyes for the final bit of the flight. I try to plan out what I'm going to say, how I'm going to beg her to forgive me. I'm starting to drift off with thoughts of the amazing makeup sex I hope we have as the captain comes over the PA system to announce we are making our final descent. The city rises up to meet us as we circle lower.

Parker and I make our way through the crowd to the gate of our connection. Awaiting passengers mill about as we take a seat and waste some time. Suddenly, the board announcing our flight flicks to canceled. Parker and I look at each other, shock written on both of our faces.

"Drive?" I ask.

"Drive," he confirms.

Luckily, we both have carry-ons and can avoid baggage claim. We finally get to the front of the line of the rental car company, both of us about to strangle anyone to get out of this city.

"Hello, sirs, how can I help you?"

"Hi, we need a car, any car. We are going to North Carolina, one way," Parker says, flashing the smile that made all the viewers love him.

"Of course! Now, we do only have one car left at this time and it might be a tight fit for you and your husband, but with the unexpected cancellations, all the other companies are also on the last legs of their fleet," the woman says typing on her computer.

"Great, whatever you've got is fine," I interject.

We sign all the paperwork and take the keys and follow her directions, searching for the car.

"These numbers are going down. We are going the wrong way," I say checking the sign before turning and going the other direction.

"If you were a good husband, you'd help me with my bags," Parker says, needling me.

I look over my shoulder at him, giving him a droll look as I pick up the pace, not wanting to waste any more time.

"I would just like to remind you that you punched me in the face which has led to me getting *many* funny looks. You can carry your own bags."

Sure, him punching me in the eye knocked me back into my senses as far as Charlie is concerned, saving me, but that doesn't stop my eye from throbbing with each step.

We both come to a stop as we spy the lone car remaining, in the spot we are assigned, a tiny hybrid awaiting us. My knees will be in my throat, but I don't care. I've already been without Charlie too long.

"She did say it'd be a tight fit," Parker says, eyeing it. We shove our bags into the miniscule trunk before he slides into the driver's seat.

We ride in silence, through small town after small town in the mountains of Georgia. My elbow rests on the open window as my hand loosely holds the wheel. The wind is cooler here, where the warmth of the sun is blocked.

My muscles get tighter and tighter the closer we get until, finally, we pull up in front of Charlie's building. My grip is so tight around the steering wheel, I'm not sure I will be able to let go.

"You have to relax, man. Knock the stick out of your ass and come apologize to your girl," Parker says, climbing from the eco-friendly clown car.

Charlie's favorite saying calms me, almost as if the turn of phrase is a sign I'm doing the right thing, so I throw open the door and follow him into the apartment complex.

The finicky elevator Charlie complained about in our time together is working, thankfully. I didn't want to be winded asking the gorgeous woman to take me back.

Parker stands in front of the door, hand poised to knock before he whispers to me.

"Remember to stay off to the side. She's probably still mad at you and we need to get in the door."

"Yeah, yeah. I know," I say, stepping to the side a little more, butterflies settling into my stomach.

I know this is going to work. It has to work. As Parker goes to knock, the door is ripped open.

CHAPTER FORTY-SIX

CHARLIE

THE MORNING AIR IS crisp. It will burn off by the afternoon, but the hint of autumn right around the corner brings a smile to my face. The line before me moves at a glacial pace, but the pastries are worth the wait. For a moment, I marvel at this. Instead of having to fight through rush hour traffic, I can stand here and enjoy the morning and take all the time I need.

My feet hurt in my heels, but it feels nice being dressed in my usual pencil skirt and top once more. My appointment to sign the contracts for the various brand deals I decided to go with isn't for another hour or so. The same attorney who walked me through my contract for *House of Deceit* was more than happy to help me with these as well when I called asking if he'd represent me once more. While I won't be making millions of dollars, combined with my winnings, I won't need to find a regular job anytime soon.

Life feels like it's settling down a little. Overall, not much has changed. I'm still, technically, unemployed. I'm still single. I still have the best parents and friend a girl could ask for. And yet, within my soul, nothing has stayed the same.

Thinking about my living situation, I finally decided what I want to do about Scott. He has been sleeping in the spare room while I decide if I want to have him back in my life. It's only been a few days since I've been home, but there's no use in trying again. He'll never beat Alec in my heart. I just need to tell him.

I wait for my blueberry muffin and piccolo with the group of half-awake commuters. My eyes flit from person to person and something settles in my chest. I'm thankful for my time in the house. Instead of standing here waiting to go to a job I hate, I have the space to try and find a dream job. Or as close to one as I can find. I have a moment where I can be picky and that's a place I never thought I'd be.

"Charlie!" the barista calls out. I thank them as I take my drink and muffin. A woman slips up next to me, stopping me from turning.

"I thought that was you. Hi, I'm Gertie, and I just want to say, I was rooting for you the entire time on *House of Deceit*. Your interviews were some of my favorites."

Turning on the person Alec helped me build, I settle into TV Charlie within seconds. Martha and I had discussed what to expect when I left the mansion in our final week together. She reminded me every interaction needs to be professional, but they are expecting the Charlie they know, not necessarily the Charlie I am.

"That's so kind, thank you so much, Gertie. Thank you for watching the show."

"I don't normally do this, but would you mind if I take a picture with you?"

"Of course, it would be my pleasure."

With a beautiful smile, she saddles up next to me and I squat down a smidgen so we are roughly the same height. Gertie holds her phone out in front of us and I make sure to smile happily.

"Thank you so much. Have a great rest of the day." I wave as I move toward the door, still a little weirded out at being recognized in public.

"Thank you, Charlie Price!" Gertie calls out, her giddiness bringing a real smile to my face. I make my way into the early mid-September sun and let myself close my eyes and take in the rays for just a moment, thinking back to a day on the sun bed with Molly.

My phone ringing cuts through the moment and brings me back down to reality. Hoping it's Martha returning my call about getting Alec's phone number, I move quickly toward my car, setting my muffin on the hood while I fish my phone out. Mere seconds before it kicks to voicemail, I answer.

"Hello?"

"Hi, my name is Devon and I'm calling for Charlie Price from Samantha Conn's office."

My mouth drops open. Samantha Conn is one of the most prolific literary agents in the game. Almost every author she represents has become a worldwide bestselling author.

"Um, hi, yes, this is Charlie."

"Ms. Price, Mrs. Conn is a big lover of *House of Deceit* and she is wondering if you'd be interested in having a meeting with her here in New York? Tomorrow at noon?"

"She wants to meet with me?" I ask, shocked. "Can I ask why?"

I can hear the smile in Devon's voice. "I think she'd like to discuss that with you herself."

"Oh, of course, sorry. Yes, I'd love to meet with her." I'm pacing in front of my car, trying to expel the nervous energy.

"Great. If you could provide me your email, I'll send you the details and a confirmation. There's a flight out of Charlotte Douglas airport that I will secure you a seat on and you'll return first thing the morning after the meeting. Mrs. Conn would like to take you to dinner as well."

"That's very generous," I say, going through my calendar mentally. "I can move a few things around with no issue."

I rattle off my email address and other various details so she can book my flight and hang up. I stare at the phone for a second in my hand before I scream a laugh and jump around. My dance of excitement is erratic and I'm left winded. Strangers stare at me, tentative smiles on their faces watching as a dream I've always had could be coming true.

The black car pulls up beside an imposing skyscraper nestled between other imposing skyscrapers. New York was a stop on my morning show parade post-winning, but this moment is so much more to me than being interviewed by people I've watched on TV for years.

My heart pounds inside my chest. I hitch my purse up higher, set my shoulders, and strut into the building. The lobby is cold marble and colorless. The security officers in their blue suits are the only specs that are not devoid of color. I walk up to the security desk and give my name as Devon instructed, per her email. They take my picture and print out a temporary badge that I attach to my suit.

A security member takes me to an elevator and rides up with me. Once on the twenty-fifth floor, he swipes his badge, allowing me into the offices of Conn, Hawks, and Ashby. This office is an explosion of deep, jewel tones and beautiful lighting that invites you to sink into one of the many plush couches scattered throughout the waiting room. Exactly the sort of thing I love in a room.

The pristine receptionist stands and smiles at me, not a single hair out of place. Her manicure is muted but perfect. Her dress is romantic and feminine and stands out perfectly against the deep blue wall behind her.

"Ms. Price, welcome to Conn, Hawks, and Ashby. Ms. Conn's assistant, Devon, will be right with you. May I offer you any refreshment?" She indicates a tray of various drinks and sparkling waters.

"I'm fine, thank you so much."

"Of course. If you wouldn't mind taking a seat? I'll tell Devon you've arrived."

I nod, moving toward a couch to the side as a woman walks in with no-nonsense shoes and sure steps.

"Devon's here," the woman says. "Ms. Price, would you come with me?"

I stand back up and follow her, thanking the receptionist on my way past her. "Mrs. Conn is extremely excited to speak with you today. She's just finishing up a call, but she wanted me to go ahead and bring you back."

I make a noise of acknowledgment as we make our way through the various cubicles. Each one is personalized to the owner with pictures. Some have wallpaper on the small walls. Fuzzy chairs, pretty knickknacks, and small comforters like blankets are throughout. Everyone seems deeply at ease and I see smiles and unhurried phone calls.

Devon stops outside of the large corner office. Samantha Conn stands, looking out on the city through the glass walls of the office. "Please take a seat and she'll be right with you," Devon whispers as I pass her.

"Patrick, my noon appointment is here, but we will continue this after lunch. Have Devon put time on my calendar." She hangs up and turns around.

Samantha's raven hair is tied back in a sleek bun. Her suit is immaculate and she is an imposing presence.

"Charlotte Price, thank you so much for taking the time to meet with me. Please." She indicates a chair in front of her desk.

"Thank you. You can call me Charlie." I take my seat and set my purse next to me, trying not to pick at my nails in my nervousness.

"Charlie"—her smile is warm—"I can't tell you how excited I was to watch your win. So many people had counted you out there at the end, but I knew from the beginning. You have that look about you."

"Well, thank you. I appreciate you saying that."

"I'm sure you wonder why I've asked you here."

"Only a little," I joke. She gives me a small laugh.

"When I found out you were a journalist, I looked up your pieces. Your writing is snappy with good humor, and your observations are on point. The human element of your stories is fantastic. Needless to say, I became a fan."

"Wow, that's so incredibly flattering, thank you." She waves away my thanks, her golden bracelet catching the midday light.

"I'm going to cut to the chase, Charlie. I would like to be your agent."

"My agent?"

"Yes. I want to represent you to publishing houses."

"Oh, I'm sorry, there's been some misunderstanding. I don't have any novels to sell."

"You don't, not yet. But you will. And with me, it'll be a best-seller." I'm not sure what to make of this meeting. Samantha Conn is not one to waste her time.

"You want me to write a novel? About what?"

"*House of Deceit*, of course."

"What?" I ask, struck dumb.

"I want your firsthand account of everything that happened in that mansion. Especially whatever happened that wasn't aired."

"Oh, um." I think of Alec thrusting away behind me and I hesitate. "I wasn't planning on writing a book, and I'm sure there's something in the contract that precludes it."

"Funnily enough, I was able to ascertain a copy of your contract. You see, I mentioned wanting to meet with you to an old friend, Tom Cochran, a phenomenal director, and he just so happens to have a new protégé who used to be a wrangler on *House of Deceit*. He sent it over without any hesitation."

Samantha sets off a bomb within my chest. I don't want to believe it, but there's no one else it could be. Even now, Alec is still trying to take care of me. Unaware my heart has stopped, she continues.

"I have had our attorneys look at it, and the only deal with your contract is you can't sell your story for a year. Due to the amount of time it will take to write, I believe we can have it ready to be published at a year and a day, if we push hard."

"I don't want to sound ungrateful, just being in this office is a dream to me. But, Mrs. Conn, every day for months, every breath I breathed, every moment I lived was recorded and dissected."

I want to pick at the polish on my nails, but I think about Alec reaching over to stop me months ago. I think about sharing our private moments, and I know my answer. "Not every one of those moments made it to the general public and was watched by millions, but there were still people behind the scenes watching every single one. There are some things I just don't want to share. Thank you, for taking the time to meet with me, but the answer is no."

Disappointed, I grab my purse and stand. I make my way out of her office and as the cold metal door handle meets my hand, her words stop me dead.

"Cain is taking advantage of the opportunities he has had land in his lap. From what I've heard, your story will be told. I'm merely offering you a chance to tell it in your own voice." I turn toward her.

She seems like she is laying out the facts, but I can see the truth behind her eyes. Not only will my book be quite the feather in her company's cap, I can see she genuinely wants to help me. "Not many people know this, but before I was *the* Samantha Conn, I was just a girl who had her story used against her. I know what you're in for if you don't get ahead of the curve. Will it be lucrative for me? Absolutely. I'm nothing if not self-serving. But I know what it means to have your story stolen from you. Let me help you own yours."

"Scott?" I call out as I walk into the apartment. I drop my keys in the bowl like always and slide my backpack underneath the entry table to deal with later. "Scott?" I call out again, déjà vu hitting me.

I hear his muffled voice from his bedroom. The cracked door lets out just enough of his voice I can hear his conversation.

"She was just offered a free week-long vacation at some hotel on the beach. They want her to film some commercial there." I hear his footsteps and I press myself against the wall. "Yeah, that's my plan."

There's a pause while the person on the other side of the phone speaks.

"I figure I'll ride it out a little longer. She's getting all sorts of promotional deals and things like that. I'm sure it will last a bit longer. It's like payback for all the times I had to cover her when her job didn't pay well enough."

My body goes numb before a sweeping sense of vindication brings a smile to my face. I knew Scott was here for a reason, but I couldn't put my finger on why. Sure, I won some money, but it's not like I was going to buy a yacht any time soon. For some reason, all the perks of notoriety never entered my mind.

"Yeah, well, when I saw her on the show and then Kim kicked me out, I figured I could crash here while I let her cool off."

I pull out my phone and see Molly tried calling me. We have plans for me to come visit in a few weeks and I am so excited to take Courtney with me. They really bonded at the after-party that night.

Swiping out of her message, I open my thread with Court and let her know what's going on, trying not to laugh as she sends me image after image of her extreme eye roll.

"I dunno, maybe a few more weeks? Kim has quite the temper, but she always forgives me. Once Charlie's fifteen minutes run out,

I'll try to get her back. She's a tomcat in the sack, why would I want to let that go?"

And that's all I can take. I open the door and lean against the jamb, crossing my arms over my chest.

"Get out of my house," I say, my tone sweet as the bananas foster French toast I'm obsessed with at the cafe down the street.

"Charlie, you're home," he says, hanging up the phone.

"Shut the fuck up and get out. I heard all of that," I say, all sweetness and warmth gone.

"Heard what? You're taking everything out of context."

"I'm taking it out of context?" I laugh. "Kim was the work 'friend' that you always told me not to worry about. Sounds like that was a lie. Is she the one you left me for originally? And then, you figured 'Hey, Charlie isn't at home right now, maybe I'll just go stay there.' Is that it?"

I walk out to the living room and run a finger along the arm of the couch I love so much, his footsteps following me, before setting the bottle of champagne I stopped to buy on the coffee table.

"No, sugar. I was confused and we were in a rut. I just needed to take time. You know how much I love you. I was thinking about marrying you and it just scared me. You know how I feel about marriage and to have someone that made me want to do that, it freaked me out!"

I turn toward him, no feelings toward the man standing before me.

"Why do you have champagne?" Scott asks, noticing the bottle.

"I got a book deal," I tell him.

"What? Charlie! That's amazing! Congratulations. I didn't know you were writing a book."

"I wasn't, but I am now. However, it's no longer any of your concern. Get out."

I shove him toward the front door as he tries to take back all the awful things I heard him say. I rip the door open and shove him with all my strength straight into Parker's unsuspecting arms.

CHAPTER FORTY-SEVEN

"PARKER. WHAT ARE YOU doing here?" I ask him as he bear hugs my ex-boyfriend.

"Apparently catching whoever the fuck this guy is." He turns Scott around in his arms and grabs a fistful of his shirt. "Who are you and why are you in Charlie's house?"

"She's my girlfriend! I'm Scott." He tries to look affronted, but Parker's grip on him diminishes the effect. Parker smiles at me.

"This is the stupid fucker?"

"Yup, that's him."

"You're no longer welcome here. If I find out you have darkened her doorstep again, you'll regret it," Parker threatens as he flings Scott to the ground behind him. He turns to me. "Hey." His smile glues together one of the cracks in my heart. "Can I come in?"

I smile back and move out of the way. "Of course, you're always welcome."

He walks in, ignoring Scott's pained groan behind him. Right as I move to close the door, a blur of black snaps out and stops my forward progress.

"What about me? Can I come in?" Alec looks miserable.

I take him in head to toe, noting one of his beautiful gray eyes is blackened. Deep shadows rest under the other. His perfect hair is in disarray and his clothes hang on him a little too loosely. I consider denying him, but the hangdog look of the man who was in control around everyone except me makes my heart squeeze in pain.

"Oh, I might have brought you a present," Parker jokes behind me.

"Okay," I whisper, holding the door open. He gives Scott a swift kick, earning a yelp, as he walks by him. I shut the door and press my forehead against it, giving myself a few moments to collect my thoughts.

"Are we celebrating?" Parker asks, picking the champagne up off the coffee table.

"What are you doing here?" I ask.

"Ah, okay. We'll get back to that then," he says, setting the bottle back down. "I'm here because I knew this dumbass wouldn't be here otherwise." He hooks his thumb over at Alec who shifts nervously.

"And you?" I ask Alec.

"I came to explain why I broke things off with you."

"This should be good." I sit down on the couch while they both take the chairs across from me. I lean back and cross my arms over my chest.

"After week two, I didn't care about the job opportunity," he says.

I scoff and he smiles sheepishly. "Okay, I didn't *only* care about the job opportunity." His face goes solemn.

"Cain's wrangler could tell he was going to get eliminated. You and Parker were always favorites of both the competitors and the audience. They knew the people remaining would never vote him out. They tried to get you removed. Apparently, Cain's wrangler was working late, knowing Cain was going to try something. He was watching the live footage and he saw us, so he decided to make a copy of our time together before we finished."

He continues.

"I never should have gone into the house, but when I saw Cain put his hands on you, I lost it."

"What happened with it? Why didn't they leak it to the media? That would have worked."

"I don't think they thought you *wouldn't* get kicked off. He was new and had no idea how it would go down, so he gave the only copy to my boss and my boss gave me an ultimatum. My options were to end it with you and take the job I had turned down with Tom Cochran or be fired for inappropriate conduct. They would have blacklisted me. The only reason why they didn't is because Sheila knew this had never happened before. That I loved you.

"The attorneys combed our rulebook and your contract looking for any piece saying a wrangler can't have relations with their contestant. Granted, it's frowned upon, obviously, and a lot of people would have been screaming we cheated, but there was nothing. I had to protect you. If there was a hint of any inappropriate relationships, you could have lost your brand deals.

"I wasn't lying when I said it was the better option. I never could have lived with myself if it got out and people thought you cheated."

My heart is pounding and I'm afraid they both can hear it.

"So you ended it."

"I admit I could have done it better, but I knew no matter what I said, you'd think I used you. I leaned into that because I *had* to end it. It broke my heart. Every word. I hate myself for hurting you."

I nod, appreciative that Alec wanted to protect my reputation. He had never once stopped taking care of me and I knew there was no other path forward for me, but one.

"Loved."

"What?"

"You said you *loved* me. Past tense." His smile is tentative as I uncross my arms and stand up.

"It was always, and still is, present tense," he says as I climb into his lap, wrapping my arms around his neck.

"Oh yeah?"

"Charlie Price, you are a frustrating, funny, smart, caring woman. I loved you the first time you asked if I was Batman and owned footie pajamas. My life is duller without you. Please, take me back and let me spend every moment for the rest of our lives making up for the lost time."

I look over at Parker and see him smiling at us, completely at ease.

"Why did you do this?"

"If I could have a single second more with Brittany, even just to ask her why she left, I would take it. No questions or hesitations. I knew this dumbass didn't break your heart for fun. We were partners in that house, Charlie. We looked out for each other. I didn't want you to go a single day more missing someone. It's just not worth it."

Tears gather in my eyes as I look back at Alec.

"He flew to my house, kicked my ass, and dragged me here even though I was convinced you would never want to see me again." I smile at Parker and reach my hand out to him which he grabs immediately.

"That explains the black eye. Thank you for kicking his ass," I tell Parker.

I look back at Alec again. "I love you. I don't want to waste any more time." I kiss Alec and my heart's pieces heal as his tongue tangles with mine.

Parker quietly leaves the apartment, but Alec's kiss demands all my attention. We break apart, panting.

"Take me to bed and keep me up all night," I tell him.

He stands, his arms flexing as he shifts me, my legs wrapping around his waist. With purposeful steps, he carries me down the hallway, kicking the partially closed door open. Spinning, he falls back on the bed, letting me settle on top of him, the bed groaning beneath us in a concerning way.

I rip my shirt off before fusing our lips together, his tongue seeking mine immediately. My fingers are frantic as I pull at my bra, exposing my breasts to him before reaching down to his belt.

He stills my hands and I look at him, questioning.

"Let's take it slow. We have all the time in the world."

My face almost splits from my smile. We do. We don't have to worry about being recorded or caught or anyone else in the apartment. It's just us. Just me and him. It always has been.

"Yes, we do, don't we?"

A hard cock presses into the small of my back. My entire body is sore and used in the best way. I wiggle my ass backward, eliciting a grunt.

"If you wanted to wake me up, that's a fantastic way to do it," Alec whispers in my ear. He grabs my leg and lifts it over his hip. His fingers trail down my stomach and begin stroking my clit in a slow manner. "Mmm," he groans in my ear. "You're so wet already, baby. Did you not have your fill last night?"

"I was without you for too long. I need more."

"You can have as much as you want." He adjusts behind me before thrusting up and into my dripping pussy. "My cock missed you and your needy pussy."

Each thrust is harder than the one before. As he pulls out, the head drags against my g-spot. I reach behind me, grabbing a fist full of his hair as I grind down onto him.

He knows just how to touch my body. How to wreck me with pleasure over and over again.

"Tell me you were desperate for me. Tell me how much you missed me. How you can't live without me," I tell him.

He pinches my nipples painfully, eliciting a small cry from me.

"I could never live without you." He punctuates his statement with a thrust. "My cock wept for your wet pussy every night." He drags himself out inch by excruciating inch. "My love for you makes me feral. I'm yours, forever."

He starts picking up speed as he fucks me. He twists my tender nipples ferociously, making me cry out and tears prick my eyes as he begins relentlessly pounding into me. His fingers go to my clit and begin expertly massaging me as his other hand spreads me open even more.

Groaning, my orgasm dances on the edge. I can't believe for even a second I considered letting Scott back into my life. The man behind me is everything I've ever wanted. Love fills me as he peppers kisses along my neck.

"Perfection. Oh, God," he moans. His fingers dig into my thigh as he pounds into me.

"I'm going to come, Alec," I say, my voice a breathy moan.

Quick as lightning, he rolls me onto my stomach and hikes my leg up, pressing his entire body down on top of me as he slides back in. The new position has him hitting the perfect spot.

I groan. "Just like that, baby. Oh, God, just like that. Don't stop," I beg. "Please don't stop."

He grunts in my ear as he gives me his cock in a way that drives me wild. My pussy clenches and I scream out my orgasm as he paints my insides with his come.

"You're such a good girl," he pants into my hair before kissing me. As he rolls over to the other side of me, he slaps my ass, eliciting a squeak from my tired throat.

We lie there together, basking in the glow of our morning. Alec slaps my ass once more before getting out of bed, standing naked and looking down on me.

"I'm going to make breakfast. You want bacon?" he asks.

"How do you know I have bacon?"

"I might have looked in your fridge last night between rounds when I was getting us some electrolytes."

"Bacon would be great, thanks." He smiles at me, more at ease than I ever saw him in the house. "You might want to put on pants!" I call out as he makes his way down the hallway to the kitchen. I giggle as I hold the blankets to me, happiness pouring out of me into the morning light.

Throwing back the blankets, I move to take a quick shower, my body sore in the best ways. Still a little damp, I tie my robe around me.

Between rounds last night, Alec told me how Parker had booked a hotel room with two beds, just in case I wanted to boot Alec out on his ass. They had left their suitcases in the car. Before he left, Parker set Alec's in the hallway, texting me to let me know it was there.

Grabbing my phone, I move to sit on the well-used bed.

"You're up early," Parker says, his voice thick with sleep as he answers my call.

"Thank you for bringing him back to me." There's nothing else I could say that will convey the depth of my gratitude.

"Anything for my fake girlfriend," he jokes. "And...for my real friend."

Taking a breath, I make a gamble. "You deserve to be happy, too, Parker. Even if that means moving on, you deserve to be loved. If you want to find her, ask her what happened, I'll help. But either way, I want you to be happy."

We sit in silence and I listen to him breathe for what feels like an eternity.

"I'll think about it. Either way, thanks for the offer." He hangs up after saying a quick goodbye and I sit for a moment more, watching the day outside my window.

I pad out into the living room and watch my wrangler. Alec has my floral apron on, a compromise to needing to cover his manhood but not wanting to put on pants, and nothing else. He is pulling the bacon from the pan and setting it on a paper towel covered plate. Music plays from his phone and I move into the kitchen.

"Will you dance with me?" I ask him as a slow song plays about the singer's first love.

He smiles at me before setting everything down and sweeping me into his arms. He spins me around the kitchen, kissing me like he'll never get enough.

"This looks amazing," I say looking around at the food as we continue to move. I give his bare ass a tap. "So does this."

"I could say the same about yours, but it's currently covered by those inconvenient shorts," he says, slapping my ass, adding to the collection of stings. "Grab some plates. The pancakes and eggs are in the microwave," he instructs as the song ends, always bossing me around.

I grab some glasses from a cabinet and pour orange juice into each, knowing Alec doesn't drink coffee, but not having any tea in the apartment. After I've placed those on the table, I grab plates before moving to the microwave to pull the eggs and pancakes out as Alec brings the plate of bacon over. He sits in his chair, keeping the apron on.

I grin at him before piling pancakes and bacon onto my plate, suddenly famished from the vigorous nightly activities.

"Thank you for cooking," I say, kissing him.

"Of course, babe." Alec says, grabbing my chin. "I love you."

"I love you, too," I say, not used to the novelty of the words yet.

We take a second, grinning stupidly at each other and our confessions. Everything in me is light and bright. Without his hands on me, I would float away in the cloud of happiness hearing those words from his mouth.

"Will you move to California to be with me?" Alec asks, hope shining brightly in his beautiful eyes. "I know that's asking a lot. I'm asking you to leave your family and Courtney and that's a lot, but I want to give this a shot and with my job, it'll be hard to have a bi-coastal relationship."

I smile. I want to make him squirm, play with him a bit, but I don't have it in me. I'm too happy.

"My parents are retired and I now have enough money between the show and my brand deals I can fly them out to see me. Same with Courtney. Hell, maybe I'll just try to convince her to move her family, too. I would have to fly back to New York periodically to meet with Samantha Conn for my book."

He grins at me. "I knew she would get you to do it. And?"

"Of course, I'll move to be with you, but there will be some stipulations if I'm going to keep you around," I joke.

He looks up at me, love and humor lighting his face, remembering our talk in the hotel room what feels like forever ago.

"Yes, to whatever you want. So long as I have you, I'm coming out the winner."

He stands, pulling me with him and presses a hard kiss to my lips before picking me up and spinning me around, a happy laugh echoing around my apartment.

Our story started all thanks to a drunken night with my best friend and ended with my soul mate in my arms. The *House of Deceit* turned out to be the best game I've ever played.

EPILOGUE

TWO YEARS LATER

ALEC

I SIT ON THE daybed outside overlooking our patio. The house is finally finished after about a year of building. There are many little nods to Charlie and Parker's time inside the mansion. From the outdoor decorating and pool layout to the fountain that stands in the front of the house, she wanted to memorialize the things she loved about that time under the summer sun.

When Charlie and I decided to build a house, Parker was the only one we trusted with the job. He left everything he knew, including his business, and started a new construction company in California, where he's now thriving. Luckily, his right-hand man decided he was ready for a new start too and followed him. Between the two of them, they hustled hard to gain contacts and build their reputation in the new state.

Around the time his company began to take off, Charlie's manuscript was completed. The many sleepless nights as her deadline neared were worth every bit of stress they caused me while watching her. Samantha ensured there was an auction and Charlie received a mid-six figure deal which she quickly earned out. She's been on every bestseller list as well as every talk show. This time, you can tell she is enjoying the experience, unlike on House of Deceit.

I took my opportunity to learn as much about the directing process as I could under Tom Cochran. After being scouted by another network, I was able to gain an assistant director position. During filming, there are many nights I'm not home until late. But Charlie always waits up for me now that she doesn't have to work an office job.

Through everything, Charlie and Parker's friendship has deepened. When I saw how he cared for her, how he became the brother she never had, I couldn't do anything but befriend him. When Parker first moved to California, I offered to let him stay with us until he was on his feet. Within about six months of steady work coming in, he was able to find his own place. Charlie, Lorelei, and Courtney went on a shopping spree and fitted out Parker's new apartment. His credit card hasn't recovered, but his place looks amazing.

Only two weeks from the house being done, Parker and Charlie are finishing up the last touches while I take a break from filming. They love the work and relegated me to relaxing after a particularly grueling schedule this year. My phone rings and I pick up with a smile on my face.

"Samantha Conn, how's it going?"

"It's going well, Alec King. Is Charlie around? I can't get ahold of her and I have news."

"Yeah, she's unpacking the library. Let me grab her." I stand up from the daybed and begin moving through the house. "Has Charlie invited you down next month for the housewarming slash anniversary of her and Parker being on the show?"

"Yes! Brian and I are really looking forward to it. We have enlisted my in-laws to babysit while we enjoy a parents' weekend away."

"That's so great, we look forward to seeing you both. Hold on one moment."

Charlie unpacks all of her books into her library. That was the only thing she required of our new house. Parker made sure the house had everything my love wanted, butdidn't know she needed. I watch her slide the ladder down and climb back up with a new armful of books. She refuses to let me or Parker help her, saying she doesn't want our boy cooties in her sanctuary.

"Hey, babe? Samantha is on the phone."

"Oh, great!" She sets all the books in her arm on the shelf she was putting them on, climbs down, and bounds over to me. She gives me a firm kiss as she takes the phone from my hands. "Hey, Samantha. What's up?" Her smile widens and I feel my face answer her happiness. "Hold on." She presses the speaker button as she calls for Parker who comes bounding in from the officehe's finishing for me next door.

"Can you say that again, Sam?" Charlie asks as Parker slides up next to us.

"Cost Communications called. They have agreed to let House of Deceit be used so the movie based on your book has, officially, been green lit. Congratulations!"

Tears fill Charlie's eyes as she thanks Samantha and hangs up the phone.

"That's amazing!" Parker says, sweeping her up into his arms. I give her a deep kiss once he stops spinning her around.

"This calls for a lot of champagne," I say, holding the love of my life in my arms.

TWO MORE YEARS LATER

CHARLIE

T HE NIGHT AIR IS thick with the smell of rain. Thunder rumbles, but I don't mind. It's my favorite weather. Alec arranged for us to have the House of Deceit mansion for a private viewing party of the movie based on my book. I stand on the gravel driveway, alone just like I did four years ago.

I always knew this house would change my life, but I never could have fathomed how much.

Footsteps crunch on the gravel behind me.

"Are you ready?" Parker asks.

"How was filming? I didn't think you'd be here!" I exclaim as he wraps me up into a hug.

"Filming was fine. I got in last night. We taped the last talk show spot instead of doing it live. Something came up for the interviewer."

I never expected for the relationship I have with Parker to bloom so much once we left the house. Watching him and Alec bond and become friends has brought me a deep joy. Parker has gradually become friends with Tank as well, joining him and Alec on guy's' nights while Courtney, Molly, and I have fallen deeply in love with Lorelei. Twice a year, we girls all get together and enjoy a relaxing long weekend while Alec bunks at Tank's.

I pull back from him, searching his eyes.

"I'm here to talk. You've barely answered my texts since you stopped filming. Alec was willing to kidnap you to get you here tonight for me," I say.

"I don't want to talk about it. Plus, tonight is about you. Are you ready? Alec is waiting."

"Yeah, just taking a second to appreciate the view," I tell him, smiling at the mansion. A drop of rain hits my nose.

He takes my garment bag from me before offering his arm. Linked, we reverse the journey we took the last time we were here and walk into the entryway. The first day I walked in, nerves gripped me so tightly. I was afraid of this house and everything that could happen inside. But I shouldn't have been. This was where my life started. Where I learned to be unapologetic with the risks I take. To trust myself.

On the entryway table is a card. I pick it up and immediately recognize Alec's handwriting.

"I'm going to go put this in the kitchen. See you in a bit." Parker leans down to kiss my cheek and walks off with my bag containing my outfit change for the premier as I open the card.

On thick, cream card stock, Alec wrote out his common phrase over the announcement system.

Price, to the interview room.

I carry the card with me as I move through the different hallways. The last time I was with Alec in the interview room was the worst moment of my life, but I know that's not the case this time. Alec and I worked through the hurt he caused with the choice he made, but in the end, I understood. With the options he was given, I would have done the same thing.

The glow of candlelight meets me as I open the doors. The smell of warmth and vanilla permeates the room. Standing next to his normal chair, Alec dons a tuxedo. It clings to his form and enhances his beauty. He's always been one of the most beautiful men I've ever seen, and he still takes my breath away every day.

The camera that was in the room with us every time we met is there now, the red light bright in the dim room.

"Price, it's time for your final interview," he says. "Take your seat."

I feel slightly underdressed in my favorite sun dress compared to his tux, but the gown I have for tonight will complement him well. The chair is comfortable. Welcome. A reminder.

"Where did the camera come from?" I ask, since he told me the house was stripped down after shooting so it'd be ready for the next show.

"Sheila. As a favor. Now, Charlie Price, how do you feel your life has been since you won season ten of *House of Deceit*?" he asks in his patent wrangler, now director, voice.

"I would say it has been very blessed. The best years I've ever had."

"Do you regret anything from your time on the show?"

"Not spending as much time with some of the contestants as I should have. I've become extremely close with a few since leaving the mansion that I didn't really connect with, like Jayden, during our time here." He rests his ankle on the opposite knee, crossing his arms. I'm taken back to our first interview where we ended up yelling at each other. His hair is a little longer now and I can read every line of his face, but he is still the same stern, intimidating man.

"Is it true you fell in love while you were on the show?"

I smile. "I did, yes."

"Do you still love them now?"

"I do."

The line of questioning makes butterflies begin to take off in my stomach, but I wait to see where he's trying to lead me.

"What would you say if that person said their life would never be complete without you?"

I look at him for a long second. "I'd say the feeling is, and always has been, mutual."

He stands from the chair and gets down on one knee in front of me, taking my hand in his. The butterflies fully swarm as tears gather in my eyes.

"Charlie, my life was missing something. Love and companionship and laughter. Someplace I could be me, and I found that with you in this room. Our last time in here was horrible and I wanted to replace that memory with another. You are the light of my life. I can't breathe without you. I want it to be you and me forever. Would you do me the honor of becoming my wife?"

Tears stream down my face as I say, without hesitation, "Yes! Of course!"

He takes a box out of his jacket pocket and opens it. The ring is a beautiful sapphire, and he slides it on my left ring finger before snatching me up in a hug. As he spins me around, the laugh that comes out of me is pure happiness.

"Best interview ever," I say as I press a hard kiss to his waiting lips.

"As much as I want to kiss you all night long, and I definitely will later, you need to go get ready for the premiere," he says, shooing me from the interview room so he can clean up. "Go find Parker. I'll see you soon." With a final kiss, I leave.

I make my way through the house, memories popping up as I move around. Keith acting out his favorite movies and all of us laughing and heckling him. Dinners in the dining room where Ava inevitably ended up crying from something someone said. Molly and I playing pranks on people who were napping.

Parker is standing in the living room with his back to me. His tuxedo is as well tailored to his large frame as Alec's is. He turns toward me and his face lights up.

"So, did you say yes?" he asks.

My jaw drops and I swat his shoulder. "You knew?"

He throws his blond head back and laughs. "I went with him to pick out the ring. We flew Courtney out to help, too."

"I can't believe you lied to me, your fake girlfriend! And I will be having words with Court."

"Don't be too mad at her. It was for a good reason," he says before leading me to a room to change.

Patting my hair into place, Alec follows me from the house, fixing his clothes. As I take in the backyard, I gasp at its beauty. Between the flowers and lights strung everywhere, it gives the illusion of a fairy garden. I simply hope the rain can hold off a little longer.

Cameras are everywhere for the event. Stars from the movie walk the red carpet through the gate in the backyard and into the house. The organizers wanted the event to feature some of the spaces Parker and I were in the most. Parker, Alec, and I stand right at the back door so I can greet guests.

Lore, Tank, and my parents stand off to the side, letting us greet people as necessary. Upon meeting Lorelei and Alec, Mom has become a bit of a surrogate, making sure they feel loved and cared for.

Molly walks in on sky high stilettos making her a head taller than attendees, Danielle on her arm. Just like I suspected, Danielle's relationship didn't last long once Molly was out of the house. Camera bulbs flash as people take pictures of my striking friend.

After a year, Molly was tired of long distance and now only lives an hour away from me and Alec. Danielle proposed a year later at a party celebrating Molly getting a new job. Now a talk show host, she features stories of people who are trying to better the world. From women's issues to inequality, and everything in between, Molly shines her effervescent light on organizations that need more help in their battle to make our world a better place. She has also become the face of a size-inclusive, eco-friendly clothing label, ensuring women of any height and weight have beautiful clothing to drape themselves in.

As she makes it to the end of the photographers, she immediately heads toward my group. My face goes straight into her boobs as she crushes me in a hug.

"I'm so glad it was you. I've always said that. Find me later, okay? I want to see that ring."

"I will. Thank you for coming. I've missed you," I mumble against her tits.

"It's only been a month since I saw you," she teases. "But I miss you, too."

I give Danielle a quick hug after she finishes her catch up with Alec. They both move through the crowd, Lorelei squealing and launching herself into Molly's arms as she nears.

"Red, I never thought I'd be back in this house, but I'm glad it's for this."

Keith is decked out in a black suit, bolo tie, and a cowboy hat. His wife is on his arm and in a beautiful maroon dress. They have invited me, and, once they knew about him, Alec, to Texas on a few different occasions and we loved getting to know them both in the real world. I give Keith a hug and kiss his wife's cheek.

"I wouldn't have been able to be here without you. Thank you for coming."

"I see you still have that strapping man. Is he taking care of my girl?" he asks in a whisper that I know Alec can hear based on Parker's smothered laugh.

"He takes very good care of me," I say in an exaggerated, sexy voice.

"Don't be gross. We'll catch up with you later." They both move through the sliding glass doors into the house.

Courtney is dressed in a gold dress, her hair in soft waves. J.D. walks beside her in a navy suit. She hugs me tight before grabbing my arm and pulling me to the side as the guys all talk. They have all bonded well over several vacations we've taken together.

"How many times have you had sex in here today?" she asks.

"None, don't be ridiculous," I say.

"You think I believe that he finally put that planet of a rock on your finger and you didn't bone him? Please. I'm not an idiot."

"Speaking of, I can't believe you kept this a secret from me! I would have dressed nicer if I had known," I scold. She just looks at me until I roll my eyes. "Twice. Not that it's your business." I keep all joking from my tone, but she knows I am.

"You are my business."

We join the guys once more, J.D. tucking Courtney into his side.

"Hey," Courtney says, "you know what I just noticed? You're the only one who hasn't made out with Charlie in this group, babe." She looks from guy to guy, an annoying smile on her face, but before I can throttle her or any of us can die of embarrassment, she gets distracted.

"Is that James St. Paul?" she asks, pointing out the actor who plays Parker through the glass. "He's on my pass list." She reaches her hands down the top of her dress and pulls each boob up so they sit even higher.

I snort at her antics as Alec and Parker avert their eyes.

"I'm pretty sure he's in a relationship," Alec says, looking up at the sky.

"I'm going to flirt with him. I'll see you later." She starts to walk away but pauses. "And Charles? Proud of you." She flicks away a fake tear before turning to go talk to St. Paul.

With a singular purpose, she walks straight up to him. I watch as she throws her head back and laughs at something he says, and J.D. shakes his head.

"She's incredibly proud of you," he says as we all watch her. "She'll never admit it if you ask her, but she tells anyone she can about your book. She carries copies of it in her car and will give it to anyone who is even slightly interested. She is your biggest fan."

"Likewise." I smile up at him. "I'm glad you guys could come."

"A rabid gorilla couldn'thave kept us from this mansion tonight. Now, I'm going to go make sure my wife doesn't embarrass herself with James St. Paul. Or worse, leave me for him. I'll see you all later." He disappears into the crowd as Alec presses a kiss to my cheek and Parker scans the crowd.

"I want a small wedding. No cameras. In our backyard. Next month," I tell Alec, his gray eyes filled with love.

"Sounds perfect," he says.

"Let me know what I need to build for it," Parker adds.

Parker goes rigid. Following his line of sight, I see the most beautiful raven-haired woman in a cream-colored dress.

"Is that her?" I ask him and he simply nods. "Go talk to her!"

Throwing back his champagne, he stomps over, the woman's gaze zeroing in on him immediately.

"Well, well, well. This should be fun," Alec says, as we watch the stilted exchange.

Laughing softly, I hold my hand out. His lips are warm as he presses a kiss right above the new ring adorning my finger and we walk in the mansion that started it all, ready for every day of the rest of our lives.

PARKER'S STORY

House

of

Desire

COMING IN 2024

Pre-order now on Amazon

ACKNOWLEDGEMENTS

Writing a book has brought me the greatest joy in my life, and yet, I never thought I would actually publish it. Sure, I talked about it, but the fact that you're holding it in your hands right now is something I never believed to be possible.

First, I'd like to thank you, dear reader, for having faith in me that I could deliver a story for you. For taking a chance on someone you've never heard of before. It's so easy to pick up a book from an established author that has proved themselves repeatedly, but you gave me the greatest gift of all. Your time. I don't take that lightly and I hope you found something in these pages that was worth that price.

Next, I want to thank my writing group Sydney, Dani, Julie, Maddie, Selbe, KP, Jae, Kayla, and Karissa. You have been with me for every word written, plot hole fixed, comma moved, and encouragement needed. I would not be where I am, and I would be a lesser person and writer, without you all in my life. Thank you for loving and supporting me in a way I never thought possible. You all are the lights at the end of the dark tunnel.

Courtney, thank you for being my friend even though I abandoned you to move closer to my family. Also, for having synchronized panic attacks with me about home renovations. I wouldn't have made it through such a stress inducing time without you.

To my ARC readers who are too many to mention, your reviews and enthusiasm for this book is the only reason it didn't end up in the trash.

To my beta readers, Natalie, Karla, Wendy, Becca, Sydney, Maddie, and Julie, your input was invaluable and I loved reading your most unhinged comments, they made me smile when I was deep in the weeds of editing. Your ability to rip apart my manuscript while simultaneously making me feel like the story I was telling was important, was something I couldn't live without.

The book that you hold in your hands was edited by Makenna, Sarah, and Jenny. They worked hard on these characters, story, and making sure I finally learned how to tag dialogue correctly. Any remaining errors, issues, etc are completely my fault. They were unfailingly encouraging and correct in all their guidance, no matter how stressed their notes made me.

And last, but not least, my family. For giving me my sense of humor, supporting me in the dark and light, and roasting me in a way that only family can. I genuinely hope you skipped the sexy bits.

About the Author

N.E. Butcher was born and raised in a suburb of Kansas City, MO. Recently returned home after 13 years away, she's enjoying putting down roots while spending time with her loved ones. When not daydreaming up stories, you'll find her engrossed in a gripping book, knitting gifts for loved ones, or embracing her creative side with home DIY projects.

An unabashed Taylor Swift enthusiast, N.E. Butcher finds inspiration in the singer's lyrics and melodies and always has her music playing in the house that she shares with a lovable dog and an adorable cat.

Join her on a romantic journey as she delves into tales of love, heartbreak, and second chances, captivating your heart with every turn of the page.

Made in the USA
Monee, IL
02 September 2023

42018464R00239